Inherent Justice

INHERENT JUSTICE

Bili Morrow Shelburne

INHERENT JUSTICE by Bili Morrow Shelburne

Book 2 of the *Justice Series*

First Edition

Published by Wendover Press

Copyright © 2025 Bili Morrow Shelburne

Author Services by Pedernales Publishing, LLC.
www.pedernalespublishing.com

Library of Congress Control Number: 2025913840

ISBN: 978-0-9967430-9-9 Paperback Edition
        978-0-9967430-8-2 Hardcover Edition
        978-0-9967430-7-5 Digital Edition

Printed in the United States of America

For Ralph, my inherently lovable mate.

Chapter One

He was on his knees with his head bowed, but I recognized him from about thirty yards away. I knew what he was doing; a repeat of what he had done over a year ago. I killed the rental car's engine and made my way to the pauper's section of the Martinsville, Tennessee Cemetery.

"Hey, Joe Bob." I spoke in the most reverent tone I could muster.

My old friend looked up at me and swallowed. Tears leaked from his eyes, and he cleared his throat. I didn't say another word, but Joe Bob must have felt a need to explain.

"Nobody else was gonna put flowers on his grave," he said. "Nobody else gives a tinker's dam that crazy old Jimmy Banks got run over and killed."

"The flowers are really pretty, Joe Bob. I think Jimmy would appreciate the gesture."

Joe Bob cleared his throat, stood, and shook my hand.

"I reckon you're here to visit your mom's grave," he said.

I nodded.

This was the first time I had been back to my hometown since my mother's funeral. Looking back on the short time I had spent here made me think twice about returning. All hell had broken loose during that week and a half. I had simply wanted to give my mother a proper southern sendoff, then get back to Denver and my law practice, but one thing after another seemed to conspire against me.

My hot-headed pregnant sister tumbled down a flight of stairs in a fit of rage and lost her baby. My friend Bernie's wife cheated on him. My father decided to show up after having been absent for years, and Mother's attorney kept postponing the reading of her will. To make matters worse, Beth, my ex, decided she wanted me back in the worst way. She spread the rumor that we were getting back together all over town. All the while, my old friends and I were under the erroneous impression that Joe Bob had hit and killed Jimmy Banks. Joe Bob, Bernie, my Uncle Stuart, and I fled the scene of the accident.

Denver hadn't felt the same when I returned to my law practice. For one thing, the city had somehow lost part of its charm. But the main reason was that the huge windfall Jack, my law partner, had been so sure was going to fall into our laps, hadn't materialized. Handling divorce cases wasn't going to cut it. Finally, we had to admit to ourselves that we were sinking fast. Thinking that we could build a successful practice had been a pipe dream, so we closed our doors and choked down our medicine. Jack stayed in Denver and went to work for a mid-sized firm, and I came back to Martinsville to decide what I want to do when I grow up. Thanks to my dad's generosity, I could breathe easy. I'd had no idea that he had set my sister and me up with trust funds.

"You here for a while, Matt?" Joe Bob asked.

"I'm not sure how long I'll be here. Jack and I shut down our practice and parted ways. Maybe you and I can get together later and catch up. I'll tell you all about it."

"Sounds great."

"Do you think Bernie might want to join us?"

"I'm not sure. See, Matt, Bernard's not exactly footloose and fancy free now."

"What do you mean?"

"What I mean is that on top of runnin' his dry cleanin' business, he's pretty much tied down with that little kid of his since the divorce. The judge give him custody of her except for a coupla weekends each month."

"Well, good for him, I guess. Who got the house?"

"I don't know how they split things up, but his ex is livin' in it. Bernard told me he never wanted to set foot in that house again, 'cause that's where his tramp-of-a-wife cheated on him."

"I understand. Hey, I want to go see Trudy now, Joe Bob. You remember our housekeeper. She's living in the house since Mom died. That sweet woman spent more time in our house than she did in hers, and she gave it a lot of TLC.

"I'll call you later and let you know where I'll be staying."

Joe Bob gave me a lazy salute, turned, and stepped gingerly over the graves of Martinsville's paupers on the way to his truck.

It felt kind of strange to ring the bell of my own house, but I hadn't let Trudy know I was in town. I didn't want to drop in unannounced.

My old friend came to the door with a dust cloth in her hand. She opened the door wearing a red bandana on her head and the biggest smile I had ever seen. There were tears in her brown eyes as she threw both arms around me.

"Matty, why didn't you let old Trudy know you were comin' home?"

"It was pretty much a spur-of-the-moment decision."

"Well, come on into the kitchen and tell me all about it."

I followed her through the living room and down the narrow hall into the blue and white kitchen that always felt like Trudy's room. I sat down at the table and Trudy pulled out a chair across from me. She reached across the table and took my hands in hers.

"Listen, I want you to tell me the honest truth. Have you changed your mind about lettin' me stay in this house? I think you might have made a hasty decision about that because you were in such a hurry to get back to Denver."

"Of course I haven't changed my mind. I'm delighted you're living here. You've taken care of this house your entire adult life. Does the house need any repairs?"

"Nothin' needs to be repaired, and if you're positive you're okay with this arrangement, I'm very happy here."

"Now that we have that settled, tell me what's been going on in this thriving metropolis while I've been gone."

"I'm sure you know your friend, Bernie Zuckerman is a single father now."

"Yes, Joe Bob told me. I stopped by the cemetery to put flowers on Mother's grave, and Joe Bob was doing the same thing for Jimmy Banks."

"I've always liked that boy, Joe Bob. He's somethin' of a mystery though; always has been, but he has a good heart."

I laughed. "What do you think is mysterious about him?"

"Well, the way he talks for one thing. You can tell he's intelligent, but he speaks like he just crawled out from under a rock. Also, people say he has plenty of money, but he lives out there in that trailer park. He wears nice clothes when he's not in his mechanic coveralls, and he wears his hair in a ponytail like a throwback from the sixties."

"That's all true," I said. "He's definitely a strange cat, but I think he's true to himself."

"Speakin' of strange people, it was a miracle that you boys ran into that weird Fred Peyton at the police station that day. If it hadn't been for him, Joe Bob would be locked up tighter than a drum."

"You're right. He was ready to turn himself over to the police for something he didn't do."

"Well, that's all in the past. Why are you here, and how long do you plan to stay?"

"I'm here to relax and try to decide what I want to do. Jack and I closed our doors. We should've never tried to make it on our own. Our two-man law firm was never going to get off the ground. Maybe being here in Martinsville with its slow-paced lifestyle, I'll be able to figure out how to make a decent living."

Trudy's face lit up like a sunrise.

"Matty, you won't believe this. I do have another piece of news."

"It must be something you're excited about. What is it?"

"You're gonna to be one happy guy."

I had no idea what she was about to tell me.

"We have a new Methodist preacher in town. He's single and a real looker. Guess who has her cap set for him."

"How would I know?"

"Your ex. I don't expect she'll be botherin' you anymore and spreadin' lies all over creation."

"Are you serious?"

"I can't say for sure, but that's the rumor. Everybody's talkin' about it."

"Well, I hope it's true. I'm in the market for some good news. It'll be nice not having Beth and her crazy schemes to distract me. Maybe this preacher can walk her back to being the person she used to be before she went off the deep end."

"Listen, Matty, I don't know what your plans are, but I can

refresh your old room in about ten minutes. Go get your bags and put them in there while I get clean linens."

"No, don't do that. I'll get a room at the Greystone for a few days while I check out places to rent. I saw a nice apartment complex the last time I was here."

"You'll do nothin' of the kind, Matt Stevenson. I haven't sold my house. I'll move back into it and come here every day to keep this house in order for you."

"That's the silliest thing I've ever heard. Look, I don't know how long I'll be here. I want you to live in this house. Consider it yours. I'm just going to pay the property taxes."

"You know me well enough to understand that my mind's made up. I won't be changin' it. Now, you do what I told you to do, and don't argue with old Trudy."

I did as I was told and put my bags upstairs in my old room while Trudy bustled around changing sheets. She never stopped talking while she worked.

"I know you'll want to see your old friends this afternoon. You and I will have plenty of time to catch up later. I'll leave your supper in the oven."

"Listen, I'll stay here because you're insisting, but you are not going to be preparing my meals. I'm meeting Joe Bob in a few minutes. We'll eat dinner in town and talk over old times."

"You're still my stubborn boy," she said, and handed me a house key.

"I have two more in case you lose this one." She chuckled to herself as she walked away.

I unpacked one of my bags and changed into jeans and a tee shirt, then drove to Morgan's Restaurant to meet Joe Bob. Morgan's was one of his favorites haunts.

He sat alone in a high-backed wooden booth facing the front

door so he would see me when I came in. His muscled forearm shot out in a salute when I stepped inside, and I didn't bother stopping at the reception desk.

"I see Bernie couldn't make it," I said.

"Well, he could have if he hadn't been on such a high horse."

"What do you mean?"

"I took it upon myself to help Bernard out, and he turned up his nose at the offer."

"What offer?"

"I knew he'd need a baby sitter if he met us, so I asked Lucy what she'd think about takin' care of the kid for a few hours. She said she'd be glad to do it. I called Bernard and told him that you wuz in town and wanted to meet with the two of us, and not to worry about gittin' a sitter because I already had one lined up for him. When I told him who it was, he nixed it asap."

"Wonder why?"

"I know why. Since Bernard's from up north, you wouldn't think he'd be a bigot, but he is. Lucy don't hold it against him 'cause he's Jewish."

"Maybe it has nothing to do with her race. He might have a sitter he uses a lot—someone the kid is used to and likes."

"That's not it. He would have told me if he had a regular sitter. He just said he wouldn't be able to make it and didn't give a reason. He's always been kinda uppity."

I decided that continuing that conversation wasn't going to get us anywhere, so I dropped it.

"Hey, I'm parched. Let's order a beer."

Joe Bob summoned the waitress, and in no time, we were relaxed and having a friendly drink.

"Tell me all the scuttlebutt floating around Martinsville since I left."

"Well, let me see. Fred Peyton's still keepin' the roadsides cleared of pop bottles and cans. He's still wearin' that same old dumbass coat. It can't be the same one he wore fifteen or twenty years ago."

I shook my head. "No, I wouldn't think so."

"Oh, speakin' of Fred, part of The Red Onion burned up. Fred's little hut burned to the ground. He'd be out on the street, but that sister of his owns a house. She took him in. Fred's lucky to have her. She's a secretary at one of the schools."

"Good for Fred. He'd probably have a pretty tough time if he had to go it alone. I'm sure he didn't have much of anything in that hut he lived in, but it was still his home. How did The Onion catch on fire?"

"If anybody knows, they're not tellin'. There's talk about condemnin' the whole thing, razin' all them little red brick-sided lean-tos. I guess that would put everone who lives there out in the cold."

"I guess The Onion made it longer than it should have. It's always been a firetrap."

"Yeah." Joe Bob grinned. "Another little bit of town gossip might interest you, Matt."

"Well?"

"Your smokin' ex appears to be hot on the trail of our new preacher man. Can you believe it?"

"That works for me. Now she won't be stalking me."

Joe Bob had just taken a healthy swallow of his beer. He looked toward the front door and his face took on a look of surprise.

"I'll be damned," he said, in what appeared disbelief.

I leaned out of the booth and turned to learn what his

expression meant. Bernie Zuckerman was headed toward us, and there was no moss growing under his feet. His face was red, and his forehead was covered with beads of perspiration.

"Hi, guys," he said, sliding into the booth beside me. He sounded out of breath.

Chapter Two

Joe Bob and I had no idea why Bernie had changed his mind and decided to join us, but it didn't take long to find out. He spat out his tale like a rushing river, never pausing to take a breath. Then, he took off his glasses and began to sob.

Joe Bob attempted to quiet him while I sat there dumbfounded, wondering why I had come back to a place where trouble awaited me the minute I arrived.

When Bernie had gotten hold of his emotions enough to speak, his words came out in staccato bursts. "I cannot do this," he said, sounding somewhat like a robot.

Joe Bob and I raised our eyebrows.

"What can't you do?" Joe Bob asked.

"I can't live like this. Whenever I see Lee Ann, imagining her with that guy, I want to die. It drives me crazy."

"You told me you never wanted to be in the same room with her, that she was history."

"That's true. The only time I see her is when I have to give up my baby girl two weekends each month. I hate Lee Ann, but in some strange way, I still love her. I know that sounds crazy."

"You got that right," Joe Bob agreed. "Sounds to me like you need to toughen up. She wuz the one who cheated. You might want to remember that before you go all soft on her."

I didn't want to get in the middle of this thing with Bernie and his ex. The only reason I had come back to Martinsville was to settle my nerves, chill out, and decide what to do with my life. I didn't need to take on someone else's aggravation. This town's laid back, slow paced lifestyle was supposed to help me get my head on straight instead of filling it full of other people's problems.

"I've been trying to move forward, get on with my life, and forget the past. I've even been seeing someone," Bernie said, sniffling.

"Now you're talkin'. That's a step in the right direction. Who's the lucky woman?" Joe Bob asked.

"You guys don't know her. And, I'm not exactly seeing her. Well, I've been sleeping with her a little bit." He shrugged.

I hadn't contributed one word to the conversation. If Bernie had come here seeking advice concerning his love life or any other sticky thing he was involved in, he'd have to get it from Joe Bob.

"Well, Bernard, nobody's gonna give you grief for takin' care of your personal needs. It's no big deal. Right, Matt?"

"Guys, I'm back in this one horse town because I need to settle myself down; calm down from the rat race of city life. I've screwed up a hunk of my adulthood with a failed marriage and feeble attempts at making a living. I'm not a good one to turn to for any kind of advice. I'm thirty-eight years old without a roadmap for the rest of my life."

"I apologize for dropping this in your lap, Matt," Bernie said. "I'm just thinking of myself."

"Now we don't need to be placin' blame here," Joe Bob reasoned. "Sometimes we just git too much on our plates, and it throws us for a loop. Seems like both of you guys got more'n you can handle right now."

What he said made me feel kind of ashamed. The three of us had been friends for a long time. We should be able to go to one another with our problems whenever we felt the need.

"Joe Bob's right," I said, "but we're grown men; we can work out our problems. Tell us about this new woman in your life, Bernie."

Bernie gave his eyes a swipe and sighed.

"Her name is Juanita Ramirez, and she's my new housekeeper/ babysitter. She's great with Claire, and my baby girl took to her immediately."

"That's good," Joe Bob said, nodding.

"Remember how spoiled and whiney Claire was? Well, she's not like that anymore except after she spends a weekend with Lee Ann. She comes home a brat, but Juanita has her back in shape in no time. She's even taught my Claire a little Spanish."

"Since your divorce has been finalized, I hope you'll be able to get over Lee Ann. It sounds like you have a good thing going," I said.

"Juanita moved out of her apartment and into the room over my garage," Bernie went on. "That way she can be there to take care of Claire when she wakes up each morning."

"Makes sense," Joe Bob said. "So what's the problem?"

"The problem is that Lee Ann knows about Juanita. A week or so ago she drove by the little park where Juanita takes Claire to play. She pulled to the curb and sat in her car staring at Juanita and Claire. She didn't leave her car and approach them; just stared daggers at Juanita."

"So she knows you have a babysitter who takes your kid to the park. So what?" Joe Bob said.

"Juanita doesn't want any kind of trouble. She needs this job, but she let me know that she isn't willing to put herself in jeopardy to keep it. I can tell that she's beginning to care for me, and she seems to adore Claire. She told me that she doesn't want anything to do with Lee Ann, but she expects trouble from her."

"Maybe Lee Ann just wanted to see how Juanita was treating Claire," I said.

"I'm sure that wasn't why she gave Juanita threatening looks. She wants her gone."

"Sure you're not jumpin' to conclusions?" Joe Bob asked.

Bernie sighed. "The last time I picked Claire up, Lee Ann didn't even let me inside. She ushered our child through the door and stepped out onto the front porch. Then, she put her hands on her hips and practically hissed, 'I don't want my child speaking Spanish. Do something about it!' She went inside and slammed the door in my face."

"I don't git why she'd care if the kid knew a few Spanish words," Joe Bob said.

"I don't either," Bernie said. "Claire brought her sippy cup to me the other day and asked for agua. I don't know how many Spanish words she knows, but I know she's smart. Maybe she'll be bilingual."

"What do you think Lee Ann might do?" I said.

"I don't know, and I don't know what I should do."

"I say hide and wait," Joe Bob opined. "Maybe she's just bein' her normal sweet self. That's kinda the way I remember her."

"I agree," I said. "If Lee Ann's all mouth and it doesn't affect Claire, I think I would bide my time. Hopefully, she'll cool down and drop it."

Joe Bob motioned to the waitress, and minutes later Lucy Combs appeared with a pitcher of beer and three steins. She delivered smiles to Joe Bob and me, and appeared to look right through Bernie.

"Lucy, I have a regular sitter," Bernie explained. "I didn't take you up on your offer to stay with Claire because I didn't think I could leave work to meet the guys. As it turned out, I could."

Lucy gave him a nod and walked away.

I've heard that when a man gives himself up to the drink his true feelings come out. He says things he would never utter if he were sober—things which might be buried in his subconscious mind that he wouldn't have the intestinal fortitude to express. I don't know how much of that is true, but I do know that any mind altering substance can change a person's thinking and actions.

With that in mind, after we had drained two pitchers while filling awkward silence with small talk, I suggested that we order dinner. I never wanted to relive the drunken experience the three of us shared in a room at The Greystone the last time I was here in my hometown.

We had just finished our dinner and were lingering over coffee when Bernie's phone chimed.

"Bernie Zuckerman," he said. "Slow down. I can't understand what you're saying. Take a breath, and tell me what happened."

Joe Bob and I looked down at our coffee cups as though that might keep us from listening to Bernie's side of the conversation.

"Just calm down. I want my friends to hear this. I'm going to put you on the speaker," Bernie said, attempting to slow his speech and stop sounding panicked. He pushed a button on his phone and placed it on the table.

"I must speak quietly. Claire is asleep in the next room."

"Okay. Repeat what you just told me," Bernie said. "Don't talk so fast."

The volume on the phone must have been turned up all the way, because it seemed that Juanita was shouting.

"Bernie," I said, "turn off the speaker."

My friend hit the button and donned a questioning expression.

"I'm still here," he said into the phone. Hold on a second."

"I don't think you want everyone in this place to hear the phone conversation," I cautioned.

Bernie nodded and spoke calmly into the phone. "I'll be there in just a few minutes."

He slid out of the booth, hiked up his pants, and stood, heaving a sigh.

"I don't suppose you guys would want to accompany me," he said.

"Well, sure, Bernard. I'll ride shotgun with you," Joe Bob said.

I told myself to stay out of other people's messes, but Bernie was my old friend, and I could almost hear the plea in his voice. I didn't have anything on my agenda since I had just gotten into town. The only thing I intended to pursue was a possible relationship with Sidney Edelman, the new veterinarian who had captured my attention the last time I was here.

"Count me in, too," I said, wondering if I would be kicking myself down the road.

Joe Bob left way too much money on the table to cover our tab, and we hurried out of the building.

"We'll follow you in my rental car, Bernie. I'll bring Joe Bob back here to get his truck."

Bernie was in his Caddie and out of the parking lot before Joe Bob and I could get our seatbelts fastened.

"Wonder what's happened?" Joe Bob said.

"I have no idea, but we're about to find out."

"Well, I don't know what his ex is capable of doin'. You wouldn't think she'd do anything to hurt the kid, but we both know she don't have no love left for Bernard. Remember how she yelled at him that day we wuz there?"

"I remember. There's no way I would have stayed in that marriage. That kind of treatment would have killed any love I had ever had for her."

"The only thing that woman had goin' for her wuz her looks, and man, did she have 'em."

"Here we are," I said.

I parked on the street, and Joe Bob and I hurried up the driveway to see Juanita rush into Bernie's arms at the door.

Juanita was visibly upset. She pulled her right arm from around Bernie's neck and wiped at her eyes with a small fist.

"Look what she did to my car!" she wailed.

Joe Bob and I had to walk past an old Kia parked at the curb. Neither of us had paid any attention to it.

"Let's go inside," Bernie said.

He motioned for us to follow them into the house through the garage, and we trailed through the laundry room and kitchen, ending up back outside on the patio.

"Juanita, these are my two best friends, Matt and Joe Bob. We've known one another since high school. You can feel safe telling us all what happened from the start," Bernie said.

Juanita sniffed. "Please to meet you. Sit." She indicated lawn chairs which were situated in a semicircle.

"Where to start?" she said. "Sorry bad English."

"When did you notice your tires had been slashed?" asked Bernie.

"Claire was fussy. It was hard to get her down for nap."

Juanita interrupted her story to burst into another spate of tears. She dropped her elbows to her knees with her face in her hands.

Bernie got down on a knee and wrapped an arm around the girl's shoulders.

"Don't be afraid, Juanita, and don't worry about the tires. We're not going to let anything happen to you or Claire, and I'll get you new tires."

He pulled a handkerchief from his back pocket and handed it to Juanita, and she pulled herself together with palpable effort.

"Claire finally wore herself out, and I put her down. When I sure she asleep, I go out to get mail from box. That's when I see what she did to my car."

I didn't feel comfortable asking questions or giving advice to this girl I had just met, and I knew Joe Bob didn't either, so we let Bernie do the talking.

"What made you think Lee Ann was the one who cut your tires?" he asked.

"She did it. She call the house before—two times today."

"What did she say?"

"She just breathe into phone. I know it was your ex wife. She hate me; don't want me work here."

"Did she say anything?"

"No. I look at caller ID. It say caller unknown, but I know who it was."

"How many times have you gotten calls like this?" Bernie asked.

Juanita shrugged. "Not sure how many. She been call here since the day she stare at us in the park."

"I understand why you think she's the one who slashed your tires and made the calls, but if she didn't say anything and you didn't see her, she might be innocent. There are a few unsavory teenage boys who live around here. They pull pranks they think are funny, like pushing over a porta potty at the construction site of a house that's being built. I wouldn't put it past them to cut someone's tires for the fun of it."

"What about the calls?" Joe Bob asked.

I assumed that he was ready to join the conversation.

"Kids make crank calls all the time. You know that. We used to do it," Bernie said.

"Yeah, we did," Joe Bob admitted, "but we said stupid stuff; we didn't just breathe into the phone. Seems like to me if somebody does that they're tryin' to scare you."

"I think I'll stay home tomorrow, maybe even for a couple of days. My manager can run things at work. Maybe I can figure out what's going on. If it is Lee Ann pulling this shit, I'll catch her in the act."

Chapter Three

It seemed that there was something foul in the air in Martinsville each time I returned to my hometown. I had hoped this time things would be different; that I would be able to bask in the sun of this small southern town with its slow, laid back lifestyle. But this was now, unlike the Mayberry of my childhood. Attitudes had changed. Innocence had morphed into more worldly thoughts and actions, and everyone seemed a little more guarded than before.

I was beginning to think that nearly everybody in Martinsville had secrets. The last time I was here, Joe Bob had confessed to indulging in afternoon delights with a married woman and having had a brief fling with Lucy Combs, a black waitress at Morgan's. Beth, my ex, had completely changed after she divorced me. She had turned into a conniving shrew, all the while feigning innocence. Then, there was Bernie who, despite the fact that he still had feelings for his cheating ex, was bedding down his housekeeper/babysitter on the sly. The only person I felt sure was true to herself was Trudy, the woman I considered my second mother.

Simply out of curiosity, I thought I might want to meet the new Methodist preacher. If Beth had her eye on him, I had no doubt that it wouldn't take long for her to lure him into her trap. I would pity the poor guy if she managed to get him into an embarrassing situation, which she eventually would if it meant getting something she wanted.

After I left my friends, I went home and climbed the stairs to my old room. Trudy had unpacked my bags and turned down my bed. I stripped down to my boxers and got into bed, luxuriating in the fresh scent of linens that smelled like they had been hung to dry on a line in the sunshine.

I abandoned the unsavory things that had been cluttering my mind and turned my thoughts to the fresh-faced, kindhearted, and ever so alluring, Sydney Edelman. I had kept her business card, and the address of her apartment I had scribbled on a scrap of paper. I was glad she had been willing to see me before I left to go back to Denver. It enabled me to explain that Beth and I had no ties, nothing in common, and that my ex was a sick woman. Sydney and I had a cordial goodbye. Now I wanted another chance to at least be friends. No; I wanted a chance to woo her.

I had told my friends my reason for returning to Martinsville was to take my time in deciding how and where I wanted to spend the rest of my life. I hadn't bothered to check into whether or not the Tennessee Bar had reciprocity with that of Colorado. I had been an attorney my entire adult life, but I wasn't sure that was what I wanted to do until I retired. Real Estate might be an option, but I wasn't sure it would appeal to me. The one thing that might help me decide where I wanted to tackle this new endeavor was whether or not Sydney Edelman remembered me and would be willing to see me again.

I stared at the ceiling remembering Sydney's lovely smile. It was fresh in my mind as if I had seen it moments ago. And her gait—a thing of beauty. I'd never seen a female walk the way

Sydney did. She moved with purpose, yet it was extremely sexy. I would bet she had never considered herself sexy. I closed my eyes and watched her move into the distance as I fell into a deep sleep.

The aroma of coffee pulled me out of bed. The clock on my bedside table told me it was nearly eight o'clock. I hadn't slept that late since I was a teenager. I threw on a pair of running shorts and a tee shirt and went to join Trudy in the kitchen.

"Good mornin', my sweet boy," she said.

"I told you that you are not to make my meals, Trudy. You don't work for me."

"Since when do you tell your old Trudy what to do?" she said in her no-nonsense tone.

"I just want you to enjoy your life. You've taken care of my entire family as far back as I can remember. It's your turn to relax."

"Sit yourself down at the table," she ordered, setting a plate of bacon, eggs, and two fluffy biscuits in front of me.

"Yes ma'am."

Trudy pulled out a chair and took a seat across from me. She doctored her coffee and took a sip.

"Have you made any plans for today?" she asked.

"Nope. I'm going to eat this wonderful breakfast. Then, if I'm not too sluggish, I'll go for a run. Is there something you need me to do?"

"Not a thing. I want you to do whatever strikes your fancy."

"By the way, do you still have that evil dog, Fifi, hidden around here somewhere?"

"No. I'm afraid Fifi isn't with us anymore. She passed away last year, but she had a good long life; lived to be seventeen. That's a long time for a dog. Why are you askin' about the dog? You couldn't stand her."

"You're right about that. She was a mean little thing. I just wondered if she was still around. I won't have to worry that the little sneak will appear out of nowhere and bite my ankles."

If the dog had still been here, I might have come up with some excuse to take the poor old thing to a certain vet.

I should have gone for a run before eating a big breakfast. So instead of running, I went for a leisurely stroll around the neighborhood. Martinsville had always been lovely as small towns go. The lawns were well-maintained with bright patches of flowers and neatly trimmed shrubs. Most of the houses were small, but the curb appeal was inviting.

I hadn't realized how far I had walked until I found myself in front of my ex mother-in-law's house. I promised myself that I would never again be lured into that house since the night Beth had plied me with champagne, talked me into smoking a joint, and made me her prisoner, handcuffing me to her bed naked. If Joe Bob hadn't sprung me, I could only imagine what she might have done to me.

I glanced toward the house, and there sat Beth's mother in the porch swing. Hoping she wouldn't see me, I quickened my pace, but I was too late.

"Matt Stevenson, is that really you?" she called.

I pretended not to have heard her, and kept walking with increased speed until I was out of her line of vision. It made me feel like a kid playing such a juvenile game with an adult, but I wanted nothing to do with Beth or her mother. I wanted them out of my life.

The house was quiet when I returned. I showered, put on a pair of Jeans and a golf shirt, then headed for Joe Bob's garage. I found him sitting on the corner of his desk talking on the phone.

"Okay. Bring it by in the mornin'. I'll take a look at it," he said, taking a drag on his cigarette and hanging up. "Hey, Matt. What brings you slummin'?"

I laughed. "I was just wondering if you might want to go someplace for a bite of lunch."

"Sure. Let me git out of these coveralls. Any place in particular you want to go?"

"That little diner has pretty good lunch fare."

"Works for me."

I was hoping Sydney Edelman might be having lunch at the diner since it was close to her place of business, but I knew it would be a long shot. Even if she happened to be there, she might be with someone else.

Joe Bob and I were led to a booth by a window. After we were seated, my friend crossed his arms over his chest and looked at me with raised eyebrows.

"What?" I said.

"That's my question. Guys don't do lunch. You must have somethin' on your mind you want to discuss."

"I was going to ask if you'd heard from Bernie this morning."

"No, and I don't expect to hear from him unless he learns more about what's goin' on at his house. It don't make sense for his ex to threaten the babysitter or slash her tires. She might not want her kid speakin' Spanish, but I doubt she knows Bernard's been boinkin' the girl. Even if she knew about their relationship, it's plain she don't want Bernard or she wouldn't have cheated on him."

"Maybe she's changed her mind and wants Bernie back."

"I'm thinkin' you're barkin' up the wrong tree. You know it's possible that our buddy could be keepin' somethin' from us."

"Like what?"

"I don't know. Most people got a secret or two. Open books don't exactly abound here in Martinsville. Oh, there's gossip about almost everbody, and it's hard to find the truth in most things you hear. Bernard and yours truly don't find ourselves in the same sandbox very often. I ain't seen hide nor hair of him more than twice since you wuz here last year. He hasn't called me or come by my place even once. I saw him one time when I went to pick up my dry cleanin' and another time when I bumped into him on the street."

The little bell over the door tinkled, and I looked up to see none other than the lovely Sydney Edelman enter the diner with a tall handsome guy about my age. The two were smiling at one another as he guided her past our booth toward the back of the diner. She didn't bother to look in my direction.

"Hey, do you ever see the lady vet around town?"

Joe Bob grinned.

"I catch sight of her ever now and then, and I see her when I take my cat in for a checkup. Why?"

"You know why, Joe Bob. I wonder if she even remembers me."

"I reckon you'll have to find that out for yourself. Why don't you give her a call? Can't hurt."

"Maybe I'll just do that. I guess you didn't notice when she walked right by our booth a few minutes ago."

"No. I didn't see her. She's a real good vet. You can just tell that she cares about the critters she doctors."

"I know she's probably a great vet. You don't need to sing me her praises. What I want to know is if she's involved with someone. She just walked past our booth with a tall good looking guy."

"I don't know nothin' about the woman's personal life, Matt. She's always friendly when I take my cat to her clinic."

Joe Bob and I finished our lunch and left the diner. He said he needed to get back to work, so I was left to while away the afternoon alone. I could spend a little time finding out if the Colorado and Tennessee Bars had reciprocity if I wanted to do something productive. But if Sydney Edelman was hooked up with someone, I might want to look elsewhere to hang my hat.

I wondered if Bernie was having any luck trying to find out who was out to get his girlfriend/babysitter/housekeeper. I didn't think he would be at his shop. He had said he planned to stay at home in case his ex tried more mischief. I thought about going to his house to find out if he had made any progress but changed my mind. He hadn't asked for my help, and even though I was curious about his situation, I didn't want to get bogged down in his problems.

I remembered where Sydney Edelman's apartment complex was from the last time I was in Martinsville, and knowing she would still be at work, I drove there. Getting out of my rental car, I went into the breezeway on the first floor to check the bank of mailboxes. It was ridiculous to feel excited to see her name in next to the last slot: S. Edelman. That meant she still lived here.

Just as I was about to leave, I heard people talking. They were coming up the walk toward me. I had never felt so childish, rushing to the other side of the building and disappearing around the corner. I sneaked a peek and saw a man and a woman waiting for the elevator. Their backs were facing me. I hadn't been here for about eighteen months, but I recognized Sydney's stance, the shape of her legs, and the cut and color of her hair. The elevator door opened, and she and her gentleman friend stepped inside.

I fervently wished that I hadn't come to the apartment complex. Twice in one day I had seen Sydney with the same man. Whatever their relationship was, I was becoming convinced that it didn't bode well for my chances of pursuing a relationship with her. Coming back to Martinsville to sort things out and decide if this was where I wanted to be, suddenly seemed like a bad idea. I was feeling more than a little depressed.

Realizing that I had been doing nothing but spinning my wheels and getting down in the dumps about Sydney Edelman, I decided to do something useful—doing a bit of research. It didn't take long to learn that because I had practiced law in Colorado for five years, the State of Tennessee would accept me on reciprocity. That knowledge, and the fact that Trudy was well and happy, were the only bright spots since I had come home.

I went up to my old room and flopped down on the bed to ponder what to do next. As one possibility after another came to mind, I was still at a loss. I fell asleep spinning my wheels. My father had given me a tidy sum which would more than tide me over until I was able to make a decision as to where I wanted to be and what I wanted to do.

The aggravating sound of a leaf blower woke me. I had slept most of the afternoon reminiscent of lazy wasted days I had idled away doing nothing when as a teenager.

Trudy was in the kitchen chopping vegetables when I came downstairs. She smiled as I came into the room.

"I hope you're chopping those for something you're making for your dinner," I said.

"I'm makin' a chicken pot pie. You're welcome to enjoy it with me."

"There's no point in my trying to explain to you that you don't need to take care of me, Trudy. I'm not eight years old anymore." I sighed.

"I'm not doin' anything I don't want to do. I'd like to have chicken pot pie for dinner. You're welcome, but if you want to dine somewhere else, that's fine."

She wiped her hands and came over to give me a hug, and it

made me feel like scum. I hugged her back and told her that I was going to see a friend, but I'd try to be back in time for dinner.

I figured Joe Bob would be home from work by now, so I drove to the trailer park. Lights shone through the small windows of his double wide. It didn't look like he had company. There wasn't a vehicle parked outside, so I climbed the two steps to his door and knocked.

My old friend opened the door wearing a terrycloth robe and a towel wrapped around his head.

"Hey, Matt. Come on in. Make yourself at home while I throw on some threads."

I had no sooner sat down than Joe Bob's big yellow cat headed straight for me. The animal knew I wasn't a fan of felines, but that didn't keep it from leaping into my lap. I noted that its hair had grown back since Sydney Edelman had patched it together after some jerk ran over it and left it for dead. The animal looked perfectly healthy.

Joe Bob returned to the living room carrying a couple of longnecks and offered me one.

"Git off Matt's lap, you dumb cat," he said, scooping his pet up and cradling it in his muscled arm. He dumped the cat to the floor to see who was banging on his door and opened it.

"Well, hey there, Bernard. This is beginnin' to look like old home week."

Bernie swallowed.

"Not exactly. I'm afraid I've got real trouble."

Chapter Four

Perspiration poured from Bernie's forehead and ran into his eyes. His glasses were fogged. He pulled them off with one hand, grabbed Joe Bob's beer with the other, and took a long pull.

"Bernard, you're 'bout white as a sheet. Take a load off and tell us what's goin' on."

Bernie dropped down on the couch and swiped the sweat from his brow with the back of his hand.

"Mister Floppy's missing. There was no way he could just disappear. Somebody's trying to send me a message."

"Mister Floppy?" I said.

"After Lee Ann and I divorced, I needed to do something to distract Claire, so I bought her a pet. Mister Floppy is one of those long-eared rabbits that are so popular. You've seen them. This one is also cuddly—you know, happy to let you hold him and treat him like a doll or something."

"So he went missin'?"

"I put him in his outdoor wire pen for some fresh air after lunch. When I went back to bring him inside, he wasn't there. There was no way he could have gotten out. Somebody had to take him."

"Them things cost much?"

"That's not the point, Joe Bob. Why would anyone steal a child's pet, and, more to the point, who would do it?"

"No idea who would steal a rabbit, but you prob'ly don't know that much about critters. They can squeeze through little bitty spaces. I'll bet he just got tired of bein' treated like a doll and escaped. Buy the kid another rabbit."

"Claire would know it wasn't Mister Floppy. My child isn't stupid. Besides, that doesn't address the big problem; that being who did it."

"Have you seen Lee Ann near your house since you've been staying at home?" I asked.

"Nope. I haven't even seen her drive by."

"But you think she took the rabbit," I said.

"Yes. Who else would do it?"

"Who else knew Claire even had a rabbit?" I asked.

"Nobody. So Lee Ann had to take it."

"I'm sorry, Bernard. I know how humans can git attached to animals. Y'all know how I feel about my old cat."

Bernie nodded.

"I left my child crying her little eyes out. She loved that rabbit."

"Here's the thing, Bernie," I said. "I don't think there's anything we can do about this. You can accuse your ex of the crime, but can you prove it?"

Bernie shook his head. "How can I do that?'

"If you can't prove it, it's slander. You know that. Either you prove it, or you need to let it go and make the best of it."

"I have a bad feeling this is another step in Lee Ann's plot to make me fire Juanita. First, she slashed Juanita's tires, now this. I can't imagine what she might do next."

"We don't actually know Lee Ann slashed the tires," I reminded him.

"She did it. I know she did."

"'scuse me for askin', Bernard, but if you're so concerned about your kid and Juanita, why'd you leave 'em alone to come over here?"

Bernie puffed up like a wet hen.

"I didn't leave them all alone, Joe Bob. I have an acquaintance hanging out at the house while I'm gone. He's a menacing looking figure, but he wouldn't hurt a fly."

"You don't have to git all bent outta shape, Bernard. I didn't mean nothin' by it. I just wondered."

"I have an idea," I said, attempting to insert a bit of calm. "It's almost dinner time. Why don't the three of us go someplace, maybe have a drink, and enjoy a nice meal."

"You up for that, Bernard?"

"I guess so," mumbled Bernie.

He had enjoyed being talked into doing something since he was a teenager.

I volunteered to drive us in the rental car. Since Morgan's was pretty much a greasy spoon, but had a fairly extensive menu, that's where we decided to go. We felt sure we wouldn't run into Bernie's ex. We knew she wouldn't be caught dead in such a place.

Bernie wanted to cruise by his house on the way to dinner to make sure everything looked normal. Joe Bob and I had only been to his new place the night Juanita had called him all distraught. A guy about the size of a silo was sitting in the front porch swing staring at the scenery, doing nothing.

"Wow!" Joe Bob said. "Did you git a look at the size of that guy, Matt?"

"Yeah, I got a glimpse of him. He is pretty scary looking."

We pulled into the parking lot at Morgan's just in time to see a couple entering the restaurant. There was something familiar about the man's posture, but that didn't merit much attention.

Lucy Combs was waiting on our section of the restaurant. She wore a big smile as she came to our table, dragging her lame foot.

"Well, look who's here," she said. "It's good to see you guys. You didn't tell me what brings you to Martinsville, Matt?"

"Oh, nothing in particular. I just decided to come down to get a dose of the South."

"Well, we're glad to have you back. Y'all want to order drinks?"

"What a good idea," Bernie said. "I'll have a Manhattan."

Joe Bob and I ordered bourbon, and he inquired about the specials.

"Two specials," Lucy said, "fried chicken and pot roast. They're both to die for."

Joe Bob opted for the fried chicken as fast as he could get the words out of his mouth, but Bernie and I asked for a few minutes to peruse the menu. I decided I wasn't going to gain weight like I did the last time I was here and chose grilled salmon and a spinach salad. Bernie studied the menu until after we had finished our drinks. He ordered another Manhattan and the steamed vegetable plate.

I had the distinct feeling that Bernie's dinner order with his choice of adult beverage might easily turn out to be a bad combo, but he was a grown man, so I kept my concern to myself. If he wanted to get smashed in order to forget his troubles, that was his business.

When our meals arrived, Joe Bob ordered a beer, and I asked for a glass of chardonnay. Bernie had knocked off most of his second Manhattan. He looked down at his steamed vegetables and began to cry.

Joe Bob spoke around a mouthful of fried chicken. "Bernard, you want some of my chicken?"

Bernie shook his head and took another slug of his drink. He pulled a handkerchief from his back pocket and dried his face.

"I'm sorry, guys," he blubbered. "I'm afraid I'm a complete mess."

"I don't think you're a mess, Bernard; you're drunk, but you're not a mess."

I put down my fork and tried not to appear as disgusted as I felt.

"Bernie, eat your dinner. You'll feel better," I said.

It was then that I came to the realization that the missing rabbit wasn't the only reason Bernie was so emotional and, for lack of a better description, off balance. He was still hung up on his ex, the cheater. It had been quite a while since his divorce, and he still hadn't gotten over her.

Bernie speared a cauliflower florette. He sniffed and aimed the fork toward his mouth, missing its mark. I pretended not to have seen it, and Joe Bob stifled a snicker.

"Bernard, you stabbed that thing like you wuz mad at it."

Bernie swallowed and appeared to be focused on something, or someone at the back of the restaurant. His sad condition had just been outranked by something more interesting. I looked in the direction he seemed to find so intriguing.

"What is it, Bernie?"

"That guy looks like Freaky Fred, but he's all cleaned up. He's with a woman, and they're coming this way."

Bernie picked up an asparagus spear and nibbled at it, his eyes trained on the couple coming toward us. Then, the pair was passing our table, and Joe Bob's eyes grew big.

"Hey there, Freddy," he greeted, around a mouthful of food.

That looked like the couple I saw entering the restaurant when we first arrived. The man definitely resembled Fred Peyton, and he was about Fred's size. I assumed the woman accompanying him was his sister, the one who took him in after The Red Onion burned to the ground. It appeared that she had cleaned him up very well. His long greasy hair had been cut and looked clean, his clothes were neat, and he was missing that ratty old gabardine coat.

The couple didn't stop, and the man, if he was indeed Fred Peyton, didn't react to having heard his name being called.

"If that was Fred, his appearance sure has improved," I said.

"That was Fred alright," said Joe Bob. I seen him several times since he went to live with his sister, but he didn't look like this. Looks like she's cleaned him up real good, but I can't imagine how she's gonna git the wild out of him."

Bernie seemed to have lost interest in Fred and resumed attacking his vegetables with a bit more luck. He got Lucy's attention and asked for a cup of coffee.

"I don't know much about that sister of Fred's," Joe Bob said, "but I know she's got a decent job, and I heard she's one of them funny religions. She don't wear no makeup like other women. I'd say she's got her work cut out for her tryin' to turn Fred into a normal person."

"Who knows?" I said. "She might be able to work wonders with him. We all know he's a genius in a couple of areas, and he has a conscience. He proved that the day we saw him at the police station."

"That's right," Joe Bob agreed. "He saved my rear end; kept me outta the big house. I was ready to turn myself in for hittin' Jimmy Banks with my Buick and killin' him when I was innocent all along. God bless Fred for showin' up when he did."

"Wonder why he didn't look in our direction when you spoke to him?" I said. "He must have heard you."

Joe Bob shrugged. "Why does he do anything he does, or don't do? He's Freaky Fred."

Bernie had managed to eat most of his dinner. He was on his second cup of black coffee and decided to join the conversation.

"Come to think about it, I haven't seen him picking up bottles for about a week, but I'm not sure I would have recognized him without that old coat. Maybe the sister burned the coat and has taught him some sort of trade."

I had been so concerned about Bernie that I had completely forgotten about Trudy's dinner invitation.

"Guys, I hate to cut this short, but I'm probably in the doghouse. I promised Trudy I'd be back in time for dinner. I'm probably in for a benevolent dressing down."

"Well, we can't have that, can we? Let's beat feet," Joe Bob said.

I dropped my friends off at Joe Bob's place and went to face the music with Trudy. She was sipping wine and watching a game show on TV.

"Hey, Trudy."

"Hey, yourself," she said, and smiled at me while holding up a hand, telling me to wait until she answered a question the game host had posed.

"I apologize, Trudy. I should have at least called to let you know I wouldn't be here for dinner."

"No apology is necessary. I've learned to enjoy meals by myself. Would you like a glass of wine?"

"No, thanks. When did you start indulging in alcoholic beverages?"

"After your sweet mama passed, I was alone in this house at night. It was so quiet, and I was powerful lonely for her. That's when I became friends with a bit of wine. I find that I like it."

I smiled at my old friend and bade her goodnight.

Lying in bed I did my best to banish Bernie's problems from my mind and turn my full attention to thoughts of Sydney Edelman. I hoped she was available and that the man I had seen her with was not a threat to my chances of pursuing a relationship with her. I tried to imagine possible reasons she might be accompanied by a man other than a romantic one. The guy could be a relative, or an old friend. He might be involved with the plans for the house she was having built. But why wasn't that house built by now? She had bought a lot when I was here before. Why was she still living in the apartment? Both times I had seen Sydney and the man together they had been smiling at one another. I fell asleep having made the decision to be bold enough to approach the pretty vet and find out who the mysterious gentleman was. It would be my first order of business in the morning.

Chapter Five

The aroma of coffee called me downstairs. Trudy was taking a pan of biscuits from the oven. Her face lit up like it did when I was a kid the minute she saw me.

I had already showered and dressed in khakis and one of my nicer golf shirts.

"Well, young man, what are you up to this fine mornin'?"

As a child, and even as an adult, I had always felt comfortable confiding in my old friend. She had never seemed to judge, but if she thought I might be in need of her sage advice, she was more than glad to offer it.

"I plan to do a little fishing if I can work up the nerve," I said.

"You don't look like you're dressed to go fishin' in the lake. What kind of fishin' might you be wantin' to do?"

"I met a certain lovely lady when I was here last. She's the vet who took Doc Green's place. Her name is Sydney Edelman. I was fortunate enough to escort her to dinner one evening, but that was right before I left to fly to Denver. I'd like to pursue a relationship with her if she's available."

Trudy smiled. "I've met your Sydney Edelman. She was so

kind and gentle with Fifi. The poor little dog was in so much pain that she wouldn't eat or drink. I couldn't stand to see her suffer anymore, so I took her to the lady vet, and she made Fifi's pain go away. She put her into a twililght sleep before givin' her the lethal injection. Sydney Edelman is a wonderful vet. She's the kind of person I've been hopin' you would find."

I had failed to inform Trudy that I had seen Sydney in the company of a good looking guy on a couple of different occasions. Subconsciously, I was afraid she would withdraw her approval of my pursuit if she thought I was attempting to break up what looked like a happy couple.

"That makes two of us. By the way, I'm glad you approve. Your opinion means a lot to me."

Trudy grinned. "Think you can eat an omelet without spillin' some of it on your clean shirt?"

"Since you're determined to feed me, bring it on."

It only took a few minutes for my old friend to produce a perfect fluffy omelet and slide it onto my plate. It was chock full of bell peppers, sweet Vidalia onions, chopped ham, and lots of melted cheese. Nobody could make an omelet equal to Trudy's. There wasn't a hint of brown on it, and it was delicious.

"What you gonna use for bait? You don't have a pet to take to the clinic."

"I guess I'll have to depend on my good looks." I grinned.

"Let me know how that turns out."

I wasn't sure why, but Trudy's approval gave me more confidence than I'd had before breakfast. In front of the mirror in the bathroom, I put on my most sincere expression. I wanted Sydney Edelman to look at me and realize that I am truly interested in her and that I'm seeking more than a one night stand. I hoped she would look into my eyes and see integrity. Then, another thought came to mind. Maybe I should swap the golf shirt for a dress shirt with the sleeves rolled up. Women seem to like that look.

Trudy knocked on the door.

"I think you're pretty enough, Matty. Come out here and listen to me."

I was sure I looked like a ten-year-old who had been practicing kissing the bathroom mirror. I opened the door, stepped out into the hall, and grinned.

My old friend led me down the stairs and into the kitchen. She pointed to the chair I had vacated minutes earlier, and I sat down. This was the very spot where she had brought me for one of her lectures that didn't seem like a lecture when I was a kid.

"Don't go obsessin' about approachin' the lady. Just be yourself. You might not know it, but the good Lord gave you a gift when you came into this world. You've got natural charm, and it's honest. You've never had to work at it. You don't have to take a pet to the clinic. There's no law that says you must have a reason to approach the vet."

"I guess you're right about that, but don't you think it's kind of nervy to show up considering the time that's elapsed since I took her to dinner? If Beth hadn't shown up at the restaurant that night and ruined Sydney's impression of me, things could have turned out much better. Beth gave Sydney the impression that she and I were still an item, and that was when Sydney gave me the gate. She had no interest in being part of a love triangle."

"Forget Elizabeth. She's got her hook baited to snag the new preacher. You know she's a lot like a pit bull when it comes to gettin' what she wants. I think she's a busy girl on a mission."

I took Trudy's advice and drove straight to the animal clinic. There were several cars in the parking lot which made me think

Sydney must be pretty busy. I sat in my rental car and watched one person come out of the clinic toting a small animal carrier and young woman tugging on the leash of a great dane, trying to coax the dog into the building.

I was afraid that if I sat there much longer I would lose my nerve and leave, so I screwed up my courage and went inside. The receptionist was busy with someone, and I was able to slip past her desk and find a seat in a far corner of the room, hoping she wouldn't spot me and ask if she could be of assistance. I picked up a magazine and held it close to my face.

After a few minutes, Sydney Edelman entered the waiting area with a cardboard box. She placed the box on the desk, telling the receptionist something in a voice so quiet that I couldn't hear what she said. Then, she did an about face and left the room without so much as a glance in my direction.

Three more people took their pets in to see the doctor, then left the clinic. I wondered how many more pets the good doctor would see until the waiting area was empty except for yours truly. It was nearly noon by the time she finished with the last one.

This was my chance. My throat was dry, and I felt blood pumping in my ears. I stood up, dropping the magazine onto a coffee table, and cleared my throat. Sydney appeared not to have heard me. She grabbed her purse from behind the desk and headed for the front door.

"I'll be back by one o'clock, Joyce," she said over her shoulder, and went out the door and down the steps to the sidewalk.

I followed her from the building to watch her get into a silver Mercedes. I recognized the guy behind the wheel. He was the same person I'd seen her with at the restaurant and again at her apartment complex. This did not bode well for my quest.

I got into my car and drove out of the parking lot, feeling

more than a little bummed. It's true that misery loves company, so I drove to Joe Bob's garage hoping to bend his ear and whine.

My friend was in a bay with the door open. He was dunking an inner tube into a tub of water.

"Hey, Matt. What's up?" He showed off his pearly whites with a big smile.

"Not much. I'm just here to vent."

"Go ahead," he said, pushing the inner tube to the bottom of the tub.

Freaky Fred was strolling past the garage dressed in a pink golf shirt and creased jeans. He waved at us. Joe Bob and I were both curious about the change in his appearance and behavior. I felt sure he would tell us all about the transformation if we asked. But he didn't stop; just kept walking down the street.

"Somethin' weird's goin' on with Fred, and I got no idea what it could be."

"I'm sure we'll find out soon enough," I said. "There's something else I'm more interested in right now."

"What's that?"

"I want to get reunited with the lady vet, but I've seen her in the company of a guy about our age a few times."

"So?"

"So I want to find out what their relationship is. If they're a couple, I guess I'll forget about her."

"Well, Matt, I doubt she's gonna look you up and explain in much detail what's goin' on between 'em. Why don't you just go to her clinic, wait to catch her comin' or goin', and flat out ask her?"

"Don't you think that would be pretty presumptuous of me since we haven't seen one another in more than a year? Add to that fact that we were only together for dinner one evening and a lunch that I practically begged for."

"I reckon that would be pretty nervy; but then, you can be a pretty nervy guy." He grinned and pulled the inner tube out of the tub and marked the air leak.

"I did go to the clinic this morning. I waited for her to finish with everyone in the waiting area before approaching her. Actually, she didn't give me an opportunity to approach her. She grabbed her purse and flew out the door before I had a chance to let her know I was there. I watched her get into a Mercedes with that same guy and drive out of the parking lot."

"Maybe you ought to try callin' her. That might be easier than seein' her in person. Remind her who you are, tell her you're here in town, and ask if you could take her to dinner for old time's sake. The worst thing she could do would be to tell you to buzz off."

Joe Bob turned his gaze toward the sidewalk.

"Here comes Fred again," he said.

I turned toward the street to see Fred ambling along carrying a plastic bag. He was swinging it back and forth in rhythm with his feet, and he looked straight ahead.

"Hey, Fred," called Joe Bob, "come over here and shoot the breeze."

Fred stopped and looked down at the bag he was carrying. Then, he headed over to the garage.

"How's it goin,' Fred?"

Fred donned a serious expression.

"I've got a job," he said, lifting the bag from the hardware store for us to see.

"You're working at the hardware store?" I asked.

Fred shook his head.

"This is just one job," he said. "I go a lot of places; do a lot of things. That's my job."

"So you run errands?" I asked.

"Other stuff, too," he answered.

"What kind of other stuff? Joe Bob asked.

"Gotta go," Fred said.

He turned and took off at a trot.

"I'm thinkin' his job is stuff he's doin' for his sister. She prob'ly told him that's how he can pay rent to live with her."

"I don't know. He seemed awfully mysterious about it."

"I've got work to do," Joe Bob said, lighting a cigarette. "Go dig up that woman's number and give her a call. I don't recall you ever havin' a lack of confidence. You're a big boy; just do it."

There were so many things I should be doing if I intended to stay in Martinsville. I needed to get rid of this rental car. I would have to go to the closest town with a dealership and buy one of my own. I also needed to decide what I wanted to do to make a living.

But all I could think about was Sydney Edelman. I recalled her smile that produced the dimple in her left cheek, the way her eyes sparkled when she was the least bit excited or happy, and the trust she exhibited in a total stranger, sharing the pain she had experienced of having a miscarriage. She had shown me her real self. There was nothing phony about her, and there wasn't a speck of guile in her.

I had to learn what Sydney's relationship was with the tall good looking guy, and I was hoping—almost praying that it wasn't romantic.

Trudy was in Mother's rose garden when I got home. She had a flat basket of roses she had snipped for the cut glass vase that never left the small table just inside the front door. She looked up when she saw me.

"You've had two phone calls from your friend, Bernie Zuckerman," she said. "He said for you to call him as soon as you can."

"Did he tell you what was so important?"

"No, he didn't."

I went up to my room and flopped down on the bed, wondering why Bernie had called the land line instead of my cell. He knew I always had my phone with me. I hit the quick dial for his number. He answered on the first ring.

"Matt," he said, sounding out of breath, "can you come over to my place right away?"

"Sure. What's going on?"

"Just come to my place. I don't want to talk about it over the phone. Ok?"

"On my way."

Bernie had always been a worrier. I assumed something else strange had happened, and he was determined to pin whatever it was on Lee Ann. He had been on pins and needles ever since I came back to Martinsville a few days ago. There was no evidence that his ex was behind the tire slashing and the disappearance of the rabbit, but it was clear to me that he thought she was the culprit. If Juanita was a fly in the ointment, he might want to get rid of her. There were other baby sitters and housekeepers. And as for his little trysts with Juanita, he hadn't mentioned that he had feelings for her. It sounded as if she were no more than a convenience.

I hurried up the walk and rang Bernie's doorbell.

He opened the door and nearly jerked me inside.

"Thanks for coming, Matt. I think I'm going nuts. You won't believe her latest threat."

"Whose threat?"

"Lee Ann's, of course. Follow me."

We walked through the house to the door leading out to the patio. Bernie stopped, and instructed me to look down when he opened the door.

Just outside the door was a huge coiled snake. I took a couple of quick steps back.

"Scary looking, isn't it?" Bernie said.

All I could do was nod. I had never been fond of snakes, even harmless ones.

"It's dead", Bernie assured me. "I sprayed it with the hose on the most powerful setting. It didn't move. This is just another scare tactic to get rid of Juanita. I know it, and you know it. You just have to help me stop my demented ex from doing these despicable things."

"You're working from home. How could anyone do these things without either you or Juanita seeing them?"

"I can't stay at home all day every day, Matt. It seemed that things were almost getting back to normal, so I've been at my business several hours each day. Then, this happened. What if Juanita had been taking Claire out in the yard to play? Seeing that snake could have scarred my child for life."

I sighed. "Well, you know you can't accuse Lee Ann of pulling these mean pranks unless you have proof."

"I know, but there has to be some way to trap her. You're one of the smartest people I know, and you're my friend. I'm counting on you to come up with some brilliant plan to catch her, or, at least scare her off."

Chapter Six

I had come back to my hometown for three reasons: to clear my head from being stuck in a no win rat race, to get to know Sydney Edelman, and decide whether or not Martinsville was the place I wanted to hang my hat. I was tired of feeling like a hamster on a wheel, going nowhere.

I hadn't looked into available legal positions or office space should I decide to go it alone. I hadn't returned the rental car or checked out dealerships to buy a car. The only thing I had done was spy on Sydney and still not get a feel of what was going on with her. Who was that guy I kept seeing her with?

The one constant since my return was an ever present problem of one kind or another with one of my old high school pals. Joe Bob had been about to be sent up the river for something he hadn't done the last time I was here. Now Bernie was paranoid, thinking his ex was out to get him. Whether or not that was true, he was convinced that she was.

It was true that mysterious things were happening at Bernie's home. I had no idea whether they held any relevance, but I had the feeling my friend wasn't comfortable being a single dad. He had been used to having a wife, albeit an unfaithful one, to share his home, love their child, and be by his side at social events. Now, he was no doubt feeling guilty about having a fling with someone he was paying to babysit and clean his house. He wasn't used to the idea of living a life in secret.

I called Joe Bob.

"Hey, Matt, have you called the cat doc yet?"

"No, not yet. Joe Bob, I have to get off my butt and get some things done. The first thing on the list is buying a car. How busy are you?"

"I'm always busy, but I'll make time for you. Whadda you need?"

"Do you know where the closest decent car dealership is?"

"Yeah. There's one in Grayson, 'bout twelve miles from here."

"Would you mind going with me to check out the inventory; maybe help me choose a good slightly used one?"

"Be glad to, buddy. Give me about a half hour to clean up."

"Okay, I'll come pick you up at your place."

Joe Bob's hair was still wet from the shower when he came out of his doublewide. He pulled a pack from his shirt pocket, whipped out his Zippo, and lit up without slowing his stride en route to the idling rental car.

I had always thought Martinsville was a one horse town until I got a load of Grayson. It sported two small clapboard churches, a couple of service stations, a mini mart, and a tiny building with what looked like a piece of plywood attached to the front with US POST OFFICE painted on it. Adjacent to the building was a flagpole with a ragged American Flag.

The main drag was the only street in town. It was lined on each side by a conglomeration of small one story clapboard, brick sided, or shake shingle houses—all sitting on concrete blocks, some with lattice work between the bottom of the house and the ground.

The tiny front yards were mostly sand with a few random patches of green. Some of the houses had front porches. An occasional straight backed chair sat on a couple, and the porch at the edge of town was home to a rusted metal glider. But one porch claimed my attention immediately. A wringer washing machine sat just outside the front door.

"This doesn't look like a very prosperous town, Joe Bob. And I don't see anything resembling an automobile dealership."

Joe Bob grinned, his pearly whites flaunting their perfection.

"Now, don't go gittin' your panties in a wad, Matt. You'll be seein' it in just a sec."

We had barely driven through the little burg when the lines of colored plastic triangles flapping in the slight breeze came into view. Below them sat a fairly large lot which looked to be filled to capacity with a variety of vehicles.

I pulled into the lot and parked in an out-of-the-way spot with a visitor parking sign.

"So you're lookin' for somethin' that's barely used, right?"

"Right. I figure you know enough about cars to make sure I don't drive away with a lemon."

"The salesmen are gonna come flyin' at us like a swarm of bees as soon as we git out of this car. Don't say nothin' to 'em. Just start lookin' around."

"Shouldn't I let them know what I'm looking for and my price range?"

"You don't want to give 'em a chance to drag you all over this lot, tellin' you how great each car is and what a bargain it is."

"Okay."

"Just follow my lead, Matthew. Have I ever steered you wrong?"

"You shouldn't have asked that question, but since you're knowledgeable about cars, I'll let you handle this deal."

He appeared to know what he was doing. The second our feet hit the ground, three guys came hurrying out of the building and descended upon us, nearly tripping over one another's feet. The one who outran the others donned a big smile, exposing every tooth in his mouth while extending a hand in welcome.

"Just lookin'," Joe Bob said, before the salesman had a chance to utter a word.

We were walking through the rows of vehicles, showing no interest in any of the inventory, and the salesman walked with us. Joe Bob finally stopped and appeared to be seriously looking at a 2017 Ford Explorer. He knew I wouldn't be interested in buying anything that old.

I didn't say anything, but I looked at the price on the windshield: $23,999.

Joe Bob walked around to the driver's side and opened the door. He got in behind the wheel and checked out the interior. Then, he popped the hood, stuck his head under it to look things over. After a couple of minutes, he closed the hood and got back behind the wheel.

The hungry salesman stood still as a statue, looking expectantly at Joe Bob who got out of the car, totally ignoring him. That was when it hit me that my old pal was whetting the guy's appetite to make a sale. He had always been a prankster.

Joe Bob addressed me, "The price ain't bad, but it's got 75,000 miles on it. I wouldn't take it on a bet."

I didn't know whether I was supposed to speak or not.

Joe Bob turned toward me and winked. "Was that about what you're lookin' for?"

"I was thinking of something a little more upscale and a later model, but I don't want to spend a fortune."

At hearing that, the salesman abandoned Joe Bob and fell into step with me.

"Sir, I have just the vehicle for you," he said.

Joe Bob shut the guy down fast.

"What you got in a late model with low mileage for a decent price?" he asked. "We ain't gonna look at the whole lot. Just git to it."

"Right this way, gentlemen," the salesman said, and led us to an entire row that fit the bill.

I spotted a good looking SUV immediately. It was the third in the row.

"Let's look at that one," I said, walking toward it.

Joe Bob stepped in front of the salesman and elbowed me to take it easy.

"I said, let me drive," he hissed.

He looked at the price tag, under the hood, and the mileage. He left the door open. The new car smell was still present.

Joe Bob glanced at the salesman, then around the lot, and spit onto the gravel like he was thinking about what he wanted to say. He looked at me.

"How 'bout we take this one for a spin?"

"Sure," I said.

"I'll be back with the keys in a New York minute," the anxious salesman said, and took off.

As soon as we were alone, Joe Bob said, "We ain't gonna take this one. We're just makin' him a little hungrier. I see the one I think you're gonna like if it checks out."

The salesman was all smiles when he returned with the keys. I figured he was too afraid to speak, because he handed Joe Bob the keys and stepped out of the way.

We got into the SUV and left the lot.

"He thinks he's just made a sale," Joe Bob said, laughing.

"I really like the looks of this one," I said. "How does it drive?"

"It drives okay, but I'm gonna pull off the road and look at its innards. Then, we're gonna go back and look at the Caddy I spotted that's got your name on it."

"I guess you're the boss, but I want to at least drive this one back to the lot."

We had been gone for nearly a half hour before returning to the car lot, because Joe Bob was having so much fun tormenting the salesman.

"Don't smile, and don't say nothin'," he warned.

We knew the salesman was champing at the bit, but he put up a pretty good front presenting his most professional demeanor. He didn't hurry or fidget.

"Well, gentlemen?" He said.

It never ceased to amaze me how Joe Bob could beat the living hell out of someone by asserting his authority. He took the keys from me and handed them to the salesman. Then, he maneuvered his features into an insulted expression and looked directly into the salesman's eyes.

"How can you sleep at night if you try to sell that piece of shit to some unsuspectin' customer?

"I don't know what you mean," the nervous guy stammered.

"Either you're tryin' to take advantage of some poor slob, or you're too stupid to know a junker when you see it."

"Well, I'm sure we have something that's just perfect," said the befuddled salesman. "I take it you're interested only in an SUV."

I nodded.

Joe Bob ambled over to a gunmetal gray Cadillac.

"You want to git us the keys to this one," he said. It wasn't a question.

"Right away," said the salesman, turning and breaking into something like a trot.

The guy was back in seconds, and I reached for the keys. I had asked Joe Bob to come with me, but I was getting a little tired of his playing the alpha dog.

"I want to get the feel of it so I'll know if we're wasting our time," I said.

When we were well out of sight of the car lot, I pulled off on the shoulder and we switched positions.

"Whadda you think?" Joe Bob asked.

"I like the way it drives, but you need to make sure it doesn't have any hidden sins."

We stopped at a garage with several bays, and Joe Bob didn't waste any time. He pulled the Caddy into an empty bay and began checking it thoroughly.

"Well?" I said.

"Sweet!" Let's go buy you a ride."

I drove back to the lot to find the salesman pretending to look pleased while speaking with another customer. He glanced in our direction and waved a hand, taking his time to come back to us for the kill. It was obvious that he was doing his level best to conceal his anxiety.

I handed over the keys, and Joe Bob rubbed a hand across the back of his neck, looking first at the SUV and then around the lot. He walked a few paces, then returned. He made the salesman endure a time lag before speaking.

"The mileage ain't bad for a two-year-old model, and the XT5 is an okay Caddy, but that $37,000 pricetag's a real rip. If you don't lower that, you ain't gonna sell this baby."

"Sir, this car is in excellent shape, and 22,000 miles is like new. I don't think I can get my manager to lower the price."

Joe Bob's expression told the salesman he'd better.

"Try," he said. "I bet you can."

"Joe Bob, what are you doing? That's not a bad price. I want that car."

My friend looked at me like he wanted to hit me in the mouth for being so stupid.

"I know you want the car. I want the car for you. If you want to pay that price, be my guest, but I've done a lot of horse tradin', and I know I can git him to come down on the price."

The salesman came back smiling and shaking his head side to side as though what he was about to say was truly astonishing.

"I still don't believe this, but my manager says he's willing to part with this great car for $34,500. He wants the total amount up front. Does that work for you?"

I looked at Joe Bob, and he gave me a nod that was almost non perceptive.

"You've got yourself a deal," I said. "Let's take care of the paperwork."

Joe Bob grinned.

Chapter Seven

One down, two to go. I had bought a car, gotten rid of the rental, and now I had to tackle the big stuff. Sydney Edelman was my top priority. Without her, my desire to be in my hometown would wither. I wasn't sure how to go about it, but I had to learn what her relationship was with the guy who seemed to be her constant companion. If it turned out that their relationship proved not to be a threat to my mission, I would have to find a way to attract her. I wanted to get to really know her, to find out if she was the person I believed her to be from the little I knew about her.

My wish list of possible scenarios marched through my mind. Sydney hadn't mentioned a brother or male cousin. Either of those would have been perfect. It was possible that the guy was simply a friend, and theirs was no more than a platonic relationship. I've had many female friends. I was going to have to ramp up my courage and remind the lady who I was and invite her to dinner as though I had never seen her with Mister X.

I drove to the animal clinic determined to make headway, even if it turned out to be negative. As I stepped inside the reception area, I took a seat beside the coffee table where I had tried to hide the last time I was here. Instead of a jumble of outdated magazines, a large cardboard box sat in the middle of the table. I peered into the box and saw a rambunctious litter of kittens playfully tumbling over one another. A hand printed sign beside the box read: Free kittens to good homes—weaned, immunized, and medically sound.

I reached into the tangle of fur and picked up one which was trying to climb out of the box. As if on cue, Sydney Edelman appeared from the back of the clinic.

"Well, if it isn't Matt Stevenson," she said. She was smiling as she approached me.

I was holding the kitten with both hands. It was purring and kneading my neck with sharp little claws.

"I see you're in the market for a pet," she said.

I smiled.

So Sydney actually remembered me. For some reason, that gave me a glimmer of hope.

"Cute little rascals," I said.

"Yes, they are. How have you been, Matt?"

"I'm fine. Thanks."

I gingerly extracted the claws and brought the kitten away from my neck and put it back into the box.

"You don't want a kitten, do you, Matt?" she accused.

"Ahem. Well, they are cute, and I might want one, but that isn't the reason I'm here."

"Oh?"

"Sydney, could I possibly take you to lunch? I'd like to catch up a bit; tell you why I'm here in Martinsville."

"That's very nice of you, Matt, but I'm afraid I already have a lunch engagement. As a matter of fact, I'm running late."

She grabbed her purse from behind the reception desk and

walked toward the door, giving me a fluttery finger wave over her shoulder.

I left the building in time to see the elusive lady vet get into the same car with the same guy I had seen her with several times. Let's see; late model luxury car, good looking guy, probably rolling in dough. I couldn't imagine why she would choose him. She hadn't even been curious as to why I was back in town.

I got into my almost new Caddy and started driving. Sydney used to like the little diner not far from her clinic. I drove slowly past it checking to see if Mister X's car was parked on the street. Failing to spot it, I drove around aimlessly for a few minutes, ending up on Bernie's street. He must not have been home, because the giant bodyguard sat in the porch swing.

I glimpsed the back of a guy walking down the sidewalk ahead of me. He turned down a side street and disappeared. His gait and posture looked familiar, I thought. Then, it hit me that his build resembled that of Fred. Fred would have no reason to be in this neighborhood, so I decided that I was imagining things.

I arrived at the house in time for lunch with my favorite girl. Trudy stood at the stove, ladling her homemade lentil soup into a bowl. She was watching the local news on the small TV on the kitchen counter. She was so intent on watching the program that she didn't see me.

"Oh, good Lord!" she said aloud, and dropped the ladle, splashing hot soup on her hand. She hurried to the sink and stuck her hand under cold water while keeping her eyes glued to the TV.

"Trudy, are you okay?" I asked, rushing to her.

"Shhh!" She didn't seem surprised that I was in the room, and nodded toward the TV.

I focused on the screen and saw a small crowd gathered outside the Martinsville Police Department. Two handcuffed men were being taken out of a police cruiser and escorted into the building. The taller of the two had a long ponytail hanging down his back, and I recognized my friend when I got a glimpse of his profile.

"And now for the weather," said the reporter.

I clicked off the TV.

"Trudy, what's going on? That was Joe Bob being arrested."

"Yes, it was. The other man was bein' arrested too. I don't know who he is or how it started. I didn't turn the TV on in time to hear the first of the story, but I heard somethin' about assault and battery."

"How's your hand?"

"It's all right. I can tell it's not gonna blister. Are you hungry?"

"I wasn't, but I am now. This soup smells fantastic. Sit down; I'll serve us."

The housekeeper didn't argue. She took her usual seat and let me take care of her for once. I don't remember that ever happening.

"I'm going down to the police department right after lunch and find out what's going on with Joe Bob. Whatever happened, I'm sure it wasn't his fault. Maybe I can spring him."

"Of course it wasn't his fault. He's a good boy. Seems like he's always gettin' blamed for things he didn't do. You go down there and get him out."

Trudy's lentil soup seemed to take my mind off Joe Bob's predicament for the time it took for me to polish off a second bowl. Then, it was back to the new normal of trying to untangle one of my old friends from some sort of mess.

I called Bernie, hoping he would go with me to the police station. Maybe he knew more about what had transpired than the smattering that I did. He could at least lend moral support,

"Hey, Matt, what's up?"

"Have you seen the local news?"

"No. Why?"

"Joe Bob's been arrested."

"I'm aware of that, but I didn't know it was on the news. Yours truly saw the real thing, or at least most of it."

"I'll come pick you up," I said. "You can tell me what happened on the way to the police station."

Bernie looked flushed when he came rushing out of his dry cleaning business. He jumped into the passenger seat and buckled up. He must have recognized me sitting behind the wheel when I pulled up to the curb, because he didn't know I had bought the Caddy. He didn't bother to mention the car, and that miffed me a little bit.

"Strangest thing," he said. "Good old Joe Bob can't seem to win for losing."

"What happened, Bernie?"

"I had just come back to work from lunch and was about to open the door when I saw some big brute beating the hell out of a smaller guy. Somebody yelled, 'Hey, stop that' and got between the two. He pulled the big guy off, but the bully went right back to punching the little guy."

"Did you recognize any of them?"

"Not at first, but when the big guy turned away from the fellow he was pounding, I got a look at the newcomer. He was real easy to recognize. Know anybody who wears white coveralls and has a ponytail?"

"So Joe Bob was trying to help the little guy?"

"Yeah. At least that's what it looked like. You know Joe Bob. He's always trying to save somebody, or something. The little guy was able to get out of the way while the other two exchanged a flurry of blows. Somebody must have called the cops, because it didn't take more than a minute for them to show up."

I found a parking place close to the front of the building and was opening the door to get out.

"Nice ride," Bernie said. "When did you get it?"

"Thanks. I got it yesterday. Let's go inside and see if we can cut Joe Bob loose."

Inside the station, I went straight to the desk. Bernie followed me, but kind of hung back.

"Good afternoon. I'm Matt Stevenson. I'm here to see my client, Joseph Robert Kincaid."

I didn't burden him with the fact that I hadn't yet bothered to seek reciprocity for admission to the Tennessee Bar.

"Have a seat. I'll check to see if they're finished booking him."

We took seats by a far wall lined with straight-backed chairs.

"Maybe we'll get to see who the other guy is," I said. "I'll bet they don't have more than a couple of cells back there."

Bernie began fidgeting and looking uncomfortable.

"What's the matter? Are you nervous or something?"

"No. I'm not nervous. I just don't think we should both go back there. I'm not a lawyer. I'll wait here. If he needs bail money, I'm your man."

The desk sergeant came back into the room and motioned to me. Bernie didn't move when I headed to the desk.

"You can go back to see your client now. I imagine you'll want to arrange for his bail, but for now he stays put."

I followed a guard into the small cell block and saw Joe Bob pacing back and forth in his enclosure. He was massaging his jaw.

"Hey, Joe Bob."

"Hey, Matt. I'm guessin' you want to know what caused me to land in here."

"There's a thought."

"I'd been to the diner to grab lunch. I'd just walked around the corner when I saw that sumbitch over there poundin' the daylights outta some guy." He pointed his chin in the direction of a guy in a cell across from his.

I wanted to see what the bully looked like, but I couldn't get a good look because he was lying on his cot with his back to me.

"So you decided to play the good guy and rescue the underdog."

"Right. The cops didn't seem to care how it started, or who started it. They just cuffed both of us and hauled us in."

"I'll see about posting bail and getting you out of here as fast as I can. You're not really hurt, are you?"

"Just my feelin's. Thanks, Matt."

I went back to the desk sergeant to ask how soon I might be able to post bail. I knew Joe Bob would have to go before a magistrate before that could happen. As it turned out, Judge Kelly was holding court that very afternoon and Joe Bob could enter a plea and have bail set then.

Bernie stood, wearing an expectant expression as I approached him.

"Well?" he said.

"We can probably get him out this afternoon. Joe Bob explained the whole thing just like you did. This should be a piece of cake."

"Did you see the other guy?"

"I saw his back. I never got a look at his face, but he was a mountain of a man. I'm kind of surprised that Joe Bob wasn't in very bad shape. I think he was more mad than hurt."

"When we find out the tab, I'll be glad to go to a bail bondsman for the bail. Poor old Joe Bob."

"Not necessary," I said. "I have plenty of cash with me."

We left the police station and I was driving Bernie back to his place of business when I saw Fred Peyton and a woman who must have been his sister leaving the only doc-in-a-box clinic in Martinsville. Fred was limping, and his left arm was in a sling. It looked like the sister was supporting him and guiding him down the sidewalk. Then, it hit me that nobody had identified the guy who was getting beaten up.

"Look at that, Bernie. That's Fred Peyton and his sister. I'll wager it was Fred that big guy attacked."

Bernie turned in the direction I pointed.

"Huh. That does look kind of like him from the side, but the woman's blocking my view. I'm not sure that's Fred."

"I'd bet on it," I said, and continued driving Bernie back to work.

My current focus was on getting Joe Bob free and the charges dropped. I went home to catch Trudy up on what had transpired. Then, I planned to go to the courthouse and sit in on Joe Bob's hearing. It would be open to the public. I was pretty sure that the Judge would set bail at a reasonable rate and that I could get my friend out free and clear this afternoon.

"Oh, Matty, I'm glad you're home," Trudy said as I came into the house.

"What's up?"

"I think you'll be pleased," she teased.

"Well?"

"You had a phone call on the land line a little while ago. I didn't call to tell you about it then, because I knew you were busy at the police station. The nice lady vet left a message for you to call her at your convenience." The housekeeper's smile lit up the room.

"Did she say anything else, like what was on her mind?"

"No. She just asked that you call her."

I couldn't imagine why Sydney would be calling me shortly after practically blowing me off. She had been downright rude when I was at her clinic. She would have to wait in line for my attention. For once, she wasn't my top priority; Joe Bob was.

I called Bernie to see if he wanted to meet me at the courthouse, but he declined, saying that he was swamped. He wished Joe Bob the best and reiterated his offer to go to a bail bondsman and take care of the bail. I passed.

It turned out that my eyesight and my hunch had been right. The victim in the street fight was none other than Fred Peyton. He and his sister sat in the front of the courtroom when I arrived. They were seated right behind Joe Bob who appeared to be composed and ready to tell his tale to Judge Kelly.

When Joe Bob's case was called, the Judge asked my friend how he pled. I fully expected him to reply, "Not guilty," and call that good. But instead of giving the Judge a succinct answer, Joe Bob swiveled his head around at Fred Peyton, looked back at the Judge and said, "Ask him; he can tell you all about it."

The Judge didn't seem to take umbrage at Joe Bob's response.

Fred Peyton stood and faced the Judge. He started talking before he could be sworn in.

"Big guy beat on me. Don't know why. Joe Bob saved me."

The Judge banged his gavel and called for order. He didn't bother having Fred sworn in. He reiterated his question to Joe Bob. That time, he got a short answer.

"Not guilty, Your Honor."

"Case dismissed."

Chapter Eight

I still hadn't gotten anywhere with Sydney Edelman, but Joe Bob was once again a free man. Immediately after he was cleared, he went right back to work in his garage as if nothing had ever happened. That was the thing about Joe Bob—he seemed to be able to dismiss the past and get on with his life.

I went home to tell Trudy the good news. She and I were sitting at the kitchen table drinking sweet tea.

"Wonder why somebody would want to beat up on Fred Peyton?" Trudy asked.

"That's a good question. I'm wondering the same thing. As far as I know, Fred's never had any enemies. He's always kept pretty much to himself, picking up pop bottles by the roadside until his place burned and he went to live with his sister. Nobody has seen him picking up bottles for several days, and his sister has cleaned him up. He doesn't wear that old coat anymore, and his clothes are clean and pressed."

"I'm glad to hear that. I've always felt sorry for him. I know you told me he's a genius in some areas, but he sure is strange.

Everybody thought of him as the town weirdo, but they seemed to accept him because he didn't cause any trouble."

I climbed the stairs to my room and sat at the desk I had used when I was in high school, pondering the question Trudy had asked regarding Freaky Fred as my mind drifted to more pressing matters.

I needed to address the biggest decision I must make—one which would affect the remainder of my life. I was practically middle aged and felt as if I were spinning my wheels. I felt nothing like the confident young lawyer I had been fresh out of law school with a new bride and a demanding position with a large firm. My craving for success had still been robust after my divorce. I didn't hesitate to pack up kit and caboodle to move to Denver and start a new practice with a friend. The two of us pushed forward with nothing more than confidence, but eventually we faced reality and let go of that dream. Look at me now. My lack of confidence was consuming me. Where was my will to be a success? Where was my spine?

I realized that I had to face facts, number one being that I was absolutely needy when it came to Sydney Edelman. Since I knew so little about her, why was I enchanted with her? Why did I feel that I had to have her? The woman had poured out her soul to me the evening we had dinner, and that had made me feel that she was nearly transparent and that I knew everything about her that was worth knowing.

It was nearing the cocktail hour, and another day had flown by. I was no closer to mapping out the remainder of my life than I was the day I arrived here. It was too late to attempt approaching the lovely Sydney Edelman. I would have to try again tomorrow.

I tapped in Joe Bob's cell number, thinking I'd catch him at his garage, but the call went to voice mail. Deciding that he must have already closed up and gone home, I drove to the trailer park. Lights were on in his doublewide, so I figured he was in the shower since he hadn't answered my call. I sat in my car a few minutes, giving him time to finish his ablutions.

Joe Bob was in his late thirties like Bernie and me. He seemed truly satisfied with his life as a single man living in a trailer park with an old cat. He owned his business and didn't have to answer to anyone. The money seemed to be rolling in as he went about the business of doing whatever needed doing to any ailing vehicle that came limping into his garage. Joe Bob was something of a mechanical genius in white greasy coveralls. The guy was humble but happy, always wearing a genuine smile.

Bernie, on the other hand, seemed to get out of one mess just to step into another one. I had no idea what he planned to do about his ex wife if, indeed, she turned out to be the culprit who was making his life miserable. But I was certain of one thing; I didn't want to get very involved in solving his problems.

I got out of my car and breathed in the sweet aroma of honeysuckle that climbed a trellis separating Joe Bob's small lot from that of his neighbor when a light inside the doublewide flickered, then went out. I assumed that Joe Bob would come out the door any second on his way to get a drink and dinner, but that didn't happen. Maybe the day had gotten to him after all, and he had opted to crash on the couch with his spoiled cat, have a beer, and nod off watching something inane on his big screen.

I hated to bother him if he was tuckered out and just wanted to be a couch potato, but I was selfish enough to do it. I knocked on the door and waited for him to open it, wearing his best scowl. No answer. Maybe he had a woman in there.

I heard a loud thump, or bang, and didn't know what to make of it. Since there was no visible activity from the front of the doublewide, I crept along the front of it to get a look at the back area. The wrought iron table and chairs sat in their usual spot. I looked to the left and saw that the back door was wide open. I was about to venture inside to make sure my friend was okay when I saw him coming out of the trees by the stream that ran along the back of the property. He was carrying a baseball bat, breathing hard, and uttering curses as his breathing allowed. I rushed to him wondering what in the world he had been doing.

"Joe Bob, what the hell?"

He stopped walking, dropped one end of the bat to the ground, and leaned on it trying to catch his breath. His face was red, and he was sweating profusely.

"I almost caught the sumbitch," he huffed.

"Who?"

"Don't know. Couldn't see his face. He had on a hoodie."

"Was he inside when you got home?"

"Yeah. I just got home a few minutes ago."

If I had been paying attention, I would have noticed that Joe Bob was still wearing his work clothes. He hadn't even had time to get a shower. The intruder must have escaped out the back door as Joe Bob was coming in through the front.

"What do you think he was doing here?"

My friend looked like he wanted to smack me upside the head.

"How do you think I'd know, Matt? Like I said, I just got home. But I do know he had no business bein' in my home, scarin' my cat."

"He didn't hurt your cat, did he?"

"He'd better not have. If he did, I'll hunt him down and show him what hurt feels like."

We were nearly back to the doublewide.

"How do you think he got inside? You don't leave your doors unlocked, do you?"

"No, Matt," he said, looking at me and shaking his head as though he thought I might be demented. "I'm thinkin' maybe Lucy coulda accidentally left it unlocked when she come by to give the cat a treat and play with him. She does that sometimes. I made her a key a long time ago."

We went in through the back door, and Joe Bob began calling his pet. It occurred to me that the animal might have dashed out the open door and disappeared, but I didn't dare mention that to Joe Bob.

"He'll still be in here somewhere. He knows not to go outside without me," Joe Bob said as though he knew for a fact that his pet would follow the rules under any circumstances.

So I assumed that the cat was still frightened and refused to come out from his hiding place. Moments later Joe Bob came from his bedroom carrying the frightened cat. Its eyes looked huge, and it had both front paws wrapped around Joe Bob's muscled forearm. Joe Bob looked relieved, so I figured it would be okay to ask more questions.

"What do you think the guy wanted? Do you think he wanted to steal something?"

Joe Bob sat down on the couch and scratched the cat's ears and rubbed his belly. He seemed in no hurry to look around to see if anything was missing.

"Matt, I don't keep nothin' worth stealin' here. The guy wouldn't have found anything to steal except beer, frozen dinners, or cat food. I've got a safe at the garage and a safety deposit box at the bank. I'm not stupid enough to leave anything valuable here. It's not too hard to break into a doublewide. Speakin' of breakin' in, go over there and check out the front door to see if it's been jimmied."

I didn't see any sign of the door having been tampered with, so we ruled that out.

"He must have come here on foot," Joe Bob said. "I didn't see a vehicle of any kind parked close by."

"What about his size? Could you tell if he was a big man?"

"Like I said, he had on a hoodie. I couldn't tell if the thing fit him or if it was just flarin' out when he took off. He was pretty tall though."

"Do you think it could have been the guy who was beating up on Fred?"

"No idea."

"This is the reason I usually discount the testimony of witnesses," I said. There could be three of them, each one telling a different story. Sometimes they just see what they want to see, and sometimes they swear to what they think they saw."

"Want to go down to the police station and see if that big guy is still there? It's possible that somebody sprung him and he still had it in for me. It wouldn't have been hard to find out where I live."

"We haven't really checked to see if anything has been disturbed, Joe Bob. Even if you don't keep valuables here, he might have been looking for something else."

"Like what?"

"I don't know; maybe a piece of mail or a bank statement. It could be something you'd never think of hiding from an intruder."

Joe Bob seemed to have calmed his pet down enough for him to stop reassuring it, and he got up to look around to see if anything seemed amiss. He came up empty.

"I'll grab a shower. Then, let's mosey on down to the station and take a look," he said.

Joe Bob and I walked into the station together, and the desk sergeant seemed surprised to see us. He looked even more surprised when I asked if the other prisoner had been released.

"No, why do you ask?"

I didn't want to go into detail about what had transpired. If the guy was still in jail, he wasn't a suspect. We didn't need to get the cops involved in something which might turn out to be a wild goose chase. For all we knew, whoever had broken into Joe Bob's trailer might have been some vagrant who happened to stop by a trailer park in hopes of stealing anything he might find of value, or possibly just to raid a refrigerator.

We left the police station no more informed than we had been, wondering who could have had an interest in breaking into Joe Bob's doublewide. Was it a random break-in or was my friend really the target?

"Hey, it's past the cocktail hour," Joe Bob said, "and I'm starvin'. Want to go to Morgan's?"

"Sure. Want to call and see if Bernie'd like to join us?"

Joe Bob swiped a big hand over his face.

"Okay, if you want to."

He didn't seem excited about the idea, so I drove to the restaurant without making the call.

"Hey, is there something you want to discuss with me alone? We don't have to invite anyone else."

Joe Bob didn't offer a direct answer.

"Let's go inside and have a drink," he said.

I didn't know why he was hesitant about inviting Bernie, but Joe Bob usually had a reason for what he did, or didn't do.

"Sure," I said.

Lucy Combs came toward our booth, dragging her crippled foot.

"Well, if it's not two of the three stooges," she said, smiling.

"How's it goin', Lucy?" Joe Bob asked.

I just knew the next words out of his mouth would be to ask Lucy if she had been by his place that afternoon.

"What did y'all do with mister high and mighty?" Lucy asked.

"I saw him earlier today, and he told me that he was swamped. I guess he's pretty busy," I said.

"Y'all eatin' or just drinkin'?"

"Both, but we'll drink first. Matt?"

"Bourbon and soda for me, Lucy."

"Same here," Joe Bob said. "It's been a tough day."

When Lucy was far enough from our booth not to hear, I looked at Joe Bob with raised eyebrows.

"Why didn't you ask if she had been by your place today?"

"I figured if she had been there she woulda told me. She always does. Besides, Lucy's responsible; always locks up."

"Is she the only person who has a key?"

"Yeah."

Our drinks came, and Lucy rattled off the daily specials.

"Bring me the chicken-fried steak with mashed potatoes and fried okra," Joe Bob said.

I settled for a grilled chicken breast and a side salad, remembering the weight I had gained the last time I was in Martinsville.

"Here's to good friends," Joe Bob said, raising his glass.

"To good friends," I echoed, meaning it.

Joe Bob didn't impress me as the kind of person who would hand out keys to his property to just anyone, so I decided to let that topic rest for the time being.

We each took a healthy drink of our bourbon. I looked

into my friend's blue eyes and saw something like discomfort, or maybe sadness.

"What's the trouble, buddy, besides having your home broken into, I mean?"

"It's just a feelin'."

"About?"

"It's about Bernard, Matt. I can't put my finger on it, and I feel kinda mean spirited sayin' it, but I don't feel like he's really my friend. He don't give me the time of day when you're not around. I know that seems kinda childish on my part."

"He could be awfully busy with his business plus having the little kid, even with a sitter," I said.

"I reckon that's possible, but he seems to make time to hang out with us when you're here."

My mind backtracked to earlier in the day. Bernie had been willing to accompany me to the police station, but he didn't seem anxious to get overly involved. He declined to go back to the cell with me, but he did offer to go Joe Bob's bail. Then, I remembered that he only wanted to do that using a bail bondsman which I thought was a bit strange. The only reason to go that route would be to remain anonymous.

We finished our drinks just as our meals arrived. Then, I switched to wine and Joe Bob opted for beer. He claimed that wine didn't agree with him; gave him a headache.

We didn't engage in much conversation during the meal. Joe Bob attacked his food with gusto, hardly coming up for air. He had finished and heaved a contented sigh when I was only half finished. His hand automatically went to his shirt pocket to retrieve a cigarette. He glanced at me and, realizing that I was still eating, appeared to change his mind.

"Hey, Matt, just forgit what I said about Bernard. Okay? I'm prob'ly imaginin' things."

"Done," I said, but I knew I wouldn't forget about it.

I dropped Joe Bob off back at the trailer park, then drove around town. I buzzed by Bernie's house. Lights were on, so I assumed that he and Juanita were having dinner in the kitchen since it was too early to put the kid to bed. She would probably be entertaining Bernie by eating bites of hotdog with her fingers or smearing pudding on her face.

Before I went home I decided to drive to Sydney Edelman's apartment complex. I didn't know why I was doing it, because I wasn't going to ring her doorbell and stand there uninvited. It gave me some measure of comfort to see her car parked next to the curb close to her building.

Having made the rounds, I drove the familiar route to 120 Mulberry Street and Trudy. I wondered what tomorrow would bring.

Chapter Nine

I couldn't recall a time that my mind had been such a cluttered mess. Too many things were happening simultaneously. I had a feeling that at least some of them were connected, but I couldn't imagine how. There were a lot of unanswered questions, and it seemed impossible to connect the dots.

Bernie had always been something of a conundrum. At times, he seemed to be a genuine friend to Joe Bob, but in the blink of an eye, he could become contentious. I thought Joe Bob might not always be comfortable in Bernie's company because he couldn't be himself. Bernie was a little bit of a snob, something he would deny vehemently. My two friends' relationship bothered me, but I felt helpless to do anything about it.

I couldn't imagine who would want to attack poor Fred Peyton, nor could I fathom who might break into Joe Bob's home. I also couldn't stop wondering why Bernie was only willing to get Joe Bob out of jail by going through a bail bondsman. None of it made sense.

Trudy had made me one of her to-die-for breakfasts, then left me to my own devices while she went grocery shopping. I was engaged in a leisurely cruise around town, trying to free my mind of all the what-ifs. It crossed my mind to simply keep driving, leave Martinsville and all of its unanswered questions behind and end up in some friendly southern town—one in need of a slightly used attorney.

All thoughts of such a scenario disappeared when Sydney Edelman's animal clinic came into view. I recognized her car and peeled off the street into the clinic's parking lot. I parked and stayed in my car, wondering whether or not to go inside. I didn't want to appear needy because that was a sure turn-off, but I had to know if I was wasting my time.

I decided to forge ahead and went into the clinic. I didn't know whether Sydney was too busy to see me, but I hoped she would come from the back of the clinic into the waiting area. The big cardboard box still sat on the coffee table, and I could hear the kittens meowing.

I smiled at the receptionist.

"May I help you?" she asked, reciprocating with a sweet smile.

I opened my mouth, not sure what I was about to say when Sydey entered the room. She was fresh-faced and smiling as she glided across the floor. I remembered how I loved the way she walked. Her gait wasn't affected or overly sexy; it was simply alluring. She just couldn't put me down.

"Good morning, Matt," she said, offering her lovely hand.

"Hi, there," I said, pasting on a goofy grin.

"Did you decide that you want a kitten after all?" she asked.

"Actually, I'm still thinking about it. I came by to take another look at them."

"Better make up your mind, because only three of them are left. Were you thinking about a male or a female?"

"Oh, I hadn't given that much thought."

"The gray one is a male, and the black-and-white and the calico are little girls. Perhaps you'd like one of each gender." She smiled.

"They're all cute, but I'm sure one will be sufficient."

"Yes, they are. Why don't you get acquainted with them while I check on a patient. Take your time. I won't be long."

I couldn't see any way around it. I was going to have to take one of these little furballs home with me. The thing would no doubt shed all over the house, and I hadn't broached the subject of having a cat with Trudy. I had no idea how she felt about them.

I picked up the calico and held it close to my chest, careful to keep it from using its razor sharp claws on naked flesh. The first kitten I had held dug holes in my neck. This one seemed tame in comparison, so I held it in one hand and rubbed a thumb over its silky head with the other.

Sydney came back to the waiting room with an elderly gentleman and his huge German shepherd. The dog had a cone on its head and a bandage on its front leg, but it wagged its tail and didn't appear to be hurting. At the sight of the monster canine, the kitten I was holding seemed to become rigid. It let go with what I thought was an impossibly loud and angry hiss. Its calm, cuddly demeanor had radically changed.

I smiled. "I don't think it likes dogs," I said. "No offense." I nodded to the old gentleman.

"Most cats don't," he said, donning his hat and heading for the door.

The kitten, in the meantime, had sunk its claws into my hand, seeming to take its misplaced hatred of dogs out on me.

Sydney laughed as she came to my rescue, gently removing the kitten and depositing it in the box with its littermates.

"You don't have to be afraid of her, Matt. She was just scared of the German shepherd."

"If you'll let me take you to lunch, you can educate me on taking care of a kitten. I don't know what they eat or anything else about cats. I've never been exposed to one."

That was a blatant lie, and I fervently hoped Sydney couldn't detect that by my facial expression. I had been around Joe Bob's cat way too many times. I'd heard that if cats sensed that you didn't like them, it would be a signal for them to descend on you for revenge, and it seemed to be true.

"I have to see two more patients before lunch."

I assumed I would be expected to play with the cats until she was ready to go.

"Joyce, please give Mister Stevenson a list of everything he'll need from the pet store. He's a new kitten owner."

She turned back to me.

"The pet store is just down the street," she said. "You can make your purchases and be back in time to go to lunch."

The way I saw it, I had no choice in the matter. I would go to the pet store, buy anything and everything a kitten might need, and return to the clinic to take the lady vet to lunch. She would eat something healthy while telling me everything I needed to know about taking care of my pet. Then, she would ask if I had any questions. I would do my dead level best to come up with an intelligent inquiry while wondering how to segue into the conversation I really wanted to have with her.

She was all smiles when she came from the back of the clinic.

"Were you able to get everything on the list, Matt?" she asked.

I nodded. "Everything. I plan to be a good pet owner. Shall we go?"

Sydney grabbed her purse from behind the reception desk and we left the building.

"What a gorgeous day," she said.

"Sure is."

I thought she was probably one of those liberated sorts who didn't expect a guy to open doors for the fairer sex, but I wanted to do it anyway. I kind of enjoyed playing the gentleman. I wanted to give the impression that I respect women. It also somehow made me feel that I was sort of in charge.

"I'm fully booked this afternoon, so I can't be away from the clinic very long," Sydney said.

"Is there anywhere in particular you'd like to go for lunch?" I asked.

"Let's just go to the diner down the street. The food is good, and the service is fast."

The diner wouldn't have been my first choice, but I wasn't about to disagree with her.

I drove us the short distance, parked, and hurried around to open the door for Sydney before she had a chance to do it. Then, I escorted her into the venue wearing a happy smile.

We were seated at a small table beside a window and given menus.

Sydney left no room for pleasant conversation, but began perusing the menu. I knew she would choose something disgustingly healthy, and she did. That made me feel obliged to follow suit.

Our salads arrived so quickly that Sydney had barely had time to give me the basics about how to care for a kitten. I'd figured all I would have to do would be feed it, show it the litter box, and pet it once in a while. That didn't seem so bad, but the lady vet went through a long list of chores required to give the thing a good home and keep it healthy and happy. These requirements even had sequential steps to follow. When was she ever going to shut up about the damn cat and let me broach the subject I wanted to discuss?

We were nearly finished with our salads when Sydney glanced

out the window. She smiled and waved at someone. I followed her gaze and saw the back of a very familiar figure—the man I had seen her with on several occasions. This was my opportunity to find out who the mystery man was, but I didn't quite know how to ask without appearing rude.

"Ahem," I managed.

"Oh, Matt, I didn't realize how late it was. I need to get back to the clinic. You must have a million questions to ask about the kitten, but we have simply run out of time. Thank you for lunch. I enjoyed this very much."

I paid the bill and drove Sydney back to her clinic where I would collect my cat and take it home to introduce Trudy to it.

"Just take the carrier inside, Matt. Joyce will show you how to transport your kitten. Feel free to call and ask any questions you have. And, thank you for offering our little orphan a good home."

I'd done it again—let her cut me off without a whisker of hope. I vowed to fix that at the next possible opportunity. True, she hadn't shown the slightest bit of interest in me except for my willingness to take one of the kittens off her hands. On the positive side, she didn't appear to feel any animosity toward me. She had been friendly and seemed glad to see me, albeit having no interest whatsoever in why I had come back to my hometown.

The kitten slept peacefully on the ride home. She was curled into a tiny ball in her carrier. I hauled all of the pet paraphernalia into the house. That way, Trudy wouldn't be slapped in the face with the real thing. I deposited my purchases inside the front door and followed the aroma of apples and cinnamon to the kitchen which seemed to be where Trudy was most of the time.

"Wow! Something really smells good," I said.

My old friend smiled her special smile she had always saved for me.

"The pie won't be done for another half hour," she said. "If you're hungry, I'll whip up somethin' quick."

"No, thanks. I've already had lunch. And, I have a surprise."

"What in this world?"

"Sit down and close your eyes. I'll go get it," I said, having no clue how Trudy would react upon learning that the surprise was a cat.

I retrieved the carrier from my car and toted it into the house, deciding to show it to her while protecting it in case she despised felines. Although I thought it wouldn't be a very sanitary thing to do, I set the carrier on the table. It was just a little kitten, and there was no way for it to contaminate the table from inside a brand new carrier.

"Okay, open your eyes," I said, wearing a big grin.

Trudy stared at the carrier and didn't say anything for a minute, and I looked at her expectantly.

"What's in that cage?" she finally asked.

"It isn't a cage. It's a pet carrier."

"You know, I didn't ask you for a pet. If I'd wanted a pet, I'd have bought one."

"May I open the door and show you the pet?"

Trudy nodded, but looked skeptical.

I opened the door and gingerly lifted out the kitten. It yawned and stretched its furry little body out in my hand.

"That's a little cat."

"Good guess," I said, being the smartass I am. "Isn't it cute?"

"I've never had a cat. Don't know anything about them. Does it bite?"

"Of course not; it's just a baby. Would you like to hold it?"

"Not particularly."

I held the kitten toward her and told her to cup her hand so she wouldn't drop it. Reluctantly, she accepted my gift.

"Be gentle, and lightly rub it on the head," I instructed.

The housekeeper followed my direction, and the kitten began purring. I could barely hear it, but the vibration must have startled Trudy because she held the kitten away from her for fear of an eminent attack.

"It likes that," I said.

Trudy brought the kitten back in close proximity to her body and a smile played at the corners of her mouth.

"I don't know how to take care of a cat," she said.

"It's easy," I assured her. "I'll teach you. There's nothing to it. I went to a pet store and bought everything a kitten might need."

At that point it seemed that Trudy was going to be willing to accept the pet, so I spent the next half hour teaching her things I didn't know about caring for a kitten. I showed her the things I had bought and read pertinent passages from the instruction manual that Joyce, the receptionist had given me.

"Ok, I'll keep it," said the housekeeper.

She headed to the living room and sat down with the kitten, continuing to pet it.

"You go on about your business, Matty. The little cat and old Trudy'll be just fine without your help."

That was all I wanted to hear. I dropped a kiss on the top of her head and hurried out the door.

I wasn't sure why, but I had a feeling of well being for the first time since I had come back to Martinsville. I drove straight to Joe Bob's garage and found him under what looked like a junker on his back.

"Hey, Joe Bob, you real busy?"

He rolled himself out, sat up, and lit a cigarette.

"I am, but it can wait. What's up?"

"Oh, not much. I just wanted to report in on my progress with Sydney Edelman."

"Yeah?" he grinned.

"I took her to lunch. Uh, and I took one of her orphaned kittens home with me."

"Sounds like a kinda bribe to get her to go out with you. Matthew, I think you need a talkin' to. That woman is takin' over your brain. You need to go to work and quit moonin' over her. Let your mind rest."

"I can't think about work until I know if I have a chance with her. She's one of the main reasons I came back here."

"You're soundin' like a fourteen-year-old; just got smacked with a hormone overload. It don't much matter what you do right now. Just do somethin'."

"I don't know anything about anything but law. The only firm I know of that's looking for a lawyer is Herman Watkins. The old goat's a shyster. There's no way I would consider working for him."

"How 'bout workin' on your own? You've got enough cash to tide you over 'til you find somethin' else if it don't work out. You've got to git that woman out of your head for a while."

"Even if I wanted to try that, there's no place to do it. This town doesn't have many places to set up a law practice."

"I've got one."

Chapter Ten

It had never been a habit of mine to allow other people to tell me what to do or how to do it, but I had been stuck in a rut. My friend, Joe Bob, might have hit upon a solution to help me out of it. I needed to have a purpose in life, something to work toward instead of mooning over someone who had thus far been elusive.

Joe Bob had offered me the use of one of his properties for free. It was a red brick building which was a cross between a house and an office. It resembled Sydney's animal clinic. I could furnish it with office furniture and the equipment I would need to set up a law practice.

My old pal had talked me into applying for admission to the Tennessee Bar on motion, and I had done the paperwork. I would have plenty to do while waiting to be admitted. If it turned out that this was not a good idea, being able to practice law in the state might still come in handy.

Joe Bob Kincaid never ceased to amaze me. If he didn't own what I needed, he knew someone who did. He just happened to have a friend who owned a furniture business in a nearby town. Hansen's New &Used Furniture carried a line of office furniture, and Joe Bob said that he could get me a good deal on the pieces I would need.

"I'll ride over there with you and introduce you to Ross," Joe Bob said. "He's a good guy, and he'll do right by you."

Ross Hansen's New & Used Furniture was not just a furniture store; it was a huge warehouse. I was able to get what I needed to furnish an office as well as good looking pieces for a waiting room. And Joe Bob had been right—I was given a heck of a deal. Ross even offered to deliver the furniture to my new place of business for free.

"You couldn't beat that deal with a stick," Joe Bob said, laughing.

We had just gotten back to Martinsville when I happened to glance to the left.

"Hey, is that Juanita?" I said, motioning with my chin.

"I didn't git a good look, but it's a man and woman. Looks like they're havin' a disagreement. Both of 'em shakin' their fingers in each other's face."

"The woman sure looked like Juanita. I'm going to drive back around the block. See if you can get a good look."

We both had our eyes peeled, but when we turned the corner, the couple had disappeared.

"I'm almost certain that was Juanita," I said, wondering who the man could have been.

After I dropped Joe Bob off, I made a quick pass by Bernie's shop. His car was there, so I assumed he wasn't the guy who was having an argument with the Juanita look-alike. It was none of my business, and I wanted to be at my new office when the furniture arrived. Ross had told me that it would be delivered that afternoon.

Joe Bob had seen to turning on all of the utilities and had given me a couple of keys to the building, and I had made arrangements with the phone company for hookups the following day. The simple act of readying my new place of business had managed to fire up my confidence regarding opening a one-man law office in this small southern town. I had gone so far as to order a sign for the front of the building and new business cards. There was going to be a new lawyer in Martinsville.

By going down this road on not much more than a push from a friend, I was putting my main reason for returning to my hometown on a back burner. But Joe Bob had been right; I had been spinning my wheels while getting nowhere with Sydney Edelman. I wouldn't have to stay in the practice if I decided to go elsewhere. There was also the possibility that Sydney was not actually involved with someone else and that I still had a chance.

The furniture van arrived as I sat on the bottom step of the staircase in my empty building wondering if this venture would work. My mind had sped ahead, and I was thinking that if my practice turned into the semblance of a lucrative business, I would furnish the rest of the rooms. I could move out of the house with Trudy and move in here with my cat unless, of course, she had gotten too attached to it to part with it.

Two brawny men unloaded the furniture and placed it in the two front rooms. They behaved as though they actually enjoyed hefting furniture around, and they refused the generous tip I offered.

Trudy was sitting in her favorite chair in the living room when I got home. She was sipping a glass of wine and petting the purring kitten curled in a ball on her lap.

"Looks like you've gotten over being scared of the little furball," I said.

She took a sip of wine and smiled.

"I think it likes me," she said.

I hadn't told her about my plan to open a law practice here in town, because I didn't want to get her hopes up. I knew she would be happy for me to stay in Martinsville. Now that I had decided to give it a try, I opened up and told her my plans and what I had done to get the ball rolling.

"I know you'll be successful, Matty. You know a lot of people in town, and they'll remember you. Your mama had so many friends who still live here. Where's your office gonna to be?"

"You've probably seen it. It's on the corner of Church and Seminary Streets, about a half block from the Methodist Church. Joe Bob owns it."

"Lord knows how much money that boy has. Lives in a trailer and talks like he never darkened the door of a school. Mmm. Mmm."

I laughed.

"He sure is a conundrum."

"Matt Stevenson, about to open a law practice in Martinsville. How about that? Does that mean you finally made some progress with the pretty vet?"

"Not exactly. I just think I should give it a try and see if it works for me."

"So you thought I needed a little cat to keep me company," she said, grinning. "I know where you got it. Are you sure it's not a bribe to get a date?"

"Of course not. But it was a legitimate excuse to go to her clinic and ask her to lunch."

I had let Trudy know my plans about opening a practice and that I had an office, but I saw no reason to burden her with my future plans. I loved her like a second mother, but a grown man needs a place of his own.

I called Joe Bob to see if he would like to meet me for dinner.

"Sure," he said. "I'll come pick you up in a half hour."

He had never turned me down, and it occurred to me that he was probably lonely and welcomed the company. I knew that he and Arlene Watkins had hooked up for afternoon delights in the past. I had no idea whether they were still seeing one another.

It occurred to me that the three old high school pals were bachelors. Bernie had a thing with his housekeeper/babysitter, but none of us had a wife. Speaking of wives, or exes, I hadn't seen Beth since I got here. I assumed she was busy stalking the new preacher. Since my new establishment was in near proximity to the Methodist Church, I figured it wouldn't be long before I saw her front and center.

I was getting a call on my cell just as Joe Bob pulled up at the curb in front of my house.

"Hey, Bernie," I said, opening the passenger door.

Bernie's voice sounded whiney as it often did, but I didn't give him an opportunity to tell me his plight.

"If you're not busy, Joe Bob and I are on our way to dinner at Morgan's. Meet us there in a few minutes."

"Is he gonna come?" Joe Bob asked.

"Yeah. Wonder what he's got on his mind this time?"

Bernie came into the restaurant a few minutes after Joe Bob and I were seated. He spotted us and headed straight to our table.

"Hey, there, Bernard, glad you could join us. I haven't seen you for a while. You been real busy?"

"Yeah, you could say that."

"Was there something you wanted to talk to me about?" I asked.

"Oh, nothing in particular," Bernie said, but his facial expression betrayed him.

"In that case," I said, I have a bit of news."

Bernie raised an eyebrow.

"I'm going to open a law office here in town. I've already got the ball rolling, thanks to one Mister Joe Bob Kincaid."

"That's great news, Matt," Bernie said without much enthusiasm.

"Joe Bob owns several properties in Martinsville, and he was kind enough to let me use that little red brick number at Church and Seminary."

"When's opening day?" he asked.

"It'll be another two or three weeks from now before I'm admitted to the Tennessee Bar. In the meantime, I'll need to let folks know I'm here and ready to go to work."

"You're not going to put one of those tacky ads on TV, are you?"

"Of course not. I'll put a tasteful announcement in the local paper and those in fairly close proximity to Martinsville and hope to build a modest clientele. If that works out, I can branch out."

I had been looking forward to a laidback dinner with Joe Bob, but Bernie's presence changed all of that. It was obvious that he didn't want to share what was on his mind with Joe Bob. Conversation was going to be stilted, and an enjoyable evening was about to be shot all to hell.

"How's your love life with that cute little Mexican girl goin', Bernard?"

I was a little shocked that Joe Bob would ask that question and that he would phrase it that way. He and I had just seen Juanita having a heated argument with another man.

"Since you asked, crudely, I might add, we're just fine. What's it to you?"

"Don't git all bent outta shape, Bernard. I was just makin' conversation."

"Guys, let's order drinks," I said, hoping that these two could get along without a knock-down-drag-out.

A good looking young woman I didn't recognize came to take our order.

"Good evening, gentlemen," she said. "Would you like something to drink, or are you ready for dinner?"

"We'd like drinks first," Joe Bob said in his most pleasant voice.

I couldn't miss the appreciative look the young lady gave Joe Bob. His hair was in a neat ponytail pulled away from his handsome face, his gold chain shone brightly on his chest, his white dress shirt unbuttoned halfway to his waist. My friend was indeed a guy who easily attracted women with his sleeves rolled neatly to just below the elbow, showing off muscular forearms.

We ordered our drinks, and Joe Bob's eyes followed every step of the comely lass as she walked across the room to the bar.

"That girl sure has a great smile," he said to nobody in particular.

"She's very pretty," I said. "I've never seen her before."

"Me neither," Bernie said.

"She don't look like any waitress I ever seen," Joe Bob said. "She might be on hard times for some reason, and she's workin' here to make ends meet."

Bernie shook his head and donned his unbelieving little smile.

"I can't imagine how you come up with some of this stuff," he said to Joe Bob. "Did you just dream up that scenario in the short time it took for us to order drinks?"

"Well, Bernard, I reckon I did. It seems clear to me that she is a pretty high class person. Maybe she's married with a sick husband. Maybe she's just been through a mean divorce. She coulda just got fired, or laid off of a real good job. I don't know what her situation is, but I'd be willin' to bet waitin' tables is not her chosen profession. What do you think, Matt?"

"It hadn't occurred to me to think anything about the young

lady except that she's a fine looking female," I said, trying for a little levity.

Our drinks came, and we ordered dinner, all three of us watching with appreciation as the waitress disappeared from sight. Then, I turned the conversation back to my new venture to allow us to have civilized, albeit dull table talk.

When the girl brought our dinner, we refrained from discussing why she might be here in Martinsville, Tennessee waiting tables in a Wednesday night supper venue.

"This looks very good," I said, peering down at my linguini with clams.

Bernie had just taken a bite of poached salmon. His face took on an odd expression, and he stood up abruptly.

"Excuse…"

He took off his glasses, throwing them on the table, and attempting to make it to the restroom, he vomited all across the room. Diners abandoned their meals and stared in horror.

"Eeeeow! That man's puking all over the floor," said a little girl, holding her nose.

Bernie had been able to drag himself into the restroom out of sight. The manager hurried from somewhere and did his best to radiate calm, apologizing and telling customers that the situation would be rectified asap. He assured them that their meals would be on the house, but his speech was in vain, because people were hurrying for the front door as fast as they could go.

Joe Bob and I rushed to the restroom to check on our friend. We had to watch our steps to avoid the trail of vomit leading to the first stall where Bernie was doubled over a commode, heaving.

"What the hell, Bernard?" Joe Bob said. "You think you got food poisionin'?"

"Gonna die," Bernie gasped.

I grabbed a bunch of paper towels and handed them to a pale-faced Bernie.

"Water," he said.

The restaurant was empty when I ran to the kitchen to get a glass of water. Two busboys were gagging while cleaning the mess from the floor, and the pretty waitress and a third busboy were gathering the half-eaten meals from the tables.

The manager followed me into the restroom just in time to witness Bernie gush forth again.

"What can I do to help?" he asked.

"Nothin' to do," Joe Bob said. "We'll take care of him."

I thought I saw a look of relief wash over the manager's face as he left.

When Bernie was finally able to leave the receptacle, he struggled to a sink and washed his face.

"Give me your keys, Bernie. I'll drive you home," I said.

I assumed that he didn't trust himself to speak, because he handed me the keys and nodded his assent.

Chapter Eleven

A few days had elapsed since I drove a sick and shame-faced Bernie home. I assumed that he had decided that he didn't need to burden me with whatever he had felt the need to discuss earlier. Neither of us had contacted the other, but Joe Bob and I seemed to stay in touch on a daily basis.

It was closing in on cocktail time. I was sitting in the living room watching Trudy pull a piece of yarn around on the floor for the kitten to chase. It was plain to see that the housekeeper had fallen hard for the new furry resident. It appeared that my chances of taking the kitten with me if I moved into the apartment in my new office building were going to be slim and none.

My phone vibrated in my pocket, and Joe Bob's name popped up on the screen.

"Hey, Joe Bob. What's happening?"

"Can you come over to my place?"

"Be right there," I said, wondering what new disaster might have occurred.

"Seems like you two are joined at the hip lately," Trudy said, grinning.

"That's true. I do enjoy his company, and he's been an awfully good friend. He helped me find a dependable SUV and he's letting me use one of his buildings for my office free of charge."

"You know how I feel about him. He's a good boy, but he's always somehow had bad luck. I wish him the best. Tell him I said hey, you hear?"

I laughed.

"I'll tell him, but he's not a boy. He's my age. Don't plan on me for dinner."

I hopped into my barely used Cadillac and headed to the trailer park. Joe Bob opened the door before I had a chance to knock.

"Come in this house and have a seat," he said. "I've got news."

"I'm all ears," I said, accepting the longneck he proffered.

"You remember when we was lookin' around my doublewide the other day to see if anything was missin'?"

"Sure. You said nothing seemed out of place."

"Right before I called you, I found my hammer layin' on the floor beside the back door. I didn't think much about it 'cause I'd used it to tack down a slat on the closet door. Not sure you ever noticed, but I'm not the neatest guy in the world. I coulda laid the hammer down to answer the door or take a phone call. The tool drawer was about half open when I put the hammer back. I'm a slob about some things like cleanin' up the kitchen, but I don't leave drawers open. That's just always been a thing with me."

"What are you trying to tell me?"

"I'm about ninety percent sure I know who broke in here."

"Well?"

"Arlene's badass boy. I've always had a bad feelin' about him. I know Arlene loves him 'cause he's her child, but I also know that she's kinda scared of him. She's said as much. He hangs out with some awful rough guys. She was gittin' ready to go to the store; had the window open, and she heard her son just outside on his phone. She didn't know who he was talkin' to, but she heard him say that he was gonna let the sumbitch know he'd better back off. Said he was gonna give the guy a warnin' and smash his big screen."

"Lots of people have big screen TVs. What makes you think he was talking about you?"

Joe Bob raked fingers through his long hair, then took a rubber band off his wrist and used it to wrestle it in a ponytail.

"I'm pretty sure he was talkin' about me 'cause later that night he called his mom a whore; made her cry. He musta found out she'd been spendin' a little quality time with yours truly. Some bad actors want to think their moms are way better than they are. I know that don't make much sense, but I've seen it more than once. I'm sure my mom wasn't perfect, but to me she was a real angel."

"Since you seem so sure it was Arlene's kid, what do you plan to do about it? You can't prove it, can you?"

"No, I can't prove it, and I don't plan to do anything about it right now. I'd like to know who he was talkin' to on the phone, and I'd like to be sure his reason for breakin' in here was just about me and his mom. He mighta been doin' it to threaten me for somebody who had it in for me—somebody who was payin' him to do his dirty work."

"Joe Bob, that sounds like a reach."

"I can see why you might say that, but when Arlene was tellin' me about it she said that she knew her boy would do anything to git his hands on money to buy drugs. He don't have a job. She buys all the groceries and just gives him enough spendin' money to git by—not nearly enough to pay for a stash."

"You don't know of anyone who might have a grudge against you, do you?"

"Been thinkin' about that, and I can't come up with anybody.

That don't mean anything. It's possible that I've hacked somebody off and didn't even know it. People take things the wrong way all the time."

"I guess that could be true, but since you don't have a plan of action, I say we drop it for now and go out for dinner."

"Sounds good. Just give me a minute to change my shirt. How about we go back to Morgan's and see if that cute little filly's still workin' there."

"What about Arlene?"

"What about her? We're not in a real relationship. She's just lonely, and I'm, well, needy, if you git my drift."

Joe Bob was back within minutes decked out in his dinner attire: dress shirt—this one was blue, sleeves rolled up to just below the elbow, and the wide gold chain he wore most of the time.

"Let's roll," he said.

Neither of us brought up Bernie's name. I doubted if he would be ready to return to Morgan's any time soon.

We had only been seated for a couple of minutes when Lucy Combs came to our table, dragging her crippled foot. She grinned.

"So, I guess this means Mister High and Mighty is a little skittish about coming back here since clearing the place out the other night," she said.

"Guess so," I said. "Could I persuade you to bring me a bourbon and soda to whet my appetite?"

"I'll just have a beer," said Joe Bob. "What's mouthwaterin' tonight?"

"Everything, but the specials are chicken pot pie and meatloaf. Pick 'em."

We placed our orders, and Lucy was turning to leave.

"Hey, Lucy," Joe Bob said, "what happened to the young woman who was workin' here the other night?"

"Nothing happened to her."

"Did she quit?"

"I don't know anything about her, except that she only works part time. Why?"

"No reason."

I smiled. Lucy was smart enough to know that Joe Bob didn't ask questions for no reason.

Just as our drinks arrived, a woman hurried past our table carrying a to-go parcel. At a glance, she looked vaguely familiar.

"Hey, did you notice the woman who just passed our table?"

"Well, yeah. I was lookin' straight at her. That was Freaky Fred's sister."

"I guess he's still bunged up from that beating the other day, and she's taking care of him at home," I said.

Our meals arrived, and without preamble, Joe Bob started shoveling it in like a starved animal. He had made a substantial dent in his dinner, then stopped abruptly.

"I want to find out what nights the pretty girl works," he said.

"Since you dine here nearly every night, that shouldn't be too hard to do."

"Good point," he said, and resumed devouring his chicken pot pie.

"Do you want to know what I'm curious about?" I asked.

Joe Bob looked at me with raised eyebrows.

"I'd like to know who Fred Peyton is working for. I know it seems likely that it's his sister. That makes the most sense, because I can't imagine who else would want to hire him. But I wonder why he's so secretive about it. On the face of it, it looks like he's just doing odd jobs—running errands etc., but he led us to believe he does several things he's not anxious to discuss."

Joe Bob pushed his plate away from him.

"I reckon I kinda put old Fred and his new job, or jobs, on a back burner after the break-in at my place."

"This might mean nothing, and I could have imagined it, but a few days ago I drove by Bernie's house. A guy was hurrying down the sidewalk and peeled off on a side street. I just saw his back, but I thought it might have been Fred. I wondered why he would have been in that neighborhood."

"Well, it's a free country. Maybe Fred decided he wanted a change of scenery."

"I also want to know who beat him up and why."

"I can't imagine why anybody would want to beat him up. Everbody knows he's harmless. Reckon it could have somethin' to do with his new job?"

"That's the only reason I can think of, because as you said, the whole town knows he's never been in any trouble; he pretty much keeps to himself."

"I'm tired of beatin' that dead horse right now," Joe Bob said. "Why don't we mosey on over to your new office. You can show me how you've got things set up."

I wasn't about to argue with the guy who was furnishing my office space for free. We paid the tab and drove to my new establishment. I would be open for business in just a couple of weeks, and I had to admit to myself that I was a little excited about it.

Joe Bob was impressed with the way I had managed to turn a rather small brick house into an upscale professional looking law office.

"Tell you what," he said, "I'd be proud to send anybody I know who needs a lawyer to you, my man. I don't doubt for a minute that you've got all your ducks in a row."

He punched me on the arm and grinned.

"As soon as I'm up and running, I'm going to start paying you rent," I said.

Joe Bob looked insulted.

"I didn't ask for rent, did I?" he said. "I don't need your money, Matt."

"I know that, Joe Bob, but you didn't take me to raise. I'll just feel better about using your building if I'm renting it instead of taking charity. That didn't come out the way I meant it, but you know what I mean. I'm a grown man; I want to act like one."

"Whatever," he said, and walked over to look out the front bay window.

"Joe Bob, you understand, don't you?"

"Yeah, I guess so. I just wanted to do you a favor. You've always been a good friend. Forgit what I said."

"Done. Let's go back to your place; sit out back with a beer and a cigar."

"You read my mind."

It was a moonlit night, and it reminded me that there was no light pollution here in small town America. I looked up to admire the heavens as Joe Bob unlocked the door. The night sky was a mass of stars.

"Damnation!" Joe Bob hissed.

I hurried to the doublewide and saw what had gotten my friend's dander up. His big screen had been smashed and most of it lay on the floor in shards.

"I saw you lock the front door when we left. Are you sure the back door was locked?"

Joe Bob smacked his left palm with his fist.

"The last time I remember goin' out that back door was when I chased that SOB into the woods."

"Is it locked now?"

Joe Bob checked the back door. It was locked.

"Maybe your hunch was right. The little we know points to Arlene's kid, but how could he have gotten inside? Did you give her a key?"

"No. Lucy's the only one I give a key."

"I hate to ask this, but is there any reason Lucy might have done such a thing?"

Joe Bob huffed out a laugh.

"Lucy? You gotta be kiddin'."

"It couldn't have been her anyway," I said. "She waited on us at Morgan's."

"Right. Think we ought to clean up this mess?"

"Do you plan to call the cops? If you do, we shouldn't touch anything."

"I don't think so. If I can't figure out who did this, they can't either."

"Your call," I said.

"Gotta find my cat," Joe Bob said, and began looking in every conceivable nook and cranny.

He found the frightened feline wedged into a corner of his bookcase bed behind a stack of Playboys, scooped it out, and held it to his chest.

"He seems to be okay," I said.

Joe Bob nodded and scratched the cat's ears.

"Now I gotta go shoppin'," he said. "I'm gonna find the bastard and teach him a lesson about breakin' in and destroyin' other people's property. Mark my words."

Chapter Twelve

One question mark after another defined the strange events which had taken place since I came back to my hometown. I had as yet to learn the identity of the culprit who was tormenting Bernie Zuckerman. That was the first of many unusual conundrums.

Fred Peyton, an unlikely suspect in anything the least bit complicated, posed another unknown. It appeared that his sister had cleaned him up and was attempting to take care of him. Who had hired Fred and what was he hired to do? He seemed so innocent that I couldn't imagine who would want to give him a beating, but I couldn't keep from thinking that he, and possibly his sister, were somehow involved in the strange goings on.

I couldn't decide how I felt about Bernie and his baby sitter/housekeeper/bedmate. Juanita seemed to be no more than a convenience for Bernie while she wanted more from the relationship according to him.

As far as I knew, Joe Bob was well liked and admired by many of the townspeople, so I couldn't imagine who had broken into his doublewide and destroyed his TV. Was the intruder searching for something? Was he trying to give Joe Bob a warning? Joe Bob was treated like a king at the country club and other business establishments. Admittedly, my old friend was an enigma. He was a do-gooder, had expensive tastes, had plenty of money, and lived in a trailer park. He certainly appreciated the fairer sex, but gave the impression of being a confirmed bachelor. His grammar was atrocious, but he was highly intelligent. As far as I was concerned, Joe Bob Kincaid was a straight-up kind of guy and the best friend a person could have.

I had been admitted to the Tennessee Bar and I was sitting in my tufted leather chair at my glass top desk, looking at my brand new computer thinking about everything except whether or not I could make a decent living in this small southern town. Could returning to my roots be yet another notch on my belt of misadventures?

I had put a tasteful bare bones ad in the local paper advising the town that there was a new law office in Martinsville. The ad stated the name of the firm, address, services available, and phone number. Now, all I had to do was wait, which I had been doing for the last three days.

Trudy had told me not to get discouraged, and that she had the utmost faith in me.

"You know how slow things are down here," she said. "Nothin' moves very fast south of the Mason/Dixon Line."

I knew what she had said was true, but that didn't keep me from being anxious to get to work, see if I could begin building a clientele, and start making some money. I needed a jumpstart to get my confidence back. I knew I had the skills, but would this town have enough demand for another lawyer?

I was still staring at the blank screen on my computer when the front door opened. In stepped Beth, my ex, looking like a movie star. She had on a summer Chanel suit and glided into the room on Manolo Blahnik heels.

"Beth, this is a surprise."

"Hello, Matt." She smiled. "Don't worry; I'm not going to try seducing you. I wanted to stop by to wish you the best of luck." She surveyed the surroundings. "I see you've done a bang-up job furnishing your office."

"Thanks. Um, how did you learn I was opening a firm in Martinsville? I assume you saw the ad in the paper."

"No, I didn't see the ad. You know word travels fast in our little town."

"That's a given," I said.

"I'm sure you've heard that I'm dating Mark Winters, the new Methodist minister."

I nodded. "Yes, I believe someone did mention that. I'm happy for you."

"Well, I must go. I'm meeting Mark for lunch. Again, congratulations and best of luck."

She turned on her expensive heel and fluttered her fingers over a shoulder, then left the building. Much to my amazement, I realized that I honestly was happy for her.

Ever hopeful, I thought there might still be a chance to snag a client before the day's end. I wanted to hire a secretary/receptionist, but I didn't dare do that until I had at least a handful of clients.

It was nearly five o'clock, and I had about given up on the possibility of anyone who might need an attorney walking through the door. I rolled back from the desk in my chair and stood up just as Bernie Zuckerman rushed inside. He was breathing heavily as seemed to be his custom lately. I stood where I was and waited for him to catch his breath.

"Water," he rasped.

I went to the cooler and hurried back with a cupful. Bernie gulped it and dropped into one of the two chairs in front of my desk.

"I need a lawyer," he said, pulling off his glasses to swipe the back of his hand across his wide forehead.

I sat down, and waited for him to let me in on what new horrible thing had happened to wreck his life. He held the cup toward me, and I was quick to refill it.

After a couple of minutes, Bernie looked at me. He resembled a broken doll.

"What's happened, Bernie?"

"Just when I thought things were beginning to settle down at home, Lee Ann struck again. I couldn't believe she would stoop this low, be this aggressive, this cruel."

"Bernie, what did she do?"

"You won't believe it, Matt."

I waited.

"She tried, and almost succeeded in kidnapping my baby girl."

"Walk me through it; what did she actually do?"

Bernie took a deep breath.

"Juanita had taken Claire to the little park down the street to play. She takes her there every day the weather is good. They were about to leave the park to go home for lunch. Juanita held Claire's hand as they approached the sidewalk. Out of nowhere, Lee Ann came up behind them and grabbed Claire."

Bernie was so beside himself that he had to pause, wipe tears from his cheeks, and blow his nose.

"Juanita turned and ran after them. Claire was crying and screaming for Juanita. People in the park were watching, and one of them started running in the direction of the fiasco. Juanita had caught up to Lee Ann and reached for Claire. Lee Ann let her go and took off down the street. Juanita said it took a long time to calm my child down."

"Why would Lee Ann do such a thing?" I asked. "Claire is with her mother every other weekend, isn't she?"

"Yes, but since she tried to kidnap Claire, I'm afraid to let her go. Lee Ann might leave the state with her. She might even take her out of the country. You have to do something to stop her."

"I don't suppose Juanita knows the person's name who tried to help her."

"No. She said it was a total stranger, just someone who saw what was going on and wanted to help."

"You have to settle down, Bernie. I need all the information you can give me. Do you know if Juanita is a US citizen?"

"I know she has a green card. Why?"

"She'll probably have to testify to what happened."

"I see."

"I'll petition the court for a modification of its previous child custody order to provide that the mother shall be limited to one hour of supervised visitation with Claire each month at a time and place to be reasonably determined by you. I'll also seek a restraining order prohibiting Lee Ann from any contact with you or Claire outside of the supervised visits."

"When can you start? I've stayed at home since this happened. Juanita is afraid to leave the house. She won't even take Claire out in the back yard to play, and Claire has started having bad dreams."

"I'll get on it first thing in the morning. Try not to worry."

"I'll try. You don't know how much I appreciate this, Matt. I'll go home now and tell Juanita and Claire that everything's going to be okay. Please stay in touch. I don't know anything about the law, but I trust you to lead me down this road."

I walked him to the door.

"Bernie, you're my friend. I won't let you down."

I had been on pins and needles, hoping for a prospective client to walk through the door before I left for the day, but I never could have guessed it would be Bernie Zuckerman. The ice had been broken—I now had one client, but I wasn't sure how I felt about it. Bernie was an old friend, but his life seemed to be one big tangled mess.

I drove home and let Trudy know that I finally had a client. Her face lit up like the morning sun.

"Anybody I might know?" she asked, sitting down at the kitchen table, looking excited.

"Bernie Zuckerman."

"Oh, Lord," she said. "I'd hoped it would be somebody important that the bigwigs would pay attention to and follow suit when they need a lawyer. From what little you've told me, Bernie Zuckerman's nothin' but trouble."

I nodded. "He does seem to have more problems than the average guy, but he's an old friend, and it's a start."

"Will you be here for dinner tonight?" Trudy asked.

"No. Joe Bob and I are going to try one of the new restaurants. He called earlier to tell me he heard it was very good and wanted to check it out."

"Which one?"

"Maison Jolie. It's the one everyone was surprised to see open in our small town. The menu looked way too sophisticated for Joe Bob's taste. It didn't mention meatloaf or chicken fried steak." I laughed.

When I had looked at the website I had seen that jackets were required, and I wondered if Joe Bob had paid attention to that small detail. It appeared that he had, because he showed up on my front porch in an expensive looking coat and even a tie. I didn't know that he owned either. His long hair was pulled back in a neat ponytail.

"Wow!" I said. "Look at Mister Fashion Plate."

Trudy had ventured into the living room and joined me at the door. She looked Joe Bob over and smiled.

"Mm, mm, mm, where are you goin' to preach?" she said.

Joe Bob grinned.

"I believe you prob'ly seen me in a coat and tie a coupla times, Ms. Trudy."

"I do recall once. 'course it was at the funeral home," she said. "You sure do look handsome."

"Thank you, ma'am."

"You two try to stay out of trouble, and don't spend all your money at that fancy restaurant."

We arrived at Maison Jolie a few minutes early, and Joe Bob pulled up in his pickup truck behind a Lexus and a Cadillac in the valet line. He didn't appear to feel a bit out of place.

The restaurant had an ultra modern décor. If you didn't pay attention, you might walk into a floor-to ceiling wall of glass.

We were welcomed by a six-foot tall reed thin beauty with coal black hair down to her butt. She donned a perfect smile and introduced us to a young lady named Lauren who picked up two sizeable menus and told us to follow her. She seated us and told us that a waiter would be with us shortly.

Joe Bob swallowed, and his hand went to his neck to loosen his tie, then re-tightened the knot.

"It's her," he squeaked.

"Who?"

"Lauren's the girl we saw waitin' tables at Morgan's that night."

I'd thought the pretty girl looked familiar, but I hadn't been able to place her.

"You're right," I said. "How'd you find out she worked here?"

"I hear things. I've got my ways of findin' out what I want."

"It seems that you do," I said. "Did you look at the menu online?"

"No. Why? I don't care what I eat. I just wanted to make sure this is the place she works. It suits her a whole helluva lot better than Morgan's."

"No argument here."

I wondered if Joe Bob had bothered to look at the linen clad table. It sported quite an array of glasses and silver. I knew he had grown up using cheap silverware and dishes sitting on oilcloth. His parents had very little money, and his father was a mean drunk who couldn't keep a job. I recalled how Mister Kincaid used my friend for a punching bag until the day he died. Both parents died in an automobile accident when Joe Bob was a teenager. His Uncle Jake grabbed Joe Bob by the scruff of his neck, pulled him out of a deep depression, and put him on the straight and narrow. He was my friend's savior, and Joe Bob never forgot it.

A stuffy looking waiter appeared and introduced himself. His name was Maurice, and he seemed to take pride in his pronunciation of it.

"Maurice, is that French?" Joe Bob asked.

The waiter nodded curtly and left.

"I sure could use a beer," Joe Bob said.

"I looked at the website. It appears they don't serve any alcoholic beverages but wine."

"I reckon I can live with that this time."

We turned our attention to the menus which were written in French.

Joe Bob stared at his menu, then at me.

"What sounds good to you?" he asked.

"I think I'll start with the snails, then have the fish," I said.

"I'll skip the snails. The fish sounds good though. I'm not very hungry," he added.

The sommelier appeared and suggested an outrageously expensive chardonnay.

"Thank you, but we'll have a bottle of Macon Lugny Les Charmes."

"Very well, sir," he said, sounding a bit peeved.

I glanced at Joe Bob as I was extracting a snail from the shell. He was grimacing, but we made it through the meal without an embarrassing moment.

We left the dining room and were making our way to the front entrance. Lauren was meeting us as she ushered a couple to their table. She smiled the way I was sure she smiled at everyone. I noticed that Joe Bob barely brushed against her, but it looked like an innocent, albeit clumsy mistake.

We were waiting for the valet to bring the truck. Joe Bob was wearing a satisfied smile.

"What's going on?" I asked.

Joe Bob looked like he had just won the lottery.

We loaded up, and I could tell that he was about to let me in on his big secret.

"That pretty little filly's got my phone number on a cocktail napkin in her cute little pocket," he said.

"Are you telling me that you slipped it into her pocket when we were on our way out of the dining room?"

"Yes, I am. I'll have you know that I could pick your pocket, and you wouldn't know a thing about it."

"For some reason, I don't doubt that, but what makes you think she'll call you?"

"Intrigue, my brilliant friend. Women can't resist intrigue."

Chapter Thirteen

Taking care of Bernie's legal problems had been a walk in the park. I slipped back into the legal profession as easily as sliding my foot into an old comfortable loafer. Lee Ann had been advised that she could be present in the courtroom during the proceedings, but she had declined to do so. Everything had gone without a hitch, and Bernie could breathe easier.

Trudy continued reassuring me that I was going to be successful.

"You just opened your practice. These things take a little time. Be patient; you'll see."

I went to my office every day as though I had a full schedule, and did my best to keep the good thought. Clients began dribbling in one at a time, most having been referred by a friend or acquaintance, and within a week-and-a-half I had managed to build a very small clientele.

If this was going to work, I knew I would need to be more visible. I would put an ad in the local paper each week and join the country club. Since Joe Bob was a member and my good friend, I figured that might give me a slight edge in meeting potential clients.

I was sitting at my desk, trying to think of more ways to flaunt my talents when a guy in khakis and a golf shirt came through the door. He approached my desk and smiled, extending his hand. I rose to take it.

"I'm Mark Winters," he said.

"Matt Stevenson. How may I help you?"

"I've been meaning to come by, welcome you to Martinsville, and invite you to come to church. I'm the minister just down the street at First Methodist."

"Thank you for the invitation. I might just do that."

Mark Winters smiled, letting me know he'd heard that one before.

"I know you're Beth's ex," he said. "She's told me what a good guy you are, and that the two of you split amicably. I hope you won't let the past stand in your way. I promise I won't badger you to join my church."

"Thanks for stopping by," I said. "I appreciate the invitation."

Mark smiled and headed for the door.

"See you in church," he tossed over his shoulder, and left.

I liked this guy right away. He didn't look like any minister I had ever known, and he wasn't pushy. I hoped that Beth had changed her ways and that she wouldn't stomp on this guy's heart the way she had mine.

It was nearly lunchtime, and I was feeling pretty good about my beginning practice.

I drove to Sydney Edelman's animal clinic and managed to go inside without a single butterfly in my stomach. Joyce, the receptionist, greeted me. I got the idea she considered herself my mentor since she had instructed me in the care of the kitten.

"Hello, Mister Stevenson," she said, smiling. "How are you and your kitten getting along?"

"Fine, thanks. Please let Doctor Edelman know I'm here when she has a minute."

She nodded and pressed a button on the intercom, delivering my message, and I took a seat in the waiting area.

I glanced up from the outdated magazine I pretended to be reading and thought I must be seeing things. The good-looking guy I'd been seeing with Sydney walked in from the back of the clinic. He said something to Joyce, then went back to the patient area, acting like he owned the place.

Minutes later, Sydney appeared.

"Hello, Matt. What can I do for you?" she asked, smiling.

"Nothing. I mean I don't need anything. The kitten's fine. I thought you might be free for lunch."

"As a matter of fact, I am free, and I would love to join you for lunch. Just give me a couple of minutes."

Now I was really confused. Suddenly, Sydney was very friendly and available. I wasn't about to question what had caused this turn of events. She seemed almost giddy as we walked to my car, and I was more than happy to live in the moment.

"Where are we going?" she asked.

"I'd like to take you to one of the new restaurants if you're not in a hurry to get back to work."

"I'm not pressed for time today. I'd like to try something other than the diner. I go there a lot because it's close to my clinic."

"Great. I found this place online that specializes in local fare. It's called *The Lite Stuff*. Sounds like your kind of place for lunch."

We were seated at a small table by a window with a view of a charming garden with a duck pond.

"This is lovely," said Sydney.

We both ordered the salad special and water. Then, Sydney seemed to have a change of heart about the drink.

"I'll have a Six-ounce glass of your house chardonnay as well. Oh, and the freshly baked sourdough bread."

This was the old Sydney, the girl I had taken to dinner when we first met.

"Sydney, what's come over you? You're not in a rush, and you're having wine with lunch."

I raised my hand and the waiter returned.

"I'll have the chardonnay, too," I said.

"Nothing's come over me, Matt. Everything has just gotten much easier. I'm not obligated to work every minute of every day. I've taken on a partner at the clinic, and he's been a godsend."

"Oh?"

I couldn't believe the relief I felt, realizing that the mystery guy must be Sydney's new partner. This revelation saved me the embarrassment of having to come out and ask her who he was.

"I had no idea there would be this much work when I took over Doctor Green's practice," she explained. "If I hadn't been able to find a competent vet to help with the work load, I don't know what I would have done. Luckily, Joe Lawson showed up just in the nick of time. As a matter of fact, the two of you arrived in town at about the same time."

"I'm awfully glad that worked out for you," I said, then, abruptly changing the subject, I said, "I'd really like to get to know you better, Sydney. I admit that I never forgot how charming you were when we first met."

Sydney looked up from her salad and peered directly into my eyes.

"That's one of the nicest things anyone has ever said to me, Matt. Does this mean you've been thinking about me the entire time you were gone?"

She wore an amused expression as she buttered a small piece of sourdough, and I had the impression that she was messing with me.

"It might," I said.

We both declared the restaurant a great place for lunch, and as we drove back to the clinic, I asked Sydney how the house she was having built was progressing.

"What makes you think I'm not living in it?"

I cleared my throat, scrambling for an answer to keep her from learning that I had been snooping around her apartment complex.

"I guess you must have mentioned it during one of our conversations."

"The house is nearly finished," she said. "What makes you ask?"

"Well, I thought you would have been excited to bring it up."

"I'll be able to move into it in about a month. I decided to make several substantial changes in the plans midstream. That's what has taken so long."

I nodded. "That makes sense. By the way, do you happen to read the local paper?"

"Of course."

"I was wondering if you had seen the ad about my one-man law firm. I just opened my doors a little over a week ago, but I already have a few clients. I'm kind of excited about it."

"Oh, I don't know how I could have missed it, Matt." She donned an impish grin. "Of course, I saw it, silly. I assumed you would tell me about it as soon as we left the clinic, but since you didn't mention it, I thought maybe things weren't going so well for you."

I drove Sydney back to the clinic, and she was about to open the passenger door.

"Matt, come inside with me. I'd like to introduce you to Joe. I think you two will probably want to get acquainted. He's really a nice guy, and I would guess you're about the same age and probably likeminded."

I accompanied Sydney inside, and she led me to her office where two desks were facing one another. Joe Lawson sat at one of them taking an enormous bite of a submarine sandwich. He looked up as we entered the room and stood while attempting to clear his mouth enough to speak.

Sydney laughed.

"Joe Lawson, I'd like you to meet Matt Stevenson," she said. "I have a feeling the two of you might have a few things in common. I imagine you're both a little short on friends since you haven't been here long."

The new partner swallowed, and he and I shook hands. I couldn't help seeing that Joe Lawson was even better looking up close than he had been from a distance. He was sharing the same office with Sydney and appeared perfectly comfortable with the situation.

"Nice to meet you, Joe. Please finish your lunch. I'm about to run late for an appointment," I lied.

Joe nodded, scribbled his phone number on a prescription pad, slid it across the desk to me, and gave me a little salute.

I didn't know exactly how I felt about this guy. I was glad Sydney wasn't being worked to death and that she had some free time, but I wasn't wild about the fact that they would be spending time together on a daily basis.

I drove back to my office and checked to see if there were any messages on my voice mail. There weren't any, and keeping my chair warm by staring at my computer screen wasn't going to get me anywhere, so I cruised over to Joe Bob's garage.

I found him sitting with one hip on the corner of his battered desk looking at his cell phone.

"Hey, Matt. What's happenin'?"

"I just had lunch with Sydney Edelman. Things seem to be looking up a bit. Also, I learned who the mystery man is—Sydney's new partner. I met him at her clinic, and he seems like a nice guy."

"How about that!"

"I don't suppose you've gotten a call from the waitress you tracked down the other night," I said.

"Give the girl time. She'll prob'ly need to mull it over a little bit before she gits bold enough to call."

I laughed. Joe Bob was the eternal optimist, but he might luck out with the pretty girl. I remembered her taking her time looking him over the first night we saw her.

"Hey, have you seen our tortured friend, Bernard?" Joe Bob asked.

His query caught me off guard. I hadn't counted on either of us bringing up Bernie's name. He was a client; and friend or not, I wasn't at liberty to discuss his case.

"Yeah, I've seen him a couple of times since the fiasco at Morgan's. Why?"

"I just wondered. I ain't seen hide nor hair of him. Maybe he's gone into hidin'. How about we invite him to play golf with us this weekend. I got to admit that I felt kinda sorry for him that night. You think he'll want to go?"

"Only one way to find out. What would you think of inviting Sydney's new partner to join us?"

Joe Bob grinned. "Sure. I git the idea you want me to meet the guy and feel him out. Right?"

"I guess I'd like to know your opinion of him, and I'd like to get to know him better. You can learn a lot about a person on the golf course. Plus, I think we would probably make an interesting foursome—four individuals in different professions, all of us about the same age."

"Okay. You do the invitin', and I'll make the tee time at the club."

I drove home to tell Trudy my good news. She was sipping a glass of wine and petting the kitten.

"You see what old Trudy told you. Everything's gonna work out fine. I sure do like that sweet little lady vet. She's a good match for you."

"This is not a done deal, you know. I'm just happy to learn that the new guy isn't a love interest. I didn't know that until today."

"Matty, I've always thought that everything happens for a reason. You'll see."

I went out to the back yard. It seemed a lot smaller than it did when I was a kid, but that was true of the entire town. Trudy had made a new flower bed, and it was thriving. I took in the beauty of her handiwork while I texted invitations to Joe and Bernie.

Minutes later my phone vibrated. It was Bernie.

"Who's this Joe Lawson guy?"

"He happens to be Sydney Edelman's new partner at her clinic. I thought it would be a nice gesture to invite him to join us since he's a newcomer in town."

"So I guess this means you're a believer in the old adage *keep your friends close and your enemies closer.*"

"That's not it at all. I wouldn't mind getting to know the guy. Okay?"

"Sure. Hey, you haven't said anything about my being your client to Joe Bob, have you?"

"You should know I wouldn't do that, Bernie. I take my profession very seriously."

I wondered if I was lying to myself. Maybe I did hold misgivings about Joe, and I probably did want to get Joe Bob's first impression of him. I was probably reading too much into what my friends had said and decided to give myself the benefit of the doubt.

Bernie had accepted the invitation while we were on the phone, and by late that afternoon Joe Lawson had followed suit. Joe Bob made a tee time for Saturday morning at nine o'clock, and I had let the invitees know that we should meet at the country club at eight-thirty.

Joe Bob and I went to Morgan's for dinner, and Lucy greeted us with her usual bright smile.

"What are you two drinkin' tonight?" she asked.

"Bring us each a bourbon. We're sorta celebratin'."

Lucy raised her eyebrows and gave us an eye-roll as she walked away.

"What are we celebrating?" I asked.

"We're about to have us a reunion of sorts. I've been thinkin' about Bernard and my conscience has been botherin' me. He'll always git on my nerves; that's not gonna to change. But I reckon he might feel the same way about me. I pick on him—always have, but he makes it so easy. He usually don't give me the time o' day unless you're around, but that road goes both ways. I could call him, but I don't. I wait for him to make the first move."

"And you plan for this reunion to take place on the golf course?"

"Sure. Why not? And I won't mention that little Mexican girl he's bangin' in front of the new guy. That might not go over very well. I plan to behave myself."

Our drinks arrived. I raised my glass, Joe Bob raised his and we clinked.

"To the reunion," I said.

Joe Bob flashed his bright, white teeth in the slightly crooked smile he used when he felt really good.

"I think I'll have the chicken fried steak," he said.

Chapter Fourteen

The first thing I learned about Joe Lawson was that he was punctual. I saw him pacing back and forth in front of the pro shop as I walked toward the building.

"Good morning, Matt," he said, smiling and offering his hand.

"Glad you could make it," I said.

I saw Bernie pull up to drop off his bags and waved to him.

"Bernie Zuckerman's the guy leaving the bag drop," I told Joe. "Joe Bob's the member here, and Bernie's our fourth."

Bernie hurried up the stairs, and I made the introductions.

"I'm sure Joe Bob's already inside," I said.

We entered the pro shop and were greeted by an assistant pro who looked to be all of seventeen.

"Good morning, gentlemen," he enthused. "Are you by chance guests of Mister Kincaid?"

"We are," I said, "but we'd like to pay our own greens fees."

I hadn't discussed this with Bernie or Joe, but I felt it was the right thing to do. Joe and I didn't have clubs, so we would have to rent sets.

"Mister Kincaid has already taken care of that," said the young man. "Maybe he'll let you buy him a beer." He smiled like he had just done us a favor. "You'll find him on the driving range, and your range balls are waiting for you."

Before I had a chance to inquire about rental clubs, he came from behind the counter with two golf bags containing what looked to be brand new sets of clubs.

"Here you are," he said. "I'm sure you'll be more than pleased with these."

I thanked the young man, and we headed to the range.

Joe Bob had just sent one splitting the wind down the middle of the range. He was about to tee up another ball when he looked up and saw us. He put on his million dollar smile as if he were about to be introduced to a bevy of beauties and extended his hand to the newcomer. As usual, his golf attire was top-of-the-line.

"Joe Bob Kincaid, Joe. Glad to meet you," Joe Bob said. "I don't reckon we'll have any trouble rememberin' one another's names."

The two shook hands.

"You guys prob'ly want to hit a few, then stop by the puttin' green," Joe Bob said. "We can git on the course whenever you're ready. Take your time. I'll be back in a few."

"Joe Bob must carry a lot of clout around here," Joe Lawson said, as we left the range and walked to the adjacent putting green.

"Looks like," I agreed.

Two shiny new carts were waiting for us as we left the putting green. They were equipped with tees, bottles of water, ice, and fresh towels.

"How 'bout you ride with me, Joe," said our host.

I took that to mean he planned to find out as much as possible about the newcomer.

The four of us loaded up, and the starter gave us the high sign, letting us know that we could go to the first tee box.

"Okay for you guys to play from the blacks?" Joe Bob asked.

Bernie was the first to decline the offer.

"I'm fine with the blues, but the blacks are a little more than I can handle," he said.

I assumed that Joe Bob had been attempting to find out what kind of golfer the new guy was, not that it mattered.

"I'm with Bernie on this one, Joe Bob," I said.

Joe Lawson hadn't said a word, and I took that to mean that he would have gone along with the majority no matter his preference. He was simply being a cordial guest.

We moved up to the blue tees, and armed ourselves with drivers.

"Joe," said our host, "show us what you got."

Joe Lawson teed up his ball, took a practice swing, and put the little white orb straight down the middle bypassing the large sand trap which covered a good portion of the fairway. He left the tee box wearing a bland expression as if a three-hundred-yard drive was run-of-the-mill.

"So, I guess you make time to play quite a bit," Bernie said.

"Actually, I haven't played for a while," Joe said.

Bernie stepped up to the tee box. He didn't bother to take a practice shot, and nearly came out of his shoes with a baseball swing that sent his ball left into the woods. He walked to our cart shaking his head in disbelief.

"I never go left," he said, "but I haven't played lately either. Crazy things can happen when you only play a couple of times a year."

"Okay, Matt, you're up," Joe Bob said.

My ball flew down the middle of the fairway, but it didn't

make it to the monster trap. I wasn't unhappy with my shot since I hadn't played much since I came back to Martinsville. I was planning to join the club, but not just to play golf; I wanted to meet prospective clients.

Joe Bob's tee shot wasn't as long as Joe Lawson's, but it was admirable. He hit it down the middle and made it over the trap.

Bernie was in a snit from the get-go. I was sure he felt inferior to the rest of our foursome, and it made him try too hard. Instead of improving, he played worse and worse. His frustration manifested itself by showing its owner's true colors. At one point, Bernie threw a club barely missing Joe Bob, and his vocabulary reached an all-time low, spewing a string of expletives after each swing of his club.

As the round progressed Joe Bob's game remained steady, and mine was spotty. Bernie couldn't do anything right, and Joe Lawson's game actually improved.

Joe only had one bad shot, and it was a doozy. He had hit another sterling tee shot, but his second shot sailed over a bunker and landed out of sight. Joe Bob drove to the place we thought the ball would be. Neither of them spotted it at first. Joe Bob stayed in the cart, and Joe was on foot for a closer look.

Bernie and I watched from the cart path.

"I've got it," Joe said. "It's under a leaf, kind of hidden."

Joe Bob had been close at hand and watched as Joe gingerly lifted the dead leaf.

"I don't see how you can possibly hit that ball," Joe Bob said. "It's awful close to the fence."

Joe was right-handed, but he grabbed an eight iron, addressed the ball backward, and gave it a sharp smack with his left hand. It wasn't a pretty sight, but the ball sliced through dead leaves and bumped over twigs and onto the fairway. Joe Bob and I applauded.

After the last ball fell into the cup on the eighteenth hole, we all shook hands. Since it was just a get acquainted game we hadn't been betting.

"The nineteenth hole's my favorite, guys," Joe Bob said. "Let's go tackle it."

"Great idea," Joe Lawson said. "It was sure nice of you guys to include me. I'd like to buy a round of drinks."

I would have bet that Joe Bob would have refused the offer, but he didn't. He gave the newcomer a light slap on the back and said, "Thanks, Joe. 'Preciate it."

We only stayed for the one round of drinks discussing the game of golf. Then, we went our separate ways.

I was anxious to find out what Joe Bob had learned about the new guy, so I called him late that afternoon.

"Want to grab dinner in a bit?" I asked.

"Sure. Should we invite the sourpuss? I couldn't believe the way he acted today. He's a spoiled kid."

"While I agree with your assessment, we probably should ask him to go. I'll call him. Morgan's okay with you?"

"Sure. See you guys there around seven o'clock."

What little I had been in Joe Lawson's company, I thought he seemed like a real nice guy. Of course, I had only observed him during a round of golf and hadn't had an opportunity to converse with him. Joe Bob was good at sizing people up, and I would bet that he had formed a pretty solid opinion of the guy.

Bernie had said he might be a few minutes late, but that he would meet us at the restaurant. I had planned to offer him a ride and try to tamp down his attitude on the way there, but I changed my mind. He was a grown man and needed to behave like one. He might still be embarrassed about clearing out the dining room the last time he was there.

I was the first one to arrive at Morgan's. I asked for a booth so it would be quiet enough to carry on a conversation. I had always liked the old high-backed wooden booths here. There was something nostalgic about them. Joe Bob, Bernie, and I came here when we were teenagers. We'd watch the girls who happened to pass our booth and rate them from one to ten.

"You flying solo tonight?" Lucy asked.

"Hey, Lucy. No, the other two are on the way. I just got here first."

"Joe Bob and the grouch?"

"Yeah."

At that moment I spotted Joe Bob coming through the door and motioned for him to come to the booth. He stepped close to Lucy and planted a quick kiss on her cheek.

"Stop that, Joe Bob, and get your bad self in this booth. You want me to get fired?" she said.

Joe Bob laughed and slid into the booth across from me.

"Bernie's on his way here," I told him.

"I hope he's in a better mood than he was today. Wonder what kind of impression he'll have of Joe. Make you a bet."

"Yeah?"

"It won't be good. He'll have somethin' snotty to say about him. Dollar?"

"No bet. And speak of the devil, here he comes."

"Sorry I'm late," Bernie said. "I had to tie up a couple of loose ends."

Lucy magically appeared at our booth.

"Drinks, gentlemen?" she asked.

We ordered, and while we waited for Lucy to bring our libations, I reiterated my thanks to Joe Bob for the round of golf.

"You're welcome, my friend. Well, I guess we ought to do what we're here for," he said. "What'd y'all think of the new guy?"

"Since it was my idea to invite him, I'll go first," I said. "I didn't have a chance to get to know him because we didn't ride together, but from the little I've seen of him, I think he seems like a stand-up kind of guy. You were with him the entire round. How did he impress you?"

Lucy came to our booth with a tray of drinks.

"Bourbon and soda, dirty martini, and beer," she said, placing the drinks before us. "Ready to order dinner?"

"How 'bout comin' back in a few minutes?" Joe Bob said.

Lucy nodded and left.

Joe Bob took a long pull on his beer and smiled.

"I really liked the guy," he said. "He's got a ton of education. You have to spend a lotta years in school to be a vet. But this guy is the real thing. He's plain as a old shoe. He likes to play golf and fish, and he don't shy away from a little gamblin'. Matter of fact, he wants to git a few guys together and start a poker group. I told him I knew you guys would want to be in on it."

"It sounds like you grilled him all morning," Bernie said. "Is he married, or divorced?"

"Neither. His wife died a few years ago. Had the big C."

"Bummer," said Bernie. "Sure looks like he's gotten over it. He was all smiles today."

"Bernard, I'm not sure, but I'd guess there's a heart somewhere in that body of yours. The man lost his wife, but he's still here. He's got a right to git on with his life."

"Just saying," Bernie said. "So did he play straight up? Maybe noodle the ball to get a better lie? Did the ball move when he moved the leaf or whatever was covering it?"

"He played straight up, Bernard, and he didn't noodle the ball. I watched him move the leaf, and the ball didn't move a whisker. What else do you want to know?"

"Nothing, thank you. It's perfectly natural to be inquisitive about a stranger's golf habits. Don't tell me that you don't sort of keep an eye on other golfers, especially the ones you just met."

"I don't usually care what another guy does on the course unless I'm bettin' with him. Then, yeah, I pay more attention. I don't go lookin' to accuse anybody."

I was getting pretty sick and tired of listening to these two bicker every time we were together. I was on the verge of letting them know that I didn't enjoy their verbal dueling when Joe Bob's phone rang.

"Yes, this is Joe Bob Kincaid."

He put on that special smile, and his face lit up like that of a five-year-old at his birthday party.

"Sure, I remember who you are. It's good to hear from you." His voice had taken on a sexy drawl.

He got up and walked out of the restaurant with his phone glued to his ear.

"Wonder what that's all about?" Bernie said.

"How should I know?" I said, knowing without a doubt who was on the phone.

Joe Bob was back a few minutes later, still wearing that smile. He slid into the booth and motioned for Lucy to take our dinner orders.

Bernie and I ordered from the Lite Menu.

Joe Bob looked up at Lucy and said, "I'm so hungry I could eat the south end out of a northbound mule. Bring me the fried chicken, mashed potatoes with gravy, and corn. Oh, and a biscuit."

It never failed to amaze me how much the man could eat and look like the picture of health.

"I forgot what we was talkin' about," he said, " but it don't matter. Just old friends hangin' out."

"Cheers," Bernie said, and we clinked our glasses.

I would never understand how Joe Bob seemed able to draw women to him like a moth to light, but I had to admire the guy. It was my humble opinion that he would never become involved in holy matrimony; he was having too much fun playing the field.

As for Bernie, I didn't think he would ever change his negative attitude. I assumed that he had simply had the bad luck to be born with that unfortunate trait.

I had always been the buffer between my friends. I hadn't chosen that path; I just fell into it. Joe Bob couldn't hide his goodness, and Bernie couldn't keep a lid on his bad side. We were quite the trio.

We left the restaurant in good spirits, and I sent our unlikely friendship to a back burner to think about the lovely Sydney Edelman.

Chapter Fifteen

My decision was made. Martinsville, Tennessee would be my home unless something terribly untoward happened to crush my plan. All appeared to be well within my small circle of friends. Bernie had Lee Ann exactly where he wanted her. He wouldn't have to wonder when or where she might show up to threaten his family, and he would be present to supervise any visits she would have with their daughter. Juanita would no longer be terrorized by the devil woman.

Joe Bob was in the process of luring in another prospect of the feminine persuasion. He seemed to be in a perpetual state of happiness.

Trudy smiled a lot. She had grown quite fond of the new house pet and her proclivity for sipping a bit of wine seemed to agree with her. She was also delighted that I was back in Martinsville.

As for yours truly, I was pretty sure I had a chance with Sydney. She had magically turned into the woman I had longed for since I first met her about a year ago, and it seemed that a lot of the credit for the transformation belonged to none other than Joe Lawson, her new business partner. He had cut her work load in about half, and she didn't feel compelled to take care of every animal in Martinsville.

My practice was beginning to grow little by little. I had just forked over the hefty initiation fee to join the country club. Joe Bob had been a real asset, introducing me to many of the town's upper crust. He and I had already played golf with a couple of doctors and the mayor. For the life of me, I didn't understand how my friend had become so highly esteemed. He certainly didn't have a white collar job. He did own his business, but every day one could find him covered in grease working on the innards of some vehicle.

Trudy was waiting for me in the kitchen when I came downstairs for breakfast.

"Well, if it's not the handsome new lawyer in town," she said.

"Top o' the morning to you, beautiful lady," I said, proffering my best smile.

"I see you've got on a suit," she said. "I reckon that means you're goin' to your office instead of the golf course."

"I have a new prospective client who's meeting me in about a half hour. Things are really beginning to look up, Trudy. I think I'm going to make it."

"Of course, you are. That's what I've been tellin' you. You're gonna be the shinin' star I knew you'd be by the time you were about seven years old."

This morning's breakfast was oatmeal, bacon, and toast. Trudy used to make a smiley face on my oatmeal with raisins when I was little.

I had just finished signing up my new client when Joe Lawson called. He was anxious to get enough guys lined up for the first poker game.

"Are you sure Joe Bob and Bernie are in?" he asked.

"Yes. They both said to count them in. Do you have some other guys lined up?"

"I only have two more, but we don't have to have seven players. Six works just fine."

"Great. When's the first game?"

"How about seven o'clock next Friday night at my place?"

"I'll let my guys know. What's your address?"

I scribbled the address on a pad and stared at it. It looked familiar. Then, it hit me. This was the address of Sydney's apartment complex. So that was the reason I had seen Joe and Sydney together at the elevator the day I had gone to find out if she still lived there. They lived in the same building and worked together at the clinic. My mind raced when Joe told me how great it was to make some friends in such a short time. Sydney was the only person he had been acquainted with until the day she introduced the two of us, so it made sense that he had been spending some time with her, especially since they were business partners.

I knew I had to decide not to be jealous of Joe no matter how much something inside me kept pulling me in that direction. His relationship with Sydney was nothing more than business. Oh, I'm sure he liked working with her, and he would have to enjoy her company. Who wouldn't?

"That sounds great, Joe. See you then."

Joe's apartment was on the second floor. Joe Bob and Bernie were waiting for me at the elevator and we rode up together.

None of us knew the two other players Joe had rounded up. I thought they both seemed okay. Stan told us that he was an insurance salesman, and Charles was a nurse at the hospital.

"A nurse, huh?" Joe Bob said. "That must take a ton of dedication."

Charles nodded. "I consider it a calling. I have friends who tell me they couldn't possibly do it, because they wouldn't have the heart. I could cut someone's head off and sew it back on if it would help them."

It appeared that nobody thought selling insurance was interesting enough to discuss, so we gravitated to the bar to get drinks.

"Gentlemen, shall we?" said our host.

Joe didn't have a poker table, so he had covered what I assumed was a round dining table with felt. It worked just fine.

"Who'd like to deal first?" he asked.

Bernie reached for the deck.

"Five card draw," he said. "Ante up."

Stan took three cards, Joe Bob, Charles and I took a couple, Joe took one, and Bernie took three. All of us folded quickly except Bernie and Joe. Bernie ended up with two pairs, and Joe won with a full house.

We played High/low, Texas Hold 'em, Seven card stud, Omaha, and a couple of crazy games I'd never heard of. We played until eleven o'clock, and Charles turned out to be the big winner for the evening. We decided to play once every two weeks, and Joe offered to host again.

I called Joe Bob the next afternoon to see if he wanted to meet me for dinner. I wanted to get his impressions of the new guys.

"Sorry, ole' buddy. Got other plans with the pretty girl you thought wouldn't give me the time of day." He laughed.

"Good for you. I'll catch you later."

I knew it would be rude and a bit presumptuous of me to extend a dinner invitation to Sydney at this late date, but that didn't stop me. I lucked out, because she was free and accepted my offer. I made a reservation at a small Italian restaurant that hadn't been here the last time I was in my home town.

The scene I witnessed as I pulled into the parking lot of Sydney's apartment complex summoned the green-eyed monster in me. The hood of Sydney's car was up. She was standing beside the car, and Joe Lawson backed his head out from under the hood, wiped his hands on a rag, and closed the hood. I couldn't hear what he said, but it produced a beautiful smile from Sydney. Joe took her elbow and guided her to the elevator where the two disappeared before I could get there.

Sydney opened the door when I rang the bell, and at that moment Joe came from the hall which led to the bath and bedroom.

"Hi, Matt," Sydney said with a smile. "I'll be ready in just a couple of minutes."

Joe and I looked at one another.

"Hey, Matt."

"Joe."

Joe cleared his throat and expelled a little laugh.

"Uh, you might be wondering what I'm doing here in Sydney's apartment," he said.

I didn't want to show my juvenile side, so I shrugged and smiled as if to say I hadn't thought about it.

Joe hurried to explain, "Somebody had undone the coil wire on her car. She was going to run a quick errand, and the car wouldn't start. I had just pulled into the parking lot and took a look at it for her. Hands are clean now."

"I guess you put her back in business," I said, and smiled.

Sydney came into the room looking like the picture of summer in a yellow linen sundress.

"What are you two cooking up?" she said.

"We were just holding down the fort until you were ready for your date," Joe said. "See you both later."

He exited the apartment, and Sydney smiled at me.

"I'm so glad you called, Matt. I'm famished."

"I hope you like Italian," I said. "I looked at the menu of this small restaurant online. It's very extensive. Shall we try it?"

"Sure. I've never had an Italian meal that wasn't delicious."

As it turned out, the food was great, and Sydney lived up to the description of her hunger. She ate more eggplant parmesan and pasta than I assumed such a small person could hold. Then, she ordered desert and polished that off as well.

It was still pretty early when we left the restaurant, and I didn't want to take the lovely lady home right away. I wanted to spend time with her and get to know her.

"How would you feel about driving around our small town for a while?" I said. "I can give you a little bit of history since I grew up here."

"Sounds like fun," she said. "Someone told me that there's a beautiful lake close by. I'd like to see it."

"That would be Henderson Lake. I'm afraid I don't know how it got its name. I haven't been there since I was a kid. It has, or had a small manmade beach. My buddies and I used to swim there a lot. Sometimes we took our girlfriends there at night and built a bonfire on the beach. It was the thing to do in a small town back then." I laughed.

Minutes later we parked beside a path which led to the little strip of beach.

"Let's kick off our shoes and go for a walk in the sand," Sydney suggested.

She didn't wait for my response and took off her sandals. I hadn't considered digging my toes in the sand, but if that was what Sydney wanted to do, far be it from me to argue. I got rid of my shoes and socks, rolled up my pants, and we made our way down the path, holding hands.

The moon cast silvery light on the sand and made the lake water glitter.

"I don't think I've ever seen so many stars," Sydney said, "and the moon is actually silver. This place looks magical."

"It's really pretty tonight," I said. "There's no light pollution out here. All we need now is a blanket and a bonfire to pretend we're teenagers."

I tightened my grip on her hand and pulled her to the water's edge. We each tested the water with a toe and decided it wasn't quite warm enough to splash in the water's edge.

When we had walked to the end of the beach, Sydney turned to me. The moon shone so brightly on her face she had to shade her eyes. I assumed she had turned to start back the way we had come, but I soon realized that was not the case. She leaned into me and put her head on my chest. I could feel blood pumping in my ears, so I was pretty sure she could feel my rapid heartbeat.

I swallowed. "Sydney, I…"

"Yes, Matt?"

I was a thirty-eight-year-old man who had been married, and I found that I couldn't speak.

Sydney looked up and pulled my face down to hers and delivered the most delicious kiss imaginable. Then, she pulled slightly away from me.

"Am I too bold for you, Matt?" she asked, wearing a mischievous grin. "I mean we are two consenting adults. Besides, I know you've wanted to kiss me for some time."

"And how, may I ask, did you know that?"

"Who else would adopt a kitten just to get a date?"

"As it happens, I did take the kitten for that specific reason, but it worked out fine. My housekeeper fell in love with the kitten almost immediately. The two are inseparable. Trudy has been my family's housekeeper since I was a toddler. When my mother passed away, I told Trudy that I wanted her to live in the house, and that's what she is doing."

"That's wonderful. Now, where were we?"

She leaned back into me, the length of our bodies meshing with our feet beginning to sink into the sand. I wasn't about to let her outdo me in the bold department. I cupped the back of her head and kissed her the way I had wanted to for more than a year. She responded in a way that let me know she was very interested in having a romantic relationship with yours truly.

I was feeling enormously chivalrous, and I put an arm around her back and the other under her knees and carried my maiden through the sand and up the path to the car only panting a tiny bit and hearing one of my knees pop twice.

"Oh, Matt, that was an absolutely gallant thing to do. You have to put me down now so I can get the sand off my feet. I don't want to mess up your beautiful car."

I hated to admit it, but I was more than a little ready to put her down. My arms were beginning to ache. I opened the passenger door and told her to take a seat and stick her feet out. Then I proceeded to sacrifice my socks to clean her feet.

"What about your feet?" she asked.

Off came my shirt. Then, my tee shirt became the second sacrifice. I stuffed my still gritty feet into my loafers feeling happier than I had in a very long time.

Chapter Sixteen

I felt like I'd been reborn. I could almost feel my life changing for the better. Coming back to Martinsville was turning out to be a real boon. After having floundered around for several years, spinning my wheels trying to make a living and getting nowhere, I was finally beginning to make headway.

Just feeling Sydney Edelman in my arms had made me forget how devastated I had been as a younger man when Beth had put a dagger in my heart. I had thought I would never get over losing her, but I did. After I met Sydney, there wasn't a trace of the heartbreak I had felt. I was a new man; ready to start a meaningful relationship with the woman I wanted by my side forever.

Joe Bob was waiting for me when I got to my law office. He stood on the small porch smoking a cigarette.

"Hey, Joe Bob, what's happening?"

"You 'bout ready to open up?" he said, pinching the fire from his cigarette, then putting the half- smoked Marlboro in his shirt pocket. I knew he had plenty of money, so I couldn't imagine why he would do such a thing.

"Hold your horses. Let me get the door unlocked."

The two of us went inside together, and I turned on the lights. Joe Bob looked as though he were about to burst to tell me something. I had always been envious of his movie star smile. It was his best asset. But I had never seen him smile this way. His entire face was taking part—his mouth, showing every pearly white it owned, his cheeks pulled back almost to his ears, and his eyes fairly shone. It was the look of a very happy man.

"Matt," he said, "I'm in love."

"Joe Bob Kincaid's in love?"

"You know I never had a problem findin' female companionship. Right?"

"Yeah, I know that. You've never seemed to be suffering from a lack thereof."

"I've always enjoyed women's company, if you know what I mean, but I've never felt like this."

"May I ask who the lucky lady is?"

"Well, damn! Are you dense? It's Lauren, the fox who works at that fancy restaurant. I can't tell you how the girl makes me feel. I just can't describe it. She's on my mind day and night. I can't even change a tire or look under a hood without seein' her face."

"That's great, Joe Bob. I think I might feel the same way about Sydney Edelman. We sound like a couple of lovesick teenagers, don't we?"

"Yeah, I reckon we do. Does the vet know how you feel about her? I mean, did you come right out and tell her?"

"No, not exactly. Did you tell Lauren?"

"No, not yet, but I'm goin' to. We've just had the one date. I'll tell her soon as things heat up a little bit. I wouldn't want to chase her off before we even git started."

"I get that, but after last night, I'm ready to turn up the heat.

It's taken me too long to break the ice. I had a hard time coaxing Sydney to agree just to go to dinner with me."

"Well, I reckon I'd better git over to the garage and go to work. My whole mornin's booked. You know when you've got somethin', or in my case, somebody on your mind, it's hard to git any work done." He laughed.

"Hey, before you go, I was wondering what you thought of the new guys Joe recruited for poker?"

"To tell you the truth, I hadn't thought much about 'em. They both seemed like okay guys. I didn't see anything out of the ordinary about either one of 'em."

"That was my take too. I just wondered, because you're so good at reading people as soon as you meet them."

"Later, my friend," Joe Bob said, and let himself out of the office.

I watched him get into his truck and re-light his half-smoked cigarette, thinking that must be how the wealthy get that way. Then, my eyes traveled down the street where Joe Lawson stood on the corner, waiting for the light to change. I squinted into the bright morning light and saw a guy who looked sort of like Freaky Fred standing beside Joe. I couldn't tell if the two were carrying on a conversation, because they were too far away.

When the light changed, Joe continued walking toward my office, and the Fred look-alike turned and went in the opposite direction. I wondered why Joe was on foot. If he had been coming to see me, I would have thought he would be driving since my office was nowhere near the animal clinic.

I was making coffee when Joe came into the office.

"Hey, Joe, it looks like you're out taking your morning constitutional on my turf. How about a cup of coffee?"

"Sounds good," he said, accepting the proffered mug. "I'm

playing hooky this morning. I have a couple of things to do before I go to the clinic. It's such a gorgeous day I thought I'd walk around town for a while."

"Was there something you wanted to discuss with me?"

"No. I just thought I'd come take a look at your new digs. This is very classy, Matt. You've done a great job."

"Thanks. By the way, was that Fred Peyton with you waiting for the light to change?"

"I don't think I've met anyone by that name. That guy was some kind of nut case. He was talking to himself about cracks in the sidewalk."

"Yep. That was Fred alright. He's a fixture here in Martinsville. He used to wear an old gabardine coat summer and winter, picking up pop bottles by the roadside. When he was a kid, he tried to dig a tunnel under the street close to his house so he could escape from the truant officer. He skipped school a lot. He's a genius in a couple of areas; otherwise, he's on another planet."

Joe gave the Fred Peyton conversation a dismissive shrug.

"Matt, I never thought I'd find myself living in a little town like this, but I have to tell you that I'm really enjoying it so far. I have a job doing exactly what I want to do, I've made some new friends, and I don't have to tell you how great Sydney is. Working with her is a real joy. You're a lucky guy."

"I do feel like a pretty lucky guy, but Sydney and I have only had a few dates. You couldn't exactly call us a couple at this point."

"Well, for my money you seem like a good match. I'd better get going. I have a couple of things to do before I go to the clinic. I'm sure I'll see you soon."

"Thanks for stopping by," I said, wondering what could have motivated him to walk across town to stop by just to say hello.

Why did I have a feeling that something might be a little off about Joe's visit? He had led me to believe that he had never before met Fred Peyton, so I assumed that their meeting at the traffic light had been pure coincidence. He had given an explanation as to why he had shown up on foot so far from the clinic, but I couldn't come up with a reason for Freaky Fred to be in this part of town. I told myself that I had an overactive imagination and put that on a back burner to review the tort case involving my first client of the day.

By lunch time I had met with two of my new clients and was feeling rather puffed up; enough so that I called Bernie to ask him to meet me for lunch to catch up. I hadn't talked with him in a while, and I thought it might boost my ego to let him know how well I was doing. He'd always had a habit of letting it be known that he wasn't hurting for money.

We met at an uninteresting sandwich shop close to Bernie's dry cleaning business. He was waiting there when I arrived wearing his usual mad face. I'd never known how to interpret that look—was he upset about something, in a hurry, or did it mean anything at all? He was almost always perspiring.

"Hey, Bernie, how've you been?" I asked, taking a seat across from him.

"I don't want to jinx my luck, but I've gotta tell you that things have never been better."

"That's great."

"Matt, I know you've been reluctant to believe that my ex actually did all of those things like slashing Juanita's tires and planting a dead snake just outside my back door. But there haven't been any more stunts like that since the judge ordered her to keep her distance."

"I'll admit that those particular things don't seem like something a woman, especially one like Lee Ann, would do. I'd think she would consider such demeaning things beneath her dignity, but I suppose she could have hired someone to do the dirty work. Regardless, you say you haven't had any more trouble, so that's good."

"There's more, and you won't believe it. She was scheduled for a visit with Claire last weekend, and she chose not to be involved. It's clear to me that she doesn't love our child. She knows I adore my baby girl, and I think she was just using Claire to hurt me."

A young woman wearing a very tight, very short dress appeared at our booth. She held a pad and pencil and batted her fake eyelashes first at me, then at Bernie.

"Hey, guys, know what you want?"

"I wouldn't mind seeing a menu," Bernie said.

The girl motioned over her shoulder toward a chalkboard on the wall. Bernie and I glanced at the offerings. The choices were pretty limited.

"Bring me a tuna sandwich and iced tea," said Bernie.

"Just double that," I said.

"So, what about you, Matt?" asked Bernie.

"Things are going very well. I have a good start on building a clientele and I'm feeling pretty positive about several more prospects. I think I've made a good move, Bernie."

"Any trouble from your ex?"

"Nope. It seems that she's more interested in the Methodist preacher than rekindling a relationship with yours truly. I also have an interest in a certain young woman, the lady vet who took over Doc Green's clinic. She's a lovely person. I met her briefly when I was here last year and I've taken her out to dinner a couple of times since I came back. She lives in the same apartment complex as Joe Lawson."

"That's all good news, Matt. Speaking of Joe, I guess I'll see you at the poker game next week. He seems like a nice guy, but we still don't know much about him. We might find out more if Joe Bob would invite us to another round of golf. You should mention it to Joe Bob. He always seems ready to do whatever you suggest."

"I might just do that, but back to you. I assume Claire is adjusting well to life without her mother. You'd told me that she and Juanita bonded almost immediately."

"They did, and if Claire misses Lee Ann, she's doing a fabulous job of hiding it. Juanita is really good with her. Claire laughs all the time and doesn't whine or throw temper tantrums like she did when Lee Ann was in charge."

"Can I assume things are going well between you and Juanita?" I asked, knowing it was none of my business.

"You can assume that. Juanita doesn't speak perfect English, but she is very intelligent. I think a great deal of her. The only fly in the ointment is her belligerent brother who shows up every now and then. He doesn't come into my house; always happens to catch Juanita when she is outside and alone. She doesn't talk about him much; just says she wishes he would stay away from her. They're obviously not close."

"I don't recall you ever mentioning that she had family here."

"There was no reason to mention it. She hadn't said anything about it until just the other day. She was in sort of a snit. I asked her what caused her to be in such a bad mood. That's when she told me about the brother."

We were seated by a window, and I happened to glance outside.

"Hey, I think we might want to cut this short. Look at the sky."

We both stared out the window as though we were transfixed. The sky was darkening by the second.

"Forget lunch," I said, tossing some bills on the table. "Let's get out of here."

"This is really eerie," Bernie said.

"You're telling me."

Bernie kept his eyes on the ominous sky.

I looked down at the sidewalk and saw a chewing gum wrapper hopping along as if were alive. It would hop, drop down, then hop again. It did that all the way to the curb where it flipped down into the gutter. With the imminent danger all around me, all that came to mind was the old jingle: Double your pleasure, double your fun with double good, double good Doublemint Gum. Then, reality hit.

"What do you think we....?"

Golf ball size hail suddenly rained down in a rush, pelting parked cars, rooftops, aluminum awnings, and the side of Bernie's head, breaking the earpiece of his glasses.

"Inside!" I yelled.

Bernie grabbed what was left of his glasses, and we stumbled inside the sandwich shop.

"Let's get away from the windows," I said.

Bernie settled his glasses on his nose, holding them in place with one hand.

"We can stand back a little and still see what's happening," he said. "I want to watch; I'm kind of fascinated with storms."

Before I could argue, a loud noise that sounded like a freight train came out of nowhere, and a mass of debris smashed through the windows, sweeping chairs, tables, and human bodies across the room and into a far wall. I was able to pull Bernie out of the way a second before we became part of a mass plastered against the wall. He seemed to have gone limp, and I had to half-drag him down a narrow hallway and into a restroom where two cooks huddled together in a corner.

"Do you think this is about the center of the building?" I asked.

Neither of the cooks answered. They didn't even shrug. Bernie was trembling and hyperventilating. This didn't seem to be a likely place to find a paper bag, so I tried to yell above the horrible noise.

"Bernie, stare at an object and try to breathe normally."

Then, there was a strange sound above our heads in addition to the roar. I could see things flying overhead through a hole in the ceiling. This was almost surely a tornado. It must have ripped off the top of the building, and maybe an attic.

The noise ceased as quickly as it had started.

"Breathe, Bernie," I urged.

My friend was still shaking, and his face was deathly pale. A streak of blood ran down the side of his face, and he must have lost the remainder of his glasses somewhere en route to the restroom.

"It's over," I said. "We're safe, now."

Bernie slid down the tiled wall. He was able to take a deep breath, but he was still trembling. He began to sob.

"It's all right now," I said. "Let's get you up and out of this restroom. We need to check out the damage."

"I thought we were going to die for sure," he said, as I helped him to a standing position.

"If we hadn't made it to the restroom, we might have."

We had to climb over piles of debris in the hallway: a couple of chairs, part of a table, glassware, dishes, and just as we got to the dining area, we had to step over a partially severed leg.

I had never witnessed such carnage. Dead bodies lay in a heap amid furniture and broken glass pushed against the back wall away from the gaping hole where the front of the building had been. I didn't hear a moan or a whimper, let alone a plea for help.

"We have to call 911," I said. "Do you have your phone? I left mine in my car."

Bernie looked lost and confused. He patted his pockets.

"My phone—it was on the table. My phone and my glasses are both gone!"

He started crying again.

I couldn't believe he was whining about inanimate objects after we had just negotiated a roomful of dead bodies. I guided him to my almost new Cadillac which looked like it had been through a war. I was able to get the door open and strap Bernie in the passenger seat.

I spied my phone resting in a cup holder, grabbed it, tapped in 911, and gave the address and the few details I knew. I thought we should probably stay where we were, but Bernie couldn't see how to drive without his glasses. Instead of checking on his car and waiting for help to arrive, I peered through a small part of my windshield that I could see through and headed straight to the hospital ER. I was pretty sure Bernie was in shock.

Sitting in the waiting area I called Trudy. She was crying.

Chapter Seventeen

Martinsville looked something like a disaster checkerboard. The tornado had split apart and touched down in what appeared to be designated spots around the town: a liquor store, a bakery, and a one-hour photo shop, all on the same street. The one which had devastated Trudy happened to be on the street where we live. Our side of Mulberry was intact, but from our front window all that could be seen across the street was a continuous pile of rubble.

I had talked with the doctor on call in the emergency room, and he had informed me that Bernie was very shook up, and that he was keeping the patient in the hospital overnight. He said that Bernie would probably be released the next morning. Having learned that, I had driven straight home to check on Trudy, thinking that if she was safe, I would make a beeline for Sydney's clinic, then to Joe Bob's garage.

Trudy stood rigid as a statue, clutching the cat to her bosom. Her face was streaked with tears.

"It's over, Trudy. You don't have to be afraid now. You're safe."

She moved from the corner of the kitchen where she had

gone after the storm and stumbled toward me. I opened my arms, and she walked into them. Then, a new spate of tears erupted, spilling down her cheeks and chin to drip on the frightened cat and my shirt.

"I think you might be squashing the cat," I said, trying for a little levity.

The housekeeper didn't appear to be in the mood for fun. She backed up a step and stroked her pet.

"We hid in the powder room by the guest bedroom, prayin' to keep from bein' picked up and blown away," she said. "I never heard anything that loud in all my years."

"The only thing that matters is that you're okay. As a bonus, the house seems to be intact. I'm fine, but my car took a beating by the hail. It might be totaled. I'll get in touch with my insurance agent as soon as I check on Joe Bob and Sydney."

"You're right. We need to be thankful to be alive, and believe me, I am. I just had a weak moment, but I'm fine now."

My phone vibrated.

"Joe Bob, are you okay?"

"I'm happy to announce that I am. You sound fine, so I guess you are too. How 'bout Miz Giles?"

"Yes, she's fine—just shook up. Our side of Mulberry wasn't touched, but the other side of the street is wiped out as far as I can see. The hail did some serious damage to my car. I won't know if it's totaled until the insurance adjuster looks it over. I haven't seen my office yet. I don't suppose you have."

"I have. It looks like it didn't know that big funnel cloud had come for a visit."

"That's a relief."

"I'm guessin' you'll be gittin' new wheels. I've got a loaner for you while you're walkin'."

I laughed. "Is there anything you don't have to back me up when I need it?"

"I doubt it."

"Bernie and I were about to have lunch at a sandwich shop close to his business when the tornado decided to wreak havoc on the town. He kind of went off the deep end, and I had to drive him to the hospital. He's okay; just pretty rattled. The doc's keeping him there overnight, but he should be released in the morning."

"Bernard sure is easy to come unglued."

"Yeah, he's kind of high-strung."

"Well, I just wanted to hear that lawyerly voice of yours to make sure you wuz okay. In case you're wonderin', Lauren's out of town, so she's safe. I'll bring my old Buick over after a while."

"Thanks. I appreciate it."

I hung up thinking that Joe Bob Kincaid was the best friend a guy could have. In the short time I had been back in Martinsville, he'd come to my aid every time I found myself in a bind.

I went upstairs to shower and change into clean clothes. Then, while staring out my bedroom window at the wreckage across the street, I called Sydney Edelman.

"Oh, Matt, it's so good to hear your voice. Can I assume you're okay?"

"Yes, I'm fine. What about you? Where were you when the tornado hit?"

"I hunkered down in the basement here at the clinic with half the residents of Noah's Ark, Joyce, and a groomer. That's where we keep our overnight guests. It's quite homey, but animals become agitated when there's any kind of storm brewing. They all decided to voice their discontent at the same time, and it took a while to settle them down."

I felt as though a huge weight had been lifted from my shoulders, knowing that Sydney was unharmed.

"I'm so glad you're safe," I said, realizing that my voice trembled. Do you have any damage?"

"No. This entire street looks perfectly fine. The apartment complex is all right too. Joe called a while ago and told me. I assume he went home for lunch. I'm going to check on my house that's under construction after work."

"If you haven't made dinner plans, you could drive to your apartment after work, and I can come pick you up, check on your house, and we can go someplace for a low key dinner."

"Matt Stevenson, you certainly do come up with some wonderful ideas. I'll be at the apartment by six o'clock."

I had never witnessed a tornado or any kind of epic storm, and I wondered how much it would end up affecting the town. Devastation of this kind had a way of making people pull together in a spirit of community to right things, but I knew it could also turn otherwise upstanding folks into looters and thieves. I figured I would find out more about our townspeople tomorrow after the dust settled.

I called my insurance company and learned that I would have to take pictures of my car from different angles and submit them along with online forms before I would learn their assessment of its condition. It seemed that everything which was supposed to be a convenience for the customer had suddenly become more work for the individual.

Sydney opened the door looking a little tired. I was sure that she had had a very stressful day what with dealing with crazed, sick and injured animals. She had naturally felt huge responsibility for them.

"I know you must have felt overwhelmed with all of those frightened animals. Can I assume they're settled down now?"

"I think so. The clinic was pretty quiet by the time I left. I'm ready for some unhealthy food and lots of wine."

"I didn't make a reservation, but if that cozy little Italian place we found is still standing, I thought we might go there. I learned that they don't require reservations."

Joe Bob's old Buick was parked just outside the apartment building, and I guided Sydney to the passenger side. She raised her brows in a question.

"It's old, but reliable," I said. "My car got hit pretty hard by those big hailstones. This is my transportation, compliments of my friend Joe Bob Kincaid."

As it turned out, the Italian restaurant was intact, and we were fortunate to be seated at a corner table on the veranda with a lovely view.

I began looking over the wine menu for a bottle that I thought Sydney would enjoy when she reached across the table and touched my hand. I looked up from the menu.

"Matt, I feel like I need a real boost. I think I'd like to start with a vodka martini, up."

"Whatever Sydney wants, Sydney gets. I won't be quite that brave since I'm driving my friend's wheels."

Sydney laughed.

"By the looks of that car, I don't think you could hurt it if you crashed it into a brick wall. Too bad they don't build cars like that anymore."

My date was quite happy by the end of the meal having consumed a martini and a half bottle of wine. I knew I would probably need to assist her in making it into her apartment safely, and that turned out to be the case.

I drove home in the trusty Buick and parked it on the street where Joe Bob had left it, but unlike him, I took the keys into the house. Then, I climbed the stairs to my old room, stripped down to my underwear, and flopped down on my bed to think about this day from hell.

I had been so concerned about the people closest to me that I hadn't let my mind travel beyond my inner circle. Bernie was no doubt doped up in the hospital, and I hadn't bothered so much as to call his house or drive there to check on Claire and Juanita. I didn't know if his house was still standing.

If all was well at Bernie's place, Juanita and Claire would probably be asleep. It was too late to call their landline. I thought about getting dressed and driving to the house, but what could I do when I got there? I should have called to tell Juanita about Bernie after I had taken him to the hospital, but my brain must have taken a hiatus; it never occurred to me.

I'd heard every lawyer joke that had ever been told, but this small town attorney still had the conscience of the kid he had been, sitting in Sunday School. I was so tired that my shoulders ached from tension, but I got out of bed, threw on jeans and a golf shirt, and drove to Bernie's address. I breathed a sigh of relief as soon as I saw the house. It hadn't been touched. I would be able to give Bernie that report when I went to spring him from the hospital in the morning.

I hadn't set an alarm, but the loud mouthed bird in the tree just outside my window let me know that time was wasting. A bright shaft of slatted light shone across the room through the open wood blinds. I hadn't remembered going back to bed after my late night drive, but as the shower needles stung my skin, I began to put a schedule together for the day.

Trudy had brewed coffee and was taking a pan of biscuits from the oven when I came into the kitchen.

"Good mornin', my sweet boy."

"Good morning to you," I said, and poured a cup of coffee.

"When I look out the living room window and see nothin' left but a pile of rubble, I just want to cry. I can't help but wonder what happened to our neighbors. Where are they, and what did they go through? The early news didn't report how many casualties there were. Nothin' was said about injuries. Gladys Jean from right across the street and I had planned to go to lunch one day this week."

"I'm going to go to the hospital after breakfast to check on Bernie's condition. If the doctor releases him, I'll drive him home. I'll try to find out how many victims of the tornado were brought there last night if they will give me that information."

"You know they won't give you the names of the injured until they've contacted family members."

"I know that. I'll get whatever information I can and let you know what I find out."

Trudy made sausage and eggs to accompany the biscuits, and a little smile played at the corners of her mouth as she watched me devour the breakfast.

Bernie was dressed, pacing the floor when I arrived at the hospital.

"Oh, Matt, am I glad to see you. I'm worried sick about Claire and Juanita. I tried calling the land- line at my house, but all I got was a dial tone. I can't believe it, but I never bothered to learn Juanita's number. I have it on speed dial, but I don't seem to have my phone. I can't see. I guess my broken glasses are somewhere under the rubble in the sandwich shop."

"Has the doctor released you yet?"

"Yes, and I've signed the release forms. I doubt anybody can read my signature. I was getting ready to call you, hoping you could pick me up and drive me to the house."

"That's why I'm here. Let's go."

"Hey, this is Joe Bob's old Buick."

"And I thought you couldn't see," I said. "Yes, it is. I guess you don't remember, but my windshield was smashed when I drove you to the hospital yesterday. Joe Bob lent me this old tank. After we go to your house to check on Claire and Juanita, we should go and have a look at your car. I didn't see any point in looking at it yesterday since you couldn't see how to drive."

"Just drive to my house. Okay? I'd like to know it's still standing, and I want to see my baby girl."

"Sure. Just so you know, I drove to your house last night. I don't think the tornado touched down on your street. I didn't ring the bell or call your landline, because the house was dark. I assumed Juanita and Claire were asleep."

I pulled to the curb in front of Bernie's house, and we hurried up the walk. The house looked perfectly fine as Bernie fished in his pants pocket for a key. He set off the house alarm by opening the door.

"Oh, shit! Punch in 3359, Matt. I can't see the numbers on the screen."

I punched in the code, and the alarm went silent. Bernie began calling out Juanita's and Claire's names as he went from room to room. Nobody answered. I could tell from my friend's movements that panic had set in. He stumbled as he hurried through the house. It wasn't very bright inside, and I thought he was probably having trouble seeing without his glasses, so I switched on a lamp. Nothing happened.

"The power's off," I said.

We checked every room, constantly calling their names, but the housekeeper and the child were obviously not there. Bernie picked up the phone on the kitchen desk and held it to his ear. The line was dead.

He made his way to the island and sat on a kitchen stool with his face in his hands. Then, he started to hyperventilate. I didn't know where to look for a paper bag, so I jerked his hands from his face and gave him a sharp smack. He shook his head as if to clear it and stood.

"We have to find my daughter," he said, his voice trembling, and headed through the laundry room to the garage.

"Juanita's car's not here. She's been parking it in the garage since all this madness with Lee Ann started. Where could she have taken my child, and why would they have left the house?"

"Maybe Juanita tried to get in touch with you but was unable to reach you. You lost your phone during the storm. Did you leave anyone in charge of your business when you left to meet me for lunch?"

"No. This has been a real slow week. I locked the place up, intending to go back after lunch and leave early. What does that have to do with any of this?"

"So, Juanita couldn't have reached you at your business if she had tried?"

"No, but she knew I was coming home early. I told her that before I left to go to work."

"But you didn't go home, because I took you to the hospital."

"Will you please drive me to the police station? I think I need to tell them to put out a missing persons report."

"Sure. I'll take you down there."

Bernie was sweating profusely on the way to the station. His hand trembled as he swiped moisture from his broad brow. I didn't try to make conversation with him, because he was in such a state.

He still couldn't see three feet in front of him when we entered the police station, but that didn't keep him from roaring in like a mad bull. He lumbered toward the desk sergeant and began demanding that he put out an APB on two missing persons without identifying himself or giving the names of those who were missing.

The sergeant looked up from his work and focused on Bernie's face.

"Excuse me, sir," he said, "but you'll need to take this form and have a seat at that desk to my left. After you fill it out, I'll pass it on to someone who will ask you for details."

Bernie snatched the form from the sergeant's hand and made his way to the desk. I tagged along to assist him since he didn't have his glasses.

"Matt, would you mind?"

"Happy to help, Bernie."

I took the form and the pen. Then, I read each inquiry to Bernie and filled in his answers. I returned it to the desk sergeant, explaining that I assisted my friend in filling it out since he had broken his glasses.

Bernie was perspiring profusely as we were ushered into a small room with a lone table and two metal chairs—one on each side of the table. I stood in a corner of the room while Bernie told his story and answered questions. He didn't have any pertinent information to give the detective.

My friend had lost his bravado by the time he learned that unless foul play was involved, it was too soon to take any action. He then resorted to tears as was his custom when he felt a sense of helplessness.

"I think we should go to your ophthalmologist and see if he can give you a pair of temporary glasses as close to your prescription as possible until you can have yours replaced. You can't function like this, Bernie."

"I'm so worried I can't think. Let's go look at my car."

"Do you remember where you left it?"

"I left it in the parking garage a couple of doors down from my business. I walked to the sandwich shop."

I drove to the garage, and we found Bernie's Caddy safe and sound. The garage hadn't been hit by the tornado. We also found his prescription sunglasses in their case, resting in a cup holder.

"This is the only thing that's gone my way since lunchtime yesterday," he said.

"What's next?" I asked. I knew he was half crazy, worrying about Claire.

"I have to think where Juanita could have possibly taken them. I guess she must have driven them in her car since it wasn't in my garage."

"I think you should drive your car home and leave it there. I'll follow you. Then, we can go to my office and make a list of possibilities. We have to at least have some idea where to begin looking as the police will enter the information into a national data base and put out an Amber Alert after twenty-four hours if we haven't had any luck.

Chapter Eighteen

As it turned out, Bernie couldn't come up with much information to help us locate his missing child and sitter. As far as he was aware, Juanita didn't have a close circle of friends. Bernie said that she never discussed doing anything with girlfriends or casual acquaintances she might have met in the park where she took Claire to play. She and her brother, whom Bernie had only seen from a distance, were supposedly estranged, and she had chosen not to discuss anything regarding their relationship.

Our search for Claire and Juanita was pretty non-existent since we'd had no idea where to start. We did go to the little park and question people who were willing to look at photographs of Claire, but none of the participants were able to identify the child. Even though we had nothing to give the authorities, I felt certain that there would be a search in progress soon, and I tried to console Bernie with that assurance.

Too many things were happening simultaneously. The wrecked side of Mulberry Street was teeming with the owners of the destroyed houses, digging through the wreckage in hopes of finding any small item which had been spared. After a few days of the devastated homeless in their fruitless quest, the street was clogged with machinery to eradicate the detritus prior to any rebuilding. It was nearly impossible to navigate the busy street to leave one's home, and the noise created by the many machines was maddening.

After several days of the mayhem, Trudy told me that she was taking the cat with her to her small house on the edge of town until living on Mulberry Street got better. She invited me to stay in her guest room. I declined her offer, opting instead to furnish the upstairs of my law office. I figured that Joe Bob, with his many connections, could help me get that done in nothing flat.

The insurance company had advised me that my Cadillac was indeed totaled and could not be replaced for at least another month. In the meantime I would have to make do with Joe Bob's old Buick.

I made a mental priority list. First, I would help Trudy relocate. She hadn't lived in her house at all since moving into my mother's. She told me that she went there twice each week to clean it and make sure everything was in working order. She had put a sign in the front yard offering it to short term renters and had enough success to keep the utilities.

As soon as Trudy was settled, I called Joe Bob about the furniture I would need to make the upstairs of my law office habitable. As expected, he assured me that he could get the job done that day if I was free to accompany him to his friend's warehouse.

I drove to my office and studied the upstairs, making notes of everything I would need to make it livable. I had planned to take Bernie to his ophthalmologist to see if he could get temporary glasses close to his prescription until he could have new ones made, but that turned out to be unnecessary. He had prescription sunglasses that would suffice in the meantime. I told him that I could be available to drive him wherever he needed to go at night. He said that there was no way he could go to work and run his business until he found his child, and he put his most trusted employee in charge of running the place for the time being. He spent his days scouring our small town, hoping for any scrap of evidence to help him find Claire and bring her home safe.

Joe Bob showed up at my office right after lunch. He had called his buddy at the furniture business and let him know we were on our way to the warehouse. Ross Hansen was waiting for us and asked for a list of the pieces I would need.

"I'm not looking for anything real expensive. I'll be living on the second floor of my law office. I want it to be comfortable and good looking enough to invite a friend over."

"Are you interested in man cave kinds of pieces, or something that's suitable for the general public?"

"Basically, the latter, but it should be feminine enough that a lady wouldn't turn up her nose at it."

I was able to check off everything I thought I would need in a couple of hours, and Ross said he would have it delivered by late afternoon.

"Joe Bob, I can't thank you enough," I said as we headed back to Martinsville.

"No thanks necessary. You'd do the same for me."

"I'll never have as many contacts as you do. I can't imagine how you collected so many."

"It's called livin' in a little southern town. You haven't been back here very long. You just opened your practice and you've already got several clients. You just got to be a little patient; this is the South." He laughed.

"Hey, have you talked to Bernie today?" I asked.

"No. I kinda hide and wait for him to git in touch with me, if you know what I mean. He seems to like it that way."

"Well, he's coming up empty trying to find his missing daughter. I tried helping him make a list of possible places Juanita might have taken Claire, but he was no help. If Juanita has any friends, Bernie's not aware of them. The only person he could come up with is Juanita's brother, and he thinks they're estranged. He's not getting anywhere with that and he's letting one of his employees run his dry cleaning business while he looks for the kid."

"You don't reckon Lee Ann could have anything to do with the kid's disappearance, do you? I mean, the judge made it clear she better not dare come within spittin' distance of either one of 'em."

"I feel sure Lee Ann's not involved. She might be nuts, but she's not stupid."

"You're prob'ly right. It's a real shame a woman with her looks turned out to be such a she devil."

"Hey, if you don't have plans with your foxy lady, might you want to meet me for drinks and dinner? I should have my living quarters squared away before the cocktail hour."

"Sure. I think this is pot roast night at Morgan's. I really like their pot roast. It tastes just like my mama's did. And I'll come by and pick you up. How 'bout sixish?"

"I think your friend Ross is fairly true to his word, so I'll be ready to go by then."

When Joe Bob dropped me off, I climbed the stairs to my new home and drew a map of the rooms so I would know exactly where I wanted the furniture placed. I had just finished and gone downstairs for a beer when the furniture truck pulled up outside. The same two guys who had brought the office furniture were back and did another first class job. They told me they were through for the day so I persuaded them to accept a beer before heading back to the warehouse. Once again, they refused a tip.

When I went back upstairs to look things over, I realized that I hadn't thought about linens, or toiletries or anything else. Instead of fighting with all of the machinery on Mulberry Street, I nixed the idea of going to the house to get my dopp kit and everything else I would need. I called Joe Bob and told him that I might be later than I had thought because I needed to purchase several things before going to dinner. Then, I made a quick trip to a drugstore and on to a department store for linens.

Joe Bob showed up as I was hauling my purchases into my new home.

"Could you use a hand?" he asked, and relieved me of part of my load.

We took it all inside and dumped it on my brand new king size bed.

"Want me to help you put things away?" he asked.

"I can do that later. Let's head over to Morgan's. I'm hungry, and I could use a drink."

It wasn't yet twilight, but there was a thick cloud cover when we arrived at the restaurant. I was feeling pretty good about moving into my new digs as we walked toward the front door. I happened to glance to my left and saw who I could have sworn was Juanita disappear into a Dollar General store about half a block away across the street.

I had to find out if it really was Juanita, and without saying a word to Joe Bob, I took off across the street at a run. Inside the Dollar General I scanned the open area, then I started down one aisle after another until I had covered the entire store. No Juanita. Maybe my eyes had been playing tricks on me, but the glimpse I'd had of the small dark complexioned woman had me believing I had seen the real thing.

I went back across the street to find Joe Bob standing outside the restaurant waiting for an explanation. He stood with hands in his pockets and raised eyebrows.

"I didn't have time to explain, Joe Bob. I was almost certain I saw Juanita go into that Dollar General store down the street. I was afraid she would disappear before I could catch up to her. As it turned out, she did just that. I don't know how she could have left the store without my seeing her, but she did."

"Let's go inside and git you a drink," he said. "You look like you could use one."

We were seated at one of the wooden booths with the tall backs and hard seats. Lucy appeared wearing a bright smile.

"What's up, guys?"

"We're mighty thirsty, Lucy," Joe Bob told her. "And tell me you've got that famous pot roast tonight."

"You're in luck. We do have pot roast. Your usual drinks?"

We nodded, and Lucy left the booth.

"You got a theory, don't you?" Joe Bob said.

"I might. It's going to sound like a real reach, and I could be way off base."

"Lay it on me. See if I can buy it."

"It occurred to me that there could be a small possibility that Juanita isn't the person we've been led to believe she is. Bernie doesn't seem to know much, if anything, about her background. He knows that she has a brother, but he doesn't seem to know anything about said brother. It could be barely possible that Juanita took Claire with her to her brother's place after the tornado. Don't ask me why, because I have no idea. It's just a thought."

Our drinks arrived, and we ordered the pot roast. Then, as if on cue, both of us took a healthy quaff.

"Bernard told us Juanita and the kid think a lot of one another. I don't think he could be imaginin' that, do you?"

"I don't know. Also, Bernie seems to think quite a bit of Juanita. He's never said he has deep feelings for her, but he told us he thinks she has very deep feelings for him. He gave me the impression the relationship is sort of one-sided."

I was at the point that I didn't know what to think about any of this mess. Bernie couldn't seem to rid himself of one bad situation just to get in the middle of another one. Baby sitting my old friend hadn't been the way I had planned to begin my new life.

"Do you plan to tell Bernard that you think you spotted Juanita?" Joe Bob asked.

"I don't think so. I can't tell him that I definitely saw her, so I don't think I should mention it. If he thought there was a remote possibility that Juanita was the person I saw, he would hound me about details, and I don't have any. All I saw was the back of a person about Juanita's build go into a store half a block away. The slightest glimmer of hope would buoy him up for nothing."

"Speak of the devil," said Joe Bob, nodding toward the door.

I swiveled my head to see who held his attention and saw Bernie heading in our direction. He looked a little unsteady on his feet and wore the pained look we had become accustomed to lately. He was wearing sunglasses.

"Hey, Bernard," Joe Bob greeted. "Do you wear them things day and night?"

"In case you haven't noticed," Bernie slurred, "it isn't dark yet. But, yes, I have to wear them if I want to see until my prescription arrives."

I slid over to make room for him in the booth beside me.

"I see you're nearly finished with your dinner," Bernie said.

"We are, but we're in no hurry. We'll visit with you while you eat. I apologize for not inviting you to join us. You see, I'm moving into the second floor of my law office. I just had furniture delivered this afternoon by one of Joe Bob's friends. Then, we decided to come here for dinner. Busy day."

"Why are you moving into your office? Your house wasn't damaged, was it?"

"No. The house is fine, but the street's a mess. It's crawling with heavy equipment cleaning up the debris on the other side of Mulberry."

"I see," he said, motioning for Lucy.

She hauled her bad foot over to our booth and peered down at Bernie.

"Why you wearing shades in here?" she asked.

"Why is everybody so interested in my appearance?" Bernie hissed. "They're the only glasses I have at the moment. Bring me a Manhattan, water with lemon and the pot roast."

I sincerely wished that he hadn't ordered a Manhattan. It was clear that he had already consumed quite a bit of alcohol.

"Coming right up, your highness," Lucy said, and left the booth.

"You havin' any luck with your search, Bernard?"

"No. I'm beside myself, guys. I don't know where else to look, and I don't know anything else to do. I'm helpless, and I'm going insane wondering where my baby is and if she's scared or being mistreated. I'm in a living hell."

Joe Bob and I looked down at our plates. We knew Bernie was beyond suffering, and there was nothing we could do to alleviate his pain.

Lucy appeared with Bernie's water and Manhattan, and our friend ignored the glass of water, lifted the drink and downed a huge gulp. He took off the sunglasses and mopped his forehead with a napkin. I knew he was at his wit's end, and I hoped he didn't think that he could find the answers he was so fruitlessly searching for in a bottle of booze.

When Lucy brought Bernie's dinner, it seemed that he had lost his appetite. He threw back the rest of his drink and ordered another one.

"Bernard, you ought to try the pot roast. It's really good."

"When I want your opinion, or suggestion, I'll ask for it. You always think you have the answers to everything," Bernie snarled.

"Guys, guys, let's cool down," I said. "Getting all upset isn't going to solve anything. Bernie, try to eat some of your dinner. It'll make you feel a little better. Physically, I mean."

Here I was in the middle of another of their tiffs, trying to play Henry Clay, the friendly peacemaker, and sounding like a bumbling idiot.

Bernie refused to eat his dinner, and he sneered at Joe Bob. Lucy deposited his new drink wearing a disgusted expression, and Bernie downed it in one gulp, spilling a good bit of it on the front of his shirt. Then, he slumped down on the wooden bench.

"Help me get him up, Joe Bob," I said.

I grabbed Bernie's keys and sunglasses. Then, Joe Bob and I hauled him out of the booth and into the passenger seat of his Cadillac. I drove him to his house where we got him inside and put him to bed on a couch. I left his belongings on the kitchen counter, and Joe Bob took me back to my law office. We moved everything off my new bed and made it up with new linens which smelled new since I hadn't had a chance to wash them. Then we toasted with a couple of longnecks I happened to have in my mini fridge.

"You reckon Bernard'll go off the deep end?"

"I'm afraid he's real close."

Chapter Nineteen

I was watching the local midday news while wolfing down a turkey sandwich. I'd been unusually busy all morning, and I hoped that was a good omen. I had yet to let anyone know how badly I wanted my new practice to succeed. Of course, everyone who knew me assumed that. A grown man doesn't want his acquaintances to think he's needy.

I had just washed down a bite with diet coke when I learned that an amber alert had been put out on Bernie's child. I hoped this move would prove successful in finding her safe and sound and that Bernie could once again breathe easy.

Joe Bob called just as I was finishing my lunch. He wondered if I might stop by the garage sometime this afternoon.

"I have a meeting in a few minutes. After that, I'm free the rest of the afternoon. I'll be there in about an hour and a half."

My meeting was with a prospective client, a well known gentleman in the real estate business and promised to be quite profitable. Not bad for a small town lawyer struggling to make a new start.

I squared things away feeling a bit smug and headed over to

Joe Bob's garage. I found him sitting on a stack of tires talking on the phone. Upon seeing me, he cut his conversation short and dropped the phone on his cluttered desk.

"What's up?" I asked.

"Somethin' kinda strange happened this mornin'."

I raised my brows in a question.

"Freaky Fred come in here and asked me for a job."

"What kind of job? He doesn't know anything about automobile mechanics that I'm aware of."

"Oh, he don't want to work on anything mechanical. He just wants to make some money doin' odd jobs, runnin' errands, sweepin' up and such."

"I thought he was already doing those kinds of things for somebody. He was probably laid off for a while after being attacked, but when I saw him not long ago his arm wasn't in a sling. I assumed he was back at work."

"He told me got fired and needed to make some money."

"Did he tell you why he was fired?"

"Nope. I asked him, but he wouldn't even give me a hint."

"I don't suppose he told you who fired him."

"Nope. When I asked him who it wuz, he just shook his head."

"What do you make of all this?"

Joe Bob swiped a big hand across his face.

"No idea," he said, "but I hired him. I told him to be here at nine o'clock in the mornin'. I figure if I spend a little time with him, he'll let some stuff spill. He sure is a strange cat."

I hadn't thought much about Fred Peyton since I saw him on the corner with Joe Lawson. It had appeared that the two of them were having a discussion, but Joe debunked that; said he didn't know Fred.

"Did I tell you that I saw Fred standing on the corner about a block from my office with Joe Lawson the other day?"

"No. Why?"

"Joe claimed not to know Fred, but it looked like they were having a conversation. They were both on foot. I couldn't imagine why either of them might be taking a stroll in that part of town."

"That is a tad strange. And didn't you tell me you saw Fred over in Bernard's neck of the woods a while back?"

"I said I saw the back of a guy I thought looked like Fred there. I didn't see his face."

"He sure is bein' mighty mysterious, and it makes you wonder if he has anything to do with some of the crazy stuff that's been goin' on, but I'm not sure he's smart enough to carry out any kind of plan even if his boss is tellin' him what to do."

"Maybe he'll let something slip in casual conversation tomorrow."

"Yeah, maybe. Hey, I'm about ready to close up for the day. Why don't you come on over to my place and have a couple of cold ones?"

"Good idea. I'll follow you."

As soon as we stepped inside the doublewide I couldn't help but notice that Joe Bob's habits seemed to have changed drastically. There were no dirty dishes in the sink or on the counter; the living room looked as though it had just been spiffied up, and magazines were neatly arranged on the coffee table. I saw that Playboy had been replaced by Golf Digest. I wondered if my friend had hired a maid since I was here last.

"The place looks great, Joe Bob."

"Thanks. Hey, would you mind if I grabbed a two-minute shower. I'm kinda grubby."

"Take your time. I don't have a bus to catch."

As soon as Joe Bob left the room, his big yellow cat appeared out of nowhere and leaped onto my lap. The feline knew I didn't like it. I knew that was the reason it was so attracted to me. It was daring me to knock it off my lap.

Joe Bob was back in no time, wearing a terrycloth robe and a towel wrapped around his head. He stopped by the fridge and grabbed a longneck, opened it, and brought it over to me.

"Git off Matt's lap," he said, and swiped the big cat to the floor. "He sure likes you, Matt. Don't know why, but he does. I'll be right back."

He was towel drying his long hair as he went to get dressed.

The cat eyed me, and I would have bet anything it was about to leap back on my lap. I looked at it, wearing my meanest expression and hissed at it. The animal took off to parts unknown just before Joe Bob re-entered the room. He was dressed in a golf shirt and khakis.

"So, are you going to make me drink alone?" I said.

Joe Bob laughed. "'course not."

He went to the fridge and grabbed another beer.

"In case you might be wonderin', I've invited Lauren over here for dinner tonight. I paid Lucy to neaten the place up, and I'm havin' dinner catered by that little Italian restaurant. You know the kinds of dishes women like, but I don't. I thought about lasagna or maybe some kind of pasta. What do you think I ought to order?"

"Women like lots of Italian dishes. You don't happen to have a menu, do you?"

"I do," he said, and produced it.

I scanned it, then suggested the veal just because it was the most expensive item listed.

"Anything but that," he said. "I don't think I could make

myself eat a little creature that's had to live in a itty bitty pen and never git to run around. You know they keep the little calves in jail like that. It's to keep their muscles from developin' so their meat'll be tender."

Every now and then I failed to remember how tender-hearted Joe Bob was. He was always for the underdog in every situation. It was surprising that he had been such a star on our high school football team.

"Well, any of these entrees will be fine."

"How 'bout wine?"

"This lady must really be special. You don't drink wine."

"She sure is, Matthew. I can't tell you how special she is to me. I've never felt like this about any other woman. It's almost scary."

I turned the menu over to read the wine list.

"Unless you're ordering seafood, I see a wine that would pair well with most anything else on the menu. It's called Fortello. If they don't have that in stock, you could go with a nice Chianti. They're all in the same price range."

"Ok. I reckon I can manage now. Thanks. I went to the Home Store and bought a set of wine goblets and some nice lookin' dishes. They're not the good stuff, but they're better'n what I had. I've even got some cloth napkins and a table cloth. They belonged to my mama. I had 'em laundered. Mama always used them when we had company."

I thought about helping him set the table, but decided against it. If Lauren didn't appreciate my friend's efforts, even if they happened not to be up to par, she wasn't worth his time.

We finished our beers, and I wished my friend good luck with his new conquest.

"Not that you'll need it," I said. "I don't think you need any luck with the fairer sex, Joe Bob. You're a natural Romeo."

Joe Bob flaunted his pearly whites and laughed.

As it turned out, his romantic evening couldn't have turned out any better. He called me to meet him for breakfast the following morning, because he thought he would burst if he had to wait to tell me all about it.

Truthfully, I had been missing Trudy's lovely breakfasts something fierce since moving into my apartment. I had gotten used to her pampering. I called her often to make sure she was well and that she didn't need anything. She always seemed to be in good spirits, but said that she missed living on Mulberry Street. As soon as the construction mess died down, she wanted me to help her move back into the house she loved.

I met Joe Bob at the diner. He waved as I came through the door. He was in a booth in the back, grinning at a coffee pot and a couple of mugs, his elbows on the scarred table top, and his big hands clasped, propping up his chin.

"You're looking awfully chipper this morning," I said.

"With good reason, good buddy. I coulda swore I'd died and gone to heaven last night."

"Are you going to enlighten me, or make me guess?"

"Let's just say that I'm not gonna to tell you ever little detail, but you'll git the idea."

Joe Bob's hand trembled slightly as he lifted the coffee pot and filled our mugs. I had never before seen him appear nervous in the least.

"Well?"

"The woman's amazin'. That don't come close to doin' her justice."

"Okay. I'll play your game. What makes her so amazing?"

"I hadn't told her where we wuz goin' for dinner. I picked her up and drove around a little while before I brought her to the trailer park. Matt, she didn't even blink when I parked beside my double wide. Guess the first words that come out of her sweet mouth."

"I have no idea. Just tell me."

"She stepped inside, looked around, and said, 'Charmin'.'"

I doubted that seriously, but I got the idea.

"I got out that old book that Mama used to look up stuff about manners and where to put everthing on the table. I didn't have nearly all the glasses and knives and forks and such that wuz in the picture, but I thought it looked as right as it could with what I had."

"I'm sure it looked great," I said.

"When she saw the flower arrangement I bought at the grocery store, she walked right over and stuck her pretty face right in the middle of the bouquet and sniffed. 'Lovely,' she said."

"Sounds like you must have done everything right. I'm glad it worked out well for you."

"Me, too. And, Matt, you won't believe this, but she even liked my cat. The cat kinda ignored her, but she got down on her knees and scratched him behind the ears. He started purrin' and lookin' all happy. She got to her feet and scooped him up, then they set on the couch with her pettin' him until time for dinner."

"Hey, I hate to cut this short, but if we're going to have breakfast, we'd better order. I have a meeting in about an hour."

"Oh, I'm sorry. I just had to tell you how fantastic Lauren is. I can't ever remember bein' this happy."

I was happy for Joe Bob. He deserved to have a good life. I'd never heard anyone say anything derogatory about him. I hoped he wasn't leaping into something that might not turn out the way he thought it would. The guy was smitten.

We ordered and ate a quick breakfast, then took off to make

our livings. Joe Bob was on a cloud, and I was hopeful about landing another new client.

Bernie Zuckerman was parked on the street in front of my building. He got out of his Cadillac as I parked.

"Hey, Matt. Got a minute?"

"As a matter of fact, that's all I have. I have a meeting with a prospective client at nine o'clock. What's up?"

"As you know, there's an amber alert out on Claire. I got a call from a woman who lives in my neighborhood last night. She told me that she saw someone leading a little girl about Claire's age on a side street not far from my house. This woman takes her kid to the little park where Juanita took Claire. You can see my house from the park, so she saw where they lived. I don't know this woman, but she knows who I am. Maybe she can give me more information to tell the cops. I thought you'd want to know."

"Of course, I want to know. Let me know what you find out."

We parted ways, and I went into my law office to wait for my would-be client, dismissing all thoughts of Bernie and his quest to find his daughter.

I had just made coffee and gotten behind my desk and turned on my computer to look busy when my phone rang.

"Matthew Stevenson," I said. "How may I help you?"

"Good morning, Mister Stevenson. I'm Joanna Parker's husband. She won't be meeting with you this morning. You see, she's decided that she doesn't want a divorce after all. Does she owe you anything because of the cancellation?"

I'd had my hopes up for nothing, but I knew things like this were going to happen. Good luck couldn't last without a hitch every now and then.

"No. There's no charge. Good luck to you both."

Chapter Twenty

I fervently hoped this little southern town would soon calm down and resemble the quiet cocoon I remembered before I decided to head for the city lights right after law school. Most of the town looked the same with the exceptions of a few new housing developments and several fairly nice restaurants, but the atmosphere had definitely changed. There was an uncertainty in the air.

I felt positive about the prospect of a successful law practice. Also, a relationship with Sydney Edelman was looking promising. My dear friend, Trudy, seemed happy after a bout of depression brought on by my mother's demise. Her easy smile had returned to the kindest face I had ever seen. Joe Bob was embarking on a new romance, and he was on a cloud. Hopefully, it would work out well for him. But poor Bernie Zuckerman was mired in quicksand. He had been sinking deeper every day since his little daughter had disappeared. The latest person to throw him a lifeline was a stranger who offered a glimmer of hope about his child's possible whereabouts.

If Bernie had many friends, I didn't know who they were. I

assumed that was the reason he was clinging onto our teenage friendship with such fierceness. Yours truly seemed to be his only real confidant. Joe Bob had been a strong third in our high school threesome. As adults, I could tell that he was willing to be a real friend, but Bernie constantly seemed to be at odds with him. I wanted only the best for both of them, but I didn't like the idea of being Bernie's savior at every snag in his unfortunate life. Truth be told, I was more of a sounding board than anything else.

Since Joe Bob seemed to have had a good result with his intimate dinner in his home with his new love interest, I decided to try my luck. I had put a lot of thought into furnishing my living quarters, striving to garner feminine appeal without overdoing it. After deeming the furnishings acceptable, I went shopping for the things I would need to make the dining area as romantic as possible. I purchased a rheostat to dim the lights, plus candles. My mother's house was loaded with linens, china, silver and crystal, so I braved the construction mess on Mulberry Street and borrowed what I would need.

I hadn't given Sydney the nickel tour of my law office/apartment, and I hoped to gain her approval. She wasn't aware of my talent as a credible cook, and I planned to surprise her with one of my never-fail dishes.

I didn't want to rush into this romantic endeavor. I wanted it to be as perfect as I could make it. There was no deadline. I was sitting at my desk, making a list of everything I would need at the last minute: flower arrangement for a centerpiece, music selections, wine and ingredients for the entrée and dessert. Thinking about the outcome made me feel like a hopeful teenager.

Bernie Zuckerman rushed into my office like a tsunami and stood panting in front of my desk. Perspiration streaked his flushed face as he fell into a chair facing me. It took him a couple of minutes to catch his breath.

"You okay, Bernie?"

Bernie took off his glasses, pulled out a handkerchief and mopped his face.

"Better than okay," he huffed. "I met with the woman who called me about the sighting. Matt, I'm nearly positive she saw Claire and Juanita. She described my daughter to a tee."

"So she saw Claire's face?"

"Well, no, but her description sounded right. You know; the size and hair color. The child was with a woman who fit Juanita's description. I'm sure my baby girl is here in town. Matt, I'm going to turn this place upside down until I find her."

Bernie was one of those people who seemed to have extreme highs and lows. I sincerely hoped he would be able to find his child and get her home safe and sound. If that didn't happen, I would hate to be around when he came down from this high.

"I'm going to start by scouring the area where the woman said she thought she saw Claire and Juanita. I don't care if I have to go door-to-door."

"I wish you the very best of luck, my friend. Let me know if there's any way I can help."

Bernie heaved himself up from the chair, reached across the desk and shook my hand.

"You're a good friend, Matt. I'll let you know."

He turned and strode to the door with purpose.

I had been in such a good frame of mind minutes before, imagining my romantic evening with Sydney. Bernie seemed to have a knack for showing up at the wrong time. He had broken the spell; now I was in no mood to plan my special evening.

I didn't have any appointments until after noon, so I decided to drop by Joe Bob's garage to find out what he had learned about his new hire. Fred was busy sweeping up and took no notice of me. He was humming while he worked.

Joe Bob was where I usually found him—under a car on his back. I tapped one of his boots with my shoe, and he rolled out and looked up at me.

"Good mornin', counselor. What's shakin'?"

I reached down to give him a hand up.

"I thought I'd come by to see if you've pried any information out of your new help. He appears to be happy with his duties."

"Don't know a thing. He don't seem to want to talk much. I've tried to strike up a conversation with him, but all he does is nod or shake his head. I almost think he might be scared of somethin', or somebody. He don't act like the Fred we know."

"He can't hear us, can he?"

"No. He's too far away; plus, he hums constantly. Weird."

"I suppose the only thing to do is to pay close attention to him and hope he slips up."

"Yeah. I figure he's bound to break at some point. In the meantime, he does a good job of keepin' the place neat, and he's run a couple of errands for me this mornin'."

I thought about telling Joe Bob my plan for a romantic evening with Sydney at my place, but I didn't want him to think I was copying him. After all, he was the self-proclaimed Romeo. I wasn't in the habit of airing much of my private life. I had given him more than an inkling about my feelings for Sydney, but hadn't bothered with details.

"I'm so hungry I could eat a horse," Joe Bob said. "What say we head over to The Dump and grab a burger and a beer?"

"What's The Dump? I've never heard of it."

Joe Bob laughed.

"It's new in town, and it does look pretty much like a dump, but it's got a damn good hamburger."

My friend wasn't a connoisseur of fine cuisine, but I would bet he could rate a hamburger with the best of them.

"I'll drive; you can be the navigator since I don't know where the place is."

We got into Joe Bob's old Buick with him in the passenger seat.

"I heard your Caddy wasn't totaled. When do you think you'll git it back?" he asked.

"As a matter of fact, I should get it back next week. I want to thank you again for lending me this old reliable tank."

"You're welcome, buddy. Turn down that next little street on your right."

I was about to drive past what looked like an alley.

"This is it," Joe Bob said.

I turned into the narrow street between two shabby buildings. Trash littered both sides of the alley, and graffiti covered the walls of the buildings. There was hardly room to navigate past trashcans en route to The Dump.

"How did you find this place?" I asked.

I was amazed that he would dare go in search of food in such a filthy area. Joe Bob had become the most fastidious person I knew since he met his new squeeze.

The building looked like a shack. It was located at the end of the alley. There was a neon *OPEN* sign in a large greasy looking window.

I gave my friend a pained expression that asked, "Are you sure?"

He didn't answer, but exited the Buick. I followed suit, and we ventured into the building.

"Grab a seat wherever you want," came from a bald guy who was wiping down the counter where a couple of workmen sat on stools, gobbling burgers.

We found a table for two by a small window and pulled out hard plastic chairs. The table appeared to be clean, but I spotted a bug, legs kicking, caught in a spider web in the right top corner of the window frame.

"Ahem."

"What?" Joe Bob said.

I nodded at the trapped bug and got up.

We then went to another table in the middle of the room and sat.

"I know what the place looks like," Joe Bob said, "but we're just gonna eat and run."

Nobody brought menus, water, or set-ups, and there were no listings of the fare above the bar. After a few minutes, baldy, from behind the bar, approached our table.

"How do you want 'em?" he asked.

By this, I assumed correctly, that the establishment served only burgers. I didn't want to tangle with the guy. He was short and past middle age, but he was built like a bulldog and wore a scowl that matched the build.

"I'll take mine medium," I said.

"The same," said Joe Bob.

I looked toward the bar area to see baldy slap two huge burgers on a sizzling grill. He left his task to bring a roll of paper towels to our table. I was astute enough to realize that the towels were meant to be our napkins. Since he hadn't offered sides, we didn't have a need for utensils.

Minutes later, the one-man server, cook, bartender brought two mugs of draft beer with foam spilling over the sides and set them before us.

I was more than a little ready to get out of this dump which was living up to its name. I gave Joe Bob a look that told him so.

"I know it's not fancy," he said, "but when did you git so persnickity? "You're beginnin' to remind me of our old pal Bernard."

I'd never known Joe Bob to be testy, at least not toward me.

Our lunch arrived. I had never seen a burger half this size. It was stuffed inside a bun of equal proportion. I wasn't sure I could pick the thing up, but Joe Bob had already taken a huge bite of his burger and gave the cook a thumbs-up. He made happy little sounds as he chewed.

I managed to heft my burger and take a bite. To my surprise, the flavor was superb. I couldn't identify the seasoning, but Joe Bob had been right about the burger. I had never tasted one to equal it in flavor and texture.

I nodded my approval at my friend.

"Told you," he said, and went back to the task of consuming his side of beef.

As we left The Dump, Joe Bob fished a pack of gum from his shirt pocket and stuffed a stick into his mouth. He began chewing like it was his job.

"You been blowin' the soot outta my old rattletrap ever now and then?" he asked.

Truthfully, I hadn't driven the Buick anywhere except around town. It had never been out on the open road since Joe Bob lent it to me.

"No. I haven't had the need to drive it anywhere except in town."

"You can't expect a car to run good if you don't take care of it. I'm gonna git behind the wheel. I'll take it out on Old Stone Road and see if it might need my healin' hand since you're not gonna take care of it."

I didn't know what had gotten into Joe Bob. He was sounding like he was more than a little put out with me. This was very unlike him. I couldn't imagine why he was behaving this way. I handed him the keys, and he got behind the wheel. Without saying anything I slid into the passenger seat.

Joe Bob backed out of the parking space and drove out of the alley. He didn't give me so much as a glance as he drove down Main Street heading for Old Stone Road.

"What's bugging you, Joe Bob?"

"Who said anything was buggin' me?"

"Something is obviously bothering you because you're as irritable as a wet cat. Have I done something to offend you?"

"Why'd you ask that? Feelin' guilty about somethin'?"

"No. I'm not feeling guilty. I thought I was taking good care of your car, but you must not think I am. I can rent a car until next week. I don't want to use the Buick if you have any reservations about it."

Joe Bob turned onto Old Stone Road and gunned it. The Buick took off like a bat. Joe Bob kept his foot on the gas until he got it up to ninety in nothing flat. The old car ran like a top. Then, he pulled into a gravel lane to back up and turn around. He was chewing furiously.

On the way back to town he drove at a moderate speed. He turned toward me, looking apologetic, and reached over with his right fist to deliver a light cuff to my arm.

"I want you to use the Buick, Matt. Sorry I'm bein' such a pain in the ass. I always liked to pride myself on bein' a man who can handle pretty much whatever I'm faced with, but it seems like I'm weak as a kitten when it comes to breakin' a habit. Looks like it ought to be easy. Nobody's holdin' a gun to my head."

Then it hit me—Joe Bob was trying to quit smoking. He hadn't lit up since I walked into his garage. I decided to keep my opinion to myself and not be quick to offer advice. If he wanted to quit the habit, nobody could assist with the task. It would all be up to him whether or not to tough it out.

"In case you're wonderin', I'm doin' this for Lauren. She hates cigarette smoke. I'm sure she hates any kind of smoke. You know I've had a cigarette in my mouth since I was a kid in high school. It ain't easy to give up somethin' that seems like a part of you. Know what I mean?"

I nodded.

"I'm sure it's not easy. I never really got the habit. I remember that we all tried it, but I could take it or leave it. Mom didn't want it in the house, so it wasn't difficult for me to stop."

"Lauren didn't ask me to stop," Joe Bob continued, "but I could tell she didn't like it. Don't ask me how I knew. I could just tell."

"It sounds like you're really smitten with this pretty girl."

"Damn straight. I think I'd do almost anything for her."

"That's great, Joe Bob. It's about time some worthy female caught you in her web. I think this is the first time you've ever been head-over-heels about a girl. You always seemed to want an entire harem." I laughed.

"This is it, Matt. Believe it or not, I don't even have the urge to look at another female no matter how hot she might be."

We were back at the garage and were about to change seats.

"You can keep this car as long as you want to, Matt. I'm awful sorry about actin' the way I did. I reckon I might need a attitude adjustment."

"There's nothing wrong with your attitude. You're just missing your crutch. That ache will go away. It might take a little while."

Joe Bob nodded toward the wide bay of his garage. We watched Freaky Fred standing at the far end of the bay. He was wringing his hands. Then, he began running his fingers through his hair, making it stand out in all directions. He paced across to the other side of the bay, then back to where he had been. We watched him try to smooth his hair, then begin the hand wringing again.

"Wonder why he's doing that?" I asked.

"Prob'ly 'cause he's Fred. Go figure."

Chapter Twenty-one

Some things never changed in many small southern towns. This was absolute in Martinsville, Tennessee. Nearly every church parking lot overflowed on Sunday mornings—the day of rest. Stores were closed with the exception of gas service stations and drugstores which opened their doors an hour or so after morning worship services.

Since it was Sunday, noise from heavy machinery had ceased on Mulberry Street for the entire blessed day. The only audible sound came from the treetops on my mother's side of the street: songbirds warbling their gratitude for a chance to be heard over the din of bulldozers.

I hadn't as yet taken the Methodist minister up on his offer to join his flock, instead taking this opportunity to sleep in. I hadn't bothered to set an alarm. The aroma of coffee and bacon wafting from the kitchen were absent in my apartment/office on this Lord's day. Such was my new life in my bachelor pad. As much as I missed Trudy's spoiling me, I was ready to get on with my new life.

I got out of bed and made do with a bowl of cold cereal and a cup of coffee. Then I talked myself into going for a much-needed run before the temperature soared. I let my mind wander back to earlier times when it seemed almost everything in Martinsville wore a cloak of innocence.

I supposed that I had been more than a little naïve when I flew the nest. I had never been very far from home until I was practically an adult. It amazed me that so many physical things in Martinsville looked the same as I caught glimpses of familiar scenery in my peripheral vision as I dashed past them.

I slowed to a walk about a block and a half from my building and breathed the honeysuckle scented air.

After my unproductive morning, I made a short list of items I might need from my mother's stash to turn my apartment into an intimate dining venue. I wanted to impress Sydney Edelman in the worst way.

Mulberry Street had been completely cleared of debris as I drove Joe Bob's Buick to my childhood home and parked at the curb. In place of the rubble of demolished abodes, a vast river of soil awaited the grader to smooth lots for new construction. A blue Chevrolet sat in the driveway. I couldn't imagine who the owner might be. There were a few cars parked on the street in front of the house next door, and I assumed the Chevy belonged to one of the neighbor's guests.

I went to the back door and used my key to enter the house. I heard muted laughter. Someone was inside my mother's house besides me. Not knowing who the intruder might be, I kept quiet as I made my way through the narrow hallway toward the noise.

I heard something like a clink produced by crystal glasses just before witnessing the scene in the formal living room. It was something so unexpected that I found it hard to take in.

I was about to interrupt a very personal moment between two consenting adults, but since I was only a step away from the room,

I felt it only polite to make my presence known. Trudy and a man I had never before seen were sitting close together on my mother's loveseat and smiling. They were dressed in their Sunday best and made quite a picture.

"Ahem!"

The housekeeper and her friend practically jumped apart and set their goblets on the coffee table in front of them. They lost the fond expressions they had worn before realizing that they weren't alone.

Trudy then collected herself and took charge of the situation.

"Matthew Stevenson, I'd like you to meet Marcus Hathaway," she said.

Mister Hathaway stood and extended his hand, and I hurried into the room to take it. I couldn't help noticing how tall the man was and how long and slender his manicured hands were. His handshake was gently firm, if such a thing existed. It was the kind of pressure one would expect from a person who might exert power without offending an underling.

"I'm glad to meet you," I mumbled, returning the gesture.

Mr. Hathaway smiled, exhibiting a set of teeth which might rival Joe Bob's.

"I've been hearing quite a bit about you, Matt," he said. "May I call you Matt?"

"Of course," I said, having found my tongue.

"Matty, would you like to join us in a glass of wine?" Trudy asked.

"Actually, I just came over to borrow a few items from Mother's dining room. I'm planning to have a small dinner party soon. I'm sorry to interrupt your visit. I had no idea you'd be here."

"That didn't answer my question." The housekeeper smiled the special smile she reserved only for me. "Join us in a glass. I'd like for the two of you to get to know one another."

She didn't wait for my answer, getting up and heading for the kitchen.

Mister Hathaway wasn't the shy sort and began telling me how he and Trudy had met and how much Trudy had come to mean to him.

They had both been grocery shopping at the same Piggly Wiggly grocery store. Trudy was testing the ripeness of an avocado, and Mister Hathaway was in the process of thumping a small watermelon for the same purpose. The two were on opposite sides of the center aisle of the produce section. They happened to look up from their testing spontaneously and looked directly into one another's eyes.

"That's the way it happened," Mister Hathaway stated, matter-of-factly. "It occurred in a split second, all because of a little squeeze and a thump."

Trudy came back into the room with a glass of wine. She handed me the glass and bent to kiss me on the cheek.

I didn't know what I was expected to do, so I decided to make the couple comfortable with my presence and, hopefully, please my dear friend.

"Here's to new beginnings," I said, raising my glass.

I couldn't tell a lot about this Mister Hathaway, but I figured if Trudy deemed him worthy of her company, he must be an alright kind of guy. She had always been a good judge of character. On the off chance that she was mistaken this time, I would make certain this tall well-groomed gentleman would regret anything he might do to cause her unhappiness for allowing him into her life.

"Hear, hear," Mister Hathaway agreed, lifting his glass and smiling at Trudy, fondness exuding from his eyes.

The housekeeper raised her goblet without comment, but did deliver a sweet smile. I had to admit that she looked unusually happy.

"Matty, have you been to the Methodist Church since you came back home?"

"No, I haven't, but I did meet the new minister. He seems like a very nice guy. He came by my office to invite me to Sunday services."

"Marcus and I went there this morning. The young Reverend did a fine job, I thought. I was favorably impressed. And before you ask, Elizabeth was perched on the front pew in all her splendor, hanging onto every word."

I chuckled. "I wasn't going to ask. She and I have nothing in common now. I feel a little sorry for the minister. I guess Beth hasn't had time to scare the hell out of him yet. Pardon the expression."

"You know it hasn't been many years ago that folks like us weren't invited into the white churches. But this young preacher welcomed us with open arms. I'm thinkin' he knows the good Lord pays no attention to a person's color. He looks at what's on the inside."

Trudy and Mister Hathaway were politely sipping their wine, but I didn't want to further intrude on their visit. Besides, I wanted to be in the dining room ferreting out what I would need for my romantic evening with Sydney. I polished off the last swallow and stood. They both rose. I hugged Trudy and shook Mister Hathaway's hand.

"I'm delighted to have met you, Mister Hathaway," I said. "I hope you realize what a treasure you have in your new companion."

"Call me Marcus," he said, "and indeed, I do."

I left the two to do whatever they had been intending to do before I crashed their party and disappeared into the dining room to dig through Mother's treasures. Filling the box I had brought, I left through the back door and headed back to my lair.

I thought about calling Sydney to set up the dinner date but decided against it. Maybe I would drop by her clinic tomorrow, invite her to lunch and casually issue the invitation then. I wanted to make sure that I had the perfect plan ahead of time to avoid a last-minute glitch. Going over my checklist, I marked off the items I had on hand. I had everything I needed except the ingredients for the meal and the wine.

I felt kind of restless and wasn't in the mood to loaf around my apartment the rest of the day. Watching sports on TV left me cold, and I wasn't particularly craving company. I thought about going for another run, but that didn't appeal either. I could pick up my almost new Cadillac the first part of the week, so I decided to take Joe Bob's old Buick for a last hoorah. I would take it out on the open road and give it a good workout; blow the soot out of it. That should make Joe Bob happy.

As I drove past the Methodist Church, I couldn't miss seeing the new minister and my ex as they strolled down the sidewalk holding hands. The poor guy, I thought, If he only knew. Just wait.

I drove through town at the speed limit, then headed for Old Stone Road. The Buick seemed to know it was playtime as soon as I pressed down on the accelerator. It took off like a racehorse breaking from the gate and never slowed its pace until I reined it in. My friend should keep this old car until it died, I thought.

I stopped at a traffic light at the edge of town and waited for the green arrow. I took my foot off the brake and eased it onto the gas pedal and began turning left just as I heard, more than felt, something like a thump. The old Buick had been struck on the right rear side. I was able to get it off the road. The other car was stalled in the middle of the street. I hurried to see about the driver.

The black late model Escalade looked familiar even in its accordioned state. I had been guilty of tailing it through the dark streets of Martinsville just over a year ago. The airbag must have malfunctioned because I could see Lee Ann clearly. Her head lolled to one side, her pretty mouth was twisted in pain and looked grotesque. Her wide-open eyes stared straight ahead. I couldn't tell if she was pinned behind the wheel, or if it just appeared that way from my perspective, looking through the driver's window. The door was jammed, and I was afraid to try to break the window.

There were no other vehicles around, nobody to assist me in getting to the helpless woman. I hurried to Joe Bob's Buick and grabbed my phone from the cup holder. With shaking hands, I tapped in 911.

It seemed that my insides trembled as I waited for an ambulance and the police. Bernie's ex could be dead. I said a silent prayer that she wasn't.

The cop car showed just before the ambulance. Then, a wrecker came on the scene. I didn't know what to do first, but I rushed toward the Escalade. Two burly guys began working on the car to get inside. I didn't know which group they belonged to and I didn't care as long as they could gain access to Lee Ann.

They had the door off its hinges in nothing flat and backed away to allow the EMTs to do their thing. I watched closely to see if I could tell whether Lee Ann was dead or alive. I didn't want to be in the way, but I pressed closer.

"Is she alive?" I rasped, hoping against hope that she was.

I was ignored. The EMTs were putting her on a gurney and hauling her away in the ambulance. The wrecker guy was attaching the Escalade to his big hook. The front bumper and a side panel fell off and made metallic thuds, hitting the pavement.

The cop conversed with the wrecker driver before bothering to acknowledge my presence. I was still Jello inside when he decided to do so. He squinted at me as though the sunlight hurt his eyes.

"You the other driver?" he asked, taking a pad from his pocket.

"Yes. I was making a left turn, and…"

"Hold on a minute, pal. I'll ask the questions. All you need to say is 'yes' or 'no'."

The only thing I could think at that moment was that some things never changed with a certain kind of guy who had a little authority. It seemed especially true in small southern towns.

"License, registration, and proof of insurance."

I handed them over.

"This is your car?"

"No."

"You're not Joseph Robert Kincaid?"

"No."

The self-important cop finally compared the license with the registration.

"Which one are you?"

This guy was dumber than a pile of rocks. Wouldn't he know the license belonged to the person who was driving?

"I'm the driver. This is my friend's car. He loaned it to me since my car is in the shop."

"You coulda saved us both a lot of time if you'd told me that at first," he grumbled.

I knew better than to argue with this jerk, but I couldn't help myself.

"You told me to only answer 'yes' or 'no', sir."

"Don't get smart with me."

"I'm not."

"How fast were you going when the accident occurred?"

"I was making a left-hand turn with a green arrow. I'm not exactly how fast that would be; maybe five miles per hour."

"How about the other car?"

"I don't know how fast it was going. It hit me on the right

back panel of the Buick. I haven't even looked to see if it did any damage. I heard it, more than I felt it."

"Let's go examine the Buick," said the cop.

We walked over to the car to examine the right back panel. There was hardly any damage. I figured Joe Bob could repair it with one hand tied behind him.

"This thing must be built like a Sherman tank," the cop allowed.

"I agree. Do you need anything else from me? If you don't, I'd like to go to the hospital and check on the young woman who hit me."

The cop took down the information he needed from the registration and my license, handed them back to me, took down my phone number, and told me not to leave town.

"I'll be checking with that young lady, too," he said.

Neither of us knew whether she was dead or alive.

I didn't feel much like a lawyer as I drove to the hospital. I was still as shaky as a frightened ten-year-old. Making myself think positive thoughts, I walked through the glass doors of the emergency room waiting area. I made myself stand tall and went to the glassed-in desk and cleared my throat. The nurse perched there and spoke through the small opening in the glass.

"May I help you?"

"Yes, ma'am. I'm here to check on a young woman who was in an accident. She was brought in about forty minutes ago. I, too, was involved in that accident, and I would like to find out if she is alright."

"The patient's name?"

I realized that I had no idea what Lee Ann's last name was since she and Bernie divorced.

"I don't know her name," I said.

Chapter Twenty-two

As it turned out, Lee Ann hadn't remarried, but she did take back her maiden name: Rivers. I learned this from Bernie when I called to tell him about the accident. Since he and Lee Ann were divorced, I didn't know why I felt obligated to call him, but I did. He met me at the hospital. I knew it wasn't beneath him to bend the truth or to lie by reason of omission. He approached the glassed-in desk and addressed the nurse on duty.

"I'm Bernard Zuckerman, ma'am. Lee Ann Rivers was in an automobile accident and was brought to the hospital about ninety minutes ago. I need to know her status."

It was as though Bernie read the nurse's mind. He spoke with authority but sounded sincere.

"I have to know she's out of danger," he said, wearing a look of concern. "Oh, I see your hesitation. My wife chose to keep her maiden name like many brides do. Rivers was her maiden name."

The nurse looked skeptical.

"I'll have to check with the doctor. Take a seat, and I'll get back with you."

Bernie walked across the tiled floor toward the bank of chairs on the far wall. The heel of his left shoe squeaked with each step. He took the chair next to mine.

"Give me a blow-by-blow," he said.

I told him exactly how the wreck had happened and that I had no way of gaining entrance to the Cadillac. I didn't mince words.

"I couldn't tell if she was pinned behind the wheel, and there was no way for me to discern whether she was alive. An ambulance, a cop, and a wrecker all arrived on the scene in a matter of minutes, but none of them would let me get very close. They wouldn't tell me anything about her condition."

"You're sure it was Lee Ann?"

"Yes, I'm positive. I saw her face. I assume the airbag malfunctioned."

After about a half hour, a doctor in green scrubs came into the waiting area. He scanned the room for a tense-looking husband. Bernie picked up on it immediately and rushed toward him.

"How is she?" he asked, sounding hopeful.

"You're Ms. Rivers's family member?"

Bernie gave a half-nod.

"I'm afraid she isn't ready to have visitors. She's sedated and resting. Maybe you can come by tomorrow and check on her progress. She has some superficial injuries and a few broken ribs. She was fortunate not to have a punctured lung because of the ribs. She also has a broken arm and nose. She has a black eye and quite a bit of facial swelling and bruising. I'd say she's a very lucky young woman."

"Thank you very much," said Bernie.

He and I left the hospital and headed to the parking lot.

"I haven't had a chance to get in touch with Joe Bob," I said. "I'm going to drive the Buick over to his garage to let him know what happened and show him the damage."

"Want to meet at Morgan's a little later?" Bernie asked without a trace of concern for Lee Ann in his tone.

"Sure. I'll see if Joe Bob wants to join us."

I didn't think Joe Bob would be upset about what happened to his car. He was pretty laid-back ninety percent of the time. I assumed that Lee Ann would have had insurance, but there was no way for me to confirm that until the police report showed there was proof of that in the car.

I pulled up just short of the open bay and went in search of my friend. Freaky Fred was busily sweeping and humming to himself. If he noticed me, he didn't bother to acknowledge it. Joe Bob wasn't under a hood, or on his back under a vehicle, so I went into his office.

He was actually sitting at his desk instead of leaning on a corner of it or lounging on a stack of tires. He wore an expression of deep concentration while writing in a small notebook. Piles of invoices and manuals had been pushed aside for something which must have been more important.

"Hey, Joe Bob."

He put up a hand, letting me know to hold my horses. I stood in the doorway while he attended to the business at hand. A couple of minutes passed before he looked up from his work.

"Hey, Matt. What's goin' on?"

"I need to let you know what transpired this afternoon. I decided to take your Buick out and give it a good workout."

"Yeah?" he said, unwrapping a stick of gum.

"I got hit at a traffic light. The right back panel is damaged. It wasn't my fault. I was turning left on a green arrow, and this Escalade came out of nowhere and rammed into me. It doesn't look like there's much damage. The car's just outside."

We went outside, and Joe Bob looked at the panel. He ran a big hand over the dent and grinned.

"If this ain't the best automobile that ever come down the pike, my name's not Joseph Robert Kincaid," he declared. "All she needs is a little rubber hammer and a dab of paint. I can make her look perfect in a New York minute. How's the other car look?"

"It's totaled. Guess who it belongs to."

Joe Bob shrugged.

"Bernie's ex."

"Git outta here. What're the chances?"

"It was definitely Lee Ann. She's in the hospital."

"But she's alive, right?"

"Yes, she's alive. She has some broken bones and some cuts and bruises. The doc who patched her up gave the impression that she'd be okay."

"If anything else happens to rile Bernard, I don't reckon he'll be able to blame her for it."

"That's for sure. Hey, let's get together at Morgan's for a drink in about an hour."

"Sounds like a plan. Can I assume Bernard'll be there?"

I nodded. "It was his idea. He sounded like he had something on his mind, but I don't have any idea what it might be."

"Uh, there's somethin' I'd like you to look over for me at your convenience. You're the only one I'd want to see it. It's personal."

"Sure, Joe Bob. Be glad to."

I wondered if whatever my friend had been laboring over when I arrived might be the thing he wanted me to examine.

I went to my office/apartment and glanced at the answering machine. The blinking light signaled that someone had wanted to reach me. Hoping it was Sydney, I listened to the message.

"Hello, my sweet boy."

I could almost see Trudy's smiling face.

"I just want to hear your opinion of Marcus Hathaway," she said. "You know you can't fool old Trudy. You have to tell me the honest truth. How did he impress you? You know what you think matters a great deal to me. Call me when you have a minute."

My old friend answered on the first ring.

"Hello."

"Hello, yourself." I let a bit of laughter seep into my voice. "I want to apologize for interrupting your visit today."

"No need to apologize. We were both just a little surprised to see you. We hadn't expected a visitor. Now, give me your impression of my friend."

I didn't quite know how to answer. I would never say, or do anything to hurt this woman who had practically reared me. My first impression of Marcus Hathaway was that he was a well-dressed perfect gentleman. I could also see that he appeared to be more than a little enamored with Trudy Giles. I couldn't honestly pass judgment on the man until I spent more time with him. If it turned out that he was sincere and a good match for her, I would be thrilled for them both. But if this Mister Hathaway happened to be a less than desirable individual, I would step in to protect her.

"You have to realize that I was only in Mister Hathaway's company for a few minutes. In that time, I found him to be polite, well-dressed, and easy to converse with. He gave the impression that he thinks a great deal of you. I don't know how much you know about him, but I know nothing. I want you to be the happiest woman alive, and no matter what his background, or his reason for being in Martinsville, he'd better be a worthy candidate."

Trudy laughed. "I know you're protective of me. I feel the same way about you. Maybe I'll be able to arrange for the two of you to get to know one another. I'll try to do that real soon."

"I'd like that."

We said our goodbyes and I took a quick shower, then went to meet my friends.

I was the last to arrive. Joe Bob was holding the door open for Bernie. I hurried to catch up to them.

"You the doorman, Joe Bob?" I asked, grinning.

"Looks that way. Git your bad self inside. My arm's gittin' tired."

We went to a booth in Lucy's section; she saw us and headed our way.

"What'll it be, guys?" she asked. "A pitcher of suds or the hard stuff?"

Joe Bob was chewing gum like his life depended on it.

Bernie ordered a vodka martini. He seemed to order kick-ass drinks when he was upset or flustered about something, and I noticed that was happening a lot since my return to Martinsville.

"Joe Bob?" Lucy asked.

"Just bring me a Coke," he said, and continued chewing.

I had intended to order a bourbon but decided not to encourage Bernie in his new habit.

"Iced tea for me," I said, feeling pretty darn wholesome.

Bernie studied Joe Bob for a few seconds.

"What's with the gum?" he asked.

It was rare that he paid the least bit of attention to Joe Bob except to ridicule him for something he'd said.

"Am I botherin' you, Bernard?"

"You don't have to be so touchy. It was just a simple question. I don't think I've ever seen you chew gum."

"I been smokin' too much. Tryin' to cut back."

"Can I assume that both of you are trying to cut back on your liquor consumption?" asked Bernie.

"It don't go too good with chewin' gum."

I wanted to talk about my afternoon adventure in Joe Bob's Buick. I had no interest in discussing our habits.

"Joe Bob thinks he can fix the Buick up like new," I said.

Our drinks arrived. Bernie took a gulp of his martini.

"I don't know why, but I think I have to go check on Lee Ann's condition tomorrow," Bernie said.

"I think you led the doctor to believe you would," I said.

"Yeah, but I don't want to see her. She's all messed up with bruises and broken bones. I don't want to feel sorry for her. I almost wish I didn't know anything about the accident."

"What difference would that make?" Joe Bob asked.

"I just don't want anything to do with her. We're divorced, and Claire's missing. Lee Ann has to have heard about it on the news. I'm not going to discuss anything about Claire with her. She'd probably blame me."

"Bernard, wouldn't she already know?"

Bernie was getting in over his head, and it seemed that he was determined to keep digging himself in deeper.

"Guys, are we about ready to order dinner?" I asked, changing the subject.

"You know what? I'm not the least bit hungry. If you'll excuse me, I'm going to go grout my tile," Bernie said, then drained his glass and left.

"Matt, I think there's somethin' bad wrong with Bernard. He acts like he don't know what planet he's on."

"I agree that he does seem confused most of the time. He's half-crazed because of his missing child."

Joe Bob made use of Bernie's unused napkin and disposed of his gum.

"My jaw's so tired I'm not sure I can eat," he said, and grinned.

"So you haven't fallen off the wagon?"

"Nope, and I don't plan to. I'm gonna do everthing in my power to make Lauren fall head over heels in love with me."

"Good for you. I'm pulling for you."

Joe Bob got Lucy's attention, and she smiled as she approached our booth.

"Well," she said, "the air in here feels fresher. What'd you do to get rid of him?"

"We weren't trying to get rid of him, but I noticed that he left without paying for his drink," I said. "I'll cover it."

"Not a problem. It's on the house," Lucy said.

"What's the special?" Joe Bob asked.

"Fried fish, and it's local. Perch, I think. It's not a bottom feeder. I had some; real good."

We both ordered the fish and a pitcher of beer. It felt like old times.

Joe Bob unwrapped another stick of gum as we left the booth. That told me what I already knew—he would stick to his guns.

It was still early when we left the restaurant, and I wasn't in the mood to go home. I wondered if Sydney had plans and if she might invite me over for a nightcap. I tried her cell phone, but she didn't answer. Would it be taking too much for granted to drive to her apartment and knock on her door? She had been more than a little friendly with me for a while. So what if I happened to find her watching the Hallmark channel in her robe?

I parked in front of her building and took the elevator to the second floor. I knocked and waited for her to come to the door. She didn't. Surely she wouldn't be in bed at 8:30. I knocked again. Sydney wasn't at home.

I took the elevator down to the ground floor. When the door opened, I nearly walked into none other than Sydney and

Joe Lawson. They appeared to be deep in conversation regarding something I hoped, and silently prayed, was work related.

"Matt," Sydney said, "what are you doing here?"

She looked surprised, but she was smiling, so I took that as a good sign.

"Sydney, Joe," I managed. "I just stopped by to say hi."

"Hey, Matt, are you up for another poker game one night next week?" asked Joe.

"Sure, if you can round up a couple of more guys. I'm pretty sure Bernie's out."

I didn't wait to be invited inside, not that anybody had offered.

"See you," I said and turned, giving the two a small wave and hurried to the Buick.

This was some record. I seemed to have had the talent to interrupt and surprise not one, but two couples with my presence in one day.

Chapter Twenty-three

I spent the remainder of the evening chiding myself for feeling like a jealous teenager. Sydney and Joe worked in the same clinic, lived on the same floor of the same apartment complex. For all I knew, they could have worked late for any number of reasons.

I was feeling positive the next morning. My one-man law firm was doing well, I thought. I had landed two more clients in the last week and had placed an ad in the local paper to hire a part-time secretary/receptionist. The latter would require a desk and chair, computer, and another phone for the reception area.

I called Sydney to see if she was free for lunch only to find out that she planned to have a lunch meeting with Joe to interview two new people for the clinic.

"I'm sorry, Matt," she said. "Joe and I need to agree on which applicants we want to hire. We need another groomer and someone who is willing to handle janitorial duties. We lost our janitor yesterday, and we have to fill that position asap."

I was more than a little disappointed, and even though I felt the green eyed monster rising up inside, I knew I should be a man about this.

I made a sandwich and sat at my kitchen table making a short list of the items I needed to order while waiting for the child in me to disappear. I would buy the furniture from Joe Bob's friend, but I would have to go to the IT store for the computer/printer.

I called the phone company to purchase and install an extension. Then, I called Joe Bob's friend, Ross Hansen to order the furniture. He promised to have it in my place of business by the next afternoon.

Some of my clients were money makers, and some were what one might think of as low bid. I was just getting started, and I figured that a client was a client. Word of mouth marketing was a good thing in a small town like Martinsville.

I had just finished handling a will for one such client when Joe Bob called.

"You ain't gonna believe this, Matt."

"What am I not going to believe?"

Instead of answering my question, Joe Bob asked, "Are you busy this afternoon?"

"As a matter of fact, I was about to call you to see if I could bring your Buick to the garage and ask you to take me to pick up my Cadillac. I had a call telling me it's ready."

"Yeah, I can make that work."

"What was it that you wanted to tell me?"

Joe Bob laughed. "I'll tell you when I see you."

I had no idea what his surprising information might be, but he had piqued my curiosity.

He was standing outside the bay when I arrived. I'd thought I would slide over and let him drive us to pick up my car, but he went around to the passenger side.

"You drive; I'll talk," he said, grinning.

"You're the boss."

Joe Bob went into great detail to preface the new piece of information. He reminded me that his relationship with Arlene Watkins had been no more than an occasional roll in the hay and that they were both good with that. He also told me that she does keep his books. I recalled the afternoon I disturbed them when Arlene was supposedly working on the books. Joe Bob had come to the door half-dressed, and Arlene was close behind him looking disheveled with the tail of her blouse hanging out and her makeup smeared. He assured me that the afternoon delights had ceased since he met Lauren.

"Arlene's a good woman, Matt. Did I tell you that her poor husband died?"

"No."

"Well, he did, and she seems to be relieved. He didn't even know who she wuz. But do you remember that Arlene told me she thought her rotten son wuz the one broke into my place?"

"Yes, but there was no proof."

"There is now. He's a real badass kid, but something must of put the fear of God in him after his daddy died. He confessed to his mama, told her he did it to make me stay away from her. You might say he's kinda reformed. He's been treatin' his mama good. The mystery's solved."

"How about that? So, can I assume you're just going to let the break-in fade into the past and pretend it never happened?"

"Yeah. It's been a while, and if he's bein' good to his mama, I can call it even. I like Arlene. She's good people."

"You have a very forgiving nature, my friend."

We had just pulled into the parking lot where I was to pick up my car. Joe Bob spotted it before I did. My wrecked, almost new Cadillac looked like it had just come off the assembly line.

Joe Bob took off in his Buick, and I drove my Caddy home.

I knew Joe Bob would have the Buick in shipshape condition that very afternoon.

I called Sydney late that afternoon to invite her out to dinner. It was too late to invite her to my place for the romantic evening I was planning because I knew I would have to spend the better part of a day in preparation for that special event.

"I'd love to have dinner with you, Matt. I'm sorry I was tied up at lunch time."

"Might there be anything in particular you're craving?" I asked.

"No, nothing in particular," she said. "Surprise me." She laughed into the phone. I really loved the way she laughed.

I wanted to be imaginative, and I came up with a simple solution that I thought she might like. I called her right after work and suggested she dress casually.

"You could wear shorts if you like. This place isn't the least bit fancy."

I bought a bottle of good wine, called ahead and ordered pizza to go. I already had a picnic blanket and paper tablecloth, plastic wine glasses, and a corkscrew loaded in my car.

Sydney came to her door in white shorts and a fire engine red tee shirt. I thought she looked to be about eighteen in that outfit and her bright white tennis shoes.

"Are you going to tell me where we're going?" she asked, smiling.

"I'd like to surprise you, but you'll soon find out what we're having for dinner."

I drove to Peppy's Pizza Parlor and pulled into a parking space.

"I hope you like pizza," I said, "because that's what's on the menu tonight. Sit tight; I'll be right back with our dinner."

"What kind did you get?"

"Half pepperoni and the other half veggie, no onion. How'd I do?"

"It sounds great. Now, take me to our secret rendezvous. I'm famished."

Sydney realized where I was taking her as soon as I exited the highway and turned onto the short drive to the lake.

"We're having a picnic!" she said. "I love picnics."

We unloaded all of the paraphernalia from the trunk. Sydney carried the blanket and the paper table cloth, and I resembled a packhorse. I added a lantern that I kept in the trunk to my load in case darkness decided to fall before we finished eating.

I found the perfect picnic table surrounded on three sides by a leafy wall with a view of the lake.

I uncorked the wine and poured. Sydney raised her glass in a toast: "Here's to your creative imagination, Matt Stevenson."

We managed to polish off most of the pizza and half of the bottle of wine. Then, we put everything back into the trunk except for the blanket and the rest of the wine. I planned to linger on the beach until the moon could light our path enough to make it back to the car. Why did I bring a lantern?

"This is a perfect night for a walk on the beach. How about going for a stroll and finding a good place to sit on our blanket and sip our wine while watching the sun sink into the horizon?"

"What a wonderful idea," Sydney said. "I seem to like all of your ideas, don't I?"

"That's because they're all great," I teased, tucking the blanket under my arm and refilling our glasses.

We left our shoes at the edge of the beach and strolled to the water's edge to splash our feet in the warm surf.

Twilight was beginning to lower its purple haze all round us, and the cicadas were tuning up to deliver their moonlight serenade as we did an awkward slow dance to the end of the little beach.

"This is reminiscent of the last time we came here," Sydney said.

"Yes, it is."

"It looks like we've missed watching the sunset," she said.

"True, but we still have our wine and each other," I said, holding up the blanket. "That looks like a good spot over by those trees. You game?"

"Sure. You're just full of good ideas."

We made our way to the cozy destination and spread the blanket on the hard packed sand. We sat facing the silver surface of the lake. Sydney sighed contentedly and leaned against my shoulder.

"It's lovely here, Matt," she said. "Do you think we might come here often?"

"Anytime you like," I said, draining my glass.

I watched Sydney finish her wine and place her glass beside the blanket.

"When do you think you'll be ready to take this relationship to the next step?" she asked, matter of factly.

This young woman was nothing but bold, and I decided I liked that about her. I'd just never before experienced it. Well, with the exception of the night Beth handcuffed me to her bed, straddled me wearing nothing, and tortured me with a bowl of ice and a riding crop.

"Believe me, Sydney, I'm more than ready."

I put my arms around her and we lay back onto the blanket. I was falling hard for this woman. Things got steamy in a rush. I was well on the road to happiness with this woman I adored, smothering her with a deep kiss and feeling the warmth of her supple body. I needed Sydney as much as a drug addict needed a fix. Then, reality hit me: I didn't have protection. I'd been in such a hurry to get dressed in my picnic attire that I had failed to raid my nightstand drawer.

I was more than a little uncomfortable and loosened my embrace. I raised my torso on an elbow.

"Matt?" Sydney sounded wounded.

I took a deep breath, wanting to smack myself on the forehead.

"Please forgive me, Sydney. I was so anxious to see you that I didn't take time to bring protection."

The pretty vet sat up and kissed me on the cheek. Then, she laughed.

"What's so funny?" I asked, feeling myself work its way back to normal.

"Actually, it isn't funny; it's sweet. You wanted to surprise me and you were so anxious that you forgot what you needed for the grand prize."

I gathered my dignity and asked, "Ms Edelman, could I interest you in coming to my apartment to allow me to show you my etchings?"

As it turned out, she was very interested, and I congratulated myself on having clean sheets and an extra toothbrush.

I thought she looked adorable in one of my shirts the next morning. The shirt came down to her knees. She stood barefoot at the kitchen counter, sipping coffee while waiting for me to cook her omelet.

"You realize I'm going to have to let Joe know I'll be coming in late this morning," she said with a sly smile.

"I'll take you home right after breakfast and you can make up your white lie while you get ready for work," I said, placing the omelet in front of her.

This girl had a healthy appetite for everything, I thought, loving it.

We arrived at Sydney's apartment building just as Joe was leaving to go to the clinic. Sydney got out of my car and gave him a little wave, then hurried toward the elevator. Joe donned a big grin and gave me a thumbs-up.

I drove out of the parking lot feeling pretty damn good in my Cadillac car.

It was still early and I didn't have a client until after lunch, so I drove to Joe Bob's garage. There he was under another car with his long legs sticking out from under it. Freaky Fred was nowhere to be seen. I figured he must be running errands.

"Mister Kincaid, you have a visitor," I said, loud enough for him to hear me over the country music blaring from a radio parked on a workbench.

My friend rolled out from under the car and sat up.

"What brings you slummin' this mornin', counselor?"

"I just dropped Sydney off at her apartment," I said, leaving the rest to his imagination.

"Well, good for you, Matthew. Now maybe you can quit bein' so miserable and git to work bein' the best lawyer in the state. I'm tellin' you what; when you've got yourself in a happy place, it fixes just about everthing."

I laughed. Nobody expressed himself like Joe Bob Kincaid.

"What happened to your garage janitor?"

"I'm not sure. I reckon he could be sick or somethin'. When he left yesterday, he said he'd see me in the mornin'."

"Huh."

"Somethin's funny though. He still hums, but not all the time. Sometimes he's started sayin' things. It's hard for me to understand though 'cause he don't make sentences, just says a word now and then."

"You can't get the gist of what he's saying?"

"I haven't been able to so far, but I'm gonna try to figure it out the next time he does it."

I couldn't help wondering what was going on with Fred. Why was he so mysterious? He had always been strange even as a kid. All modesty aside, I was the one left standing in contests like spelling bees and math with the exception of Fred. I could best him in spelling, but on occasion, he could beat me to the finish line in math before I could come up with the answer. He was fast as a cheetah doing math problems in his head.

I wondered who would hire him to do any kind of job except his sister. Who had he worked for before Joe Bob gave him this opportunity, such as it was? And why in the world would anybody want to beat up on him? He had always been harmless, albeit weird.

Joe Bob and I chewed on these questions but couldn't come up with any reasonable answers.

"If he don't show up in the mornin', I just might go hunt him down," Joe Bob said.

"That's probably not a bad idea. He's a nut case, but I wouldn't want anything to happen to him."

"Wouldn't it be a hoot if some unsuspectin' guy offered him more than minimum wage?"

"Yes, it would, but if that actually happened, he'd probably be doing something illegal."

"Yeah."

Chapter Twenty-four

Two days had passed, and I had managed to hire a part-time secretary/receptionist. Mary Grace Satterwhite was fresh out of high school. She had never had a job except wrapping Christmas gifts during the winter break at a local department store. She didn't pretend to know the first thing about the law, but she was a whiz at taking dictation and typing. Every now and then, I would have to tell her how to spell an unfamiliar word, or phrase, but she seemed to be a quick study. I was prepared to pay her a decent salary for her services, and she all but cheered at the sum.

"Don't you think you'll need someone who knows a modicum of legal terminology?" questioned Sydney.

The two of us were having dinner at a little hole-in-the-wall Mexican restaurant.

"This young woman is capable of doing the job I need her for at the present. She's polite, fresh-faced, has a pleasant speaking voice on the phone, and she has excellent secretarial skills. As my practice grows, I'll need someone who has some legal experience, but I don't need that now. I'll make sure Mary Grace doesn't make any mistakes."

"Would you have considered a male for this position?"

"I didn't mention gender in the ad I put in the paper. This young woman was the first applicant. I interviewed two others, both women, by the way, and I chose the person I thought was the best fit for the job. I hope you know I'm not a chauvinist."

"Of course not. I just wondered."

I had to smile to myself, driving home after taking Sydney to her apartment. She was jealous. Yep, I was sure of it.

It was seven-thirty the next morning when I went downstairs to make coffee. At the sound of the coffee maker beep, I poured a cup and breathed in the aroma heading to my desk to check my email. I had just turned on my computer and happened to glance out the window. My new employee was sitting in her car on the street outside my office. She wasn't due here for another hour.

I went out on the small front porch and motioned for her to come inside.

"Good morning," I said. "I'm assuming you believe the old adage, 'the early bird gets the worm'."

Mary Grace smiled. "Well, I wanted to make sure to be on time," she explained.

"How about a cup of coffee?" I offered.

"Oh, no thank you. I don't drink coffee."

"Juice?"

"That would be nice. Thank you, Mister Stevenson."

I proffered the juice, and she took it to her desk, waiting for instruction, I supposed.

"You're very early," I said. "Enjoy your juice and play a game on your phone while I check my email."

Did that sound insulting? I decided that it probably did.

After she had finished her juice, I went over to her small office space, took a seat in one of the two visitor chairs in front of her desk and started asking her a spate of questions that had nothing to do with her office duties—things I had no business asking her.

I learned that her father was deceased and that her mother was homebound. Her mother had been a nurse until she fell from a ladder changing a light bulb in their garage and managed to break both legs. She was only able to take limited physical therapy and was in a wheelchair most of the time.

The poor girl sounded like a stoic robot explaining her current situation. It was obvious that she wasn't asking for pity; just stating the facts.

I felt that I had unintentionally tortured her enough for one day, and changed the subject with my best smile.

"You're pretty much looking at the entire office, Mary Grace," I said, nodding toward the small kitchen. I keep snacks and soft drinks in the fridge. Feel free to help yourself. The restroom is just down that hall, and you and I share this area divided into our respective niches. Do you have any questions?"

"You haven't told me how many hours I'll be working or if you'll always want me to be here in the mornings or afternoons."

"I'm thinking a couple of hours in the morning and a couple more in the afternoon to start. Are you thinking of taking another part-time job in addition to this one? If so, you might want to work just in the morning or the afternoon here. If this will be your only part-time job, you might want to sleep in or do things at home and come in late. You could work a couple of hours, take an hour off for lunch, and come back at two or three in the afternoon."

"That's an awfully flexible schedule. It's very kind of you. I think I would prefer the latter option if you're sure you're okay with that."

"Tell you what," I said, "since you're here already, you can work four hours this morning and take the rest of the day off. Tomorrow we'll start with the schedule you chose."

"Perfect. I'm ready to go to work."

And was she ever ready. I dictated four letters and watched her fingers fly across the keyboard. She was finished in nothing flat. The letters were perfect. My secretary/receptionist sat primly at her desk waiting for further instruction.

"Excellent work, Mary Grace. That's all I have at the moment. You'll be responsible for greeting anyone who happens to come in and for answering the phone. If you're bored, feel free to borrow a book from the bookcase over there or spend time on your phone."

"Mister Stevenson, I can't sit here doing nothing and get paid for it."

"Sure you can."

My new hire opted for her phone since I didn't have a meeting with a client and there were no walk-ins. At twelve o'clock on the dot, she collected her purse and asked if there was anything else she could do for me before she left for the day.

"You've done a great job, Mary Grace. I look forward to our having a good working relationship. If you like, come in around ten o'clock tomorrow and leave whenever you want to go to lunch. It doesn't matter what time you return as long as it's by three o'clock. The office closes at five. Have a good afternoon."

Mary Grace was on her way out when Bernie Zuckerman burst through the door and nearly ran into her. He all but skidded to a stop and fixed his bespectacled eyes on her startled face without comment.

"Oh, excuse me, sir," Mary Grace apologized, knowing very well that it was Bernie who should be begging her pardon.

I hurried across the room.

"Bernard Zuckerman, meet Mary Grace Satterwhite, my new secretary/receptionist."

"I'm pleased to meet you, Mister Zuckerman," said Mary Grace.

It was clear to me that the young woman was having a bit of difficulty holding back a giggle.

"Mister Zuckerman isn't usually in this much of a hurry," I said, touching Mary Grace's elbow and walking her to the door and closing it behind her.

"Bernie, what the hell?"

"That girl!" he said. "She's beautiful! She looks exactly like my little Claire. I've never seen anything like it."

Truth to tell, I had forgotten what Claire looked like. I hadn't laid eyes on the kid in over a year. All I remembered about her was that she was a whiny little brat, but I had chalked that up to her mother's charming personality. Claire probably inherited that trait from Lee Ann.

"I don't have any clients this afternoon. Let's go into the kitchen and have a beer. Then, maybe you'll tell me why you came through that door like gangbusters."

I pulled a couple of longnecks out of the fridge, twisted off the caps and handed one to Bernie who had dropped into a kitchen chair. He removed his glasses and mopped his face with a handkerchief.

"Two things," he wheezed out, then took a long pull on his beer.

"I'm listening."

"First, I'm walking through my living room and happen to glance out the bay window. What do you think I saw?"

"How would I know?"

"None other than Freaky Fred bent over my recycle bin. He was going through it with both hands like he was looking for something."

"Man, that's weird. You're aware that Joe Bob hired him to do odd jobs, aren't you?"

Bernie nodded. "I heard about it. What's that have to do with him digging through my stuff?"

"I don't know how, or if, the two are connected, but he didn't show up for work yesterday or the day before. I don't know whether he went in today."

"I got outside as fast as I could, but he took off before I could reach him."

"What's the other thing that has you upset?"

"Lee Ann's out of the hospital. I went by to see her and was told that she had been dismissed. You won't understand this, I know, but I felt the need to go to her house and check on her. She cheated on me, doesn't love me, doesn't love her child and probably doesn't even care what's happened to her. I must be going insane. I don't know why I feel this way. I'm certainly not responsible for her welfare."

"No, you're not responsible, and I'm sure she has qualified help to take care of her in her home."

"She does. A nurse answered the door. I asked if I could see Lee Ann, and she took me to the den where Lee Ann was resting on a hospital bed. She looked terrible. When I said her name, she opened her eyes and growled, 'Get out!'"

"Drink your beer, Bernie. I can't imagine why you would want to see the woman, let alone assist her in any way after what she did. And, I don't know why you're telling me about it."

"You're right, of course. I guess I just needed a sounding board. I haven't had a life since Claire's disappearance, and I'm at a loss as to how to get her back. There haven't been any leads since the woman I met with seems to have been a dead end."

"You've barely mentioned Juanita since she left with Claire."

"Juanita was good for Claire. She took excellent care of her, and they bonded immediately. I have to admit that I took advantage of the situation; I used Juanita to assuage my loneliness and sexual needs. I'm ashamed of that."

"That was a two-way street, wasn't it?"

"I don't think so. Our relationship meant more to her than it did to me. I knew it. I didn't have to continue to use her. She was a convenience, and I was an SOB."

"Let's finish our beers, then head over to Joe Bob's to see if Fred showed up for work today. Maybe that will shed some light on the situation."

"I'm going to pass. I have to stop by to check on the guy I left in charge of my shop, then catch up on about a million things at home. Tell Joe Bob I'll catch him next time. And, Matt, thanks for letting me bend your ear."

"Sure thing. I'll let you know what I find out at the garage."

Bernie turned to go, looked back over his shoulder and said, "You sure have hired a gorgeous little girl to do your paperwork. That face of hers lights up the room."

I felt sorry for Bernie. He was a real mess, but there was nothing I could do to ease his pain.

I realized that I should carve out some time to leave the office for personal reasons during the hours that Mary Grace would be available to answer the phone. I could be missing out on a prospective client by locking up and taking off even though I had put a very professional message on the answering machine.

Joe Bob was sitting at his desk watching Fred sweep. He seemed to be studying Fred as he chewed his gum furiously.

"Hey, Joe Bob," I said. "I see the prodigal son has returned."

"Hey, Matt. Yeah, he wuz pacin' out on the street when I got here this mornin'."

"Did he tell you why he missed work the last couple of days?"

"Nope, but he pulled his pockets out to let me know he wanted more money."

"And you said?"

"As soon as you do somethin' to deserve a raise, I'll give you one. He just got the broom and started sweepin' and hummin' like usual. I watched him and listened to him hum. After a few minutes, he stopped hummin' and said a few words—words not connected to each other, you know. He never made a sentence. He's a crazy bastard."

"He's strange alright. Is he still doing that?"

"If he's not hummin', he's sayin' the words. Maybe you can figure out what he's sayin'. Go out there and look around at stuff on the walls like you're interested in buyin' a fanbelt or windshield wipers and listen to him."

I mosied out to the bay where Fred was working and tuned my ear as best I could to decipher his gibberish.

"Snake"…"good."

I walked around and got pretty close to him, but by then he had started humming again, so I went back into the office to report what I'd heard.

"That don't make any sense whatsoever," Joe Bob said around a wad of gum.

"No, it doesn't. I see you're still employing your chewing gum crutch."

"Yeah, and I'm gonna keep it up until I've got this smokin' habit licked. Lauren's proud of me." He grinned, and the look on his handsome face was the epitome of a guy who was hopelessly love-struck.

"I know you're a man of resolve," I said, clapping him on the shoulder. "Keep up the good work."

I was about to leave and pay Trudy a visit when Bernie

Zukerman screeched to a halt at the curb in front of the garage. He jumped out of his Cadillac, ran-walked to Joe Bob's office and burst in out of breath.

"Guess what," he huffed, bypassing any kind of salutation.

Joe Bob and I both looked at him awaiting his revelation.

"I just received a very strange and intriguing email. It came from the email address: jdoe@coldmail.com."

"Well?" Joe Bob said.

"It said, and I quote, 'Claire is safe and healthy. You'll never find her, so give up. She has a new life.'"

Perspiration and tears tracked down Bernie's face. He took off his glasses and covered his face with a handkerchief which was a wet mess. Joe Bob shoved a box of Kleenex toward him, and Bernie grabbed a fistful, dropping his handkerchief into the wastebasket.

"You didn't click on that address, did you, Bernie?" I asked.

"No. I was afraid to."

"Good. That's how a hacker got into my email. I had to move heaven and earth to get it straightened out."

"How's he gonna find out where it come from or who sent it?" Joe Bob asked.

"I don't know. We might have to give it some time and hope to get another email that gives more information. J Doe could be anybody."

"Ain't that the truth? Bernard, you can't let this thing drive you crazy. You need to calm down so you don't have a stroke or somethin'. I'm gonna send Fred home and close the garage up, and we're gonna go to my place and have a few beers. You can relax and we'll try to come up with some kind of a plan."

Bernie was a beaten man. I didn't think a few beers could

make him feel any better, but it was clear that he couldn't feel much worse.

"Let's take my car," I said. "Bernie's in no shape to drive."

Fred was mumbling as he made his way to the sidewalk. I was almost certain I heard him say the word *tires*. At the sidewalk, he turned left, then abruptly changed course. A large man in a hoodie seemed to come out of nowhere and walk hurriedly in the same direction.

I had a strange feeling that Fred Peyton would not show up for work the next day.

Chapter Twenty-five

I was getting tired of having to chauffeur Bernie Zuckerman around and making sure to get him home safe and sound. I'd felt obligated to perform this task on numerous occasions since I returned to Martinsville. The last such occasion had been over the top. First, I drove him from the restaurant to Joe Bob's doublewide where he cried and drank himself stupid. Then, I drove the two of them to the garage so Joe Bob could drive Bernie and his car home, and finally, I drove Joe Bob back to his doublewide.

As soon as I got back to my place, I looked up the closest FBI field office so Bernie could report the email with the bogus address. The Knoxville office was the closest to Martinsville. The FBI was my friend's best bet to learn the whereabouts of his child, who had taken her, and bring her home. Bernie called me the next day to tell me that he had contacted the field office and was waiting to hear from them.

I couldn't allow Bernie and his problem to occupy all of my time. I had been neglecting Trudy lately and felt terrible about it. She was dear to me, and I needed to make time to visit her. I called her on her cell phone. She was at my mother's house polishing silver. I didn't understand why she felt obligated to keep a vacant house in shipshape order.

"You haven't moved back into that house, have you?" I asked.

"No, but I do spend some time here. You know that."

"Then, why are you bothering to polish the silver? Isn't it still as noisy on Mulberry as it was?"

"Yes, it's just as bad. Some of the heavy equipment is still here and now sawing and hammering have joined the choir. Some folks have started rebuilding."

"Trudy, you don't have to polish the silver. I borrowed a few of Mother's pieces to make a special dinner for Sydney Edelman. I thought the things I took looked fine; I don't plan to polish them."

"If you must know, I'm planning to invite both you and Mister Hathaway to your mother's house for a Sunday dinner soon. There won't be any noise on a Sunday, and this house is more accommodating than mine. I thought it would be alright with you if I had the dinner here."

"Of course it's alright with me. It's very sweet of you to arrange a get-together, especially with your culinary skills. Just let me know when to show up. I'll definitely be there."

As soon as our conversation ended, I realized that I hadn't accomplished what I had set out to do. I called Trudy back to ask her to lunch so we could catch up.

"That's real sweet of you, Matty, but I already have plans. As soon as I finish up here, I have an appointment, but I would so love to see you. Check your busy calendar. Maybe we can do lunch another day."

I wasn't having very good luck at making lunch dates, but being the eternal optimist I am, I called Sydney.

"I'd love to have lunch with you, Matt. As a matter of fact, I'd like to spend the rest of the afternoon with you if you're free."

Sydney Edelman was the most forward woman I had ever known. I didn't object to this, mind you. It was just that she seemed to be beating me to the punch in furthering our relationship. Maybe I was simply an old fashioned kind of guy.

I pulled into the parking lot of her clinic at twelve o'clock on the dot and saw Sydney and Joe Lawson coming out of the building. Joe was telling Sydney something that produced a big smile on her lovely face. As they were about to go their separate ways, she pulled him into a hug and kissed him on the cheek. Then, as if I were to take lightly the scene I had just witnessed, she trotted to the passenger door of my car, opened it, and hopped into the seat, grinning.

"That was a touching little scene," I said.

Sydney smiled. "I'm so happy for Joe," she said.

"I kind of got that impression," I said, sounding like a jealous teenager.

"He's getting married, Matt. As you know, his wife died a few years ago, but before he came here, he had been seeing someone. They've been in touch on the phone and he's flown to see her several times on weekends. She'll be moving here as soon as she can land a job. She's a music teacher and has an interview lined up with the local high school. I know Joe's going to be so much happier than he has been. I've been his only real sounding board since he came here, so we've spent quite a bit of time together. He's really a great guy, but you know that."

"Of course I do. I'm happy for him."

"Where would you like to go for lunch?"

"That depends on whether or not you have clients this afternoon."

"As a matter of fact, I do not. I'm expecting my new secretary to come into the office at two o'clock. I'm kind of letting her choose when she works. I told her she could count on four hours per day. She came in at nine this morning and finished everything I had for her to do in about a half hour. The kid does good work."

"Oh. I was hoping you'd be free all afternoon."

"I can be. I'll just call and let her know I won't be needing her, but that I'll pay her for the time regardless."

"Perfect. Let's go to your place and make a sandwich or something. Then, we can play the afternoon away. How does that sound?"

"Sydney, that sounds perfect. I'm surprised I didn't think of it."

And perfect it was. I decided that Sydney Edelman was the answer to my prayers. We made love off and on all afternoon. Then, we had Chinese delivered for dinner. Sydney laughed at my attempt to use chopsticks while she looked like an old pro at the task. After dinner we padded into the living room to watch an old movie from the comfort of my new couch and eat ice cream from the carton with dueling spoons. Everything seemed right with the world the next morning when I awoke spooning with the woman I realized that I truly loved.

I made Sydney breakfast, then delivered her to her apartment. Then, I went to my law office to scrounge up enough work to fill the four hours I had promised Mary Grace each day. She was sitting in her car in front of my office when I got there, looking down at something, probably her phone, and didn't see me approach her car. I tapped on her window. She looked up surprised, then got out of her car, smiling.

"Good morning, Mary Grace."

"Good morning, Mister Stevenson. I guess I'm a little early again," she apologized.

"You're right on time," I said. "I've been running a couple of errands."

I made small talk with my eager employee while scraping

together a few unnecessary things to occupy her time until I could manage to give her some menial tasks which actually did need to be accomplished.

The time dragged by until the big hand landed on twelve o'clock. I had a client meeting at twelve-thirty which wouldn't take but a few minutes, but it would generate some much needed work for Mary Grace. She wouldn't return to the office until three o'clock today. I had realized right after hiring the young lady that I hadn't really needed her yet, but it was nice to have a lovely young thing with a pleasant phone voice and a positive attitude sitting in the office.

I skipped lunch and prepared for my client meeting, all the while having to shove thoughts of Sydney to a back burner and concentrate on the business at hand. I was all set when the client arrived. The meeting went well, and it seemed that I had performed well for this small businessman. He assured me that if he needed more legal assistance, he would be in touch.

For the first time since returning to my hometown I felt that I had made the right choice. Everything seemed to be falling into place. My relationship with Sydney was beginning to feel solid and on a pretty fast track, thanks to her. Joe Bob was a happy man now that the lovely Lauren had stolen his heart. He was willing to change an ingrained habit to please her and work on self-improvement. He no longer wished to present himself as a small town Romeo. Bernie was still crazed because of his abducted child, but I had hopes that since the FBI would now be involved, Claire would be coming home to Martinsville soon.

To my great surprise, Trudy had miraculously found a like-minded companion. I sincerely hoped that her Mister Hathaway turned out to be the missing piece of the puzzle to ensure her happiness for the rest of her life.

I had a good handful of clients and the number grew each week, but I still had enough spare time to idle away. There were a couple of hours to kill until Mary Grace returned to the office, so as usual, I drove to Joe Bob's garage to shoot the breeze.

Freaky Fred had returned to the scene of the crime, so to speak. He was using an edger along the driveway leading to the bay. He didn't look up as I approached.

"Hey, Fred. Working hard?"

He ignored me, so I walked past him and went into the garage and found Joe Bob making entries in an old fashioned ledger.

"Hey, my man, you look kind of busy."

"Matthew." He acknowledged my presence without looking up. "Be with you in a sec."

I waited for him to finish and realized that he was doing the work by hand.

"I just noticed that you don't have a computer," I said. "You should get one. It would save you a lot of time."

"I'm my own secretary/ bookkeeper here at my business. Why would I need a computer?" he asked, chewing his gum. "I've got a phone to communicate several different ways, and I've got Arlene to come to my doublewide to straighten things out if I've screwed up, and I've got that big filin' cabinet over there in the corner. I don't want my business on a computer. Nobody's gonna have a chance to steal Joe Bob Kincaid's information."

I could tell I was fighting a losing battle, so I changed the subject.

"I talked with Bernie a while ago. He's contacted the FBI about that email and he's breathing a little easier now. He said they told him they'd keep him abreast of things. If I understood correctly, they'll also stay in touch with the local authorities, but they'll handle the situation on their own. They don't want the locals involved."

"That's good news. Now, maybe Bernard'll come back to planet earth. He's been one crazy sumbitch ever since the kid got snatched."

"I see Fred's come back. Did you find out why he was missing work?"

"Nope, and he pulled out his pockets again to let me know I ought to give him a raise. He shut up when I told him if he brought it up again I'd fire him."

"Wonder what he was doing to earn money before he got fired from his previous job?"

"Like I told you, he just says a word ever so often. It don't make sense, but I think the single words he lets slide might have somethin' to do with the job he had. He said a new word this mornin'."

"Yeah?"

"Pet. He just said 'pet' out of the blue. Is that crazy, or what?"

"Maybe he had some menial job in a pet store or at an animal shelter. He might have had a job walking dogs or cleaning cages."

"Well, whatever the job was, it must of paid more than I'm payin' him."

"You want to grab some lunch?" I asked.

"No can do today, ol' buddy. I've gotta go home and git cleaned up so I can meet Lauren at the club. She wants to take golf lessons, and yours truly is gonna give her a hand."

"I'm not telling you what to do, but I've been led to understand that you shouldn't try to teach someone close to you how to do anything. I'd guess that would include giving her golf lessons."

Joe Bob laughed. He tore a receipt from a pad on his desk and deposited his gum in it, then lobbed it into a waste basket.

"You don't understand. This is me and Lauren we're talkin' about. This is gonna be fun for both of us."

"You're the boss," I said. "Let me know how it works out."

"Well, I guess I'll head back to the salt mine. I'm due at the courthouse at four o'clock."

Fred had stopped edging. He was pacing back and forth mumbling to himself.

"Hey, Fred, how you doing?"

"Big man."

"Who's a big man, Fred?"

Fred didn't answer. He picked up the weed eater and walked into the bay.

I grabbed a sandwich at the corner deli, then drove back to my office to find Mary Grace on the phone with a prospective client. I thought she sounded very professional. There was someone sitting in front of her desk, and she smiled at him. On closer inspection, I saw that it was none other than Bernie Zuckerman. He was staring at my secretary/receptionist wearing an expression of awe.

Since Mary Grace was doing her job, and Bernie was all but drooling at the sight of her, I tapped him on the shoulder and motioned for him to follow me to my side of the office and have a seat. It was obvious that he was having a hard time tearing his gaze away from my new hire, and that she was uncomfortable being openly ogled. Bernie finally got to his feet and came across the room.

"What's the matter with you?" I hissed.

"What do you mean? Nothing's the matter with me. Matt, that child is absolutely breathtaking."

"Would you please lower your voice?"

"Sorry."

"In the first place, she is not a child. She's a young woman attempting to do her job. And I'm having trouble trying to understand your behavior. You're old enough to be her father. She needs this job, and you're spooking her."

"I was just admiring her. I would never do anything to upset that ethereal being."

"Tell me that you came here for legal advice, or that you've heard from the FBI."

"I didn't come here for legal advice. I don't really have anything to tell you except that I did call the FBI field office. I wanted to know if they had made any progress regarding the email. A guy with a voice like Joe Friday on that old TV show, Dragnet, told me that when they have something to report, they'll let me know. In other words, 'Don't call us; we'll call you.'"

"Well, it's a brand new case for them. You'll have to be patient. I feel confident they'll find out who's behind the email and get Claire back home."

I suppose that if I were in Bernie's shoes, I would feel as anguished as he does. At least he's aware that his child is alive and well. He couldn't ask for more at this point.

"I hope you're right, Matt. I don't know anywhere else to turn."

<h1 style="text-align:center">Chapter Twenty-six</h1>

My old friend, Joe Bob Kincaid and I were chewing the fat while loafing around in his office at the garage. It turned out that he had, indeed, given his new squeeze a golf lesson, and he had proved me wrong. He told me that the girl was a natural. She could stroke the ball and send it sailing, and it looked effortless. According to Joe Bob, there hadn't been any tears or hard feelings. I had a feeling that Lauren was about to replace me as Joe Bob's best friend and I was okay with that.

"I'm tellin' you, she had a perfect swing. It wuz a beautiful sight to see. You know how women usually don't listen to instructions. Well, she did listen, and she followed the instructions without arguin'."

I laughed. "I'm glad it worked out."

"The next lesson's gonna be on puttin'. I bet she aces that too."

"Hey, I noticed you're not chewing your gum. You didn't give up and start smoking again, did you?"

"I most certainly did not. I've got this thing licked. It just takes a little willpower. Plus, it helps to have a good reason to give it up. I'd do anything to make Lauren happy."

"Well, my friend, you're practically glowing. If you don't have plans with your new love this evening, how about joining me for dinner? I was thinking of going to Morgan's. I like all the new restaurants, but when it's just guys hanging out, Morgan's feels like the place to be."

"Morgan's it is. I'll see you there in about a half hour. I might have a news flash or two for you."

"Oh?"

"I'd like for you to be settin' down havin' a bourbon when I enlighten you. See you at Morgan's."

I couldn't imagine what news Joe Bob might suddenly have. Usually, he hit me in the face with any tidbit he had just heard.

I drove home and changed into khakis and a golf shirt, then took off for Morgan's. Joe Bob pulled into the parking lot as I was getting out of my car. I had to admit that he had piqued my interest, and I was kind of anxious to hear his big news.

Lucy Combs was carrying a tray of drinks to a table of rowdy guys replaying their golf game. She delivered the drinks and gave us a little wave, motioning us to a booth in her area.

"Hey, Lucy." Joe Bob gave her one of his brilliant smiles.

"Well, Joe Bob, you look like the cat that ate the canary. What's up with you?"

"I'm just a happy man, Lucy. I'm in love."

"No kidding?"

"I wouldn't kid about a thing like this. You're one of my best friends, and I hope you're happy for me."

"Well, sure I am, sweetheart. I know you've got a good heart. I just never thought you'd stick with any one lady friend long enough to fall in love. That's all."

"I hate to break up this intimate little conversation, but I'm really thirsty. Lucy, would you kindly bring me a bourbon and soda."

Lucy nodded; then turned her attention to Joe Bob.

"What tickles your fancy, Mister Lovesick?"

"Bourbon and soda works for me too."

Joe Bob couldn't seem to stop grinning. He steepled his big hands, stared at them while shaking his head in what one might think was disbelief, and grinned like a Cheshire cat.

Lucy brought our drinks as I was about to tell Joe Bob I was tired of his waiting game.

"Cheers!" Joe Bob said.

We touched our glasses and both of us took a healthy pull.

"Here she goes," Joe Bob said. "I've asked Lauren to marry me."

"Congratulations! You work at the speed of light. Can I assume her answer was yes?"

"Not exactly. She said she wanted me to know all about her past. I reckon we wuz both pretty much livin' for the moment and we hadn't bothered tellin' each other our life stories. She told me she needed to tell me things that might change my mind about her. That almost made me cry, Matt. I don't care what that angel did before we met. That's over. This is a brand new beginnin'."

"I guess I agree with her, I said. You two don't want any secrets if you plan to spend your lives together."

"This wuz a real bomb, but I'm all in. My bride-to-be is a mother. I'm havin' house guests next weekend. Lauren and Annie are comin' for a visit. Annie's three years old. I'll give them the bedroom, and I'll sleep on the couch. Annie's been stayin' with her grandmother since Lauren's been here. We wouldn't want the little tyke to say anything 'bout the sleepin' arrangements to the grandmother." He grinned. "This'll be a git-acquainted visit. I plan to charm that little girl with ever tool I've got."

"Wow! How come they're going to stay at your place instead of Lauren's apartment?"

"I don't know why I wanted 'em to stay with me. I just did. Lauren didn't ask why. She said that would be fine. It would show Annie the kind of person I am. Besides, she said Annie would love my cat."

"If you don't mind my asking, what happened to Annie's father?"

"He wuz in a bad wreck. Got hit by some drunk driver. Lauren said the doctors did everthing they could, but he died on the operatin' table. They'd only been married for a little over a year. She wuz pregnant with Annie when it happened. Annie never got to meet her daddy. The reason Lauren moved here wuz to git away from all the bad memories and their old friends who looked at her with pity in their eyes."

"That's very sad, Joe Bob."

"Yeah, it is. In case you're wonderin', Lauren's been goin' back to see her little girl once ever two weeks. Cottage Grove's just about a two hour drive from here. That's where she's from. Her daddy died when she was thirteen, and her mom raised her. The mom's a schoolteacher."

"I'm sure you've thought this whole thing over," I said, not wanting to sound like I was telling him to look before he leaped.

"Yes I have. I know I love Lauren, and I know I love that little girl even though I haven't met her. Uncle Jake's the only family I've had since I wuz fourteen and my parents wuz killed in that wreck. This is what I want. I want a family of my own."

That shut me up. I remembered how Joe Bob adored his mother and how mean his father was. Mister Kincaid used his son for a punching bag, but Joe Bob missed him all the same after his death. I was never sure I understood that, but I knew it was true.

"Well, my friend, in the process of absorbing all of this news, I've worked up a pretty healthy appetite. Shall we order dinner?"

Joe Bob got Lucy's attention, and she headed to our booth.

"What's the special?" Joe Bob asked.

"Chicken 'n' dumplin's, and it's gooood."

We both ordered the special, and Lucy was right. It was gooood.

After we went our separate ways, I couldn't get Joe Bob off my mind. He was such a good human being. He was kind, generous, and good natured, except maybe for his intolerance of Bernie. In Joe Bob's defense, Bernie had the ability to test most anyone's patience.

Lying in bed, I found myself doing what I often did during quiet times. My mind wandered back to our teenage years and looked at the ways in which our lives had changed. I had barely known Bernie's parents. They had never been very visible. Joe Bob and I hung out at my house quite a bit, and I went to his house occasionally when I didn't think his dad would be there, but we had never been invited to the Zuckermans'. Funny, that had never occurred to me until now. Perhaps Bernie's proclivity for arguing and his short fuse had been inherited from one, or both, of his parents. It could be possible that each individual is born with certain traits that are inherent, and that person's behavior will instinctively follow the path that has been etched for it. One would need to work hard to overcome such a thing.

One thing I had never understood regarding Bernie Zuckerman was the obvious fact that he was jealous of Joe Bob's relationship with me. There was no reason for him to be jealous. I had never shown favoritism to one of them over the other. Their personalities were at opposite ends of the pole. They were as different as day and night, but they were both my friends. Bernie was volatile; Joe Bob was laid back.

At the sound of my alarm clock I awoke with my arms wrapped around a pillow, feeling stupid. I had barely shaken myself awake and was on my way to make coffee when the phone rang. It was Trudy.

"Good morning," I said.

"Good mornin' to you, my sweet boy. Are you up and dressed?"

"Actually, I just got out of bed, but I always have time to talk to you."

"Good, because I'm standin' on your little front porch. I've brought breakfast."

"Give me a minute to throw on some clothes, and I'll be right down."

I took the steps to my bedroom two at a time and got into shorts and a tee shirt to meet Trudy at the front door. She had a picnic basket in one hand and a pretty little bouquet in the other. I took the basket from her and gave her a half-hug with my free arm.

"If you don't have a vase, just put these in a glass of water," she said, handing me the posies. "They came out of your mama's garden. I cut them a few minutes ago."

It just so happened that I did have a vase. It was one of the items I had borrowed from Mother's cache of beautiful things for the romantic dinner I had been planning. Trudy took the flowers and arranged them in the crystal vase, then placed them on the table. A woman's touch really did make a difference.

Trudy began unloading the picnic basket. The contents smelled heavenly.

"I thought I'd bring you a little treat," she said. "We've got country ham, some buttery grits, biscuits, and my peach preserves. I hope you're hungry."

"What's the occasion?" I asked, setting the table.

"I just wanted to spend a little bit of time with you, Matty. I miss our mornings together."

"I do too, Trudy, but it seems that we both need to get on with our lives. You have a new friend in your life now, and I'm delighted for you. Your Mister Hathaway seems like an upstanding man, and you deserve a relationship with such a respectable gentleman. I'm sure the two of you have a lot in common. As for yours truly, I have a new law practice. I also have someone who's beginning to be pretty special in my life. Sydney Edelman is becoming a part of my world a little at a time. She's a lovely young woman who is passionate about her work, and she appears to think I'm worthy of her time. I'm glad I came back to Martinsville. I feel good about my work, and I have both you and Sydney close at hand. I'm a happy guy."

Trudy sidled over to me, wrapped her arms around me and squeezed me the way she did when I was a kid with a scraped knee. Then, she ordered me to sit down while she filled our plates.

"If you'll pour your old Trudy a cup of coffee, maybe I'll tell you another reason I'm here," she said.

"Yes ma'am."

"I'd like to invite you to Sunday dinner unless you already have plans. Mister Hathaway and I will be going back to the Methodist Church that morning, but that will give me plenty of time to do everything I need to do and have time left over before you join us at six o'clock for a sip of something before dinner."

"That sounds lovely."

My old friend donned an impish grin and asked, "Did I mention that I plan to invite that new lady vet to join us? It must have slipped my mind."

"Even better," I said, feeling thankful for having known such a kind and loving person for my entire life.

I thought I noticed a slight spring in my old friend's step when she left my apartment. Trudy had a boyfriend!

I found myself whistling as I got ready for my work day. Mary Grace would probably arrive early again as was her custom. I was ready for her this morning. I had saved up a substantial batch of items which called for my dictation. She would type the letters in nothing flat, but there was a list of errands I had saved for her to run. That should take up her two hours before lunch. It was beneath me to ask her to perform tasks such as making coffee.

I had just sat down at my desk when Mary Grace came through the front door looking like summer dressed in bright yellow from head to toe. Bernie was right; she was a pretty little thing. She was also quite professional and a little bit on the prim side.

"Good morning, Mister Stevenson."

"To you as well, Mary Grace. I must say you look lovely today."

"Thank you," she said, turning a little pink.

As predicted, she finished the work in less than an hour. I handed her the list of errands, most of which involved office supplies and told her that I would be out of the office for most of the day. Her afternoon duties would consist of answering the phone and taking care of walk-ins.

I called Bernie wondering if he had any news regarding his missing child, while thinking that if he had heard from the FBI, I would be the first to know. I wanted him to know I cared.

"Um, no, Matt, I haven't heard any more from the FBI. I was embarrassed after calling them the last time. They gave me a dressing down for bothering them. Remember?"

"I just thought someone from the field office might have gotten in touch with you to give you an update."

"I don't think they're going to. I think they've dropped the ball. I've searched everywhere I know to look, and the FBI is useless. I'm giving up."

That didn't sound like the Bernie Zuckerman I knew. Something was off.

"You sound like you might be busy, Bernie."

"Yeah, I am, actually."

"I'll let you go. We'll talk another time."

Something strange was going on with Bernie, and I intended to find out what it was. I hoped he hadn't become so frustrated and depressed that he might harm himself. That was probably ridiculous. He thought too much of himself to do anything that foolish.

I closed up for lunch and cruised through a drive-thru, picking up Joe Bob's kind of healthy lunch fare. He was standing in the doorway between his office and the bay where Freaky Fred counted aloud while he pointed to different items hanging from the pegboard on the walls. I approached him with the food.

"Hey, I brought lunch," I said.

"Hey yourself, and thanks. I wuz gittin' kinda hungry." He nodded at Fred. "Wonder what he's doin'?"

"I just got here. How would I know?"

Joe Bob turned around, shaking his head.

"Well, it's kinda entertainin' tryin' to figure out some of the strange stuff he does. What brings you slummin', counselor?"

He motioned me to his chair while he got a couple of Cokes from a machine in the corner.

I sat down and took our sandwiches out of the bag.

"There's something strange going on with Bernie. He said he's giving up on finding his child. You seem to know everything that's happening around Martinsville. Have you heard any rumors about him?"

Joe Bob took a huge bite of his jumbo burger and looked thoughtful.

"I can't say I've heard any rumors about him, but I know he's been visitin' his ex some. I didn't think it wuz worth mentionin'. I told you I thought he still might have a thing for her, but you nixed it."

"How do you know he's been seeing her?"

"I saw him leavin' her house with my own eyes. Don't know what he wuz doin' there, but my eyes don't lie."

"He said he didn't want to feel sorry for her, but I'd bet money he does."

"Could be, but I don't feel like gittin' all tangled up in Bernard's troubles. I'm gonna concentrate on Lauren and my new family-to-be."

"I hear you, but I have to tell you that he has my curiosity up and running."

Chapter Twenty-seven

I found myself wanting to be with Sydney twenty-four/seven, but it seemed that the majority of our time together was spent sharing meals. I craved much more than that. Granted, I knew that her job was demanding and some spur-of-the-moment interruptions in her personal life were inevitable, but that didn't make me any less unhappy about it.

I was about to open up for the day when I noticed a plain white envelope lying on the floor just inside the front door. How strange. The only thing that I had found slipped under a door in recent times was my hotel bill. I picked up the envelope and took it with me to the kitchen. A cup of strong coffee would be just what I needed before learning what lurked inside the surprise package.

I took a few swallows of the brew, then sliced open the mysterious envelope with a letter opener I kept in a cubby over the kitchen desk. It took me a few seconds to figure out what I was reading. Who would send me such a thing? It was a horrible attempt to pen a childlike poem.

Then, it hit me. This had to be what Joe Bob had wanted me to look over for him. I read the love poem slowly, then read it again. Joe Bob was my good friend. I had never lied to him. How could I give him honest feedback on this pitiful attempt to express his undying love to the woman he intended to marry? I had told him I would be glad to look over whatever he wanted to run by me, and I knew he would want my honest opinion. This would take some serious thought and I didn't want to rush into it.

Bernie Zuckerman was the man I had been thinking about as I had fallen asleep and who still occupied my mind upon awakening. My half-crazed friend who was obsessed with finding his child and bringing her home would never entertain the notion of giving up on that mission.

As soon as I could get Mary Grace settled with a sufficient number of tasks for the morning, I would go to work on digging into whatever had stopped Bernie cold in his quest.

Looking out the bay window, I saw my young employee unloading office supplies from the trunk of her car. I went outside to help her and carried in the box of typing paper. One of her tasks would be to store her purchases on shelves in the supply room and make an inventory list.

The phone was ringing as we were bringing our haul inside. Mary Grace deposited a box of supplies on her desk and silenced it.

"Good morning. Mister Stevenson's law office."

I had no idea who might be on the other end of the line, but I didn't want to talk to anyone at the moment. For all I knew, it could be Joe Bob inquiring as to whether I had read his poem. I held an imaginary pad and pencil in my hand and air wrote *take a number* on it.

"If you'll give me your name and number, I'll have Mister Stevenson return your call as soon as possible."

I grinned at her. She was going to be a crackerjack gatekeeper.

We took our haul to the supply room. Then, I asked her to

come to my side of the office so I could dictate a few letters. I figured she would have enough work to fill her morning with the typing and organizing the supply room.

Leaving my secretary to her own devices, I took off to do a bit of detective work. I drove past Bernie's dry cleaning business. His car wasn't parked where he usually left it. Then, I drove to the garage where he sometimes parked. It wasn't a large structure—only three tiers, and I viewed every floor, driving at a snail's pace. Bernie was obviously not at work.

My next stop was his home. I parked on the street, went to the front door, and rang the bell. After the second ring with no Bernie, I walked across the lawn to the garage. The door was down, and I wasn't quite tall enough to look through the high windows, so I hopped up and down a couple of times to get a glimpse inside. The garage was empty.

I was stumped. Martinsville was a small town, but I couldn't spend the day driving all over it trying to spot Bernie's Cadillac. It wasn't even eleven o'clock, so it would be a fruitless venture to stop by the animal clinic and invite Sydney to lunch.

I gave up and drove to Joe Bob's garage. I knew he would ask if I had found the envelope and read its contents. There was no way I could tell him a blatant lie, saying that I deemed it impressive, nor could I let him think an effort to express his love through poetry was a bad idea. It would kill him if Lauren made light of it, but from what Joe Bob had told me about her, she didn't seem to be the kind of person who would do such a thing.

I found my friend perched atop a stack of tires, with his chin resting on his big fists. His knees were apart, and supported his elbows. He was staring into space as though he were in a trance.

"Hello. Anybody home?"

Joe Bob blinked a couple of times and raised his torso.

"Hey, Matthew. What's shakin'?"

"Are you okay; just day dreaming?"

"I reckon you could call it day dreamin'. I wuz just sittin' here thinkin' about Lauren and Annie and tryin' to imagine what our new life'll be like. I've gotta tell you, I can't wait to find out."

"They'll be staying with you this weekend, right?"

"That's right. Lucy's comin' over tomorrow to spiffy the place up. She does a great job."

"Changing the subject, I don't suppose you've seen Bernie around town the last couple of days."

"Nope. Seems like the last time I saw him he wuz leavin' his ex's place."

"I've just driven to his business, the garage where he sometimes parks, and I even went to his house. He didn't answer the door, and his car wasn't there."

"Well, he didn't just disappear into thin air. Maybe he's at his ex's again."

"I'll make the rounds again and drive past her house this time. I don't know anywhere else to look."

Joe Bob didn't seem overly interested in Bernie's whereabouts. My friend did something he had never done before; he gently dismissed me.

"I've got to finish workin' on the mayor's car, Matt. I hate to rush you off, but I spent most of the mornin' thinkin' about my new life. Maybe we can git together later. Okay?"

"Sure. I should get back to work too, and I want to drive by Lee Ann's house."

I couldn't believe that Joe Bob and I had spent several minutes together and he hadn't mentioned the poem. I was sure he would bring it up the next time we met.

Mary Grace was about to leave for lunch when I returned to

the office. She had organized the supply room, typed the letters and had left a short stack of phone messages on my desk.

"Take the rest of the day off, Mary Grace," I said, checking out the supply room. "You've done a beautiful job."

It seemed that the young woman had given up on begging for work.

"Thank you, Mister Stevenson," she said, grabbed her purse, and left.

One of the messages was from Sydney. She wanted me to call her. I tapped in her number.

"Oh, Matt, I'm so glad you called. I just did a walk-through of my new house with the builder. It's finally finished, Matt, and I love it. I was wondering if you might be willing to help me with a few finishing touches this weekend. The appliances are all being installed tomorrow, and the furniture in my apartment is being transported to the house tomorrow as well. I've placed an order for the remainder of the furniture, but it won't be delivered for three more weeks. Is it possible that you might like to have a roommate until the house is completely furnished and everything is ready to go?"

She had laid this information on me in such a rush that it had caught me completely off guard. I hadn't gotten around to setting up our romantic dinner at my place, and she wanted to move in without preamble.

"Sure, Sydney, to all of the above."

I had intended to invite Sydney out to dinner, but my plans had suddenly changed. I had allowed my apartment to look a lot like an authentic bachelor pad by letting things stay where they landed. Many days I didn't bother to make my bed, and several items of dirty laundry hadn't made it all the way to the hamper. Toiletries littered the counter in my bathroom. The only presentable areas of the apartment were the small kitchen and Mary Grace's and my offices. I would have to spend the evening cleaning up my mess plus make room for whatever Sydney would bring with her.

I had hired a cleaning team to come do their thing once a week, but they weren't due until the following Tuesday. Trudy would disown me if she knew what a slob I had become.

I had made it a priority to return phone calls regardless of their importance. It was a professional courtesy. So I returned each of them in the order that Mary Grace had received them, and that was the extent of my lawyerly tasks for the day.

I treated myself to a cheese, tomato and mayonnaise sandwich before changing the sheets, doing the laundry, and giving the furniture a quick dust job. I didn't bother vacuuming since there was no evidence of a need. The next chore was a trip to a grocery store to stock the refrigerator and pantry. I needed mentoring in this department; my shopping ability was limited. I didn't need a list to remind me to buy beer, cereal, sandwich material and ice cream. I would have to put a bit of thought into this.

When I thought I had made a respectable grocery list, I went to the store I was fairly familiar with and made my purchases. I wasn't accustomed to handling domestic chores and didn't realize how time consuming they were. I was considering crashing on the couch with a book, or maybe even grabbing a catnap.

Just as I was putting the groceries away, the phone rang. I put my chore on hold and looked at the caller ID. Sydney was calling. She was in the process of leaving a message before I had a chance to pick up the phone, so I let her leave the message.

"Matt, I know you're busy. I hope you're not with a client. If you are, please call me as soon as you're free."

I had a bad feeling that my little afternoon respite was about to be aborted. I finished storing the groceries, then listened to

Sydney's message a second time. It gave the impression of urgency, so I returned her call immediately.

"Sydney, I just heard your message. Is everything alright?"

"Yes and no, Matt. I seem to have rushed things to the point that I've just put myself out on the street."

"What are you saying? I don't understand."

"I told the people who are moving my furniture from the apartment to the house that I was in somewhat of a hurry, and they called to tell me that they want to transport it this afternoon. I have a full schedule the rest of the day. I hope you don't think I'm being presumptuous, Matt, but I flew home and packed a bag instead of having lunch. May I please stay at your place tonight?"

"Of course you can, but I don't see a problem concerning the movers. Can't you give them keys to the apartment and the house and have them return the keys to you?"

"I guess I could do that, but that furniture is high quality. It's very special to me. I need to make sure the movers are careful, and the furniture should be checked out once it's in the house. I hate to ask you, but is there any possible way you might be able to do it in my stead? If you're too busy, I'll try to find somebody else. I just don't know who I can trust to do it."

This day was not at all to my liking. It was true that I craved Sydney's company something fierce, but having her as my roommate for three weeks suddenly felt smothering. I hadn't had another person constantly sharing my private space since Beth and I divorced, and the thought of such a scenario was making me feel invaded.

"Of course you can count on me, Sydney. I'll come to the clinic and pick up the keys now. What time do you expect the movers?"

"They should arrive at the apartment in about an hour. I can't tell you how much I appreciate this, Matt. I'll come to your place with my suitcase as soon as I close the clinic."

I drove to the animal clinic to get the keys and walked into a waiting area overflowing with whiney pets and their owners. I stopped at the desk and told Joyce to let Sydney know that I had arrived.

The receptionist smiled and handed me the keys.

"Dr. Edelman told me you would be stopping by for these," she said. "Both of the doctors are in surgery for at least another hour."

I thanked her and left to go to Sydney's apartment and twiddle my thumbs until the movers showed up. I knew I was probably being unfair, but I felt I was being used. It wasn't a good feeling.

I had only been at the apartment for a few minutes when the movers showed up. They were both tall and lanky. I didn't think either of them looked capable of lifting more than fifty pounds, but I was wrong. They went about their business like a couple of human machines, wrapping heavy quilted material around every piece of furniture. The contents of every drawer was packed into boxes and labeled. Heavy cardboard wardrobes housed closet contents. The men loaded everything into the truck without breaking a sweat. The apartment was empty except for a few items in the refrigerator, so I took the liberty of committing those to a trash bag and depositing it in the garbage chute.

I went to Sydney's new house to oversee the movers unload her possessions and to make sure the furniture was unharmed. While I wasn't thrilled about inspecting each piece, I understood why Sydney found it necessary. She owned only high end furniture.

By the time I got home, I had worked myself into a real snit. Sydney would be arriving, suitcase in hand shortly, and I needed to seem happy about it. We were an item. I cared deeply for her, and I was sure she hadn't intended to overstep her bounds. I might have been equally presumptuous had I been in her shoes. Partners should always be willing to help one another.

I was drinking a lite beer while reading my email when Sydney arrived. She wore a tired smile, but her eyes were bright the way they look when she's happy to see me. They almost look like they are smiling at the sight of me, and that makes me melt.

She set her suitcase down just inside the door. I embraced her and delivered a welcoming kiss. She returned the kiss, making it pretty damn special.

"Let's get your things put away, then go someplace casual for dinner," I suggested.

"Sounds like a plan," she said.

I carried the huge suitcase into my bedroom and opened it on the tufted bench at the foot of my bed. Then, I showed her the drawers I had emptied and the satin hangers I had bought for her side of the closet.

"This is perfect, Matt. Thanks for letting me invade your space. It means a lot to me."

I brought her a glass of chardonnay while she unpacked and got everything stowed out of sight.

She had changed into shorts and a tee shirt with *I am woman, hear me roar* scripted across the front when she appeared in the kitchen. She was barefoot, and I thought she looked adorable.

"Do I presume you don't plan to wear shoes to dinner?" I grinned.

"You may if I have my way about where we dine."

"And where might that be?"

"How about right here? Would you be willing for us to order a pizza and be couch potatoes? I'm pretty beat."

I hadn't considered that possibility, but it sounded good to me. Lounging around at home after being out of sorts might be just the ticket.

I envisioned the two of us sharing a pizza and a bottle of wine while watching a rom com on my big screen, then getting cozy on the couch. We would look at one another, laughing and rolling our eyes at the inevitable innuendos being thrown into the dialogue.

I knew that all of my ill feelings about this roommate thing would disappear as we made our way to the bedroom with my arm around Sydney's waist. But I must have been having a pipe dream, because we never left the couch. About halfway through the movie Sydney began snoring loudly.

I was bummed all over again as I lifted her dead weight and carried her to my bedroom. She was so out of it that I deposited her on the clean sheets fully clothed and turned out the light.

Chapter Twenty-eight

Sydney came downstairs rubbing her eyes and looking embarrassed. She was wearing the shorts and tee shirt she had slept in.

"Did I pass out?" she asked.

"You were really tired," I said, opening my arms for her to walk into them.

"Oh, Matt, I'm so sorry. First, I invite myself to spend the night, then I nix your dinner suggestion, and for the finale I pass out on your couch."

"Forget it, Sydney. The breakfast cook is about to show off. Are you hungry?"

The amazing Sydney Edelman switched gears in a flash, and it led me to believe she would be capable of doing just that if we had a spat. She might be hurt or angry, but she could be forgiving and loving a minute later.

"I'm starved. Let me go brush my teeth so I can give the cook a proper good morning kiss before breakfast," she said with an impish grin.

We were back on an even keel. I was at a loss as to why I had felt used yesterday, and I was looking forward to spending much more time with Sydney. I was willing to help her with hanging artwork or anything else she might need me to do beginning tomorrow. She was excited about her new house.

After breakfast we shared the kitchen cleanup. Then, I went to my office to check my email and my calendar while Sydney readied herself for work. I was pleased that she didn't spend a lot of time getting ready and that she looked like a million bucks when she came downstairs to kiss me goodbye.

After she left, I couldn't resist going upstairs to see what kind of condition she had left the bathroom. She had used a squeegee on the glass wall of the shower, hung up her towel, and put away her cosmetics. She had also made the bed. The woman was awesome.

I was a happy man when I went downstairs to begin my work day. I only had one client scheduled before noon. The guy had some kind of grievance with his neighbor regarding an easement which the neighbor claimed to have on my client's property. I assumed our meeting wouldn't take long. He could tell me the problem, and I would take a few notes. This sort of issue shouldn't take much time, and I was virtually certain the case would land on the *small potatoes* list.

I was playing a game of blackjack on my cell when the office phone rang. It was Mary Grace. She was calling to let me know that her mother had a medical problem and that she needed to take her to her doctor.

"Thanks for calling, Mary Grace. This is not a problem. There isn't anything for you to do today except look pretty and answer the phone. Take good care of your mother. I'll see you Monday."

Just as I hung up the phone, Trudy called.

"Good mornin' my sweet boy. I hope you're busy rakin' in lots of money."

"As a matter of fact, I'm not very busy. What are you up to?"

"I'm callin' to remind you about our dinner date this Sunday. I just called your Doctor Edelman and invited her. She accepted the invitation. Ya'll plan on arrivin' at six o'clock for hors d'oeuvres and a little libation. That'll give us a chance to get acquainted before dinner.

"I accept your kind invitation. Doctor Edelman and I will see you then."

This was going to be a busy weekend. Joe Bob, his lady love and her little girl were going to get to know each other up close and personal. Sydney and I would spend Saturday working in her new house, then join Trudy and Mister Hardaway for Sunday dinner.

I still wondered what had happened to Bernie Zuckerman. I had driven all over town twice in an attempt to spot his car with no success. I wasn't sure why he occupied my mind. He was a grown man and didn't need me to babysit him. He could have gone on some wild goose chase in search of his child, or he might have just decided to get away from Martinsville for a few days. Trying to come up with reasonable scenarios hadn't helped, so I hit his number on speed dial.

"You've reached Bernie Zuckerman. I can't come to the phone right now. Please leave your name and number, and I'll get back to you."

"Bernie, Matt here. You seem to have dropped out of sight. Are you okay? Give me a call."

The ball was in Bernie's court. I didn't know anything else I could do to locate him, so I made myself put him out of my mind following Trudy's advice when I was about to embark on my college career: If there is nothing you can do about a situation, drop it like a hot potato.

It turned out that I was right on point regarding my new client. Our meeting didn't last but a half hour, and it wouldn't take but a few minutes to drive to the courthouse and check for the existence of the claimed easement. It should be easy to learn which one of them needed to move his fence. No doubt this would be a quick fix but only peanuts for yours truly.

I was on my way to the courthouse when I saw Fred Peyton walking down the street. He appeared to be paying close attention as to where he placed each foot. I had never noticed anything unusual about his gait. He was so strange that I thought he might be playing some sort of game, like making sure he didn't step on a crack or something equally as weird.

I pulled to the curb and put down my window.

"Hey, Fred, can I give you a lift?"

He turned around and came over to my car.

"Hi, Matt," he said.

"Hop in," I said. "I'll drive you to Joe Bob's garage."

Fred opened the door and settled himself in the passenger seat.

"Not goin' there," he said. "Don't work there now."

It hit me that he had just strung a few words together instead of leaving a lone word hanging in midair with no explanation.

"Why aren't you still working at the garage, Fred?"

"Quit. Not enough money. "Where you goin', Matt?"

"I'm on my way to the courthouse."

"I'll go with you. Fred'll work for you."

"You can't work for me, Fred. I'm a lawyer. I don't need anyone to sweep or anything like that."

"I can do other stuff."

Since I wasn't in a big hurry, I decided to dig into learning what kinds of things Fred had been doing and who he had been doing them for before Joe Bob hired him.

"How about a milkshake, Fred. I'm not in a hurry."

Fred nodded and grinned.

I took us through a drive-thru at a fast food establishment and ordered a couple of chocolate shakes, then parked in the shade of a live oak at the back of the parking lot.

Fred puckered his lips and sucked the thick liquid into his mouth and swallowed. He looked at me and gave me a thumbs up before going back to sucking.

"Fred, if you don't mind my asking, how much money did you make an hour before you went to work for Joe Bob?"

"Not the same money for everything."

"I see. What were some of the jobs? Which one paid the most?"

Fred seemed to have a hard time deciding which job deserved the most pay. He rolled his eyes as he pulled on the straw.

"I think the pet," he said at last.

"What about the pet? Whose pet are you talking about?"

Fred ignored those questions and returned to the previous one.

"Maybe the snake. Not sure." He nodded at the milkshake. "This is good."

"Who paid you for doing those jobs?"

"Thanks, Matt," Fred said, and got out of the car.

That was as far as Fred Peyton was going to let me push him. The milkshake bribe hadn't helped much, but it hit a hot button in my mind. Fred had mentioned the words *pet* and *snake* at Joe Bob's garage. It told me that he might be connected to the threats at Bernie's home. I made up my mind to find the connection.

I put my trip to the courthouse on hold and headed to Joe Bob's garage.

My friend was wiping grease from his hands with a rag that looked like it couldn't possibly help.

"What's the latest, counselor?"

"Two things. Number one, Bernie's not answering his cell;

and two, I just had a chat with your ex employee. He told me he quit working here because he wanted more money."

"Neither one of them tells me somethin' I didn't already know. Looks like Bernard's gone off the grid and don't want our help. And as for Fred, he's just bein' Fred. He's whinin' for more money."

"Fred was actually speaking in sentences, not just throwing out a single word every now and then. He wouldn't tell me who he had worked for, but that he did different jobs some of which paid more than others. When I asked him which job paid the most, he first said *pet,* but later he said it could have been *snake.*"

Joe Bob scrubbed a big dirty hand across the stubble on his chin and shook his head.

"I know this sounds far-fetched," I said, "but don't you remember that the pet rabbit disappeared from Bernie's backyard, and that a dead snake was coiled just outside his door?"

"Do you mean you think Fred got paid by somebody to scare Bernard?"

"It's a thought."

"Yeah, I reckon so, but Bernard thinks his ex did it. I can't see her even gittin' within ten feet of Fred Peyton."

"I agree, but she could have hired a middle man."

"Yeah, I guess. Listen, I can't think about Bernard right now. I want to git home and pay Lucy for sprucin' up my doublewide. Lauren and Annie'll be here tomorrow mornin', and I want everthing to be perfect."

"Okay. I hope you and the little girl hit it off. You being such a charmer, I'm sure you will."

I drove to the courthouse after leaving Joe Bob. My research didn't take long, but my client wasn't going to be happy. The dispute over the claimed easement turned out to be in the neighbor's favor. My client could have easily made a trip to the courthouse and found this out for himself. Maybe he thought an attorney might be able to find a loophole.

I didn't know how much actual work would be involved at Sydney's house, so I made the executive decision to dine at home tonight in case we needed to get an early start tomorrow. I stopped by the butcher shop and picked up a couple of steaks to grill. It would be a no-frills dinner and an early evening.

I was about to unlock my front door with the package of steaks under my arm and a bottle of wine in my left hand while fiddling with the key when I saw a car pull up to the curb in my peripheral vision. I turned to get a better look and nearly dropped the bottle of wine.

Bernie Zuckerman exited his Cadillac and strode up the walk to my law office. I had seen this man frustrated many times, but I had never seen him appear so disheveled. He had always been clean shaven and buttoned up. I stopped working with the key and stared at him open-mouthed.

In lieu of a greeting, Bernie stood facing me. He took off his glasses, pulled a handkerchief from his back pocket, and wiped his face.

"Bernie, where in the world have you been? You disappeared without a trace. I've searched high and low for you, and you haven't bothered to answer your phone."

Bernie took the key from me and unlocked the door. He followed me inside and closed the door behind him. I waited for him to say something—anything.

"Put your stuff away. I'll wait in your office," he said.

I followed his orders, then joined him in my office.

"I've been several places doing some business."

"Are you okay? You look like you've been sleeping on a park bench."

"I guess this is how one looks if he simply doesn't give a shit about anything."

"This is not you, Bernie. You do care about things. You care a great deal about finding your child, and I think you care about your friends. You care about your business."

"Matt, I've pretty much given up on finding Claire. The people who are supposed to be conducting the search are sitting on their hands. Nobody's even gotten in touch with me to give me an update."

"Have you called them back?"

"No, and I'm not going to. That ship has sailed."

I couldn't believe what I was hearing.

"I just left Lee Ann's house," Bernie said. "I've been to see her a few times; not because I wanted to, but because I felt obligated to make sure she was okay. Don't ask me why, because I don't know. On a previous visit I informed her that you were the person she hit. She hadn't known until I told her. She asked me to tell you that she was texting at the time of the accident. She voiced no remorse; didn't offer an apology."

"I didn't expect an apology. She never enjoyed being in my company. Is she expected to fully recover?"

"That's what the doctors are telling her, so I assume it's true. She told me that she plans to move back to Philly. She said she never felt that she fit in here."

Bernie had come to me with a heavy heart, and I couldn't brush him off. I had a little time before Sydney would close for the day, and I wanted to give my old friend a chance to vent.

"What do you say you and I head out to that old tavern on the outskirts of town and have a couple of beers?"

Bernie sighed. "You just told me I look like hell warmed over, and I know that's true. I shouldn't be seen in public."

"Nobody we know frequents that place, and it'll be pretty quiet this time of day. Tuck in your shirt and let's go."

Bernie seemed to have calmed down a bit since he got to my place. He offered a tentative smile, stuffed his shirt into his pants, and we walked out the door.

The only thing I learned during our two beer conversation at the tavern was that Bernie had been out of town for several days. I feared that if I pressed him to tell me where he had been that he would clam up completely, so I steered him in other directions. I told him about Joe Bob's expected house guests and that Sydney and I were going to be roommates for the next three weeks. He seemed to be back on planet earth by the time we parted.

Sydney must have closed up shop early, because I found her in my kitchen barefoot and clad in short shorts and a tee shirt putting together a salad.

"Where have you been, you gadabout?" she asked, opening her arms for a hug.

I walked into them and embraced her, avoiding the sharp knife she wielded with her right hand.

"Wow! We've barely made it to the roommate stage, and you're playing the nagging wife," I teased.

She kissed me on the cheek and smiled.

"I thought I should rehearse a little bit before the actual performance," she said.

I didn't know how I knew it, but I knew Sydney Edelman could never be a nag.

"I just had a couple of beers with Bernie Zuckerman," I told her. "I don't think I told you that he had dropped out of sight the last several days. I had been a bit concerned about him. He's one of my oldest friends."

"I don't recall the name. The only person you've mentioned

is Trudy Giles, the lady who invited us to Sunday dinner. She's delightful, by the way. I met her when she brought her little dog to my clinic. You were still in Denver at the time. Oh, and Joe Bob Kincaid, your friend who owns the garage."

"Bernie, Joe Bob, and I were inseparable when we were teenagers—three peas in a pod. After high school we went our separate ways, but as soon as I came back to Martinsville and found the two of them here, it felt like time had stood still. Bernie had married a girl from Philadelphia where he was originally from. I became a lawyer and married Beth. We were both from Martinsville, but we lived in Atlanta for the duration of our marriage. The one who was true to his roots was Joe Bob. He lost it when his parents were killed in an automobile crash. His uncle caught him as he was about to fall off the rails and delivered some tough love to his nephew, got him straightened out, and set him up in that garage. Joe Bob's a real success story. The boy's got plenty of money."

Sydney grinned and changed the subject. "Thanks for the update, counselor. I don't know about you, but I'm famished. I happened to see the butcher's stamp on the package in the fridge and took it out so it would be room temperature. I assume you plan to grill."

"I do. I also have a lovely bottle of wine I think will be to your liking."

"Do you have plans for the rest of the evening?"

"Yes ma'am. After this perfectly prepared dinner, I'm going to carry you up those stairs and make mad, passionate love to you."

"That's another of your fantastic ideas."

Chapter Twenty-nine

Saturday morning dawned bright and beautiful. Sydney beat me out of bed. She had showered and dressed before my feet hit the floor. The aroma of coffee caused me to hasten my morning ablutions, and I hurried down to the kitchen. Sydney was perched on a bar stool at the counter eating yogurt and checking email on her phone. She looked up as I came into the room.

"Good morning, sleepyhead," she said.

"You must have worn me out last night," I teased, crossing the room to kiss her.

"I made coffee, but since you're the chef, I waited for you to do your thing. I know how to boil water, but that's about all." She laughed.

"That's not a problem," I said. "I'll make breakfast while you tell me what's on the agenda for today."

As it turned out there was a lot more than I had expected. I had thought we would be hanging a few paintings and unpacking things like linens, maybe even some books. I hadn't counted on moving furniture, lugging heavy pieces up and down the stairs. I decided that the next time I agreed to help with some final touches, I would ask for specific details.

Sydney and I were both bone tired by the time we finished the heavy lifting and decided to leave the finishing touches for another day.

"I have a wonderful idea, Matt," she said.

I hoped her wonderful idea didn't entail any more physical exertion, and I looked at her with a raised eyebrow.

"Let's go to that little ice cream parlor for a cool fattening treat. We can go in our grubbies. Then, we can go home, shower, and take a nap."

None of this sounded one bit romantic, but that was fine with me. My energy gauge read *empty.*

As we drove past Joe Bob's garage, who should I see on the patch of grass to the left of the bay but the man himself down on all fours. A tiny girl dressed in western attire sat on his back as he crawled from one side of the grass patch to the other. The child grabbed her cowgirl hat and waved it in the air at her mother who sat in a canvas chair just inside the bay.

"Is that your friend Joe Bob?" asked Sydney.

I nodded. "It is, indeed. Looks like he's making points with his future family. He's asked that pretty girl sitting in the shade to marry him. That's her little girl."

"Wow! That's quite a commitment."

"I can't argue, but Joe Bob hasn't had a family except an uncle since his parents were killed in an automobile accident. This is what he told me he wants, and I wish him the best."

Sydney leaned over and kissed me on the cheek. And that was the way our weekend progressed. We had ice cream, we showered, and we took a nap. We ordered a pizza for dinner and we both fell asleep on the couch watching an old movie. I awoke in the middle of the night, and once again, carried Sydney up the stairs to bed. Things weren't going exactly the way I'd had in mind.

Sunday morning as I was making breakfast, I had a fleeting thought of accepting Mark Winters's invitation to visit his flock and take Sydney along for the ride to get a small dose of religion. Mark seemed like a nice guy, and Sydney and I had never discussed our religious beliefs. It would warm Trudy's heart if she saw her *sweet boy* back in church on a Sunday morning.

Sydney seemed a bit taken aback when I issued the invitation over bacon and eggs. She appeared to mull it over for a minute, taking a sip of coffee, then smiling.

"That's a wonderful idea, Matt. Lets."

Since the church was just down the street, Sydney and I walked to the service. Upon entering the building, we each received a bulletin from an overly friendly member of the flock who stood just inside the door.

"Good morning," he said. "We're so glad you're here to worship with us on this glorious Lord's Day. Welcome to Calvary Methodist."

"Thank you," we said in unison and went into the sanctuary to find seats.

Visitors never want to sit close to the front, and I steered Sydney toward a comfortable distance from the altar close to the middle of the pews. I spotted Trudy and Mister Hathaway across the aisle as we walked past them and deliberately went a couple of more rows toward the front so Trudy would be sure to see us. I turned and nodded in their direction just before taking my seat. Trudy beamed.

Trudy had told me that Beth was always perched on the first pew just in front of the pulpit, and I tried to spot the back of her head as unobtrusively as possible. I must have been craning my neck from one side to the other in that pursuit because Sydney delivered a ladylike elbow and a disapproving look.

Minutes later the whispers ceased, a deacon took the pulpit to welcome everyone, and announcements were made. The congregation stood and joined the choir director in singing the Doxology. Then, came the inevitable part of the service—the offering. I never begrudged contributing because I knew it was for a good cause. I recalled setting aside a tithe from my allowance when I was a child to help orphans and missionaries, and felt myself smile at the memory.

After the choir's special music, a couple of congregational hymns, and a prayer, Mark Winters took his place at the pulpit. I was impressed from the very beginning of his sermon. The young preacher got his message across in a convincing manner. He was neither a screamer nor a fist pounder like several ministers I had been exposed to over the years.

After the benediction, Mark made his way to the back of the sanctuary to shake hands with the congregation as they exited. He donned a huge smile as he shook my hand.

"Glad to see you finally made it, Matt," he said, "and who is this lovely lady?"

"Reverend Winters, meet Sydney Edelman. Sydney runs the animal clinic here in town."

"I'm happy to meet you, Sydney," Mark said, "and Matt, you can drop the reverend. Mark's fine. I hope to see you both again soon."

"I enjoyed the sermon," Sydney said as we strolled back to my place. "I thought you told me the minister was dating Beth."

"He was. He told me so one day when he stopped by my office to introduce himself and invite me to visit his church. Maybe that's changed. I didn't see her this morning, but let's not spoil our day by discussing my ex. How would you like to spend the day until we go to our dinner date?"

"I'd like to tackle some of the unpacking at my house if you're up to it. I promise I won't ask you to move any more furniture."

I was relieved that she added the promise and agreed. Hanging pictures and unpacking a few dishes was a snap compared to the heavy lifting. I wasn't the least bit tired when we went back to my place to dress for dinner.

Sydney charmed our hostess and Mister Hathaway over cocktails in my mother's living room. It made me realize that she would be poised and at ease in most any situation. It delighted Sydney to see that Trudy had brought along the half-grown kitten.

"What did you name her?" she asked, bending down to scoop the kitten from the floor and lift it onto her lap to pet.

"Princess," said Trudy, "because that's what she is. She makes the rules and she's trained me pretty well."

Trudy had outdone herself with another of her fabulous meals, and I deemed the evening near perfect. We learned that Mister Hathaway was a retired real estate broker. He had worked for a prestigious company in Atlanta for his entire career until his retirement ten years ago. His wife's life was claimed by cancer shortly after that, and he wanted to leave the city in search of an entirely different kind of environment. He had visited several small towns before he ended up in this little burg.

I recognized Bernie's Cadillac in the beams of my headlights as I made a left turn onto my street. It was parked at the curb in front of my building. I couldn't imagine why he would show up at ten o'clock on a Sunday evening without calling to see if I was at home. I gave Sydney a door key and told her that I would join her shortly.

Bernie was slumped behind the wheel and appeared to be asleep. I tapped on his window to rouse him, thinking that I was about to hear another whiny sob story about something that he expected me to fix. He straightened up and motioned for me to get into the car to talk. It had been such a nice Sunday, and I had a feeling that he was about to ruin it. I slid into the passenger seat and waited for him to explain why he was here.

"Hey, Matt."

"Bernie."

"I've come to tell you that you won't be seeing much more of me. I've lined up a realtor and I'm putting my house on the market. The guy who's been managing my business wants to buy it. I've decided to move back to Philly; not because of Lee Ann. This has nothing to do with her."

I was stunned. I stared at him in disbelief. He wore a determined expression with his jaw set at a sharp angle as if he was daring me to try to disabuse him of the notion.

"Well, say something!"

"You've caught me completely off guard, Bernie. I don't know what to say. If you've made up your mind to make this move, I can only assume you've given it a lot of thought."

"I have. I just wanted to tell you before Martinsville's grapevine beat me to it."

"I appreciate that, Bernie. You know I wish you the best. I'll miss you."

We shook hands, and I walked out of Bernard Zuckerman's life just as he was about to walk out of mine. He had always been something of a pain, but we had been friends since we were kids. We weren't kids anymore, and each of us had to choose his personal path of the fork in the road.

It was hard for me to fall asleep even with Sydney curled up beside me. It felt so right having her close, sleeping peacefully. So why couldn't I get the thought of Bernie's departure out of my mind? I wondered if he would tell Joe Bob of his decision in person. I was sure I'd find out tomorrow.

It had been an event packed weekend involving my close circle of friends, but everything seemed to slow to a crawl come Monday morning. Sydney and I were back at our jobs, Trudy had returned to her little house with the cat, and I assumed that Joe Bob was back in his mechanic's coveralls instead of crawling around in the grass on all fours.

Mary Grace attacked the secretarial work I had amassed to keep her busy. She was as prim and proper as ever and seemed to enjoy her job. I hoped to have a chance to introduce her to Sydney, but because of their schedules, the opportunity had thus far not presented itself.

The new hire had completed the work I had given her by lunchtime, and I let her know that if she chose to return in the afternoon she would only be needed to answer the phone and take messages.

I couldn't resist driving to Joe Bob's garage to see if he was free for lunch. I wanted to learn how his weekend went with Lauren and her daughter, and I was curious to know if Bernie had paid him a visit to tell him that he planned to leave Martinsville. Knowing how at odds he and Joe Bob were at least half the time, I would have bet against it. I parked on the street and walked to the bay.

There was an old Chevy up on the lift, and Joe Bob stood directly beneath it. He appeared to be studying the car's underside and didn't seem the least bit upset when a stream of dirty oil dripped onto his face. He must have felt my presence, because he swiped a rag across his face and kept studying the oil leak as he greeted me.

"Hey, Matt, what's the latest?"

"It looks like you're in the middle of something pretty important. I can come back later."

"I'm ready for a break," he said, easing out from under the car. "This old junker's not worth fixin', but I'll sell the guy a new oil pan. He's been comin' to me for the last few years to put on one Band-Aid at a time."

"I just came by to see if you might want to go to lunch and tell me how your weekend went."

"It was great, Matt. I'm almost as much in love with that little girl as I am with her mother. I can't wait to marry Lauren and adopt Annie. I've never felt like this."

"That's fantastic. Have you set a date for the wedding?"

"No. I've decided to leave that up to Lauren. I don't want her to rush into this with any misgivin's."

"How about lunch? Are you hungry?"

"Yeah. Let's go to the Dump. I can go in these duds."

Over burgers and beers I asked if he had heard from Fred. He had not. Then, I hit him with the big question: "Has Bernie been by lately?"

"No. Why?"

I shouldn't have brought it up, because it was possible that I was jumping the gun. Maybe Bernie hadn't had a chance to let Joe Bob in on his plan.

"No reason," I lied, taking a giant bite of my burger.

"You don't ask questions like that for no reason. What's goin' on?"

I swallowed and felt heat creep up my neck and onto my face.

"Bernie came to see me last night after ten o'clock—just showed up without warning."

"Yeah?"

"He told me he's putting his house on the market and selling his business to move back to Philadelphia."

"You've gotta be kiddin'. I heard that his ex wuz doin' that. I told you he still had the hots for that evil woman."

"He told me the move didn't have anything to do with her.

He said he had given up on finding his child; that he didn't know anywhere else to get help finding her. Of course, he could stay in touch with the FBI from anywhere. I guess he just wants to get away from all the ghosts and start over."

After we finished our lunch, we drove by Bernie's house. There was a FOR SALE sign in the front yard, so we assumed that he meant business. As we continued down the street, we passed the little park where Juanita used to take Claire. There was a big burly Hispanic guy sitting on a bench. He seemed to be watching the small children play while their mothers and nursemaids sat on shaded benches talking and laughing.

"Slow down, Matt."

Joe Bob didn't tell me why he gave the order, but I eased up on the gas.

"See that guy on the bench at the edge of the park?"

"Yeah. What about him. Just a guy sitting on a bench."

"I don't think he's just any guy. Remember that day we saw some big guy arguing with Juanita? They wuz really goin' at it, stabbin' fingers at each other. That guy sittin' over there looks like the one we saw."

"The only thing I recall about that guy was that he looked too big to have been Bernie."

Joe Bob shrugged, letting the subject drop, but I had the feeling he would be doing some investigating on his own. He could be like a pitbull when he felt the need to prove himself right.

Bernie was still on my mind as I dropped Joe Bob off at the garage and drove back to my office. Martinsville had been his home since he was a teenager, but he'd had it pretty rough the last few years. Joe Bob and I had found out by accident what a despicable person his ex was. She was not only spoiled and selfish; she was unfaithful to the man who adored her. She broke his heart and then stepped on it. But the thing which killed his spirit was losing his little girl and being impotent to do anything about it. Maybe he was making the right move.

Sydney didn't question me about Bernie's late night visit. She didn't know what was going on, but she knew I would tell her when I was ready. She wasn't one to hand out free advice, but if it was requested, I knew she would give me her honest opinion.

Seeing that sign in Bernie's yard sealed his decision to leave Martinsville behind. I wondered if he would find happiness in Philadelphia. He had left that city a long time ago. It must have changed dramatically over the years, just like my hometown. I fell asleep with my arm lying across Sydney's waist, breathing in the sweet smell of her floral shampoo and feeling like a lucky man. I had left thoughts of Bernie Zuckerman before climbing the stairs but I knew they would be front and center to greet me at first light.

Chapter Thirty

I was sitting at my desk staring at the screensaver on my computer and came to the realization that my two closest friends from high school and I were about to lose our status as a trio. We wouldn't be meeting at Morgan's for a cold brew or to solve the world's problems over dinner. Bernie wouldn't be here to carp and complain about something Joe Bob had said. Joe Bob wouldn't have time for the likes of me because he would be spending most of the time with his new family.

I hadn't come back to my hometown simply to escape Denver or because Sydney Edelman was important to me. Granted, those were the main reasons, but having a couple of old friends here had helped cement my decision.

Sydney made me feel alive. My divorce from Beth had left an unspeakable void which I tried to fill by moving to a new city, making new acquaintances, dating people who meant nothing to me. I was just passing time in Denver. Sydney was everything I wanted in a mate. In addition to her good looks and sparkling personality, she had a successful business she loved. She provided a service this small town needed, and it was obvious that she didn't miss city life.

My phone rang, breaking the silence.

"Good mornin', my sweet boy."

"Good morning to you, culinary queen. What are you up to so early?"

"I was just wonderin' if you had a good time grillin' Mister Hathaway."

"I did have a lovely time at your dinner party. I wasn't grilling Mister Hathaway; just making sure he was worthy of your company. I think you know I'm pretty protective of you. I've loved you since I was a baby. There's nothing wrong with learning about a person's background."

Trudy laughed. "You're right, Matty, but give old Trudy a little credit. I'm pretty good at readin' people. If I hadn't known Mister Hathaway was a good man, I would never have allowed him into your mama's house. You ought to know that."

"He seems to be a very nice person, and you have my blessing."

"That's a load off my mind," Trudy joked. "By the way, I know why we didn't see Elizabeth in church Sunday mornin'."

"Why?"

"I heard there's a new doctor in town. He's a hotshot surgeon, and guess who has her cap set for him. She must have dropped our sweet little preacher like a hot potato. That girl's got a real mean streak."

"I've known that for a long time. I like Mark Winters. He's lucky to have escaped her clutches this early."

"I won't keep you, Matty. I know you're busy. I just wanted to tease you a little bit. Old Trudy's in such a good mood. Mister Hathaway and I made a lunch date for twelve o'clock today. He wants to take me to one of the new fancy restaurants. This housekeeper's movin' uptown."

"Good for you. I hope you have a fabulous time. Call me anytime you want to crow."

"I will. Bye bye, my sweet boy."

After our call ended, I couldn't help thinking that another person who was a big part of my inner circle might be about to make a significant change. I wanted nothing more than for Trudy to be happy. She was my dearest friend.

I couldn't sit around wondering about the paths my friends' lives might take. I had work to do. My client base was growing by leaps and bounds by Martinsville's standards. It had gotten to the point that I was almost ready to offer Mary Grace a full-time position.

As if on cue, my part-time employee walked through the door looking fresh-scrubbed and ready to work.

"Good morning, Mister Stevenson."

"Good morning, Mary Grace. I have quite a bit of dictation for you this morning. Would you like something to drink before we get started?"

"No, thank you."

The young woman took a seat in one of the two chairs in front of my desk with her steno pad and pencil at the ready. She never looked up while I dictated and kept her pencil flying across the pad the way her fingers did on her computer. This girl was a keeper.

I left Mary Grace to do her work and took off for the courthouse. I had two cases before lunch. As I walked across the marble tiled floor of the main hall, I thought it felt pretty good being a lawyer in a small town—a fairly big fish in a little pond.

I dispensed with both of the cases early, so I drove over to kill a little time with Joe Bob. I was surprised to see Fred sweeping out the bay.

"Hey, Fred, are you working for Joe Bob again?"

Fred nodded. "He's in there." He nodded toward the office.

My old friend sat behind his desk wearing a smile that showed most of his teeth. His expression told me that he was about to crack Fred wide open with just a few bucks.

"You look like you just won the lottery," I said. "Give."

"Freddie Boy's got secrets, and I'm about to find out what they are."

"Exactly how do you plan to do that?"

"I'll have to catch him off guard. You know he almost makes sentences now. He don't just say one word so you have to guess what he's tryin' to git across. I've got a list of the words he's spit out one at a time."

"How are you going to catch him off guard?"

"I'll have to listen to him while he works. You know he used to hum while he worked. If he starts stringin' words together, he makes some little sentences now. He might start singin' in sentences instead of hummin'. Use your imagination, Matthew."

"What is it that you think your strange detective work will explain?"

"I'm hopin' it'll tell me who Fred worked for before I hired him and why some of the jobs paid more than others. All I've got right now is a lot of question marks."

"Well, good luck with your plan. I don't suppose you'd be interested in joining me for lunch."

"That's not a bad idea. This conversation's frustratin' me; makin' me crave a cigarette. Maybe eatin' somethin' that's bad for my health'll stop the cravin'." He laughed. "Give me a minute to wash the grease off and lose these coveralls."

I took the opportunity to observe Fred while Joe Bob spiffied up. He had stopped sweeping and turned his attention to stacking and re-stacking tires. I walked into the bay where he was doing his busywork.

"How's the job going, Fred?"

"Gotta stay busy. Got a raise. Can't stand around doin' nothin'."

"Has Joe Bob given you important jobs to do? Is that the reason he gave you a raise?"

Fred stopped stacking tires and scratched his head, looking confused.

"No."

"The person you worked for before, was it a man or a woman?"

"Never worked for no woman!"

"Oh. Did the man you worked for give you important jobs?"

Fred grinned. "Yeah."

Joe Bob came into the bay, and that ended the conversation.

"The place looks real nice, Fred," Joe Bob said. "You can take the rest of the day off."

Fred left the garage without any kind of farewell and started down the street humming.

"If you had been about a minute later getting here, I might have gotten some information out of Fred. I found out that his previous boss was a man. He seemed offended that I thought it might have been a woman, so that means we can rule out Lee Ann for sure."

"Good work, Sherlock. Let's go eat."

We went to the diner and were seated at a table by a window. We were both studying menus when Joe Bob's head jerked up with a start.

"Here comes Bernard," he said. "I thought he left town."

"It takes time to relocate. He's probably tying up loose ends before he goes."

Joe Bob followed Bernie with his eyes as he walked toward the diner door. Bernie came inside. He didn't look left or right as he was being led past our table.

"Hey, Bernard," Joe Bob said, "pull up a chair."

Bernie turned at the invitation, looking like he'd been running from the scene of a crime. It was clear to me that he was trying to rearrange his facial expression into something other than guilt.

I pulled out a chair, and he reluctantly sat down, looking embarrassed. He was finally able to conjure a half-smile.

"My mind must have been somewhere else," he said. "I didn't see you guys."

"I'm glad you happened by," Joe Bob said. "I hear you're thinkin' about goin' back up north."

I hadn't bothered getting into the conversation.

"I reckon you got a great job offer," Joe Bob said.

Bernie fidgeted in his chair without responding.

"Have you two ordered?" he asked.

"No," I said, "but I'm ready."

I handed him my menu and took in the cold look he shot at me. He knew I'd told Joe Bob his secret. We ordered, and I tried to think of something else to talk about, but failed. If Bernie had wanted Joe Bob to know his plans and the reason for the move, he would have told him.

It was obvious that Bernie wanted to get out of there in the worst way.

"You'll have to excuse me, guys," he said. "I just remembered something I have to do."

He threw a few bills on the table and left the diner. I didn't understand why he was willing to join us in the first place. Maybe he didn't know how to refuse the offer. I assumed Bernie was embarrassed that I had told Joe Bob about his visit to me but that he hadn't afforded Joe Bob the same courtesy. None of it made sense. I looked at Joe Bob and shrugged.

"Bernard ain't changed much, has he?"

"He's always been hard to read," I said.

"Moody—that's how I'd describe him. One minute he might be laughin' and jokin'; the next second he could be cursin' and cryin' in his beer. I never understood him. I tried to like the guy, but you know he never made it easy. Can't say I'll miss him too much."

"Well, there's no point in beating a dead horse," I said. "Here comes the waitress with our lunch."

Joe Bob had meant it when he had let me know he planned to consume another unhealthy meal. He went through a plate of fried chicken, a glob of mashed potatoes with gravy which could have fed both of us, and fried okra. He heaved a contented sigh after cleaning his plate and rubbed his stomach in appreciation.

"That hit the spot," he said.

"Are you still craving a cigarette?"

"Yeah, a little, but I'll tell myself I'm not. I don't plan to ever smoke another one."

Joe Bob went back to the garage, and I returned to my law office. Mary Grace was sitting at her desk waiting for the phone to ring. She looked up from the novel she had been reading.

"You've had a couple of phone calls," she said. "The messages are on your desk."

She had written the time each call had come in. I didn't recognize the name of the first caller, but returned his call first. He told me that he was a friend of Joe Bob Kincaid's and that he needed a lawyer to help settle an insurance matter for his small business. So, one more pebble in the pitcher to raise the water level for Matthew Stevenson, Esq.

The second call was from Marcus Hathaway. After identifying himself, he suggested that I take a seat. That scared me so badly that I did just that. For some reason, I was afraid he was about to tell me that something terrible had happened to Trudy.

"What is it, Mister Hathaway?"

"You sound like you might want to take a deep breath, son," he said. "I would prefer to have this conversation in person, but I find myself a bit anxious to be done with it."

"I'm listening."

The older gentleman took an audible breath.

"I just escorted a most charming lady home after enjoying her company over lunch at an elegant restaurant. I know you are very well acquainted with the lovely lady."

"I assume you're referring to my dear friend, Gertrude Giles, but why are you telling me this?"

"My dear young man, I'm telling you this because your dear friend has captured my heart. I want to marry her if she'll have me."

Chapter Thirty-one

Marcus Hathaway's news hit me like a pail of ice water. I wanted real happiness for Trudy as much as I wanted it for myself. Mister Hathaway seemed to be a wonderful companion for her, and I was delighted that he cared so much for her. But marriage—this was a huge step for someone who had not had a mate in a very long time.

I told Mister Hathaway that he was a lucky man and stopped there. I did not give him my blessing. I assumed that he had approached me because he felt it would behoove him to do so, and I admit that I appreciated the fact that he came to me before popping the question. I wondered how Trudy would respond.

I shut down my law office early to go shopping for supplies to make dinner for Sydney. I knew from past experience that I could pull off a mean beef stroganoff. That, paired with a nice Bordeaux would probably get me points with my lovely roommate.

On the way to make my purchases I couldn't help but notice that there was a banner spanning the front of Bernie's dry cleaning business bearing the name of the new owner in large letters. It appeared that his day manager had indeed bought the business, or was at least in the process. And since I had seen a FOR SALE sign in front of Bernie's house, I assumed that soon there wouldn't be a trace of Bernie Zuckerman left in Martinsville, Tennessee.

The more I thought about Bernie's plan to leave town permanently, something about it nagged at my mind. I was actually thinking more about Joe Bob than Bernie. Joe Bob was what Trudy would call a soft hearted person. I made up my mind to make sure the three of us had a chance to say proper goodbyes. We needed to part on a positive note.

As soon as I put away my dinner supplies, I called Joe Bob.

"Kincaid here."

"Hey, Joe Bob, I've been thinking. Bernie's leaving town, and we'll probably never cross paths with him again. I know you two have had your differences, but the three of us have been friends since we were kids. What do you say we invite him to join us for a round of golf before he leaves?"

There was only silence for several seconds.

"What makes you think he wants to spend time with me, Matt? He sure acted like he wanted to get away from my company at the diner. I felt like tellin' him to go piss up a rope."

"Trust me. He'll want to join us. He's just sad and confused."

"Okay, I'll go along with it, but you need to be the one to call him. He prob'ly won't answer his phone if he knows I'm callin' him."

"Deal. I'll track him down and make the offer."

"Let me know what he says. I can make a tee time whenever ya'll want to play."

"Will do."

I drove to Bernie's house and rang the bell. He was slow coming to the door, but he invited me in. The living room looked like a cyclone had hit it. Newspapers, a stack of mail, and the remains of last night's dinner on a paper plate told me he was pretty much living in this room. I nearly tripped over beer cans as I walked by the coffee table en route to the kitchen. Surely, he planned to get the house in shape to show before he allowed a prospective buyer to see it.

Bernie offered me a seat on a bar stool and dropped down on another one. I couldn't tell anything about his frame of mind by his facial expression.

"Bernie, are you sick?"

"No. Why?"

"You can't show the house until you get this mess cleaned up. What are you not telling me?"

He waved his arm in the direction of the living room in a dismissive gesture.

"I've just been covered up with all the things I have to do before I leave town. Don't worry about it."

"I understand that you have a lot of loose ends to tie up and that you have a million things on your mind, but do you think you could make time to play a round of golf with Joe Bob and me to say our farewells?"

Bernie rubbed a hand across his face and heaved a sigh.

"I'm not in a very playful mood," he said. "Whose idea was this?"

"It doesn't matter whose idea it was. The golf course is a nice place for friends to get together, and in this case, say our goodbyes."

"I suppose I can make time to play a round. When do you have in mind?"

"Joe Bob said he would make a tee time whenever it's convenient for you."

That wasn't exactly what Joe Bob had said, but it was close enough.

"I suppose Saturday morning would work."

"Great. I'll tell Joe Bob."

After I left Bernie's, I rushed home to prepare the romantic dinner that I had been planning to make for Sydney. It had been relegated to a back burner too many times, and I was determined to do it up right this evening.

I placed the ingredients for the menu on the counter, draped the table with my mother's best damask cloth, along with her china and crystal. Then, I added a floral centerpiece flanked by silver candlesticks sporting the decorative ivory candles I had purchased specifically for this occasion.

I finished the food preparation and had it ready to assemble. I planned to prepare the meal while Sydney and I sipped the champagne I had chilling.

I saw Sydney's car pull to the curb right behind mine, met her at the door, and opened it as she reached into her purse for a key.

"Hello, gorgeous, welcome to Chez Stevenson. I hope you're hungry."

Sydney smiled and delivered a chaste peck on my cheek. Then, she brushed past me and went straight to the dining area.

"What did I do to deserve such a welcome?" she asked, smiling.

"Just being Sydney merits whatever I can do to make you happy."

I popped the champagne cork and filled the flutes, then handed one to Sydney, brushing my lips over hers. I led her to a bar stool.

"I want you to sit here and sip champagne while I cook your dinner," I said, bowing.

Sydney smiled and took a sip.

"This is a real treat, Matt. What's the occasion?"

"In case you haven't noticed, I'm madly in love with you. I want to show you just how much. I want to give you your heart's desires. Tell me what you want and I'll do everything in my power to deliver."

This wasn't like me. I was sounding downright goofy. Sydney was smiling, and a tear tracked down her cheek. It took me a few seconds to realize that she was trying, without much success, to stifle a giggle at my ridiculous attempt to express my love.

Sometimes, the best way to get past an uncomfortable moment is simply to skip ahead as if it had never happened.

I touched my glass to hers and proceeded to make the meal. While the mushrooms toasted, I pulled the salad from the refrigerator and dressed it. Then, I proceeded to make the entrée step by step while Sydney looked on.

"Who taught you to cook, Matt?"

"I taught myself. My ex wife didn't cook. I never learned whether she didn't know how, or if she was just lazy."

"Well, I admire you, and it's very sweet of you to cook for me. Whatever you're making smells divine. What can I do to help?"

"Not a thing. Sit there and look pretty while I plate this. We're almost ready to eat."

Sydney oohed and aahed when I seated her. The candles cast a warm glow, and the wine paired perfectly with the impossible to-screw-up meal. Sydney never stopped smiling between bites.

We each talked about our busy days. Sydney told me that Joe Lawson's fiancé had gotten into town and landed a teaching position at the high school. I was happy for Joe since I learned that he had no romantic interest in Sydney. He seemed like a straight up guy. Joe and Joe Bob were just a stone's throw away from holy matrimony. It appeared that the love bug had bitten several people in this little southern town including Trudy's recent admirer.

Sydney wanted to know if I had anything exciting to tell her. My day had been pretty mundane. My getting involved in setting up a golf outing was the only thing worth telling her. I didn't understand why she would take umbrage at my involvement in such a thing, but she did.

"Why do you feel obligated to make sure those two engage in a peaceful parting? You're not responsible to make them behave like adults. Zuckerman's leaving town. That sounds like good riddance to me. Everything you've told me about him is derogatory. And I understand that this Joe Bob is your friend, but why should you have to hold his hand to make sure he feels good about himself?"

"Sydney, they're my oldest friends. I care about both of them. I would feel terrible if they parted on a sour note. You don't even know them. I don't see how you can have an informed opinion about either of them, and I don't understand why you should care if I'm involved. This isn't like you."

Sydney donned a weak smile and got up from the table. Then, she came and kissed me on the forehead.

"This was such a lovely gesture, Matt. The table is gorgeous and the meal was fantastic, but I have a raging headache." She headed for the stairs.

"But I have chocolate mousse," I called to her back.

I extinguished the pretty flames, cleared the table, and loaded the dishwasher thinking that my romantic dinner had been a complete disaster.

Sydney had made it abundantly clear that she'd had her fill of my company for the evening, so I bedded down on the couch. Tomorrow would be a brand new day.

And indeed it was. Sydney was all smiles and dressed for work when she came down for breakfast. I was making omelets when she came up behind me and put both arms around me.

"Good morning, my love," she cooed.

"Top o' the morning to you. Breakfast is almost ready."

And that's how it went. Neither of us mentioned last night's fiasco. We made small talk over breakfast, then began our workdays.

I stopped by Joe Bob's garage at lunch time. He told me that he had made our tee time for nine o'clock the next morning, and he seemed a little more amenable to getting together with Bernie for a farewell round of golf than he had been.

My next stop was at Bernie's house. He came to the door in a ratty pair of jeans and a dirty tee shirt.

"Hey, Matt. Come in if you can wade through the mess. I'm just working on making a wider path. I figure I can get rid of enough of this stuff by the end of the day so a cleaning crew can get in here and do their thing."

"Looks like you're making some headway. I brought a couple of sandwiches," I said, holding up a sack. "How about stopping for lunch, then I can help you bag some of this up before I go back to work."

Bernie nodded, and we headed to the kitchen. I thought he would have soft drinks or a couple of beers in the fridge, but I was mistaken. We had to settle for water to wash down our pulled pork sandwiches. Bernie was definitely getting ready to vacate the premises.

"Joe Bob made us a nine o'clock tee time for tomorrow morning," I said.

Bernie took a bite of his sandwich and chewed while staring at the ceiling. I couldn't tell what he was thinking.

"You know the golf course might not be the best place to say our goodbyes," he said. "I assume your idea for the three of us to get together was intended to say our goodbyes on a friendly note. Am I correct?"

"Sure. We've been friends for a long time. Wouldn't you like to bid one another farewell feeling good about our enduring friendship?"

"I'll tell you what I think. I think that's some fairy tale shit. We're grown men. If we get together at all, it should be in a place where we can be totally honest—a place where we can bare our souls if we want to. I'd like to be able to say what I want to say without being ridiculed. I'd like to leave Martinsville, Tennessee with a clean slate—tabula rasa. What do you think about that?"

"What I think is that you don't want this meeting to take place on a golf course where people are playing a game. I guess you want it to be a *come to Jesus moment*."

"That's the idea."

Bernie had been on a soapbox and had barely touched his lunch. He pushed his paper plate across the counter and stood up. I followed suit.

"Let's bag some of this trash. Then, I'd better get back to the office. I'll stop by Joe Bob's and let him know golf is off the table. Maybe we can come up with a better idea."

Bernie and I worked for nearly an hour, getting rid of beer and soft drink cans, paper plates, fast-food wrappers and Chinese food cartons. We put the stacks of mail on the kitchen counter. By the time we finished, we had four sacks of garbage to haul out to the curb.

"Thanks for your help, Matt. I've kind of been a mess lately. I'm ready to plot a new course. I can't stay in this town. I hope you understand."

"Sure, Bernie. I'm not going to question your motives. A guy's got to do what a guy's got to do. I'll get back to you after I talk with Joe Bob."

I hadn't changed my mind about the three of us getting together for a last goodbye, but truthfully, I was thinking the sooner Bernie left town, the better. His being here was just muddying the waters. Where Bernie was, there was usually turmoil.

Mary Grace handed me three phone messages as soon as I walked through the door. Two of them could wait, but the third was from Sydney. I called the clinic and learned that she was in surgery, so I left word that she could reach me on my cell phone.

I told Mary Grace that I needed to leave the office again and that there was nothing for her to do except play receptionist until four o'clock. Then, she should close for the day.

Joe Bob's feet stuck out from under a car, and Fred was doing his busywork, mumbling to himself. I greeted Fred, but he ignored me and started singing. I did my best to decipher some meaning from the words he was dropping in his rendition of an unidentifiable tune.

Joe Bob rolled out from under the car grinning.

"Hey, Matt. Saw your feet and recognized them fancy shoes."

I motioned with my chin for him to get up and follow me into his office. He nodded and wiped the grease from his hands as we left the bay.

"I think I might have understood some of Fred's lyrics," I said.

"Yeah?"

"I thought he said *big man, money, kid,* and *job*. None of that makes sense, but I'm pretty sure those were the words."

Joe Bob shook his head.

"Maybe we ought to come right out and ask him."

"I guess it's worth a try."

We returned to the bay, and Joe Bob walked over to Fred and tapped him on the shoulder. Fred turned to face him.

"Fred, what wuz that song you wuz just singin'?"

"Time to go," Fred said. He walked out of the bay and down the street.

"I reckon that's our answer. He ain't talkin'."

"Hey, I think I recall that you said you were going to do some detective work about the big guy we saw sitting on a bench at that little park. Do you know anything about him?"

"No. I've been kinda busy lately with Lauren, and I dropped the ball, but I'm not givin' up."

"Do you think the big guy in Fred's song might have something to do with the guy we saw in the park?"

"I reckon it could be. I'll keep my ear to the ground. Maybe he'll drop another word or two."

"The reason I'm here is to let you know that Bernie changed his mind about the round of golf. He told me that he would rather meet somewhere other than a golf course. I got the idea that he wants to get kind of personal with you and me. He also might want to rid his conscience regarding a thing or two. I'm not sure what he wants, but I know he wants it to be private among just the three of us. Might you have a suggestion?"

Joe Bob swiped a big hand across the back of his neck.

"I gotta tell you the truth, Matt. I think you might want to have this last goodbye meetin' more than I do. You might want it even more than Bernard."

"Maybe you're right, but are you willing to have it?"

"Anything for you, Matt Stevenson. How about I cancel the tee time and give Uncle Jake a call to see what his plans are for the weekend. He's gone a lot, and I know he'd be happy to let us use his cabin."

"That's a great idea!"

Chapter Thirty-two

J oe Bob's Uncle Jake had moved into his cabin on the lake after selling his house a few years prior. He enjoyed living in nature's lap, listening to the chorus of creatures that inhabited the woods. He engaged in hunting, fishing, and various offerings of the great outdoors. But as much as he liked the solitude of his out-of-the-way domicile, he found that frequent trips to Nashville tended to refresh him in various indulgences. He appreciated the arts in a broad spectrum of venues and enjoyed most everything from the theatre to country music. When Jake visited the city, he could be found in the most expensive restaurants, sometimes with friends, and sometimes all by his lonesome. He attended car shows, motorcycle shows, and gun and knife shows. He was a renaissance man of today—that, and Joe Bob's Uncle Jake.

"Matt, Joe Bob here."

"Hey, Joe Bob. Did you call Jake?"

"Yeah, I caught him just as he wuz packin' to take off for the city. He said he didn't have time to talk 'cause he wuz runnin' late to meet a friend, so I dispensed with the chitchat and asked if it'd be okay for us to use the cabin for a few days. He said we can git the key from Mister McCauley's store like we did the last time."

"When do you want to leave town? I can go anytime, but I'll have to check with Bernie."

"You got plans for tonight? If you don't, I'd like to git on the road before dark. We can pick up the key and some supplies at McCauley's, then go on over to that cool joint with the floor show for dinner. Tell Bernard to git a move on."

I thought Bernie might balk at the idea of leaving on the spur of the moment, but he didn't. He said he had gotten quite a bit more done to get his house in shape for the realtor to show it.

I called Sydney's clinic to fill her in on my plans, but she was in surgery, so I sent her a lengthy text. I hoped she would understand that this outing was important to my friends and me. There was nothing keeping her from moving into her new house except for the fact that she enjoyed my cooking and we both kind of liked the sleeping arrangements most of the time.

Mary Grace didn't work on the weekends, so I sent her a text informing her that she only needed to play receptionist Monday. I would leave a key for her in the secret rock that I kept under the shrub second from the door on the right and that I would see her at the office Tuesday morning.

Joe Bob pulled up in front of my building at four o'clock on the dot. His duffel and a large cooler were stowed in the back of his truck under a tarp. I didn't break stride as I slung my duffel into the back, jerked open the door, and stepped up on the running board to get into the behemoth.

Bernie was pacing his driveway when we got to his house. He wasted no time hoisting a suitcase into the back of the truck. I wondered why he didn't look very happy to see us since it was his idea to spend time together someplace other than Martinsville.

Joe Bob picked me up first so I was stuck in the middle between him and Bernie. Maybe I would suggest that Bernie and I switch seats part of the time.

It was closing in on dusk when we got to McCauley's store. There were a couple of guys loading up on camping supplies when we made the little bell over the door tinkle. Mister McCauley looked up from totaling the bill for his customers and smiled at us. After the campers paid their bill, he walked them to the door and held it open for them.

"Well, if it isn't the three adventurers come back to the woods to stir up trouble," he joked. "Jake called me a while ago to warn me that you were coming. I've got a new key for you right here in the drawer. How long do you think you'll be staying?"

Joe Bob laughed.

"Well, I hope we won't git into too much trouble this trip. We're just gonna to be here for the weekend."

"It probably won't be quite as exciting this time," the storekeeper said. "The snake handlers have all been chased out of that little church, and I haven't seen any gypsies since you were here. I guess you'll have to make your own entertainment this time unless you can find another teenage runaway who needs you to deliver her infant, Joe Bob."

"Let's hope we don't have that much drama this trip," I said. "We'd like to get some supplies for the cabin."

"How about the key to the shed? Do you plan to do any fishing? The bass boat's just sitting there waiting to get into the water."

"Sure," Joe Bob said. "I've got rods and reels and my tackle box in the truck. Maybe we can catch our breakfast."

Joe Bob pulled a grocery list from his shirt pocket, and the three of us collected the things we thought we would need. Mister McCauley totaled the bill.

"I'll just run a tab for you fellows," he said. "You'll probably be back here tomorrow to tell me what you forgot. You can pay up when you return the keys."

It was obvious that Jake, or maybe the county, had made some drastic improvements as soon as we left the main road and turned onto the lane that led to the cabin. The lane hadn't been paved, but the deep potholes had been filled and gravel had leveled it. The tree branches had also been cut back from the sides of the lane.

The cabin looked the same from the outside. The hanging baskets of flowers and the rocking chairs looked just as they had when we had been here last year. Joe Bob dug out the key to the front door, and we unloaded the truck and hauled everything inside.

"Same sleepin' arrangements as last time okay with you guys?" Joe Bob asked.

"Fine with me," I said.

Bernie didn't bother responding. He just started lugging his suitcase up the stairs.

As we walked through the living room, we couldn't help noticing the addition of a big flat screen TV. It sat on a console beside a floor-to-ceiling bookcase which housed Jake's fishing trophies and a variety of leather bound books.

"I reckon Uncle Jake got kinda tired of readin' his huntin' and fishin' magazines," Joe Bob said. "Let's git our stuff put away and head over to that restaurant we liked."

Ned's Place was fairly empty when we drove into the parking lot. We entered the restaurant and the same Mae West look-alike who had greeted us the last time we were here headed in our direction. She smiled and delivered her well-rehearsed line.

"You guys been here before?"

"Yes, we were here about a year ago," I said.

"Then, you know the drill: menu's on the chalkboard, show starts at nine, grab a good table. Someone will be with you in a sec."

"Wonder what the entertainment will be tonight?" Bernie said. "Those Elvis impersonators were pretty good. Hopefully, we won't be subjected to watching a watermelon seed spitting contest."

The look on Joe Bob's handsome face told me that he was having to bite his tongue to keep from telling Bernie to lose the negativity.

"Why don't you pick us a table, Bernard?" he said. "I don't care where we sit; I'm thirsty and just about starved."

Bernie scanned the large room, then led us to a table close to the stage.

"How's this?" he asked.

"Fine with me," I said, hoping to alleviate the tension in the air.

I was more than a little tired of playing referee between these two.

A wait person dressed like Daisy Mae in the funnies came prancing over to our table. She was cracking a wad of gum as fast as she could chew, but held it at bay to give us a practiced smile.

"Hi, guys," she said. "Ya'll got the best table in the house. How about somethin' cool and refreshin' to wet your whistles?"

It seemed that my tablemates were both afraid to open their mouths for fear of upsetting one another, so I grabbed the reins.

"Bring us a pitcher while we look over the menu," I said.

The girl nodded, smiled, chomped down on her gum with a boisterous crack, and left to get the beer.

"The place doesn't look like it's changed much," I said.

Joe Bob nodded. "Same furniture and same mirror makin' it look like it's super crowded, but that big group of hifalutin city slickers is missin'."

"Maybe they'll show up later," I said. "I enjoyed watching the

Arthur Murray dancers, especially the couple who showed up all of the others."

At that point, Joe Bob couldn't keep his mouth shut any longer.

"They wuz real good, but Bernard and that pair of tight jeans wuz a lot more fun to watch. She had Bernard in a headlock. No way he wuz escapin' her clutches. Her greasy hair just about covered his face, and I wondered how he could breathe. It wuz a real sight!" Joe Bob laughed.

"Very funny," said Bernie. He wasn't smiling.

"I'm sorry, Bernard," Joe Bob apologized. "You woulda laughed too if it had been one of us."

I could have kicked Joe Bob. Now, I had to step in and change the subject.

"Hopefully, that group won't show up tonight. I'm sure they were locals, but I doubt they hang out here very much. This place is kind of pricey, and they didn't look very prosperous."

Daisy Mae brought our pitcher and three beer steins. She delivered it along with another smile that showed every tooth in her mouth and I wondered how she did that without losing a grip on her wad of gum.

"Ya'll looked over the menu?" she asked.

None of us had bothered, and her query prompted us to take a look. The offerings were extensive.

"What looks good to you, Joe Bob?" Bernie asked. He didn't wait for an answer. "I'm sure it's something deep fried and smothered in gravy."

Joe Bob didn't bite. "As a matter of fact, it is. I'm gonna have the fried chicken with mashed potatoes and gravy. Oh, and some fried okra. That's somethin' green."

I laughed hoping to bring a bit of levity to the conversation.

"I'll have the trout and mixed vegetables," I said.

"Bring me the chef's special salad with grilled chicken," said Bernie.

"Here's to a meaningful visit to the backwoods," I said, and we all raised our glasses in a half-hearted toast.

I ordered a bottle of chardonnay just as we were being served, and hoped that my friends would take off the gloves and enjoy their dinner.

We managed to get through the meal without further discord and turned our attention to the platform which served as a stage. We all wondered what the entertainment would be and whether or not we would want to stay for the show.

All at once there was a loud gong followed by the same old geezer who had been the emcee last year.

"Hello, ladies and gents," he said. "I know you're all holdin' your breath, waitin' to see what we've got in store for you tonight."

Hoots and hollers emanated from the patrons who didn't disappoint in their enthusiasm as well as their eclectic dress and demeanor. They appeared to come from most every walk of life.

The emcee held up both hands to quiet the crowd.

"It's gonna to be a surprise. I'll bring these super stars out onstage to give you a look-see. Then, you can guess who they are and what they're gonna do."

Boos and hisses filled the room.

The gong sounded again, and three men ambled out onto the stage. One black and two white men stood in the center of the stage and began laughing and punching one another on the arm. The black guy ducked out from under the punches of the other two and launched into a wild tap dance using up most of the stage. It was reminiscent of a Gregory Hines performance. Barely winded, he clapped his hands once and extended his palm toward the guy to his left who sported a fedora and a big smile. He tipped his hat and returned to his place on stage, giving the third of the trio a friendly push. This guy was the personification of laid back. He had curly black hair and a lazy smile. He simply stood there, his shoulders shaking with silent laughter and a hand held to his face to block his expression.

Enter the emcee, clapping his hands enthusiastically.

"Ladies and gentlemen, I give you The Rat Pack!"

Applause broke out but ceased as the Sinatra impersonator stepped forward and began singing his ever popular *My Way*. He was interrupted by the Sammy Davis Jr. guy who gave him a shove and began belting out *I've Gotta Be Me*. He was nearly finished when the last guy who looked a great deal like Dean Martin, stepped in front of him and began crooning *Everybody Loves Somebody Sometime*. The King of Cool was so convincing that his pals didn't bother to interrupt him. He sang it to the end.

The three told jokes, poked fun at one another, and sang some of their other favorites. Then, their time was up, but the audience begged for more.

The emcee stomped back onstage, pointed to Frank, and said, "Ladies and gentlemen, Ol' Blue Eyes!

"Strart spreadin' the news," he sang, snapping his fingers to the rhythm.

The audience loved it, nearly drowning him out with their applause.

Following his last *New York*, he turned to Sammy and introduced him as Mister Show Business.

The Candy Man erupted from his throat and had the audience on their feet, swaying and singing along.

The emcee all but clicked the heels of his run-down cowboy boots as he came back onstage.

"Ladies and gentlemen, The Rat Pack!"

The entertainers bowed and were leaving the stage when Dean turned to the crowd, smiled, and said, "Goodnight Jeannie!"as he ambled off the stage.

"Those guys were really good, weren't they?" I said. "I remember when Dean Martin had his TV show a long time ago. That's how he always said goodnight to his wife."

Both of my friends were grinning and nodding in agreement. I hoped those faces would still be smiling at the end of our little foray into the woods. I wanted things to end on a happy note.

The crowd began to disperse, and we joined them in their exit. There was no sniping as we got back into the pickup. Since everything appeared to be on an even keel, I didn't bring up a change in the seating arrangement.

Back at the cabin, Joe Bob suggested that we have a nightcap. He had bought a big bottle of Wild Turkey since that was what we drank the last time we were here.

"I bought this to leave with Uncle Jake 'cause we helped ourselves to his stash. I figured we wouldn't drink this whole bottle," Joe Bob explained.

I hadn't planned to indulge in a nightcap because that tended to get us into a world of trouble on a couple of other occasions. Truth be told, none of us could hold our liquor very well if we overdid it, but I wasn't going to be the guy to refuse.

"Good idea," Bernie said. "I think having a nightcap is in order."

We went into the kitchen for the bottle and Joe Bob opened a cabinet door to retrieve glasses.

"Wow!" he said. "Look at these fancy highball glasses. Uncle Jake must have been doin' some big-time entertainin'."

I picked one up to examine it and touched it to another glass. It had a pretty ring.

"These are fully leaded crystal," I said.

"Hope we don't break 'em," Joe Bob said, pouring generous portions into three glasses and heading to the front porch where the rocking chairs awaited us.

Bernie and I followed him out and claimed our chairs. We started sipping and rocking. It was a lovely evening. A lone owl hooted in the distance, and tree frogs issued a chorus of never ending mating calls.

"It's nice here," Bernie observed. "I'd like to live somewhere like this. Well, I don't mean just like this, but a place where everything's peaceful and slow-paced."

"That sounds a lot like Martinsville," I ventured.

"That's not what I mean," Bernie said. "I'm picturing a place where nobody knows me—a place to start over."

"I thought you wuz goin' back to Philadelphia," said Joe Bob.

Bernie drained his glass and stood. His rocking chair was still in motion.

"I'm going to bed," he said.

Chapter Thirty-three

Of all the harebrained ideas any of the three of us had ever thought of, a getaway to the woods headed the list. It materialized after Bernie decided that we needed to leave town so there would be no distractions while we bared our souls to one another before he departed Tennessee never to return.

As it turned out, the soul-searching true confession session never took place. Bernie had been out of sorts from the get-go, but the nightcap on the porch was the straw that broke the camel's back. It was abundantly clear that Bernie had changed his mind about the tell-all experience when he took off in a huff. That left Joe Bob and me sitting in rocking chairs on the porch with a bottle of Wild Turkey and nothing to do but clink our glasses and say, "Bottoms up."

The next morning as I walked bleary-eyed through the living room en route to the kitchen, I saw Bernie perched on the couch staring at the blank big screen. His suitcase was parked just inside the front door. My head hurt, and my stomach was queasy.

"What are you doing, Bernie?"

"What does it look like I'm doing?"

"I don't feel like playing games. This whole idea was yours. We're here because you wanted to get out of town so we could tell one another our deepest, darkest secrets and clear the air before you took off for parts unknown. Now, you're giving me the distinct impression that you're ready to return to civilization and keep all of your pent-up secrets to yourself."

Joe Bob came stumbling in from Uncle Jake's bedroom rubbing his eyes.

"Mornin', ya'll."

Neither Bernie nor I returned the greeting.

"He's packed and ready to go back to Martinsville," I said, nodding at Bernie.

"We just got here," said Joe Bob. "I thought we'd go fishin' today."

Bernie got up and went to stand by his suitcase.

"Well, I'm not going fishing. I'm ready to go back to town. I need to wrap up some things before I leave."

Joe Bob swiped a hand over his face, then shook his head in disbelief.

"Bernard, you're the reason we dropped everthing because you wanted us three to get away and talk. What wuz it you wuz so all fired up to talk about? I want to hear it."

"It was a mistake. I shouldn't have suggested it. There's nothing to discuss. I want to leave now."

Joe Bob stiffened and went to stand about a foot from Bernie so he was looking down at his face.

"This is the last mistake you'll make involvin' me," he said, punctuating each word by poking his index finger into Bernie's chest. "Let's git packed up, Matt. We wouldn't want to keep our dictator here waitin'."

We left all of the things we had purchased at Mister McCauley's store in Jake's refrigerator and cupboard. Then, Joe Bob returned the keys to the storekeeper, explaining our early departure with the bald-faced lie that Bernie had an unexpected emergency in Martinsville.

I was so aggravated with Bernie that I couldn't help behaving like a child.

"You're in the middle, Bernie," I said, standing by the open door of the pick-up.

Nobody spoke on the drive back to town. I was pretty hungover, and I knew Joe Bob had to feel as rotten as I did. I closed my eyes trying to catch a catnap, but that caused me to feel nauseous. Bernie stared straight ahead, and Joe Bob kept his eyes on the road while driving way too fast.

Joe Bob drove straight to Bernie's house and killed the engine. I got out so Bernie could. He went around to get his suitcase out of the back, but he was a little too short to reach over the side to get it. He stood beside the truck looking helpless, and I felt obliged to retrieve it for him.

"Thanks," he said, taking it from me. Then, he turned and headed for his house.

None of us bothered with farewells.

Joe Bob found his voice as soon as I got back in the truck.

"He's a real SOB, Matt. I've tried for years to be civil to the short little shit, but I'm glad he's leavin'. I don't care if I never see him again."

"I know you've tried, Joe Bob. Bernie's a real toughy. I guess I hate to see it end like this because we all kind of grew up together. Everybody in Martinsville thought of us as a trio since we were in high school."

We were driving down Main Street when I saw someone chasing Freaky Fred around the corner by the drugstore.

"Joe Bob, that's Fred, and that big guy is about to catch him. I wonder if it's the same guy who put his arm in a sling a while back."

Joe Bob focused on the scene. He squinted.

"That kinda looks like that big guy we saw settin' on the park bench."

He stomped the accelerator to the floorboard, and we rounded the corner just in time to see the two men disappear around another corner.

"We've lost 'em now," he said. "There's no tellin' where they are; too many alleys and short cuts to keep up with 'em."

"Fred does so many crazy things, I can't hazard a guess as to what he might have done to make someone chase him to get revenge."

"If he shows up for work tomorrow mornin', I'm gonna find out what he's been up to if I have to beat it out of him," Joe Bob said.

That was just Joe Bob's mouth spewing out his bad mood. He'd had it with Bernie Zuckerman and needed to get the anger out of his system. He would never harm Fred, and we both knew it.

My Caddy was parked in front of my building when Joe Bob dropped me off, but Sydney's car was nowhere in sight. I wondered where she might have gone on a Sunday morning. Maybe she went back to church to hear Mark Winters deliver another of his inspiring sermons.

There was a note lying on the kitchen table advising me of Sydney's whereabouts.

Matt, I'm at my house.
Sydney

Just Sydney; not love, Sydney. It was a pretty cold note. I wondered if she was upset because I had gone on the guy trip.

Without bothering to unpack, I got in my car and drove to

her new house. I didn't see her car, but another one that looked familiar was pulling up to the curb out front.

I went to the front door and rang the bell. She and I had been sleeping together, so why did I feel that I needed to ring the bell? She didn't ring the bell when she came to my front door. Those thoughts made me feel like a spoiled, defensive child.

"Coming," called a voice just before the door opened, and Trudy smiled up at me.

"Well, if it's not my sweet boy, lookin' like someone who might have had a little too much fun and no sleep. We didn't think you'd be back until tomorrow."

"May I come in?" I asked.

Trudy delivered a motherly smile and pulled me inside.

"We had a change of plans," I explained. "Might I ask why you're here?"

"Yes, you might. I'm helpin' the young lady plan a flower bed for her back yard."

"How did you get here?"

"Marcus drove me. He's gone to pick up some lunch for us. I bet he bought enough for one more hungry soul."

Sydney came bustling in from the back yard looking like a seventeen-year-old in short shorts and a tee shirt. She was covered in dirt. I looked at her and grinned.

"Matt, we didn't expect you."

That wasn't the friendliest greeting I had ever heard.

"Bernie had an unexpected issue that needed his attention, so we came back early," I lied.

Mister Hathaway announced his presence by tapping on the front door with his shoe, and Trudy hurried to admit him. He had a large bag in each hand.

"We have here enough Greek salad for an army, sourdough

bread, and a couple of bottles of a crisp chardonnay," he said on his way to the kitchen.

"That sounds wonderful," Sydney said.

"Why, Matt, it's good to see you," said Mister Hathaway. "I hope you'll join us for lunch."

Sydney left the room, then returned a few minutes later minus the dirt and wearing a clean shirt. She walked up to me, wrapped her arms around me, and delivered a chaste kiss to my cheek. That made me feel certain that everything was just dandy between the two of us.

The flower garden was ready to plant, and the gardeners left after lunch with a promise to come back and help with the planting the next weekend. Sydney told me that she wanted to shower before coming to my place. That was perfect because I needed to unpack and check my email and phone messages, then buy something to cook for our dinner.

I had just gotten home from the store when Sydney arrived. She came hurrying through the front door, without ringing the bell, by the way, wearing a Joe Bob kind of smile. She practically raced across the room to give me a real welcome home kiss.

"That kind of action might make me want to hurry dinner along," I said, smiling.

Sydney took a seat on a stool at the island and watched me open a bottle of wine. I thought she might ask me about the guy trip, but she obviously had no interest.

"I have a surprise for you," she said.

"Oh?"

"But I'm not telling you what it is until after dinner."

I couldn't imagine what her surprise might be, but I went along with her little game. All during the meal she made me guess what her surprise might be. Then, we joined forces to load the dishwasher. I thought we would take the rest of our wine into the living room and snuggle on the couch, but Sydney had other ideas.

"We have to go to my place for the surprise," she said. "I'll drive."

I grabbed what was left of our bottle of wine and followed her to the front door.

"Leave the wine here," she said, taking me by the hand and leading me to her car.

When we were just inside her front door, Sydney told me to close my eyes. Then, she produced a black scarf and blindfolded me. She led me through the house to the master bedroom.

"Don't say anything when I remove the blindfold," she said. "I want you to take it all in before you tell me what you think of my surprise."

"Okay."

I had to blink after losing the blindfold. Sydney had turned her bedroom into something of a fairy-tale love nest. The king-size bed had been turned down to reveal silk sheets scattered with rose petals, and our initials were embroidered on our respective pillow cases. Bedside lamps bathed the room in soft light. A trail of rose petals led to the adjoining bath which was lit with votive candles encircling the Jacuzzi tub, and soft music played from unseen speakers.

I opened my mouth to speak, but Sydney silenced me with a kiss. She made her way to a small bar in the corner. On it rested a bottle of champagne in an ice bucket and two champagne flutes. She donned an expression so sexy that I couldn't tear my eyes away.

Handing me the bottle to uncork, she said, "Let's christen this place."

And so we did.

In the aftermath of our lovemaking, it seemed that her entire personality became all business.

"Matt, this may not have come to your attention, but you are living in a bachelor pad apartment/law office. I have a brand new gorgeous house in a lovely section of town. Don't you think it would be more comfortable for both of us if you moved in with me?"

"I'd never thought about it," I said. "Your house is lovely, and your surprise was over the top."

"Then, you agree?" she purred.

"Don't take this the wrong way, but I'm not sure I'm ready to move out of my apartment. I just spent a lot of time and money to make it Livable."

"So you don't want to move in with me."

"What would you think about the two of us spending time in both residences?" I asked, attempting to avoid a firm commitment.

"I guess we could do that," she said, "but I think it would be kind of silly."

"Let's give it a try. I'll bring some of my clothes over tomorrow, and we can play it by ear to see how we feel after a while. How does that sound?"

"It sounds like my big shot attorney might be afraid of little ol' me, but I'll go along with your plan. Bet I can change your mind." She smiled and trailed a finger across my chest, giving me one of her *come hither* looks.

The aroma of coffee wafted into the bedroom, and it took me a few seconds to realize where I was. Sitting up and looking down at my initials on the pillowcase, it all came back in a rush. I didn't have a toothbrush, but I found mouthwash in the bathroom.

Sydney was in her very modern kitchen playing hostess. She

was taking a quiche from the oven. She placed it on the counter and came to give me a kiss. Then, she poured our coffee.

I looked at the quiche. "Did you make this?" I asked.

Sydney laughed. "No, Matt, I didn't make it. I bought it, but I happen to know it's going to be delicious. I've sampled lots of things from the little specialty shop where I bought this."

She was right. The quiche was excellent, and the large kitchen window provided a great view of the neighborhood lake. I knew Sydney was doing her best to tempt me to move in with her. I would have her drive me to my place to make a list of things to take to her house after work. Like I said, we would have to play it by ear.

I had failed to take my cell phone when Sydney and I had left my place. Picking it up I saw that I had missed several calls. Three of them were from Bernie asking me to call him. I hit the speed button for his number.

"You've reached Bernard Zuckerman. I can't answer the phone right now. Leave your name and number after the beep and I'll return your call when I can."

"Bernie, this is Matt. I'm just now seeing this. Call me."

Joe Bob had also left a message. He wanted me to come to his garage as soon as possible.

As soon as Mary Grace showed up, I gave her a list of things to do, then took off for Joe Bob's. He was sitting at his desk rubbing his chin the way he sometimes did when he was in a quandary about something.

"What's up, Joe Bob?"

"I tell you what, I'm pure bumfuzzled."

"About what?"

"Fred. You're not gonna to believe it."

"Tell me."

"That big guy we saw chasin' Fred wuz the guy he worked for before I hired him. I did give him a little raise. It must not have been enough 'cause he went back to the other guy and asked for his job back. The guy told him there wuzn't any more jobs. Fred got smart with the guy and threatened to tell somebody all about them jobs unless the guy would hire him back."

"I don't suppose Fred told you what those jobs were."

"Are you ready for this?"

I nodded.

"Fred wuz the one who did all that stuff at Bernard's house. He slashed the tires and planted the snake outside the door. I don't remember what else he did, but the big guy paid him to do all of it."

"Did he tell you who the big guy was?"

"No, but Fred's scared of him. He told Fred he'd be awful sorry if he told anybody anything about them jobs, and that sooner or later he'd catch up with him."

"So where is Fred?"

"He wouldn't tell me where he wuz goin'. He just left here a few minutes ago."

"Hey, changing the subject, have you heard from Bernie since we got back to town?"

"No, and that's fine with me. I don't care what he's doin' or where he goes."

"I understand. I had several missed calls from him, but when I tried to call him back, I got his machine. I left a message for him to call me, but he hasn't."

Joe Bob shrugged. "Lucky you," he said, and gave me a Joe Bob smile.

Chapter Thirty-four

Too much was happening all at once. Joe Bob was engaged. Trudy and Mister Hathaway were something of an item. I was thinking seriously about moving in with Sydney, and Bernie was about to beat feet.

All of the aforementioned situations seemed plausible, sort of, with the exception of Bernie Zuckerman's decision to leave Martinsville with no knowledge regarding his missing child. He had been obsessed with learning her whereabouts and knowing that she was unharmed. That obsession seemed to have abruptly ended. I wasn't sure I knew Bernie anymore.

I had spent all afternoon in court, and I was mentally exhausted by the time I got home to pack a bag with everything I thought I might need to take to Sydney's house for a couple of nights. Maybe staying at her place would work out for us. I just wanted us both to be happy.

Sydney was sipping a glass of wine, looking out her large living room window at the view of the lake when I arrived. I dropped my bag just inside the door and went to kiss her hello. Holding the glass at arm's length so as not to spill it down my neck, she returned the kiss.

"So, Matt, what's for dinner?" she asked, smiling. "I'm famished."

"I guess I hadn't given dinner much thought," I said.

Sydney laughed. "Well, Matt, you know I don't cook. If you didn't buy anything to make, I guess we'll have to go out."

"Okay. We'll go out. I just want to get out of this suit and tie and have a glass of wine. Then, let's go someplace for a low key dinner. I'm bushed."

We went to a small Chinese restaurant not far from Sydney's house. Over dinner she told me all about her day. She had been in surgery for a short while, cleaned a Basset Hound's teeth, and handled several other nonthreatening procedures. She never failed to be excited about her work.

I had been busting my butt on these two important court cases and was thrilled at having won both of them. I thought Sydney might inquire about my day, but she didn't, so I didn't bother her with details.

Back at the house, we settled on the living room couch and watched a rom-com that Sydney wanted to see. Then, we went to bed and slept like a couple of stones.

When I got to my office the next morning, Mary Grace was sitting in her car at the curb. She was early as usual. I tapped on her window, and she opened her door smiling. This young woman was a treasure, and I decided then and there to give her the news that since my clientele was steadily growing, I would like to hire her full-time. I realized that it would depend on whether she thought she could spend that much time away from her housebound mother. She had a part time caregiver for her mother, and I was prepared to offer her remuneration enough to hire the caregiver full time if she deemed it necessary.

When I made the offer, one would have thought I had offered her the moon.

"Mister Stevenson, I'm humbled by this offer, but you know I'm not a legal secretary. Are you sure you want me for the job? Don't get me wrong. I'd love to have the job and the money, but I don't have the knowledge or experience."

Before I could answer, she heaved a sigh, and tears began leaking from her eyes. Then, between hiccupping sobs, she said, "Yes, Mister Stevenson. I really want the job. I'll try to learn as fast as I can."

Mary Grace stood by her desk and resumed crying. I pulled a handkerchief from my back pocket and offered it to her, then took her in my arms in a brotherly hug.

"You're hired," I said with a chuckle. "You already know more than you think you do. You have a way of dealing with surly clients. I've seen you in action, and you are a definite asset in my law practice. You already know some of the legal terminology and you're a quick study. You're going to have on-the-job training."

My new secretary handed back my unused handkerchief, retrieved a tissue from her purse and blew her nose.

"I'm ready," she said.

I spent the morning teaching her some of the basics, and she caught on quickly. Then, I told her to take the rest of the day off to check with her mother and the caregiver to see if she could work things out with them.

I hated to eat alone, so I cruised over to Joe Bob's garage hoping he would join me.

"You must have been readin' my mind, counselor. I'm cravin' one of them blue plate specials they have at Morgan's."

I was driving us to Morgan's. Joe Bob was pretty quiet on the drive which was unlike him.

As we were getting out of the car, I glanced in his direction to see a smile cover most of his face. He was obviously elated about something he was about to tell me.

"Did you just win the lottery?" I asked as we entered the restaurant.

"That's how I feel," he said. "Yours truly has never been this happy."

We went to a booth in Lucy's section, both of us leaning back against the tall wooden backs of the old booth.

"Would you just spill it?" I said.

"If you insist. I told you that I wanted to let Lauren pick the date for our weddin'. Well, I gotta tell you I'm on a cloud. She wants to tie the knot next Saturday. We've already been to see that new preacher to see if he'd do the honors. He's a super nice guy—real down to earth. He's not like any preacher I ever knew. Do you know if preachers charge a certain fee for things like marryin' couples? I didn't want to ask him, but I sure do want to be fair with him."

"Joe Bob, hush and come up for air."

My friend gulped in air like a fish out of water.

"There wuz just so much I wanted to say and I want to do everthing right. I wuz afraid I might leave somethin' out."

This man was one of the best human beings who ever lived. He was kind and generous to a fault, and I was honored to have him as a friend. It was a privilege to know him.

"Number one: congratulations," I said. "Number two: I think you made a good choice in Mark Winters. I like him too. Number three: This is a small southern town. I doubt seriously if any minister in Martinsville would charge a fee, but I think it's customary to pay an honorarium to a minister for performing the ceremony. I think he'd be pleased with $150 or $200 to marry you and Lauren."

"That's great. Now....

"How's the world treatin' you troublemakers?" Lucy interrupted.

"We're fine, Lucy," Joe Bob said. "We'll both have the blue plate special. What is it?"

I hadn't planned to order the blue plate special no matter what it happened to be, but I decided it wouldn't kill me to let my old pal run the show since he was so wound up.

"The special's open-faced roast beef sandwich with gravy, mashed potatoes, and green beans," Lucy said. She turned to put in our orders, but looked back over her shoulder. "What's makin' you grin like a fool, Joe Bob?"

"Didn't know I wuz, but it's prob'ly 'cause I'm gittin' married next weekend."

"Hallelujah!" Lucy spouted, and headed to the kitchen shaking her head.

"Now, where wuz I?" Joe Bob said, rubbing his chin. "Oh, yeah. I wanted to ask you what would be a real favor to me."

"Sure. Anything."

"Will you be my best man, Matthew?"

"I'd be honored."

"Thanks, man. I wuz hopin' you'd say yes. You're the best friend I ever had."

Our lunch arrived, and I was glad because Joe Bob could get a little overly sentimental if given the opportunity. I had almost forgotten how good this fattening southern cooking tasted, and I thought I enjoyed it as much as Joe Bob did. That said, I would refrain from indulging very often.

After lunch I dropped Joe Bob off at his garage and went back to my office. Mary Grace had left, and all I had to do for the rest of the day was a bit of research for one case, return phone calls, and check my email. One of the emails was from Bernie Zuckerman.

Matt, I'm gone. I won't be available at this email address or my old cell phone number. I want you to know I've enjoyed our time together. Bernie

That blew me away. It seemed that Bernie had already left town. That must have been the reason he never returned my texts or calls. He had been deliberately avoiding me. He must have left his realtor in complete charge of selling his house and simply split.

I left the office early and bought the makings of a spaghetti dinner. I used my new key to enter Sydney's house. She had seemed disappointed last night because she had assumed I would be cooking our dinner. I could tell that she hadn't been wild about going out to eat. She wouldn't be home for another couple of hours, so I had time to kill before starting dinner.

I hit the speed dial for Joe Bob's cell.

"Joe Bob here."

"Hey, you won't believe this."

"Wanna let me in on what I won't believe?"

"I have an email from Bernie telling me that he's gone, as in no longer in Martinsville."

"No kiddin'? Well, good riddance. It's about time."

"I guess you're right. He sure hasn't been happy lately. I just thought he'd probably say goodbye in person."

"Reckon he'd had enough of at least one of us. You okay with me changin' the subject?"

"Sure."

"Little Annie's gonna be the flower girl at our weddin'. That little princess is cuter than a bug's ear, Matt. I just about can't wait 'til next weekend."

"I've got to tell you, I've never seen you this excited about anything."

"That's 'cause I've never been this excited. It's gonna be a small weddin'. We're not havin' a ring bearer or bridesmaids. Lauren's got a list of about fifty people she's invitin', and then there's my little list: you, Sydney, Lucy, the preacher, of course, Ms. Trudy, and Mister Hathaway. He's gonna give the bride away. That fancy French restaurant where Lauren's been workin' is doin' the reception. They're givin' Lauren that for a weddin' present."

"Wow! No wonder you're excited."

"Matt, I want to thank you again for bein' my best man. It means a lot."

"It means a lot to me that you asked me," I said, meaning it.

Sydney kicked off her shoes the minute she stepped into the house. She was in a fabulous mood—all bubbly and radiating happiness.

"Hello, my love," I said as she trotted into the kitchen where I was putting our dinner together.

She made straight for my embrace avoiding the dishtowel I held in my left hand.

"Hello, yourself," she said, turning her face up for a kiss.

"You seem to be in an extraordinarily good mood. Is there any particular reason?"

"I've had a perfectly lovely day, and to top it all off, Joe told me that he and his fiancé are planning their wedding here. The Reverend Winters will be marrying them. They're getting married next month. Isn't that exciting?"

"It is, but I think I can top your good news."

Sydney gave me a questioning look.

"Joe Bob and Lauren are getting married next weekend. Joe Bob asked me to be his best man. I've never seen him so happy. The Martinsville Romeo is about to break some hearts. He's no doubt already done that because he hasn't had eyes for another female since the minute he laid eyes on Lauren."

"I suppose your news did top mine," Sydney said. "Love must be in the air."

I handed her a glass of wine, and she sipped it while I put dinner on the table. She dug into my spaghetti with so much gusto that one would have thought she hadn't eaten for at least a week. Her appetite for absolutely everything never ceased to amaze me, and it was one of the things I liked best about her.

After dinner we took our wine to the living room and listened to music for all of fifteen minutes until Sydney decided that we would be much more comfortable in the bedroom. Maybe staying at her house wasn't such a bad idea after all.

Joe Bob was parked in front of my law office when I arrived there the next morning. He exited his truck as I pulled in behind him.

"Good morning, Mister Kincaid," I said. "Might you be in need of some legal assistance?"

"No, but I've got somethin' interestin' to show you," he said, pulling an envelope from his breast pocket.

"Let's go inside," I said, hoping it wasn't another poem.

Something seemed a little off, and I realized that Mary Grace wasn't already at the office. She arrived just as Joe Bob and I sat down in my office space.

"Sorry I'm late, Mister Stevenson," she apologized, putting her purse away. "I had to get my mom settled before I left. Her caregiver won't get to our house for another half hour."

She turned her attention to me and noticed that I wasn't alone.

"Oh, excuse me. I didn't realize that you were with a client."

"It's alright," I assured her. Mister Kincaid is a friend of mine. Please use the form letter we talked about and fill in the names and addresses of the list I left on your desk."

She nodded and went to work.

Joe Bob slid the envelope across my desk and waited to see my reaction as I read the typed letter.

It was addressed to Joseph Robert Kincaid at his home address, and it had been sent from right here in Martinsville. It was penned by none other than Fred Peyton's sister.

"She seems to have given us a lead, but we're no closer to finding the guy's identity than we were," I said.

My eyes traveled back to the last paragraph of the letter.

> *My brother has issues as I'm sure you're aware, but he has a good heart. He didn't realize the impact of the orders he was carrying out for that man. Now, he's afraid of being caught by the man. He won't leave my house. He stays in his room, afraid he might be seen through a window. His world consists of his room, the kitchen, and the bathroom. He's no match for that big man. I don't know what my brother did to incur his former employer's wrath. Fred likes you, and you must have some feeling for him since you hired him. I don't know what you might do to help sort this out, but I don't know where else to turn.*
>
> *Sincerely,*
> *Rose Peyton*

"Reckon why she sent the letter to me?" Joe Bob asked. "Why does she think I'm involved? Bernard wuz the one he wuz tormentin'."

"It doesn't make sense to me either. It sounds like she thinks you have some kind of pull to help Fred. Do you think Fred told his sister all of the things he did? And do you think she knows who the big man is?"

"I'm bettin' we do. I'll wager he's the same big hulk we saw settin' on the bench at that little park. Now, all we gotta do is find out his name and where he lives. I'm gonna pay Fred's sister a visit."

"Good luck. Let me know what you find out."

Joe Bob did, indeed, visit Fred's sister at her home. He had looked up her address online and was waiting for her in her driveway when she came home from work that same day. She told Joe Bob that she didn't know the man's name or address, but her description definitely fit that of the guy on the park bench, and she remembered seeing him there a few times on her way to, or from, work.

Joe Bob and I had too much on our plates to spend time playing detective. His wedding was only a few days away, and I was about to be involved with training my secretary while keeping Sydney happy. We needed some inconspicuous soul to tail the guy and get the information we needed. The thing that nagged at me was the fact that we would be at a loss to do anything about his threat to Fred. We couldn't accuse the man of any kind of crime, so what would be the point of knowing his identity?

Joe Bob and I were sitting in a booth at Morgan's staring at one another across the table when Lucy Combs came over to take our lunch orders. She rattled off the specials and paused her pen over the order pad.

"I'll have the chef's salad and iced tea, Lucy," I said.

"Make that two," Joe Bob said. "I've gained twelve pounds in the last month."

I laughed. "You quit smoking," I said. "It won't take you long to lose the extra weight."

Lucy brought our lunch and heaved a sigh. Then, a smile spread across her pretty face.

"You scalawags won't be seein' me for another week after my shift today," she said. "Lucy Combs is about to go on vacation."

"Good for you," I said. "Are you going someplace special?"

"Nope. I'm just gonna to kick back, be lazy, go for strolls in the park, and watch old movies."

Joe Bob looked at me across the table, and I knew exactly what he was thinking.

"So, Lucy, where is it that you go walkin'?"

"I like to drive over to that little Park over on Magnolia. It's a popular place for mothers and nannies to take little kids to play. I get a kick out of watching the little toddlers. All the adults are gossipin', ignorin' the kids. Seems like it's a good place for everybody."

"Enjoy your vacation, Lucy," I said.

Joe Bob was chewing a bite of salad and looking at me with raised eyebrows.

"Not a good idea," I said. "We don't want to get Lucy involved."

When we parted ways after lunch, I had no idea whether or not Joe Bob would approach Lucy about spending part of her vacation tailing the big guy. Granted, she was an unlikely candidate, and she could follow the guy in her car without arousing his suspicion. I decided to banish the thought. Joe Bob could pursue it if he chose to do so, but I had more important things to do than to worry about Bernie Zuckerman. He had left the building.

Trudy was waiting for me when I got back to the office. She was sitting on the front step studying my small front yard.

"Hey, how's my favorite girl?" I greeted.

"This yard needs some sprucin' up," she said. It needs more curb appeal. I'll plan a couple of flower beds for you."

"You don't need to do that, Trudy. You have more important fish to fry. You're helping Sydney with landscaping. More to the point, you and your Mister Hathaway are spending quite a bit of time together. You don't have time to mess with my front yard. It seems to me that love is in the air."

Trudy laughed. "Let me ease your mind, child. While it's true that I'm havin' a wonderful time with Marcus, and it's true that he did ask me to marry him, I'll let you in on a little secret. I told him thanks but no thanks. I tried that once, and it didn't work out. I have no intention of gettin' married again. I did tell him that he's welcome in my home anytime. He even has permission to spend the night, but he's not gonna put a ring on my finger. I like things just the way they are."

I looked into my old friend's eyes and saw happiness in the laugh wrinkles at their corners and at her mouth. I didn't know that I had ever seen such a beautiful expression on her face.

"Let's go inside and you can tell me what brings you to see your lawyer," I said.

Trudy sat in a chair across my desk from me and didn't mince words.

"You've told me that you never plan to live in your mama's house and that you're lettin' me reside there until I die. My sweet boy, old Trudy would like to buy that house unless there's some reason you might not want to sell it."

I looked at my old friend and smiled. Then, I asked Mary Grace to bring me a certain file. It only took her a nano second to retrieve it. I handed it to Trudy and told her to open it. She looked at the document and promptly released a stream of tears.

"This is the deed to the house. It's in my name. Matty, I can't accept this. Please let me buy it."

"This is a done deal," I said, coming around the desk to hug her. "It's already recorded at the courthouse. Consider me your adult child. After all, you reared me from an infant. Now, please go celebrate and let me get some work done." I grinned.

Trudy's visit had put me in something of an elated mood. After doing a bit of on-the-job legal training with my secretary, I called Sydney at work. For once, she was free to talk.

"Hey, Matt. What's up?"

"What do you say that we dine at that little Italian restaurant we like this evening?"

"That sounds great. There's something I need to discuss with you. I'll meet you at the house right after work."

"Great."

I wondered what she might have to discuss with me. I figured it couldn't be anything bothersome since she seemed to be in an unusually good mood.

The waiter at the restaurant recognized us as we entered the building. He smiled and led us to a table on the veranda. It was in a cozy spot, and soft piped in music added to the mood.

"This is one of my favorite restaurants in Martinsville," said Sydney after we were seated. "It isn't fancy or expensive, but just the place for a comfortable weeknight dinner."

"I agree. So, I assume you think this is another of my great ideas," I teased.

The waiter came to tell us the specials. We ordered drinks and placed our dinner orders. Minutes later, our drinks arrived.

"Cheers," I said, touching my glass to Sydney's. "Now, what is it that you want to discuss with me?"

Sydney cleared her throat and took another sip of her drink. "Matt, you know by now that I'm in love with you," she said, matter-of-factly.

"And I'm in love with you," I said. "I don't see that as a problem." I smiled, holding her gaze.

"I hope you'll take this in the spirit in which it's given," she said. "I think you were right in regard to our living arrangements. I know I was pushy about wanting you to move in with me, but I was wrong. I truly enjoy our present arrangement. We can still spend our evenings alternating between our homes and be as intimate as ever, but we don't have to feel compelled to give up our separate homes. We can be our own person and keep separate addresses. It doesn't change anything. We'll still be in love with one another just the way we have been. If we change our minds about living arrangements later, we'll make a decision together."

I looked into Sydney's eyes in the flickering candle light and thought, once again, how level-headed she was and how lucky I was to be in love with her. I reached across the table, took her hand, and said, "I love you, Sydney Edelman."

"I love you as well, Matt Stevenson. I think I'll keep you."

Chapter Thirty-five

I had driven to Joe Bob's garage from force of habit and interrupted his work which I seemed to do frequently. He laid the wrench he was holding on the roof of the vehicle he was repairing, careful to place it on a rag so as not to mar the car's paint.

"Matt, I'm not the type to git too fancy with this weddin' stuff," he said. "I'm not gittin' married in one of them monkey suits. That's not me. I bought a fine black suit to wear for the ceremony."

"I think that's fine," I said. "You should feel comfortable when you take the big step."

"Lauren thinks so, too. I just love that girl. I know bein' married to her is gonna be smooth sailin' from start to finish."

"That's great."

"Hey, Lauren showed me the little dress she bought for Annie. That little angel's gonna look like a fairy princess scatterin' them rose petals."

"I'm sure she will."

"Well, Matt, unless you've got somethin' earth-shatterin' to tell me, I'd better git back to it. I'm overhaulin' Bruce Dyre's engine. When I git this done, I'm not puttin' on these white coveralls again 'til after my honeymoon."

I laughed. "What are you going to do for the next couple of days?"

"Set around and feel nervous. I'm lookin' forward to it. It'll be a brand new experience for me."

"I just stopped by to chew the fat. I'll let you get back to work," I said.

"Later", Joe Bob said, turning his attention back to the Mercedes.

I stopped by my office to grab my briefcase before heading to the courthouse, arriving there ten minutes early and feeling pretty damn good about myself for being so prompt and efficient.

If I had been trying all of my cases before the same judge every time I entered that courtroom, I might have thought that I was being given unfair breaks, but that wasn't the case. Different judges presided over my cases, so I assumed that I must be doing a bang-up job. I had only lost one case.

After leaving the courthouse, I sat in the parking lot at the grocery store perusing Mediterranean recipes on my phone. I wanted to make Sydney a healthy dinner since I had been only offering high carbohydrate fare lately. Then, feeling healthy simply by purchasing fish and vegetables instead of pasta, I was aware of a slight spring in my step as I left the store.

The meal turned out perfectly. The fish was flaky, the vegetables were crisp and colorful, and the wine had just enough bite to accompany the meal.

Sydney was praising me to the heavens when my phone shrilled its ear-splitting ringtone, causing Sydney to drop her fork.

"I hope that's important," she said, sounding irritated and sarcastic.

I grabbed the thing to silence it only to see that it was Joe Bob, the groom-to-be, who wanted to sit around and feel nervous for the next couple of days. I knew he wouldn't be calling me unless it was important, but I decided to put off listening to his message until after dinner.

It was clear to me that Sydney had no interest in what was happening in the lives of my old high school friends, so I waited until she went into the bathroom to get ready for bed before listening to Joe Bob's message.

"Hey, Matt, I know you're prob'ly all tied up with your squeeze, but I need to tell you somethin'. Meet me at the diner in the mornin' around eight o'clock."

I almost wished he hadn't left a message because at that moment, Sydney came out of the bathroom wearing nothing but a sexy smile and padded toward me flaunting her wares. The girl had a way of getting my full attention. Joe Bob was definitely on hold until morning.

As soon as my feet hit the floor the next morning, Joe Bob's need to see me in person re-arranged my morning schedule. Instead of heading straight to my office, I drove to the diner to see what was so important. I found him sitting in a booth back in the corner strumming his fingers on the table.

"What's on your mind?" I said, dispensing with a greeting.

"Good mornin' to you, too," he said.

The suggestion of a grin played at the corner of his mouth, giving me the impression that he was about to unload something big. He waved a waitress over and ordered two black coffees.

"Wait 'til you hear what happened after you left my garage yesterday," he said. "I'd just got through overhaulin' that engine and wuz about to lock up for the day when Fred Peyton's sister come rushin' into my office. She wuz wringin' her hands and lookin' like she wuz about to turn on the waterworks."

Joe Bob picked up his mug and took a big swig of coffee.

"What did she want?"

"She wanted me to go with her to her house and talk to Fred. She said he'd told her a bunch of stuff that didn't make no sense; things that didn't seem to have anything to do with one another. I didn't know what she thought I could do about it and I told her so. Then, the poor woman started bawlin'. You know I can't stand to see a female cry."

I nodded.

"I told her I'd go with her, and that calmed her down some. Then, I followed her to her house. We went in and found Fred curled up in a ball in his underwear. He wuz on the floor in a corner of the laundry room, cryin'."

"I'm not understanding, Joe Bob. What did she want you to talk to him about?"

"You know, and I know, that Fred's not hittin' on all eight cylinders; never has, but he could make a sentence most of the time. He never used to spit out one word at a time. That just started this summer. Think about that thing for a minute or two."

"You're right. He jumped from one subject to another, and he didn't always make sense, but he spoke in complete sentences. Are you telling me that the big guy who was chasing him had something to do with his speech?"

"That's what his sister thinks. She also thinks it's affected his mind." Joe Bob offered a little grin. "Such as it is."

"Were you able to talk to him?"

"Yeah. His sister got him into a robe, and we took him to the livin' room. She give him a juice box. He stopped blubberin' and just then seemed to notice that I was there. I said, 'hey, Fred', and he kinda nodded."

"What's the important thing you wanted to tell me?"

"He started droppin' one word at a time, like he wuz doin' before, and his sister told him to stop that and to speak in sentences."

"So, did he?"

"Yeah. He's really screwed up, Matt. He said he knew he wuz goin' to hell 'cause of what he'd done. You know his sister's one of them strange religions. I don't know what they call it, but I've got a feelin' she's been preachin' at him, tellin' him that doin' them things wuz sinful. Seems like he thought that meant he wuz on a fast track to hellfire and brimstone."

"Are you telling me that she led him to believe he's bound for hell because of the things he did at Bernard's house?"

"Yessir. He thinks he chased Bernie out of Martinsville by doin' them things. He told me that Bernard's in Mexico with Juanita and the kid, and that he's never comin' back here. Fred thinks it's all his fault."

"Did he tell you why he thinks Bernie's in Mexico?"

"He said the big guy told him, and that's why there's no more jobs for him to do. The big guy's Juanita's brother. He threatened Fred; told him he'd better keep his mouth shut about them jobs."

"That doesn't explain why he hired Fred to do those things."

"This is what don't make sense: Fred said the big guy and Juanita wuz supposed to be workin' together at first. The brother's plan wuz to snatch little kids and trade 'em to their families for cash; in other words, hold 'em for ransom. Juanita wuz supposed to go to the park to help him some way or another. I'm guessin' he wanted her to spot people who looked like they had money—somebody who could afford a nanny, but she didn't want no part of it. The brother decided to scare Juanita away from Bernard's house. That way, she'd be out on the street without a job unless she agreed to help him. Fred didn't know whether he'd kidnapped any kids or not, but that wuz the plan."

"Joe Bob, this whole thing sounds awfully farfetched. Are you really taking Fred Peyton's word for it? And even if it turns out to be true, what do you plan to do about it?"

"I don't plan to do nothin' about it. I'm gittin' hitched tomorrow. I just thought you might want to keep a eye out for the big guy; maybe drop into the police station and try to find out if the cops might know somethin' about him."

"You do realize that we don't even know the guy's name."

"Yeah, we do. Fred said his name's Luis. I reckon his last name's Ramirez. That's Juanita's last name."

"I'm not making any promises. Fred Peyton's not high on my priority list right now, but if I happen to learn anything about this Luis Ramirez, I'll let you know."

"Good 'nuff."

I went to my office after leaving the diner and returned a few phone calls. Then, I spent the rest of the morning dictating letters to the efficient Mary Grace until lunchtime.

I was getting ready to leave the office to go out for a quick bite when my cell phone alerted me that Joe Bob was, once again, bursting with information that couldn't wait.

"Hey, groom-to-be, I don't think you're giving yourself time to sit around and feel nervous. What's happening now?"

"Seems like Fred's big sister must of talked him into accompanyin' her to the police station to spill it all. I told both of 'em yesterday that I didn't think Fred would go to jail for admittin' to them things he did at Bernard's place. He didn't hurt nobody or cause any kind of damage. I'm thinkin' she convinced him that if the cops heard Fred's story, maybe they would arrest the big guy on suspicion or somethin' like that. Anyway, Fred told the cops, and that's what they did. Fred's not afraid to leave the house now."

"How do you know about this?"

"Oh, Rose just called me. For some reason, the woman thinks I'm the guy to call whenever Fred's in trouble. She wanted to thank me for talkin' with him."

"Thanks for filling me in, my friend. Now you can concentrate on being nervous. I'll see you tomorrow."

I had gone down the street to a burger joint and inhaled my lunch. Joe Bob had taken up a hunk of my lunch hour, giving me a blow-by-blow update on the life of Fred Peyton.

When I returned to the office, Mary Grace was seated at her desk, seemingly with nothing to do. She would normally be reading a book in such an instance, but she was staring at a laptop which sat right beside her office computer. She was smiling.

"Hello, Mary Grace. What are you so happy about, if I might ask?"

She pointed to the laptop.

"This is what I bought with my raise," she said. "I've signed up for a couple of pre law courses. I can take them online. Thanks to you I know what I want to do with my life."

"That's wonderful. I'm happy for you, and just a little bit proud of you. It looks like we're pretty caught up for the day. I want you to take off early. Go home and get to work on those courses."

I was truly proud of my new secretary and had no doubt that one day she would make a first rate lawyer. I smiled to myself on the way to the kitchen fridge for a cold one when Joe Bob struck again.

"Hey, Matt, it's me again."

"What a surprise. I'm through for the day. Come on over to my office for a beer and tell me all about whatever it is in person."

"On my way."

A few minutes later, Mister Kincaid let himself in and met me in the kitchen.

"He's out already."

"Who?"

"The big guy—Luis."

"He was just picked up this morning."

"I know, but the cops couldn't prove he'd done anything wrong. They couldn't hold him. Rose said that Fred's in his room, afraid to leave the house again."

"Joe Bob, you're going to have to let this go, at least for now. You're getting married tomorrow afternoon. You can't let Fred Peyton dictate between now and then. You'll be on your honeymoon after that, but I'll be here. I'll look into this while you're gone. You have my word. Now, finish your beer and get out of here."

I cuffed him on the shoulder and grinned.

"Okay. I just feel sorry for the guy. He can't help it if he's got a loose screw."

After Joe Bob left, I drove straight to Sydney's place. All the drama of the day must have worn me out. I was tired and didn't want to cook dinner, so I made a reservation at a low-key chop house.

Sydney was tired, too, so that was fine with her. We enjoyed a quiet dinner and a bottle of wine, then went home and crashed. Maybe we were working too hard.

Then, came the big day. I spent a few minutes with Joe Bob before the service and told him that I didn't want to hear one word about Fred Peyton. My friend didn't argue. He simply nodded.

Lauren looked ravishing, and Joe Bob had bitten his nails into the quick, but he couldn't stop smiling. I assumed he had finally had time to get a giant-size case of the jitters. Little Annie, who had just turned four, wore a serious face as she scattered rose petals down the aisle, taking measured steps as if being prompted by a metronome.

I liked the Methodist preacher better each time we were in one another's company. The Good Reverend seemed so down-to-earth that I thought I could probably discuss anything with him. I thought he was the perfect choice to perform this ceremony.

"Dearly beloved….," began Mark Winters. Then, knowing the script by heart, he laid his book aside, lifting Annie so she could see her mother's face. Then, he continued a beautiful ceremony containing vows contributed by Lauren and Joseph Robert. At the words, "You may now kiss the bride," Annie clapped her chubby hands.

The reception was opulent. Everyone was in high spirits. I knew I was expected to toast the newlyweds, and it was something I truly wanted to do, so I tapped my glass for attention.

"Ladies and gentlemen, let's all raise a glass to the happy couple. Lauren and Joe Bob, may your love forever shine in your faces as it does today. Marriages are made in heaven, but so are thunder and lightning. Always keep one another safe from the storm. Congratulations!"

Crystal glasses clinked, playing a tinkling melody, and wild applause filled the large room. Joe Bob left his bride's side just long enough to approach me and deliver a heartfelt handshake.

"That wuz downright beautiful, Matt. You always know what to say and how to say it. Damn, you're good."

There were a few more toasts. Then, it was party time. Joseph Robert Kincaid waltzed his new bride around the dance-floor in elegant fashion. Other couples joined the happy couple and the festivities were in full swing.

At some point, Lauren and Joe Bob disappeared from the revelers to seal their wedding vows which they did in Joe Bob's trailer. They had an early flight to an unknown destination for their honeymoon.

I've always liked lazy overcast days, and that was a perfect description of the day following my old friend's wedding. Sydney and I slept in, it being Sunday, and I made breakfast, feeling just a tiny bit guilty for telling Mark Winters that we would be at his morning service. We could show up the next Sunday, and I was sure he'd forgive us.

Sydney was in the shower, and I was thinking of going for a leisurely jog around the neighborhood when my phone rang.

"Mister Stevenson, this is Rose Peyton. Joe Bob Kincaid gave me your number. I hope I'm not disturbing you."

"How can I help you, Ms. Peyton?"

"I'm calling to let you know that the police have arrested Luis Ramirez again. It happened while Joe Bob was getting married. Ramirez was caught in the act of grabbing a two-year-old girl away from her nanny. The policeman who called to let me know said that Ramirez was going away for good this time. I thought you'd want to know. Again, I'm sorry to bother you on a Sunday."

"Thank you for telling me, Rose. Take good care of your brother."

"I will. Goodbye."

Joe Bob would be elated to hear this news. He was probably sitting in the airport about to take off for his honeymoon with the girl of his dreams, but I couldn't help myself—I sent him a text to give him the news.

Sometimes things turn out the way they're supposed to. This was one of those times.

Acknowledgments

The first person I want to thank is my attorney husband, Ralph Shelburne, whose love and support have always been constant. He doesn't shy away from delivering constructive criticism, nor does he fail to lavish praise where it is deserved.

My sincere thanks go to my readers who have been patient for the duration of this project which I began during the Covid rampage and stumbled its way to fruition. Donna Aelmore, Ronald Moore, and Rennie Langman, I owe each of you a debt of gratitude for your fine-tooth comb attention to my work.

To Jose Ramirez without whose talent and expertise this novel would not exist, I thank you for all of your hard work and the many hours you afford me.

Last, but not least, I want to express my gratitude to all of you who buy my books and come back for more. You make me want to get to work on another idea and cause it to come to life.

Inherent Justice Book Club Discussion Questions

1. This is the second time Matt Stevenson has returned to his hometown for specific reasons. The first was for his mother's funeral. This time it is to clear his head so he can decide what he wants to do with the rest of his life and where he wants to do it. Have you ever returned to your roots? Why?

2. Matt reconnects with two of his old high school pals, Bernie Zuckerman and Joe Bob Kincaid. The three were inseparable when they were kids. Now they are in their late thirties and each has his own set of values. How do you perceive each man's attitude as an adult?

3. Bernie and Joe Bob seem to have an ongoing rivalry, and Matt finds himself playing referee/peacemaker between the two. How do you feel about his role?

4. Gertrude Giles, the housekeeper, has been like a second mother to Matt since he was small, and the two remain very close. Why do you think their relationship is set in cement? Do you have such a relationship with someone from your childhood? Explain.

5. Fred Peyton (Freaky Fred) shows up all through the novel. Do you think he is an integral part of the plot? Explain.

6. Matt is intent on renewing his acquaintance with Sydney Edelman. He goes to great lengths to achieve this and turn it into a meaningful relationship. How do you view their relationship? Do you think one or the other gives more than his/her share to make it work?

7. Bernie appears to have a love/hate relationship with his ex. Do you think this is commonplace among divorcees?

8. Claire, Bernie's and Lee Ann's little girl, seems to be the most important person in Bernie's life. He thinks Lee Ann is using the child as a pawn and doesn't care about Claire at all. Bernie turns the world upside down after Claire disappears, then he seems to simply give up. How do you view this?

9. Juanita, Bernie's housekeeper/babysitter/lover, plays a big part in the novel. How do you view her? Why?

10. Inherent Justice has a male protagonist. Do you think the novel appeals more to males or females? Explain.